Murder in
Westminster

The Lady Worthing Mysteries
Murder in Westminster

Other Titles by Vanessa Riley

Historical Romance

The Rogues & Remarkable Women Romances

A Duke, the Lady, and a Baby
An Earl, the Girl, and a Toddler
A Duke, the Spy, an Artist, and a Lie

Historical Fiction

Island Queen
Sister Mother Warrior

Murder in Westminster

Vanessa Riley

KENSINGTON
PUBLISHING CORP.

www.kensingtonbooks.com

KENSINGTON BOOKS are published by

Kensington Publishing Corp.
119 West 40th Street
New York, NY 10018

All Kensington titles, imprints, and distributed lines are available at special quantity discounts for bulk purchases for sales promotion, premiums, fund-raising, educational, or institutional use.

Special book excerpts or customized printings can also be created to fit specific needs. For details, write or phone the office of the Kensington Special Sales Manager: Attn. Special Sales Department. Kensington Publishing Corp, 119 West 40th Street, New York, NY 10018. Phone: 1-800-221-2647.

The K with book logo Reg. U.S. Pat. & TM Off.

Library of Congress Card Catalogue Number: 2022935886

ISBN: 978-1-4967-3866-0
First Kensington Hardcover Edition: September 2022
ISBN: 978-1-4967-3872-1 (ebook)

10 9 8 7 6 5 4 3 2 1

Printed in the United States of America

For my mother, to thank her for the countless hours of *Matlock*, *Remington Steele*, and *Murder She Wrote* we enjoyed.

Nothing is impossible.

I believe.

Acknowledgments

Thank you to my Heavenly Father, for imagination.

To Esi Sogah, my editor, thank you for allowing me to stretch my wings.

I look forward to shaping Abigail with you.

To my fabulous agent, Sarah Younger, I am grateful that you are my partner.

You are my ride-or-die friend and sister.

To Gerald, Marc, and Chris—Love you bros.

To Denny, to Pat, and Felicia. Thank you for helping me elevate my game, the gentle shoves, and every challenge.

The Writers of Me and My Sisters

To those who inspire my pen: Beverly, Brenda, Farrah, Sarah, Julia, Kristan, Alyssa, Maya, Lenora, Sophia, Joanna, Grace, Laurie Alice, Julie, Cathy, Katharine, Carrie, Christina, Georgette, Jane, Linda, Margie, Michelle R., Liz, Lasheera, Alexis R., Angela, Piper, Alexis G. Eileen, Rhonda, and Jude—thank you.

And to my rocks: Frank and Ellen

Love you all, so much.

Murder in
Westminster

Prologue

April 8, 1806, London

Before her youth is spent, a resourceful woman enjoys many passions—embroidered scarves, fine pearl pins, and lovers, of course.

For Juliet Henderson, affairs of the heart are a good way of keeping boredom at bay whilst a husband is at sea. But with her staid husband of ten years, Lieutenant Commander Stapleton Henderson returned, having retired from his naval career, and setting up camp in their Westminster home, why must she give up her fun? Excitement, any excitement, is simply too great of a temptation to surrender.

Sliding her finger along her ribbon necklace, she chuckles, then hums and sinks into the white velvet padding of her carriage.

Gliding a palm across the seat to her empty reticule—one she's decided Stapleton must fill—she examines her plans, her heart's desires.

Boring and given to a frigid temperament, her husband can

be counted upon to do the right or convenient thing. It's clear in his icy gaze, he wants her gone. With the tidy fortune he inherited and the riches he's won at sea, he can afford to send her away in style.

At a minimum, the pocket change he often leaves lying around his private study could buy his peace and freedom. The last time she saw him, he frivolously spent it on lumber and wrought iron to build an unnecessary fence in his ongoing war with their neighbor.

If Stapleton thought about Juliet with the same passion he had for besting the prickly Worthing woman, Juliet might consider reconciliation.

Her husband is nice to look at—tall, dark, and muscular, but suffering another boring year on his arm while he reacquaints himself to London Society—no.

Putting up with his angry pianoforte—definitely no.

Tumbling into his bed and dirtying his perfectly aligned sheets—maybe?

She closes her eyes and draws deeper into her heavy shawl. It's always best for a lover to want a woman more. Stapleton tolerated her. His sudden rush to evict her from his life shocked.

Juliet now understands the difference between lust and a desire to be with the one who quickens her heart. She doesn't want her husband anymore, but a love for the ages.

Nonetheless, this doesn't mean she wants Stapleton forgetting her. He should regret not having her at his side.

Singing softly to soothe her ego, she tries to focus on her plans, not her miscalculations. Her head is for simple pampering, not mathematics.

Thus, Stapleton's generous allowance spent too fast on gold jewelry and pretty pearls and those tawdry lovers.

She sighs and searches the outlines of buildings along Queen Street.

Her soul has grown accustomed to nosy neighbors, fine furnishings, and the regal charm of everything in Westminster. It's one of the first residences of Saxon kings and queens.

Very cruel of Stapleton to banish her to Cheapside. What is she? Cheap fabric?

The carriage parks outside old Number Eleven Greater Queen Street.

As she waits for her driver to assist with her grand return, she blows kisses into her hands, hot moist air from her lips. Bared of gloves, she feels cold but free.

Mr. Sinclair, her faithful driver, opens the door. "Miss Bumners has been saying everyone is in a frenzy that you're actually leaving town. It's not true, is it?"

Taking her time, Juliet descends and loosens her long blue scarf so it will drape along her blush-pink gown. Her shoulders are bared and she holds herself erect to make the most of her ample bosom. "It is. I won't need you anymore tonight, Mr. Sinclair. Maybe not for a long time."

He tips his jet-black tricorn back and offers the ruddy grin she's accustomed to seeing. "That Miss Bumners knows everything. Mrs. Henderson, I hate to think of you going away."

Ann Bumners, her personal maid and spy, spends half her time at Juliet's town house in Cheapside, the rest here polishing every speck of woodwork.

Feeling triumphant that the news has shaken Queen Street, Juliet puts her lips to Sinclair's, right there in the open. Any of the other Henderson servants could watch her performance from the many windows of Number Eleven.

"You've always served me well, Sinclair. Thank you."

His perfume of ale breath enhances the scarlet bloom of his cheeks, but her driver, the excitable, superstitious man, shakes his head. He takes a four-leaf clover from his pocket and offers it. "Luck for you. I wish you get what you deserve, ma'am, all the happiness."

She takes it. It's warm and squishy in her palm. He bends his head for a moment and offers a goodbye prayer. "The man in there's a hero, served good under Lord Nelson. Sailors come home different sometimes, especially when they've served long and under such circumstances. A hero and an angel deserve to have joy. He's the only man I'd give you up for."

Crumpling the clover, casting it from her palm, Juliet stills, and hopes her small desire for the musket ball that felled Nelson to have shifted doesn't show on her face. An inch or two to the right and the country wouldn't be mourning the man who won Trafalgar.

Of course, that would mean she'd be in awful widow's weeds for months, what with the admiral's most faithful physician, Lieutenant Commander Henderson, having been killed.

She shakes these thoughts. Stapleton isn't so bad. Quite amenable when cornered, he's also patient—and patronizing. It's a horrible combination, for Juliet loves to provoke. Without high passions, how does one know if they are loved?

Head up, she follows the cobbled path to the town house.

Before she's able to knock, the silver liveried footmen, Dillard and Humphrey, whom she affectionately calls Tweedle Dee and Tweedle Young, open the big black doors.

"Ma'am," said Mr. Dillard, a gangly fellow with fuzzy black eyebrows. "You're not supposed to be here. The master's out."

"That's the perfect time to visit." Juliet saunters inside, but holds to her scarf, refusing Mr. Humphrey's offer to hang it. He's a scrumptious addition to the household, mirroring Dillard's height and weight, but for her tastes—too naive.

She was once like him, young and dumb. But being innocent is a fool's luxury. A girl from Chelsea dairy country can't afford to stay stupid. Juliet has learned fast, which means she always takes more than what's owed.

Always more.

Fooling an honorable man into matrimony is the least of a pretty woman's sins.

She smooths the *J* on her necklace and heads down the sky-blue hall, treading across newly laid floors—perfectly cut, four-inch planks. Ridding the place of irregularities like wide mismatched planks of fir is the equivalent of giving away the town house's charm.

None of this matters. Juliet needs to stick to the plan—which means getting to Stapleton's private study.

She dashes down the stairs to the ground floor, his lair. Having direct access to the lawns behind the town house, the man could come and go as he pleased.

No wonder the two of them have never endured being together for more than a few hours. They've arranged the house to avoid one another.

She steps onto the new floors and shifts her weight to find one board that'll squeak.

None do. "The man is too precise."

This was the first thing he'd done since returning in January instead of discussing their marriage.

She did Mr. Dillard.

Compromising the fellow isn't something Juliet is proud of, but it passed the time and made everyone aware that she was unhappy.

Humming with glee, she lifts her hands and measures the art hanging on the walls. Each is too big to steal. Couldn't carry one out under her arm with the pair of footmen at the front door.

But through Stapleton's study and off the terrace seems possible.

Her brother, Jeorge Tanner, knows where to sell borrowed items fast in the rookery.

A few dealers have clients who'll pay good money for a dead ancestor in a gilded frame. Jeorge, the last of her living family, would do it for her without any questions.

Just a little grease for his palm is all that's required.

Cough. Cough. "Ma'am."

The forced tones are the butler's. Her favorite man to banter with, William Jyles. He's strict with salt and a pure delight when he's flustered into a tizzy.

Cough.

"I hear you wheezing, Mr. Jyles." Juliet doesn't face him.

Instead, she teases and goes to Stapleton's pianoforte and plunks off-sounding keys. "This needs tuning. Frantic music does wear the instrument."

The butler comes to her. "You're not allowed to be here, Mrs. Henderson, without the master's permission."

With both hands, she hits more strained notes. "Isn't it better that he's not here? Less arguments. Less noise. Less threats to kill one another."

"Ma'am, you're making a scene. And you're obviously dressed to go out."

She drops her scarf and makes a sultry turn before scooping to pick it up. "I thought I'd come here for fun. Can I say all is missed, even you?"

"Mrs. Henderson."

Fluffing a drooping curl that her newest admirer says is spun gold, she puts her lips to the boxy instrument.

"I'm saying goodbye." She rubs her cold hand along the freshly polished wood.

Juliet spins in circles, humming as if there's music. "I do miss Mr. Henderson's angry sonatas." The harsh tones are practically the only way to tell he has feelings.

She moves to the center right under the chandelier. "What do you do when you're angry, Jyles? Do you ignore the problem like my husband? And where is he? Did he decide to go out and partake in society?"

Draping her scarf again on both shoulders, she sighs. "Has he finally learned to pay attention to his sister?"

"They're both out, ma'am." He folds his arms over his starched black jacket and his squishy belly, that he tries to suck in. Don't men know women won't notice such things if they are charmed and satisfied?

"Mrs. Henderson, ma'am. Please. Leave."

"Don't fret. I told my husband I'm going to Scotland to give him what he wants, without dying that is." Juliet cups her hand as if they're full of coins. "And he has said yes to me."

Jyles's face sweeps into a smile. "Ma'am, I'm not privy to such news."

Liar.

Cowpox man. Everyone at Eleven Greater Queen Street knows of the couple's difficulties. And almost everyone sides against Juliet.

Crossing her scarf and tugging it tighter about her arms, she stares at him. He is Stapleton's confidant. What has he confessed since her husband's return?

The plan, Juliet. Stick to the plan.

"Jyles, dearest Jyles. There's supposed to be a little present left for me when I came to my senses. I've come." She mocks Henderson's dry tones. "Then I'm to be whisked away."

"Whisked? You mean you'll leave with one of your special friends and give the master his writ of divorce?"

"See. He still tells you everything."

She laughs, but Jyles is sometimes colder than Stapleton.

And like her husband, she knows better than to push him too far.

Stapleton could've killed her the night he found her tempting Dillard. And the butler would've helped hide the body.

Running past Jyles, Juliet whips into her husband's study and flings herself upon his desk, a good sturdy mahogany piece caught in a sea of dead gray-painted walls.

The butler follows.

His gait is slow. That dragging leg bothers him from time to time. "You should soak that foot. And cut back on port and brandy."

"You sound as if you care. Juliet Henderson cares about another living soul?"

"Did he tell you how he begged me to stay, even after finding me *busy*?"

Jyles goes to the terrace doors and draws the curtains shut. "No. Please, ma'am, get down. You may wrinkle the master's drawings."

"Did he complain I'd found someone whom I love more than Henderson money?"

"Ma'am, please go."

"I will, but I wonder what he'll think. You're alike. Tell me what you think about my going away." Playing with her scarf, she gives it a saucy back-and-forth tug at her shoulders. "My, it's warm in here. There's no fire under the mantel. Maybe crack open the terrace door."

The unblinking butler pivots. "You're only trying to cause another scene. Probably a loud one to awaken all the neighbors. You should've said Mr. Henderson is expecting you. Stay here until he comes. Touch nothing. Take nothing."

The hall door to the study closes behind him, a smidgen short of a slam, but the vibration rattles the glass terrace doors.

She sits still, waiting, but no one enters.

Looking around, she detects there's no money on his desk, as there usually is.

This is Stapleton playing a game on her. They'd agreed to a sum. It should be here. There should be enough to maybe send something to her brother.

Where would the reclusive man hide it?

Eyeing the drawing on his desk, Juliet studies the complex architectural draft of the fence she's heard he's constructing.

She flips through the stack of drawings.

"He even numbered the pieces of wood like it's a puzzle.

And he selected pine this time? What, no ancient lumber with Scottish connections?"

The plan, Juliet.

If she tore up these drawings, that might send Stapleton into a rare frenzy. One final display of temper would at least let Juliet know he cares; that she still has a hold on his icy heart.

The man frets over his sister's reputation. It's easy to ruin a girl, and if Juliet decided to stay, she'll do something horrible by accident that will hurt her sister-in-law. Mary Henderson is sweet and trusting, like her sugary portrait, with ribbons and bows, that hangs on the bookshelf behind Juliet.

Edging around the desk, she looks again at the drawings and the pages and pages of survey notes and even something that looks like surveillance. "Stapleton, you're more animated over a property line or losing to the neighbor than anything. Why?"

That Worthing woman next door has gotten to him somehow.

One note from the social-climbing shrew sends him to the wretched piano.

Church bells clang.

Living in Westminster, one gets used to hearing them. As they practice change ringing, one hears the chimes of the bell towers from the great abbey or its smaller cousin, Saint Margaret's.

The bells keep booming.

She can picture the men pulling on ropes, up and down, then tying them off, making century-old metal ring for the nation.

Ding.

Dong.

Wrapping her scarf about her neck, she sways like she's a bell readying for full peal.

A laugh bubbles as she smooths her hands over the bust of John Donne, which sits on the edge of Stapleton's desk, close to the terrace doors. "'For whom the bell tolls, it tolls for thee.'"

If she doesn't hurry, she'll miss her chance to prove to her lover that she's serious about leaving Stapleton. Nonetheless, she has to leave with a full reticule. "Where do you put your pocket change now, darling Stapleton? Hater of banks."

Moonlight streaking around the curtains falls on Donne and a dish collecting the ash of a half-smoked cigar.

She taps the ashtray. Her touch shakes hints of vanilla and burned cedar into the air.

He must not have left that long ago. At nine, would he have gone to his club?

Frantic, she searches drawers and shelves. Nothing's found, but another old relic—this one, a rapier, one Henderson swears he'll polish, but doesn't. When she looks at the sweet picture of Mary, she finds it crooked.

As quietly and as quickly as she can, she shifts the portrait until a metal door is unearthed.

Covering her lips, she almost giggles. There could be enough money to ensure her comfort for a long time. Any doubts about her lover ever losing interest or abandoning her for a wealthier, younger thing evaporates. No one will choose duty and honor over Juliet and a fortune.

"The Cliffs of Dover by the week's end, frolicking on a carpet of emerald clover. Thank you, Stapleton, darling." She yanks at the metal handle.

Won't budge. Locked.

He never locks anything.

The bells toll again.

Maybe the church team began another peal, full or quarter.

The bust of Donne seems to laugh, louder and longer with each chime.

She backhands it.

The heavy object doesn't fall, but slides on the orange oil–polished surface.

Deciding she'll send the poet to his demise and make him a crumble of marble on the new floors, she lifts it high and then stops midswing. The sparkle of a key hits her eye. "Donne might be the answer, after all."

Juliet takes metal and pushes it into the lock.

Clicks announce a fit. She braces and opens . . . an empty vault.

Nothing. Where's the money?

Stapleton Henderson is never this unpredictable.

Never.

Heart pounding, she backs away. Time to convince her lover of her commitment is running out.

They were to have one last laugh at her husband's expense.

With no money in hand, this night will look like a game, as if Juliet was causing a scene to make Stapleton jealous.

Everyone will think she wants to return to her husband.

Rotating, she spies the mirror above the fireplace. Her reflection glows of fear, clear on her pale ghostly cheeks.

She pinches them to draw color, to look as fresh and as confident as possible.

A lantern shines from the garden. Her lover is waiting.

Tugging at her scarf, wrapping up for the night air, she exits through the terrace doors.

Her husband's greyhounds greet her with kisses to each palm.

"Have you been terrorizing the neighbor's pet? Naughty boys. Come on, let's walk. Let's go be adoring. That'll buy me more time."

A grand, dangerous passion won't cool because she miscalculated Stapleton again.

Everything will be fine.

Juliet can't lose.

Clasping the *J* on her ribbon necklace, she hums with a rhythm that matches the bells' moans and nears a figure standing in the hedgerow, close to the half-done wrought-iron fence.

Suddenly she's grabbed. At first, she hopes it's a lover's delight, a reunion.

It's not.

It's hell.

Desperate, she fights, scratching and gouging the dark.

But the ribbon tightens about her throat, wrenching life from her body.

The cold night air steals her last breath. Time runs out.

Chapter 1

April 8, 1806, Opening Night at Drury Lane

Something gripped my shoulder.

Surprising and soft, tugging me backward away from the dark.

Away from the ribbon.

"Abbie."

Blinking, I filled my lungs.

One breath—I spied a hanging chandelier.

Second breath—people in theater boxes.

A third gasp—my dress, an evening gown edged with purple lace. My hands were attired in ivory gloves.

At the opening of *Ali Baba* at Drury Lane Theatre, I didn't need to call attention to myself because of nightmare. Slow and easy, I pried my hand from the balcony rail and gulped as much air as my lungs could hold. I held a portion on my tongue like it was a fine claret.

"Abbie, you were asleep and mumbling. If you haven't been resting well, we needn't have come." My cousin Florentina

Sewell sounded half-annoyed, half-fretful. "We can end things now and go home."

Sitting back and hiding my tension, I put on my best sophisticated Lady Worthing look. "My dear Miss Sewell, opening night at Drury Lane can be overwhelming."

Florentina shook her head. Her beautiful olive face held a scowl. "Abbie, have you not been sleeping again?"

Couldn't tell her I wasn't and that one of those rare dreams had started again. We had too much to do tonight to let my anxious heart get the better of me. "Just a little nap. It's not as though sleep deprivation has me running down to the stage screaming like a loon."

Or being strangled, like in my nightmare.

Gentle brown-gray eyes with flecks of fire glared at me. "I knew you were lying to me. Abbie, this isn't right."

I grasped her hand and hoped she felt my strength, my commitment to doing my part in the struggle. "I didn't sleep well last night, but I'm fine."

Then I offered a laugh, one of those good fake giggles that society women shared when shopping for gloves. "You need a night away from staring at numbers. Math, be gone tonight."

"I love mathematics, and I'm lucky to be a helper to Mrs. Edwards. Those calculations for longitude are needed for our sailors to get home safely." Her passion sounded better than the applause rumbling below. Florentina was lucky. She knew from an early age the things that would make her heart sing.

And there was no one I wanted at my side when I finally claimed the things my soul needed.

Another wave of claps started in the crowded Drury Lane Theatre as a trumpet sounded.

Offering Florentina a wicked grin, I fluttered my fan, a large thing of jet fabric and ivory feathers. "No quitting now. Ali Baba's waiting for us."

Eyes rolling, but with her lips wiggling, suppressing a laugh, she straightened in her chair. "The things you get me to do."

"Florentina, we can't be selfish. We need to put my elevated status to use."

"But we aren't staying. That's part of your plan."

"As I said, we need to put my Lady Worthing name into action, helping those who truly are in need."

"If you say so. But you were my favorite cousin when you were plain old Abigail Carrington. Not that you were ever plain."

The noise coming from the hall behind us was the cue to begin our disappearing act.

Offering a nod to Florentina, she pulled the string I'd attached to the curtain of our box. The fabric stretched, shrouding the corner.

Flat against the wall of our private box, Mrs. Smith, my housekeeper, and Miss Bellows, my lady's maid, entered. Dressed similarly to us and hidden in the dark with my legendary fans, the two would do nicely representing us. Florentina and I had other plans.

"Ma'am," Miss Bellows said in her lovely Irish brogue. "Ye not doing somethin' illegal."

"Certainly not."

I kissed the older woman's cheek. "I thought you might want to see opening night. You've always wanted to go to the theater."

"But pretending to be you, ma'am?"

It was ridiculous on face value, with her being pale white and myself not so much. My complexion was more gold than olive, unlike Florentina's. But in the darkness of the theater, behind the ridiculous plumage, Miss Bellows could pretend to be me.

The notion of Miss Bellows *passing* for a Blackamoor in itself filled me with humor.

In a way, this mirrored some of the stories my godfather, Mr. Vaughn, had told me of how people had survived by exchanging races in the West Indian colony of Jamaica, where he and my mother were born.

"It's ludicrous," I said aloud, and meant it as comment on this moment, history, and every farce one had to endure to make a better day.

Cold fingers latched to my wrist. "You're shaking, ma'am."

Was I? "Just my normal shivers." Always cold, even near the roaring fire, I dismissed these shakes as nothing, not even second thoughts. Miss Bellows had known me as a precocious child. She kept my secrets, and those of a mixed-race family caught in colonialism and a volatile home. Didn't know how I'd survived without her.

"Just hand me the cape, Miss Bellows, and then take my seat."

She did so, took my big black-and-white fan, and then claimed my theater chair.

Mrs. Smith, who'd been standing almost in the hall, watched with her usual mixture of quiet dignity and disdain. She shook her head, handed me her long cape, before exchanging places with Florentina.

"This is highly irregular, mum." Her Jamaican accent would give her away, but I counted on people offering half stares and assuming one dark face was the same as another.

Before I could reassure her, she'd whipped out a pair of my opera glasses. "I suppose you won't tell us where you two are going?"

I put a finger to my lips, then winked at her. The Smiths were a settled Blackamoor family known for their service to many of the ton, especially within the Westmorland and Jersey peerages. Nothing disturbed her for too long. Discretion might as well be her surname. "Ladies, leave in the middle of the last act. Make sure no one sees you."

"But how will we know how it ends." My maid looked disappointed, but tried to pry the glasses from Mrs. Smith.

"They all lived and loved happily ever after, Miss Bellows."

Making sure our hoods were up and that no trace of hands or faces could be seen, I prepared to leave Mrs. Smith and Miss Bellows to the joy of opening night. "Have fun. Be gone by the middle of the last act. Hire a jarvey and return to Greater Queen Street."

Grasping Florentina's hand, we escaped through the halls and down the stairs. The crowds behind us clapped like thunder.

I hesitated for a moment. That feeling of being watched sent a sensation down my neck, like the fine baby hairs of my braided chignon being touched. Craning my head, I saw no one. I accounted this to those nerves I denied, but it wasn't every day one was invited to a secret meeting.

My cousin and I donned our dark capes made of the tweed fabric my father loved as a boy in Glasgow, Scotland, and headed down Brydges Street.

No one seemed to stare, but lively Covent Garden was always filled with more extravagant distractions.

I felt invisible and invincible, two things I hadn't been since I wed James Monroe, Lord Worthing.

The night was cloudy with bits of red. I'd like to think James was enjoying the other end of these skies from his sloop as he chased his dreams across the seas. " 'Red skies at night, a sailor's delight.' "

"What, Abbie?" Florentina slowed, then came to a full stop.

I stumbled into her. "Sorry. Guess I should pay closer attention. The smells of food and spirits and the sounds have me."

Tumbling my hand forward, I got her moving again.

The farther we were from the theater, the more I caught myself looking over my shoulder. That feeling that something was wrong, that we'd been seen, returned. It gnawed at my insides.

"Florentina, turn on Russel."

"But our mews is farther."

"I know, but trust me." Unable to shake the notion that we were in danger, I led my cousin into Anderson's Eating House on the corner of Clare Court and Drury Lane.

"Abbie, your driver is meeting us at the mews now."

"Rawlins knows if we aren't there at nine-thirty, he's to wait another five minutes, then come here."

"You have a prearranged second place to be picked up. Why not make this the primary place? It's closer."

"It's too close."

"Abbie, do you want me to calculate the odds of our success tonight for this overly elaborate ruse?"

"No." I massaged my temples, asking myself why I'd made things difficult. The voice that answered in my head was my sister Dinah's: *Because you are difficult.*

"Let's get a table and wait for Rawlins." I reached into my reticule, avoiding the folded page, and brought out coins.

Someone on the waitstaff noticed the shine in my gloved palm and soon gave us a place in the corner.

Anderson's had a reputation of being crowded and not asking too many questions. "Tea, sliced beef, and cheese. A little bread." The fellow nodded, bit my gold coin to ensure it was real, and then went away.

"Abbie, you've rushed us from the theater to eat?"

"No." I pulled out my watch, a wonderful thing with brass springs and windings. It read 9:15. "We still have some time before Rawlins comes. Eating will make us look less suspicious."

"Right. Two hooded young Blackamoor women can simply blend into the woodwork."

A pot of tea, a plate of cheese and bread, dropped onto our table. "Out of beef." The young man grunted and walked away.

Trying hard to keep my this-is-how-I-planned smile from breaking, I plucked a bit of the crusty loaf. "Eat up, Florentina."

Her gray-brown eyes were wide as she nibbled a bit of cheese.

"Aren't these witnesses to us being here and not at the theater? Or is this another cog in your complex plan?"

I didn't answer. If I hadn't felt like I was being followed, we would've made it to the mews, with none the wiser. I checked my watch again. "Where's Rawlins?"

"Your driver is better than a sundial in his precision. He'll be here, as you planned." She grabbed my hand. "Abigail Carrington Monroe. Tell me what's going on or buy me a decent dinner. Something with a roast. Something luxurious and filling. Not a plate with no meat."

"Settle down." I looped my arm about her baggy sleeve. "We have an appointment."

"That's obvious. Where to and with whom?"

I leaned in close, daring not to raise my voice and attract attention—well, more attention. At least in this corner, no one could come from behind and strangle me, like the woman in my dreams.

The image haunted me these past nights. It was why I hadn't been sleeping. Couldn't close my eyes and be trapped witnessing a vision I'd not understand, nor be able to stop.

Florentina stabbed at the Stilton cheese. The blue veining and the tart smell said this was cut from a Cropwell Bishop block. "Abbie, I'm waiting. What are we doing?"

"The who is Wilberforce. The where is a private meeting at Holy Trinity Clapham."

"An abolition meeting!"

I clapped her mouth. "Hush."

She pried my fingers away. "You're supposed to leave it alone. Lord Worthing's concerned with your safety. The movement can wait."

"My husband is considerate, but he's not here." My voice sounded sharp, showing more disappointment than I wanted. "Lord Worthing is attending to his priorities. I'm doing the same for mine."

She dropped two too many lumps of sugar into my cup and passed me the tea. "Sorry, Abbie."

As much as I loved saccharine things—especially blended with chamomile's tang and the tartness of lemon—the sugar trade, white gold, did much harm.

"The cause of abolition is something I can help. Something I could fight for while Lord Worthing is off to sea for high adventure. It's something I can do while he's left me here to battle London alone."

"I'm sorry. Let's think about our doings." She offered a small smile, one laced with pity and a teaspoon of the worst medicine, the I-told-you-to-wait kind.

"Flo, cut me some Stilton. Smash it onto a piece of the bread."

She did, then offered me another sad expression.

Stuffing my mouth with delicious earthy cheese, I looked to the window. Florentina didn't need to see that her calculations of my odds at being happy were right. James was gone. In a few more months, I'd mark our second anniversary of marriage, with him away.

"More bread, Abbie. I'll save you the crusty part."

"No. I'm full. And Lord Worthing will always be concerned, but he knows me to be capable. He'll not object to me finding my own ways to battle for justice."

She shrugged and then chuckled. "If you have to choose a dump to dine, you'd pick the one with great Stilton cheese. That's signature Lady Worthing."

Florentina knew me, understood me, and in the end, she championed my choices. That couldn't be said of my sister.

"I need my causes, Flo. Something has to fill me up."

"So where is Holy Trinity Clapham?"

"In Clapham Common. We head back toward Westminster and then take the bridge. It's not much farther, once we cross. It wouldn't seem long if we were under way. Where's Rawlins?"

"It's now the time for him to leave the mews and come here. He can be counted upon." She cut another bit of the cheese. "Add another ten minutes if there's traffic. Covent Garden at night can be chaotic."

Munching on the toasted bread, she cleared her mouth, patting away crumbs. "If we're heading back to Westminster, let's stop at your house. We could change. Something sensible that doesn't say monk or theater."

"Flo, I don't want anyone else knowing my whereabouts. We've gone to a lot of trouble to have *Ali Baba* alibis."

"But we're going to a serious meeting looking like nuns on the run. We need an impeccable, unimpeachable Lady Worthing outfit." She winked at me. "You know, something that says expensive and trustworthy."

I had thought of that and weighed the risks of further involving my household. Never certain of their loyalty since having married the third baron of Worthing, I wasn't sure who to trust besides the people who came with me to Queen Street—Mrs. Smith and Miss Bellows.

Nothing could be done to jeopardize Wilberforce. William Wilberforce was a beacon of good. I couldn't compromise him, even if I looked like a missionary gone amok.

I shook my head, elevated my chin, then offered an exalted gaze. "I'm Lady Worthing regardless of my clothes. And I'm in no mood to return to Greater Queen Street to see how much of the monstrosity Number Eleven has finished. The horrid man dropped off more wood and huge sections of wrought iron. I left him the other day fiddling with his drawings and making measurements as if he planned to build a massive temple. The gall of him to do this because I asked Mr. Stapleton to keep his mangy dogs from terrorizing my Teacup."

Florentina chortled into her mug. "You sure it's not the other way around? Your terrier can be a handful."

"My little dog can do nothing to those bigger ones. They're

greyhounds of some sort. The two are massive and my Teacup is wee."

"True, but a determined mutt can do great things against purebred bullies." Her words, her clear gaze, weren't merely about dogs anymore. It was the resilience in our mixed blood, the survival coded into our flesh. It bonded us. We could move mountains. We needed to be smarter and more focused than the rest.

My cousin picked lint from her cape. "So we stick to the plan? No dinner, just cheese, bread, and warm tea. Well, that's consistent and efficient—very Abigail."

Logic and stubbornness were inherited gifts from the Scottish and Jamaican sides of our family, double portions for me. "Rawlins can't be delayed much longer. We'll miss Wilberforce's new plan. And I have what he needs to reengage parliament's debate on abolition. This time there will be action."

My cousin nodded and fixed another cup of tea.

She and I were a pair, a privileged pair. Florentina used her skills to help the navy, and I dabbled in helping individuals keep their freedom—by solving problems.

My yellow bounder stopped outside. I left coins on the table and towed Florentina and her handful of cheese outside. "They'll think we've hired a hackney."

We headed out of the coffeehouse. My driver, in his dark indigo-blue tricorn hat and ebony mantle, jumped down.

"To our meeting, Rawlins." I held out my hand, but he didn't take it.

He was motionless for a moment.

I could hear my heart pounding. "What is it?"

"Word was sent for you. No meeting tonight." He handed me a note. The handwriting was too familiar and worrisome.

"Very well, Rawlins. Take us home."

"Good, ma'am." The bronze man, with strong, aged hands, helped me and Florentina up into the chaise. Then he began navigating our carriage down all the remote streets to arrive in Westminster.

"Abigail, you look like you've seen a ghost."

"Not a ghost, but a godfather. He said our meeting's canceled and something about *other fish to hook*."

Florentina took the note from my fingers. "What does this mean? And will it be tasty?"

"He means trouble. And it's someone close to us."

My cousin covered her mouth, but not before mumbling "Dinah."

My sister.

Whatever she'd done now, I was prepared this time—to save her and me. This little scrappy baroness would win. I wouldn't be denied anything because of the changing politics of a fickle nation, a finicky neighbor, or a sister determined to find ruin.

Chapter 2

The bells tolled, and Rawlins drove as fast as he could, though not fast enough for me.

It had to be past ten.

One of the many churches in Westminster was hard at work. "Odd for them to ring at night. Do you think King George has passed? He was quite ill two years ago."

"No."

I winced at Florentina's quick dismal. "Flo, did that answer come from some sort of actuarial table?"

"Number jokes." She pointed through the slats to the empty streets. "More people would be outside with very public displays of affection. The loss of important people does that."

She dropped the hood of her cape and pushed at rich dark ringlets, the braids woven and rolled into a tight chignon. "Remember how it was for Admiral Nelson, the weeklong funeral culminating at Saint Paul's?"

"Yes. People lined the route of his coffin in miserable cold January. The man died at sea last October, but his body wasn't returned to England for months. Everyone still came"

"Same with Mr. Pitt. They waited until the following month

to have his funeral. The former prime minister lay in state for two days in Westminster Abbey. People were everywhere. Tonight is too quiet for the king or someone important to have died."

It was a harsh way of putting it, and the cross look on her pretty countenance stung.

Sitting back with my arms folded against my stomach, I prepared for my cousin's true feelings. "Out with it, Florentina Sewell. Say what you are thinking."

She rubbed her hands together as if she were cold and I already felt the frost coming from her forthcoming words.

"Dinah is not in trouble, none but the mischief caused by her own hands. When she left, we searched the streets for months. She is well hidden. You missed seeing Lord Worthing off, hoping to catch a moment with her."

"I wanted to show her she was still important to me. That all was forgiven."

"Abbie, you didn't do anything wrong. You chose to marry a man who is a national hero and who paid your father's debts. You've been elevated. That helps all of us. Dinah didn't like that she was no longer the golden daughter, or she despised Worthing's joke or whatever silly reason she happened upon."

"You make her sound heartless. She might project that to the outside world, but that's not who she is. You know her. She's in trouble."

"I know that wherever she is, Dinah Carrington is well. She left and she's still controlling you. You're changing plans, our plans, for her. Tonight was important. You made us wear costumes. Everything is abandoned because your sister wishes to send you on another wild chase."

Flo was right about a lot of things, but not about Worthing's departure. We'd argued. I chose not to go. Hunting Dinah was a better excuse than watching my husband leave me, not knowing when or if he'd return.

Glancing over her shoulder at the lamps lighting the Westminster Bridge, I calmed looking at the glow and how it turned the River Thames into an ebony mirror.

Dinah. She was the special one, the one with the brightest hopes, until I won Lord Worthing's favor. Didn't she know there was enough light for both of us to shine?

Trying to hold on to my composure or my hope, or something solid and true, I clasped the seat. "I made my choice. Wilberforce will meet again. My contact will secure more information. I'll have to find him a rare book or a choice wine."

"Your contact? Are you talking about Shaw? The handsome solicitor continues to pass you gossip he overhears at your father's firm?"

"Well, yes. But I wouldn't call him handsome. He's like my brother."

"He's not *my* brother. I can admire his good looks, even if he is one of the most arrogant men in Britain."

Wilson Shaw, Florentina, and I all grew up together in a Spitalfields neighborhood, a Blackamoor stronghold in London. It was hard to think of Wilson as anything but fun and dependable. But my cousin had been critical of everything of late, especially anything she deemed nonsensical. Wilson was seldom without a smile and a hearty laugh.

My gaze noted the silhouettes of Saint Margaret's and huge Westminster Abbey, ancient buildings with towers stretching through the clouds. They were constants, strong and formidable. If I were going to use my position to make a lasting difference, then I needed to be the same.

Tearing up over things I couldn't change shouldn't be done.

"She's all right, you know." Florentina tugged me into her embrace. "Dinah's strong-willed like you."

The carriage stopped, but I kept hugging my opinionated cousin. I descended, but she handed me her heavy cloak and stayed inside.

"Flo. You're not coming?"

"No. You need to talk through things with Dinah alone. Godfather Vaughn is right. If she's here—if she stays—that's more important than Wilberforce."

"Abolition won't be solved in one meeting. At week's end, you come here. We dine and then me, you, and Dinah will go see how *Ali Baba* ends."

"Yes. I'll be hoping for that happy ever after. Now go, Abbie. Show Cousin Dinah that you've been Lady Worthing for two years and the sky hasn't fallen."

Blowing a kiss, I closed the yellow bounder's door. "Rawlins, take Miss Sewell to her residence. Take care in the East End of London. You have special cargo."

My driver tipped his tricorn, then started on the forty-minute journey.

I stood still, preparing to see Dinah and praying for the right things to say.

Number Two Greater Queen Street, James's house and mine, sat side by side with my questionable neighbors in Number Eleven. The Hendersons' home and mine looked nothing alike.

Mine had reddish-brown bricks, theirs pale limestone.

Mine had twelve windows on upper floors, theirs fourteen.

Mine didn't have horrid arguments with their spouse, overheard by all.

Mine had no words between husband and wife at all.

Very different.

Those fancy slippers with silver lace I wore tonight didn't budge. The marriage that I knew would save us—keep our father from financial ruin, offer my sister opportunities—drove us apart.

Missing for a year, breaking my heart, binding Papa to his brandy, Dinah had taken her revenge.

All that would end tonight. I merely had to move.

After counting windows again, I marched to my door.

Slipping off my heavy cloak, I decided I'd hug her first, then wring her neck. Yet, in my heart, I vowed to fix whatever I got wrong. Blood and love meant more than weighing who was more right.

As soon as my slippers hit the last stone step, the footmen in cranberry-red liveries let me inside.

Offering the capes to one and my reticule to another, I heard barking.

My butler came from an adjacent hall. "Evening, ma'am. How was the theater?"

"Fine. Where is she?"

"Where's who? The dog? I thought your Welsh terrier was a boy."

I folded my arms about my middle, holding in those words I had for my sister and found some for Mr. Rogers. "My dog's a boy. I'm talking about my . . . sister, Dinah."

The blank look on his face—noble chin lifted allowed the light of the sconce to shine on his receding gray hairline. His thin lips shrank to naught—said she wasn't here. She was still missing.

My chest hurt, stung like it had been kicked. Were these visions of death, the blond hair splattering with blood, of Dinah?

"Ma'am, are you well?"

Rogers tried to grip my arm like I'd begun to fall.

With my hands up and waving, I made him step back. "The dog, where's Teacup?"

"Outside."

My sandy-blond Welsh terrier's whine sounded steady. He was upset.

"Mr. Rogers, why is Teacup outside? It sounds as if he's been barking all night. Why haven't you attended him?"

Rogers lifted his pointy nose. "He's difficult, ma'am."

The man looked frightened, frightened of a tiny dog. I moved past him and hunted. Though small, my boy would stand out on the dark stained pine floors or the whitewashed walls. "Where are you, Teacup?"

"Ma'am, he bites and scratches anyone who's not you. The last I saw, he went inside your parlor. I closed the door."

Running to my favorite room, I crossed the threshold to see the entrance to my terrace wide open, the way I'd left it earlier.

"Lady Worthing, I thought he'd be safe in here—"

"And you'd be safe in the rest of the house."

The man looked fresh in his onyx coat and starched, unwrinkled shirt. Didn't look as if he'd tried hard to coax or calm anything.

"Teacup is outside, Mr. Rogers. He'll tear up my tulips or he'll be attacked by the Hendersons' hounds."

His bark settled down and gave me time to look and see if he'd done any new damage. No paw prints on my off-white parlor walls. The floor-to-ceiling windows had no tongue licks, none that I could see.

Not a single ivory curtain had been tugged to the floor.

Checking the yellow fluffy pillows on my blue sofa and the two side chairs with seats covered in the same azure color, there were no new tears. My comfy patchwork reading blanket was another matter. Sections had been chewed, and batting pulled from seams. "I see this is where Teacup amused himself, the tapestry my mother made."

Mr. Rogers offered a sheepish smile. "I'll have Mrs. Smith fix it good as new. She's out tonight."

Wanting to glance at the longcase clock in the corner—and count how much time my housekeeper and maid had left to enjoy the delightful play, the play I'd skipped for naught—I resisted.

My heart sank lower. No Dinah, no Wilberforce, no Ali Baba. "Now, no Teacup."

The floorboards creaked as I moved to the terrace door. The floor on this level shifted all the time, causing little squeaks. This was the charm of an old house. It meant something to be here listening to it settle and become what time intended a house to be, well lived.

"Ma'am, I see the little fellow in the garden. How about you call for him and I'll scoop him up for a bath?"

"Brave now, Mr. Rogers? Never mind. I'll get him. Have a warm bath ready for him and me."

I slipped onto my cobblestone terrace. The beautiful square of polished stones held an oak table and two wrought-iron chairs. This was my breakfast nook. I ate here every morning until the great fence war.

My dog saw me, but instead of running to me, he took off into the lawn.

"Teacup! He's headed to the Hendersons'."

Rogers ducked inside and came out with the lantern I kept behind my sofa. "Here, ma'am. Godspeed. I'll go get those baths started."

Alone, I walked toward the rear of Number Eleven. "Teacup!"

I heard him. He was distant.

Then my dog stopped barking.

An eerie quiet settled.

Darkness shrouded my steps.

The air smelled different. Not the sweet aroma of my flower garden or the freshness of freshly trimmed grass.

"Teacup, sweetie. Come to Mama."

The light in my lantern seemed quite dim. "Teacup?"

That feeling I had at Drury Lane of being followed returned. Tightness clawing at my throat returned.

A lit torch appeared to my left.

The flame blazed high, but the figure holding it remained engulfed in shadows.

"This, I believe, is yours." The voice solid and gruff struck me before I saw him. Cantankerous Stapleton Henderson had my dog. His big palm straddled my pup's middle.

That thing in my chest calmed, my frozen tongue eased. "Yes. Where did you find him, sir? Cowering from your greyhounds?"

"This dog was on my property trying to get my dogs to play. My greyhounds have been trained not to associate with riff-raff."

Mr. Teacup, the shaggy blond, looked happy, licking the neighbor's palm, regrettably not biting the man. But Henderson's hand looked red between his thumb and forefinger. Maybe my dog did have a go at him.

"Sir, you're lucky he's not traumatized."

He held out Teacup and put him into my arms. "Do you tell yourself falsehoods enough times that you begin to believe them as truth? I'm fascinated by women that lie."

From all the rumors rampant about my neighbors, there were cruel things to be said about him and his estranged wife. But my mother said never kick a man when he's down—or when he could get up and strike you. "Thank you for finding my dog, sir."

"Lady Worthing, the terrier is the aggressor. He's been that way since the beginning."

"He's a third of the size of your dogs. Not possible."

"But my greyhounds are trained. They don't savage runts."

I'd grimace at him, but it was too dark. A well-placed Worthing frown shouldn't be wasted. "Thank you again."

"It's a little hard to ignore the scratching at my door. The pup yelps like a maddening fool for attention." He wrung his hand. "It took a moment for us to get reacquainted. I'll send you a bill for the paint chips."

"He did bite you. G—I mean, sorry."

His lips pressed to a line, and he tugged at his cravat. White and perfectly done as if he'd starched it for this visit. "Yes. You sound anguished."

He shined his lantern toward the fence for a moment. It looked half done, only complete near Saint James Park, where our properties backed.

"Your monstrosity will be done this week?"

"Once it's finished, our dogs will be separated, and we won't be meeting like this anymore. You should've borne half of the expense."

"Money problems, Mr. Henderson?" Stroking Teacup's fuzzy face, I shrugged. "I give to charity often, but not for foolish endeavors. You wanted the fence. I wanted an apology. And I've sent no bill for the damage your wolfhounds have caused digging holes about my prized tulips."

"My greyhounds are not wolfhounds. They are prized animals. Your Teacup can be vicious. Why on earth, madam, would you give a dog such a name? Especially one with a killer bite? Do you want him bullied?"

It was none of his business what I named my terrier and why. Before I could turn to my house, Teacup leapt, heading straight to Saint James Park.

"Oh! Come back!"

I chased briefly; then my lantern snuffed.

Everything became black and stifling. Unable to see in front of me, I froze. "Teacup, where are you? Come back."

Henderson grunted and caught up to me, waving his fire torch. I was grateful for the light, but hated he had to be the one to help.

"Wouldn't want you tripping on a wolfhound hole and suing, Lady Worthing. But you pick up the cretin. I'm not going to be bit again by a dog with such an unbecoming name."

"Agreed. You might manhandle him with your clumsy palms."

"Madam, you don't know the accuracy of my hands. I assure you, they are far from clumsy."

"If you say so, sir. Lead, Mr. Henderson."

He grumbled something that sounded like, *Must be hard for a woman like you to heed.*

I'd mumble a criticism in return about a brooding man, but my mother taught me better.

Unwilling to work together, but with no choice, we started

deeper into the night. Our shadows lengthened in the torch-light.

The closer we got to Teacup's bark, the closer we came to the start of the ridiculous wrought-iron fence.

Then we both stopped.

Frozen, I could simply stare.

My dog sat next to a woman. Eyes wide open, half-naked, gown wrenched open to her waist, she slumped motionless against the fence, not uttering a sound.

I didn't think she'd move, no matter how hard Teacup barked.

"Oh, God," Henderson said. "No. No. Juliet."

I turned to him, and he grabbed me as if to hold me up.

Shock and I weren't the best of friends.

But Death and I were acquaintances. We'd spent a lot of un-wanted time together.

Pulling free, I grabbed a second look.

Flapping in the air, the free end of a ribbon floated.

Silk threads frayed.

Delicate and gauzy, it hovered and tangled in the rough iron curls of the fence.

The other end tied like a noose about Juliet Henderson's neck.

Chapter 3

It took an hour for the magistrate and runners to arrive.

Henderson and his greyhounds stayed outside guarding . . . her.

He'd taken charge, ordering me to my town house, warrior-like in getting his and my servants to light the grounds. Even now, he stood with a soldier's stance protecting his wife's body.

From my parlor windows, I watched my garden turn into a trampled soup.

A death . . . in my yard. Well, mostly my yard, the rest on Henderson's stupid fence.

The creak of the floorboards accompanied my pacing. It was an odd, comforting melody; one I could recite as often as I moved back and forth near these windows. Wrapped in my patchwork of reds and oranges, I kept looking outside.

I shivered, but couldn't get warm, thinking of Juliet Henderson and that ribbon, the ribbon I'd seen in my dream.

Mr. Rogers entered the parlor with a service of tea. "Calm down, ma'am. I know it's most distressing."

"I am calm, Rogers."

He set the tray on the small zebra wood table next to the sofa. "If you were calmer, there wouldn't be a groove in the floor."

"Would a groove stop the creaking? No, never mind." I put my hands on my hips, puffing out the quilt. Bits of batting fell down like I was an old worn tent. "A woman lay murdered on my lawn. And the men who are supposed to find clues are trampling everything. They probably stomped on evidence, along with my flowers."

After fixing a cup of chamomile, he lifted it to me. "Drink this to soothe your nerves. Lord Duncan's men must be thorough."

Taking the tea, I let the heat warm my palms. I frowned at how I was safe and warm, and Juliet Henderson was cold, growing colder, and exposed.

"They're rummaging through my bushes, but no one has the decency to cover Mrs. Henderson. It's not decent."

"Ma'am, you remember Lord Duncan to be a capable investigator. He's an even-handed magistrate. He'd not do anything if it weren't necessary."

It was true; Lord Duncan tried to be fair, but the man arrested my James for murder. If I hadn't found the confession note of the true embezzler, Lord Worthing might've been hanged.

"Rogers, I've battled with Duncan before. I assisted with my husband's circumstances, and two others."

"Lady Worthing, you have a clever mind and were lucky enough to find the suicide letter that saved an innocent man. Your other two mysteries were a missing dog and stolen vintage books. I hardly think that qualifies you to discover evidence."

"I didn't ask for your opinion, Rogers."

My butler pushed out his chest. "I was always able to give

Lord Worthing my honest words. I'd like to do so for you, ma'am."

My questions of his loyalty diminished. "Go ahead, sir."

"The baron was appreciative and humbled by your assistance. The dog owner and bookseller, too, but this is different. It's your yard. The body is on your side of the fence. You may be a suspect."

What? I handed back the tea, sloshing it over the side. "She was murdered, Rogers, by someone with great anger or strength. No one can get tangled up like that, can they? How does one get caught up on a fence? With a dress ripped asunder."

With his handkerchief, he wiped his fingers, then set the cup on the table. "Doesn't sound like an accident, ma'am. And if it wasn't, someone did this to her. Which is why you need to stay inside and let Lord Duncan work."

Moving to the windows, Rogers began closing the curtains. "Be patient."

"How can I? You said I'm a suspect. Juliet Henderson's been my neighbor for nearly two years. Why didn't . . ."

"Why didn't you what, ma'am?"

My gaze lifted from my jumble of regrets. "Why didn't I spend more time trying to befriend her?"

His brows raised and an odd look creased his forehead. "Ma'am, she called you horrible names. She thought the fence dispute was a ruse. She accused you of trying to take the husband she no longer wanted."

Oh, that. In my head, I heard Mrs. Henderson calling me "a lucky wench."

Why was it that established women of the ton tried to assign newcomers the worst motives? I suppose that was like asking why the whole world movement for abolition was stopped by the emergence of a new country, the Black Independent nation of Hayti.

Staring at Rogers's calm eyes, which showed the perfect shade of cobalt blue, I realized that I might have more advocates at Number Two Greater Queen Street than I'd assumed. "I've never appreciated your candor before. It's welcomed."

A smile appeared. It was wry, almost endearing. Perhaps he could be someone to count on—if he learned not to fear Teacup.

Picking up my dog, who now looked settled and tired, as if he'd been barking all along to alert every one of the murder, I fluffed the shaggy fur on his neck. The poor boy smelled of mud and grass. "I can't stand not doing anything."

"Then sit, Lady Worthing. Have your tea. And pray this is resolved and gone as soon as possible. Scandal is nasty business."

Mr. Rogers warmed my cup, filling it again to the brim. His aim with his left hand was precise. I hadn't noticed that before, that he favored that side.

"Ma'am, here, and don't spill."

"Good chamomile shouldn't be wasted." Easing into one of the sitting chairs, I leaned against the high back. Never noticed how uncomfortable it was before. I'd have to do something about it when I wasn't a potential murder suspect.

"Thank you, Rogers."

My butler didn't leave. There was something in his face—fear, concern—something he wanted me to know.

"Out with it, Rogers."

"I apologize. I'm supposed to guide you and keep you grounded while Lord Worthing's away. I should've gone after the sniping dog. He's bitten everyone more than once. I should've been the one who found the body."

"No. Then you'd be a suspect. It takes a lot of strength to strangle or choke a person. More to string her body to the fence."

"Or someone very angry, seething."

Enraged, the meekest person can have extraordinary strength. With the scenes I'd witnessed with Mrs. Henderson, I suspected that she could drive an angel to sin.

Teacup's head flopped on my arm. He was soundly asleep. I set him on the sofa and almost draped him with the blanket, like he was a babe, but that might encourage him to keep ripping at the patchwork.

It was the last thing my mother made. It should stay with me.

When I looked up, Rogers still stared.

Did I look ridiculous, all covered up in a tattered quilt? "What else is wrong?"

His arms went behind his back, then he paced, causing the creaking to begin anew. "You discovered the body alongside the most likely suspect, ma'am. You might've been harmed. I'll never forgive that. His lordship would have my head."

"Lord Worthing wouldn't hurt . . . You think Henderson did this?"

Rogers nodded.

Hadn't my neighbor sounded shocked to find his wife?

And he embraced me as if it were natural and right to do so.

But hadn't the man argued I didn't know the accuracy of his hands. Was that a confession from a man who'd strangled his wife?

Could the arms that held my dog and me have killed?

A chill whipped through my bones. Everything inside my skin shuddered. "The man is odious and obsessed with a fence, but a murderer? No, Rogers. Horrible and testy, but didn't you tell me he'd served in the navy? That he was a hero?"

The butler bowed his head for a moment. "He served at least ten years under Lord Nelson. Stapleton Henderson was a fine officer—a hero is the talk. But he's been at war a long time. The battle can change a person."

Rogers was right. An estranged husband would be the likely killer. Turning back to my wall of windows, I wanted to pry all the curtains open to see if Lord Duncan had taken Henderson into custody.

"Ma'am, where have you been tonight?"

"The theater." I couldn't tell the surprising man about my canceled secret meeting. "Why do you ask?"

"No reason other than the costume robes."

"They're Scottish tweed capes."

"Of course, ma'am. And the giggling housekeeper and maid singing lyrics like they, too, had gone to the theater." He twiddled his fingers. "And Miss Bellows wore a dress similar to yours. Was it a foursome?"

I held my glare upon him and his starched black coat. I hoped it had the offended look I wanted to convey.

"Very well, ma'am." Rogers went toward the hall to exit my parlor. "If you ever want to solicit advice, I'm here to serve. I've been loyal to Lord Worthing, though he kept a chaotic house. I can be loyal to Lady Worthing, too."

"Duly noted. And I thank you. Seems I might need advice from time to time on Scottish robes."

"Capes, ma'am."

The man bowed and left.

As soon as the creaks from his footfalls settled, I sprang to the window and opened the sheer panels of white Burmese muslin.

One of the runners pointed at the fence.

As I squinted, it seemed as if they'd unhooked Mrs. Henderson. Still uncovered, she looked like a fallen ornament or statue on the lawn.

So disrespectful. So exposed. She might have disliked me, but if I was fighting for a world where everyone looked upon their fellow man or woman with compassion, how could I leave her like this?

Suddenly hot and fevered, I decided to use my privilege and decency for good.

Before I could talk myself out of acting, I flung open my terrace door and stepped out into the torchlights.

All eyes might be on me, but I looked at Juliet.

Head leveled, gaze focused, I marched straight to her.

"Ma'am, Lady Worthing." The rough voice giving chase was Lord Duncan's, the magistrate.

Sidestepping him and his runners, I knelt in front of Juliet's body.

Someone had at least closed her eyes, even smoothed her long hair, strands of tawny gold from her face.

For one moment, she was Dinah.

But I knew my sister was alive and hoped she lived with people who cared for her.

I took the quilt from my shoulders and tucked it about Mrs. Henderson's. The ribbon that had bound her throat had been cut away. A sharp single line like a red-and-purple band went about her throat.

The bruising about her neck, and more on her bare arms, was evidence of a struggle. Like my dream, Mrs. Henderson had been strangled, not hanged. If I hadn't forced myself awake, would I have seen her face, the face of a woman who fought until the end?

"Lady Worthing," Duncan said, "please stop."

No. My examination was beginning. Feigning prayer, I hovered over her, looking for clues. Blood was on the broken nail of her index finger.

A violent struggle.

Yet, not a button of her gown was torn. The delicate pearls of the back closure were undone and in place, not ripped. The dress was opened with care—not in an assault, but in celebration.

Imperious Lord Duncan stooped to my side. "Lady Worthing, are you tampering with evidence or making a mockery of the crime scene?"

"It's been hours. And no one has covered her up. That's a mockery, my lord."

"Lady Worthing, please go back into your house."

I tucked the quilt over her feet. "Rest, Mrs. Henderson."

"Ma'am, please."

"Half your runners are ogling her." Pulling my hands together, I again made a motion like I prayed.

This time Duncan bowed his head. I adjusted the quilt again, checking for a captured button or loose hair. Nothing. Even her rings on her fingers were intact. I was positive she wasn't clawing a random attacker, but someone she knew.

"What do you suspect happened, Lord Duncan?"

"Please stop hovering over the body. The coroner has not come."

"Did you notice, sir, that she has a broken nail and something that looks like blood pooled under another ragged one?"

"What?" Duncan waved one of his runners close. He took the man's lantern and shined more light about Mrs. Henderson.

"Yes, she fought that necklace and fence that eventually hanged her."

"Or her assailant, my lord."

He offered his arm to me. "Now, Lady Worthing, please."

"Looks as if she chose to fight her attacker and not the wrought iron. She scratched him or her."

Duncan leaned over and checked Juliet's neck and hand. Then he covered her up again.

"I think you are right." He bit his lip and nodded. It was something he did when he pondered evidence. "I remember you're inquisitive, Lady Worthing, and often take no thought of safety or cautiously proceeding."

"Your men are rampaging everywhere. How is that thoughtful or cautious? And I have been helpful to you on several occasions."

He folded his arms; his dark blue, almost black, eyes glanced at me, then Mrs. Henderson. "It has been three curious circumstances that your input was helpful, but no murders, ma'am."

His olive-green tailcoat held wrinkles. Everything he wore had them, but Duncan was a man dedicated to solving crime and never beholden to fashion. "Go back inside, Lady Worthing. When the coroner's done, I'll have questions and you can ask yours. I know you'll have some. Go on."

If he called me "lass" or "little lady," I might vomit. Instead of rebelling, I curtsied and trudged back to my house. It was easier to get information from Duncan in private if I honored in public.

Henderson sat on my terrace. He'd made himself comfortable.

I wanted to interrogate him. What did he know or suspect? But he sat there deflated in my chair. I decided to let him mourn. Yet, when I passed, he called my name.

I turned. "Yes, Mr. Henderson."

"Thank you," he said. His voice was dry and chalky. "For covering her."

"She's been my neighbor since I moved here. It's the decent thing to do."

The look on his stone face was far away. The torchlight made his dark eyes look haunted.

Again, I felt for him.

Until I noticed the scratch to his hand, the one my dog made or the one Henderson had made me think was Teacup's doing.

"Such a horrid accident. Juliet, her love of scarves and ribbons, getting caught—"

"Your wife was murdered." I lowered my tone. "You know you're a suspect. Everyone still talks about the noisy scene of you tossing her out. All of Greater Queen Street heard."

Henderson took a cloth from his pocket and wiped his mouth, his fingers. "All is not as it appears. And I can want a woman out of my house and still wish her to be happy, healthy, and free."

"Then who would do this?"

"My wife had a place in Cheapside. We were amicable. She often returned for pocket change or to tell me of her impending travels. I assume that's why she was here tonight. This has to be an accident. No one would hurt Juliet. She had no enemies."

Lord Duncan approached. "You don't need an enemy for a murder. Catch the wrong person at the wrong time and anyone can kill."

"You intend to question all of London, my lord."

"No, ma'am. Just the most likely suspects." The magistrate came fully onto my terrace and put his lantern on my table. "Where were you tonight, Mr. Henderson?"

The blinding light barely made my neighbor move. "The Drury Lane Theatre."

My heart sank and beat drums all the way down my throat.

"Lady Worthing was there, too. I saw her and her companion from my seat."

Wait? Why did he have to mention seeing me?

Both men looked at me, as if I could corroborate his presence. I couldn't.

"Yes, I was at the theater. But I must've missed you, Mr. Henderson. Everyone knows how I love plays and operas. I'm completely absorbed from the moment the production starts."

"Lord Worthing mentioned your fondness for the theater. The baroness and I have been feuding about our dogs. My attendance was meant as a peace offering. That I'd tried to understand her way of thinking." He stood, and with his hand on his lapel—the way men did to appear impervious, broad-shouldered, and above it all. "This is my fault. If I hadn't been building that blasted fence to keep our dogs apart, Juliet would still be alive. I should've listened sooner to the baroness. The blasted wall will come down as soon as the investigation is over."

Duncan folded his arms, his head tilting again at me. "What did you see at Drury Lane, Henderson?"

"*Ali Baba and the Forty Thieves.*" My neighbor thumbed his lips. "The third act was particularly amazing. The poor actor who played Ali forgot his lines momentarily. I've never been more on the edge of my seat. Kept hoping the poor lad would recover. He did. Overall, a stellar performance."

"Did he, Lady Worthing? Did the actor make mistakes?" Duncan's steely glare sank upon me.

I had no idea how the actor performed, but Henderson wasn't stupid. He'd not claim something that could be easily disproved. "Does one ever recover from flubbing a line? It ruined things for me."

"Oh, give Ali Baba another chance," Henderson said, his tone soft, but heavier than a whisper. "You must admit that once he fixed things, he didn't make any more mistakes. At least none I noticed."

Duncan seemed satisfied. His attention shifted to his runners and all the blinding torches men waved.

But I heard a confession and a threat.

The magistrate stretched and picked up his lantern. "I'll have to check these alibis for veracity."

These?

"Of course." Henderson dipped his chin, and he hummed something that was probably a part of the show. Who would believe Mr. Grunter could be gallant and social?

Not me. This was an act.

It was his life, his late wife. And somehow, I'd become entangled in his web.

My throat tightened.

"If the coroner fails to come," he continued, "utilize my medical knowledge for questions. I was the medical officer with Lord Worthing and Nelson's chief before his death."

"Before Trafalgar." Duncan took off his top hat for a second.

"Lord Worthing has charged me to look after Lady Worthing's interests while he's on his present excursion. Please don't have the runners tearing up her lawn. She's particular about her flower beds."

This civility was theater. I was more convinced than ever.

He'd done it.

And with his *Ali Baba* talk, he'd made me an accomplice, offering to Duncan the picture of a friendship and an alliance with Worthing to make it easy to assume I might be in league with Henderson.

If I could explain my whereabouts without involving two servants, a cousin, and Stilton cheese, I'd confess right here.

Disgusted, I moved from the men. "Yes, don't tear up my lawn."

When I opened my terrace door, Teacup bounded outside. He passed me, but Henderson snatched him up.

"Ouch," he said, and shook his hand in the air. "This thing bit me again. Lady Worthing, how do we teach him some manners?"

We? His cold indigo eyes glared at me, daring me to say anything that would contradict him.

I couldn't say a word, even when he put my dog in my arms.

My emotions were too heavy. I'd been caught and made to look as guilty as Henderson.

I could barely breathe and held on to Teacup as if he'd escaped a madman. My neighbor looked smug answering more of Duncan's questions.

Henderson thought he'd won.

Not on my lawn.

Chapter 4

Pounding on the bedchamber door roused me from a deep sleep. Well, it felt deep for the whole three hours that it was.

Teacup stood and stretched, then lay back down on his fluffy pillow on the floor. His fast breathing and slurp from his close water bowl sounded like permission for another thirty minutes of sleep.

Knock. Knock.

My boy started sniping. I looked over the side of the mattress and the dog vanished underneath my bed. Blinking, getting my eyes used to daylight, I called for him. "Oh, Teacup. I thought you were giving me at least another five minutes."

He growled.

And I wondered if he'd found something under my bed.

Peeking over the side as if something might snatch me, I swept the lace and bedclothes back.

Nothing but Teacup dragging and chewing on my silver slipper from last night.

When the pounding on the door started anew, he howled and dodged deeper under the bed.

"For a boy who gets me in such trouble, you seem to be a 'fraidy pup."

Mrs. Smith came into the room. "I hear ya talking," she said with her island accent more pronounced. "That must mean you're up."

"Teacup's under the bedframe. He has the right idea. Maybe if I sleep another ten minutes, we'll both be ready to rise."

She stepped inside, holding towels in her hand and humming something upbeat and refreshing.

"Is that from *Ali Baba* last night?"

"Yes. It was good. And then there was comedy."

"Oh, how so?"

"The fella playing Ali, he forgot his lines. Some in the crowd chuckled. Then the actor got on with it."

So Henderson was telling the truth. "Did you see anyone you recognized?"

Her brow furrowed as she placed the towel over the footboard. "No. We stayed hidden in the shadows. And we left before the last act."

"Good. As we planned."

"Ma'am, I see you came home to disaster."

"Indeed."

"And I heard you discovered the body with the husband."

"Yes, Mrs. Smith."

She folded up a big white towel. "That must've been upsetting. Lady Worthing, I've known you for a lot of years. I've known your mother and father. I think a lot of you. I—"

"Mrs. Smith, I didn't sneak out of Drury Lane to kill Mrs. Henderson. I was going to a secret abolition meeting. I wasn't supposed to say anything, because I can't jeopardize the movement or the leaders. They're holding on by threads."

Olive-brown cheeks brightened. "I didn't think you did, but it's nice to hear."

Flopping backward, I pulled a pillow over my face. "Don't tell anyone. I can't break the secrecy of the group. And even if I tell the truth now, no one will believe me. I'll simply look guilty."

She came to the side of the bed and tossed off the pillow. "You definitely can't hide in bed. Lady Worthing has to entertain. The baroness must go about her day like any normal innocent person."

"Well, this innocent person feels like sleeping today."

Mrs. Smith looped her finger around one of my loose paper curls and stuffed it back under the cap. "Get up. Go see about Miss Henderson. I heard she fell to pieces when she returned home."

I didn't need this piece of news from Mrs. Smith. I had seen it all.

Apparently, Mary had spent the evening at a friend's supper in Mayfair, but nothing, not even a protective older brother, could hide all the runners and torches in our yards upon her return. She collapsed against Henderson and then sobbed in my arms.

Mary came to live at Number Eleven when her father died. She and I had bonded this past year over flowers. I hadn't realized that she and Juliet had also become close.

A cold hand gripped my foot. I sprang up.

"Wake up, sleepyhead. We were talking about last night and you fell asleep."

"Just resting my eyes."

The housekeeper's full, pouty frown was sympathetic. "I'll keep to myself what you told me, and I'll make sure Miss Bellows does, too. She's been known to run on."

Mrs. Smith tugged my foot again and looked quite cross as if I was naughty, missing a tutor's lesson. "Now look here, Lady Worthing, you have appearances to make. Sleeping too long looks guilty. Get up and do what it is you do."

"You mean figure out who did it?"

"I was thinking breakfast and gardening, but if that gets you up." Mrs. Smith put her hand to her crisp white apron. "And Mr. Vaughn is downstairs."

My godfather.

I should've guessed his visit would come soon. Well, I needed his resources to find the truth about the Hendersons.

I'd also like to know how he found out about the secret Clapham Sect meeting.

His note had forced me home. I thought it was about Dinah. Perhaps it wasn't that at all.

"Ma'am, you need to move. He says it's urgent."

I rolled to my side. Rising up seemed too far a distance. "What time is it?"

"A little past nine."

"Oh, tell him I'm still asleep." I flopped back and covered my head with my lacy nightgown sleeves. "Though I suppose he won't keep until noon."

"No, Lady Worthing. He has that haunted look in his eye, the same as when it comes to business or the late Mrs. Carrington."

Mrs. Smith had been in service to my family a long time. I knew she had many secrets in her head; if she sneezed too hard, they'd escape. "He's fearful. Murder of a woman hits his heart. Hits us all. And poor Mr. Sinclair. The lady's driver is beside himself. He been crying all morning. The man loved working for her."

She made a sad, nasally *uh-huh-um* and went to my door. "I'm going to offer Sinclair tarts and tell him to stop the whiskey for a while."

"That would be good. Mrs. Smith, I didn't know you were close to the neighbor's servants."

"We all are. All the workers in the neighborhood talk. Sinclair's a good man. Loved his job. This is sad, *uh-huh-um*," she said again. "I'll send Miss Bellows in to help you dress. She had a nice time, too. The woman actually hushed long enough to enjoy other people's words."

"Wait, Mrs. Smith. A murder doesn't happen in Westminster every day. What's the talk?"

With a shrug, she moved to the window and opened the curtains wide.

The blasted sun burned through the glass pane and sparked light on every glossy surface—the vanity, the shiny mirror.

"It's not good. Half say Henderson gave the wretch what she deserved. Others think it was one of her jealous lovers."

"Lovers? As in more than one? But that's hearsay."

"Him say, too." She chuckled, then put a hand on her hip. "Plenty of men think she was involved with too many lovers. One of them killed her."

Sitting up, I pulled my knees to my chin and wrapped my arms about my legs. "I'll have to get a list to investigate."

"And you be careful of Mr. Henderson, Lady Worthing. It's not every day a man builds a fence to keep away from you. I'll send Miss Bellows to you."

The door closed.

Her warning stayed with me, and a sense of panic clawed at my spine. Sharp like my dog's unclipped nails, it sent my mind whirling. Didn't like the possibility of living next door to a killer. I loathed that my housekeeper and maybe even Duncan could read more into the stupid dog wars I had with my neighbor.

"Teacup, when you're ready to come out, make sure you get Henderson before he gets me."

I lay back and rested my eyes.

A shuffling noise and the smell of lavender stirred me. My lids cracked open and I saw Miss Bellows dancing in my closet.

"Ma'am," she said. "This heavy black crepe with shiny onyx black buttons will do nicely."

"Miss Bellows, I think—"

"I think you need to wash your face and dress. And your godfather's been here for quite a while. And there's probably a list of things you'll need to do before going to the neighbors."

"Wait? What? Mr. Vaughn stayed an hour?"

"We let you sleep for two, ma'am. A dead sleep at that. But it's time to get up."

"Well, I hadn't been sleeping well." Focusing on my closed drawer of bedside table, I blinked my eyes. If the busy Neil Vaughn stayed, the gossip was truly bad.

My maid came to my bed and smoothed my brow. "Frowning like this will give you wrinkles. You're far too young for that."

Was I? Juliet was older than me, and she didn't live long enough to have wrinkles. At twenty-two, I felt mine might be a badge of honor. They'd represent that I lived and survived all the ills of my world . . . on my terms.

Grasping my hands, Miss Bellows towed me from the bedclothes. "That's it. Let's start those limbs working. He's waiting on the terrace."

The terrace? Not the parlor. I'd stopped eating out there since fence construction began.

I supposed Godfather Vaughn was curious about the murder scene.

Looking at things in the light of day might help me piece together more clues.

How did the killer arrive?

Which way did he go when he left?

"I'll dress you appropriately for the Hendersons' gathering. They are having a . . . I'm not sure. Some Scottish tradition where everyone drinks and eats. The invitation's just come."

Wishing I had a cup of strong black tea to make me alert, I sank into my vanity and let Miss Bellows attend to my tresses.

She'd become quite good at navigating my wavy curls and my hair's uncanny ability to swell in hot ballrooms.

Miss Bellows brushed and parted and began braiding my thick hair into a sculptured chignon.

Then she brushed the baby hairs, those fine ones at the nape of my neck and around my brow, into place.

I'd look the part of an elegant baroness when I went down the stairs.

If my godfather, Prince George's power broker, had come with more news, most of it wouldn't be good. I wondered how long it would be before his words reduced me to the frightened child he'd found wandering, lost in a storm, all those years ago.

Neil Vaughn always happened upon me at the worst times in my life.

The small feeling snaking through my middle told me that this time, the sage man was here to save me.

Stepping through my terrace door, I tried hard not to look to the fence, to imagine again a strangled Juliet, arms woven into wrought iron, hanging by her ribbon necklace.

But I didn't have to fret. The monstrous fence was gone.

I squinted under the bright sun and tried to make sure I wasn't still in my bedchamber. I shifted my weight on the slate tiles and waited to awaken and find that yesterday was a dream.

"It's gone." My godfather's deep voice reached me. He pushed back in his chair, then rose to greet me. "My goddaughter has returned to the living."

"Good to see you, too." I kissed his sable-brown cheek.

Taking my hand, he studied me for a moment. "What, my girl, are you seeing?"

His steady grip on my hand didn't slacken and his question

wasn't about the missing wrought iron and sections of lumber. He still had hopes I'd inherited my mother's gift, the gift of second sight.

"Abigail, speak to me."

"Nothing of consequence, but I'm remembering Mr. Henderson showing me the plans of the monstrous fence to separate our properties. I can quote dimensions from our last argument. That was three days ago. If he hadn't built it . . . maybe his wife would still live."

He let go of my hand and drew his arms to his sides. "You think a fence could've saved Mrs. Henderson? What if someone had mentioned a premonition of her death? Do you think that would've kept her alive?"

Rubbing my flustered skull, I stepped away from him to the edge of the cobbles and stopped in my trampled garden. "I planted tulips. You think they will still grow with all those runners plodding through?"

"When your mother missed a warning . . . it would eat her up inside. She felt responsible. Magdalena often forgot she was human and everything could be given to misidentification."

"It doesn't work like that for me." I took a deep breath. "I only get bits and pieces, none ever makes sense or gives me time."

"Abigail, I'm—"

"I thought it was Dinah. I made myself look away."

Like when I was young, like when my parents argued and I wanted to run from the Spitalfields neighborhood, Vaughn embraced me and held me until I stopped shaking. "I remember when you'd show up and take me and Dinah for ices at Gunter's. We'd all stay in your carriage, waiting for servants to bring back lemon ices."

"Well, you loved them, and you girls were a package deal. I can't help but care for you both."

"Why does it feel like that was a lifetime ago or someone else's life?"

He shrugged and led me to the table. "It probably was. Seeing death catch a person who was filled with life is hard."

The sadness creeping into his countenance spoke for him. Vaughn remembered my mother. His love for her had never gone away.

Nonetheless, he wasn't here to reminisce and I wasn't trying to become like her, trapped by visions that drove her mad. Sitting next to him, I reached for his arm. "Tell me how bad things are."

His dark brown eyes, which crinkled when he laughed, appeared stark.

"That bad. Oh, the gossip must be rampant."

"Why, Abigail, can't you be happy with embroidery or volunteering with charity work?"

"I didn't ask for a woman to be murdered on my property."

"Lord Worthing's property, Abigail. It's in his name."

"I wear his name. It's all one in the same."

"Abigail, Worthing has not updated the deed to Number Two Greater Queen Street. You're the keeper of it. Status quo."

The lilt in his voice had hints of Saint Giles brogue he'd learned from the streets. The slip in his cultured, manufactured tones meant he had more fears than a murder on my lawn. I'd be scared if I weren't assured of his love for me and Flo and Wilson. He claimed us as the children he never had.

"Vaughn, you don't need to fret. Worthing will attend to things when he returns. He said he'd never leave me unprotected. Silly me. I assumed it meant he wouldn't leave at all."

My godfather picked up a glass. "It's a good match. You're protected."

"And I get to walk around all fancy as Lady Worthing and pretend I'm no better off than the simple girl who took notes for my father at his solicitor firm. That's what the ton wants. But I'm elevated and that cost me my sister."

"I take it your talk with Dinah didn't go well?"

"Never saw her." I gripped the table. "All the noise and runners must've scared her off."

Steam left his nostrils and fogged the side of his glass. "Dinah was to be here last night. That was the note I sent. I'd hoped you two had met before the chaos."

With my hands lifted together, I dropped my face to my steepled knuckles. "No. She must've seen the torches and trouble and ran. I can thank the murderer for killing my chances at repairing my family."

Vaughn's warm, rugged finger wiped a tear from my cheek. "If I'd known about Mrs. Henderson, I wouldn't've had Rawlins hurry you home, but I don't have the gift of precognition."

"I told you, I don't, either. A few images in my head that mean nothing. Now my chance at reconciliation is lost."

Vaughn flicked away another tear. "Things aren't irrevocably broken. Dinah Carrington is smart and safe and will come back to you when she's ready. That will be after the Henderson business is done."

"You know where she is? Tell me. I could . . ."

A big gulp made a third of Vaughn's glass disappear. "Don't ask anymore. I talked her into coming. I'll talk her into coming again."

"Then tell me why she ran away on my wedding day? Why does she hate that I married?"

He shrugged. "Until Queen Street is free of the magistrate's runners, she won't darken your door. I suggest you figure out what happened to Juliet Henderson."

You've helped Lord Duncan solve a mystery or two."

It was exactly three, two since my marriage, but none were murders. Vaughn knew it. Each closed case afforded me a lecture about being careful, but now that Lord Duncan saw I had a talent for puzzling things together, he occasionally indulged a wife of a peer with questions, similar to the way other wives of parliament were entertained at the Old Bailey.

"When I saved Lord Worthing's neck from Newgate's hangman's noose, you saw the benefits of my questioning mind."

He chuckled and guzzled the lemonade. "Yes, and I arranged an advantageous offer of marriage for you to the dashing family friend. It also helped your family's debt. Your father has the nerve to own a solicitor firm managing other people's money, and he can't keep his."

"You promised not to talk of my father's debts. I liked Worthing. He's dashing, but at twice my age, Papa was against it."

"What choice did Carrington have? And how could he deny a match that afforded you privileges, comfort, connections, and cash?"

I glared at him with tear-filled eyes. "You didn't say my elevation would cost me my father's love and Dinah. And maybe Worthing, too."

He reached into his impeccable indigo coat with silver buttons and pulled his handkerchief. "If they cannot honor your sacrifice, perhaps they are expendable."

This man with secrets, who had power in the dark sides of town, as well as in the shadowed corners of the ton's ballrooms, could be ruthless, but he'd always protected his three—me, Flo, Wilson—and a fourth, Dinah.

"Mr. Vaughn, when am I expendable?"

"Never, my girl. You're too clever." My godfather sipped from his glass again. "And the baroness is lovely in jet and not brown monk robes."

The mourning gown with the heavy pleating that ran the length of the front made me appear serious and grounded, the stately wife of a peer, not a creature who'd been ensnared in her neighbor's web. Or one of Vaughn's. "Thank you. My theater disguises worked until you sent a note, forcing me home to discover a murdered woman."

"I sent you home for Dinah." He swirled the cloudy liquid in the deep glass before taking a small sip. "But what caper were you up to? And why was my niece involved? You two hardly do anything without involving the other."

"Florentina and I were going to a meeting with Wilberforce to assist in getting the abolition movement started again."

"The clandestine Clapham Sect are at it again?" He took another gulp and the sourness made his lips pucker. "You and Florentina want to be abolitionists. How do you two plan to help?"

"I have testimonies of atrocities that happened this year on Antigua plantations. Powerful firsthand accounts. The Clapham Sect can issue new pamphlets, ones that will rile people more than their last. Yet, I can't put the eyewitnesses or even my husband at risk. Everyone has to be committed."

"Is what Lord Worthing sent accurate? You verified it?"

"Yes. I had Wilson check on the names and positions of slave drivers, traders. Everything is true, from the beatings to the rapes to open murder. No one could fabricate such horrid details."

He thumbed his lips. "I wish it was a ruse. That all the horrors were over."

"No ruse, Mr. Vaughn. You have to get up early to fool me."

"Abigail, you barely see the sun before noon. Many can trick you."

His mirth was annoying and endearing.

"Well, at least you're not sneaking off for an affair with Henderson."

"No." My hand waving was frantic like my fingers were on fire. "Never!"

Vaughn laughed harder. His silky baritone, which had charmed dukes and princes and the wealthiest of Europe, pitched up a little when humored. It was rare to see the serious man hunched over in a full chortle.

Yet, times like these reminded me how human he was under all his politicking.

"Go on, Mr. Vaughn. Tell me the rest."

"The rest, Abigail?"

I tapped my onyx-dyed slippers on the slate tiles. "You're here first thing in the morning after my neighbor's wife was found strangled on my lawn. You even waited for the girl that doesn't rise until noon. Neil Vaughn waits for no one."

His ripe smile soured, falling to nothingness. "There's such a thing as waiting too long."

Yes. There was. A different, thoughtful look—a regretful one—dimmed his eyes. When he pined for my mother, I knew him to be very human.

Next month would be four years since her passing. Vaughn had been a steady friend to her and all the Carringtons. That's why he helped Papa avoid ruin, all because of his undying love for Magdalena.

This look of loss and tenderness—I saw none of it in Henderson's eyes last night. If the man ever loved Juliet, those feelings had disappeared. I detected sadness in the manner of her death, but none that she'd be missed from his life.

Vaughn stared off in the distance toward the roof tiles of my house, mourning a woman whose memory was larger than life. For a moment, his dark hands smoothed my gold one; then he sat back, adjusting his pocket watch against his sea foam–green waistcoat, looking so human I wanted to sob.

Instead, I cleared my throat and sipped lemonade. "Mama always said you'd make time slow. You don't move until everything is right."

His eyes flashed. His stare sailed above my head. "I suppose that's why she slipped away. Took too long building my world."

"You know she was always proud of how busy you were and the world of influence you've created within the ton. Rumors persist you're the man the Prince of Wales enlisted to find proof of Princess Caroline's infidelity. He wants a parliamentary divorce."

This made Vaughn grin. "There's no need to slather me with Devonshire cream, Abigail. I'll always tell you what you need to know."

That wasn't exactly the same as what I wanted to hear. "Say the worst. What do you fear?"

He tapped his fingers on the table, then stopped. "You know Juliet Henderson wasn't a happy woman."

"She's definitely not happy now."

"True. When Henderson returned to London, he discovered she was having multiple, reckless affairs. He kicked her out."

Multiple? As in the same time? Bristling, I sat back in my wrought-iron chair. "Affairs? If it were one, he'd have let her stay?"

"Abigail. There's only so much a man is willing to take. I have charity for him. Recently back from an illustrious career at sea, an outstanding one under Lord Nelson, and the woman with his name was neither faithful nor discreet."

There was a message in his even tone, one I'd ignore.

"Where did Henderson banish her? I know they had an awful fight about six weeks ago. She was made to leave."

"He pays for her residence, Seven Watling Street in the heart of Cheapside. Have you been there?"

Well, well. What the neighbor had said was true. "No. Mrs. Henderson and I weren't enemies, but we weren't close."

He looked over his glass. "What of you and Henderson? I hear he served once with your absent husband. I believe them to be friends."

"My neighbor is arrogant and conniving. His dogs terrorize my little Teacup."

"Then why are you providing him an alibi?"

My eyes went wide, and I shook my head hard. I saw stars. "It's not what I wish. But to expose him is to expose myself. I left the theater early. I had decoys so that no one would know I went to a secret abolition meeting. If discovered, I look guilty. I'm sure Henderson will twist events to say I killed his wife."

Vaughn groaned. "Decoys? Abigail Carrington Monroe, explain."

Holding my breath, I prepared to blurt out my horrible luck. "Henderson went to the Drury Lane Theatre last night. He knows Florentina and I left before the second act."

That feeling of being followed. Did Henderson send someone after us? He knew my alibi to be shaky.

My godfather smoothed his clean-shaven chin. "Well, telling Duncan he saw you in Drury Lane for the entire play sounds like a solid excuse for you and him."

"He's lying, but how can I fix it and explain my leaving early?"

"You don't think people will believe you were dragging your cousin to hear a boring speech by a coward?"

"Wilberforce is brave."

"Then his cause has turned coward. One colony in a sea of unrest has thrown off their shackles. Hayti is free and now everyone is rethinking if Blackamoors should have liberty everywhere."

His voice, which rarely was raised, spiked, but this topic had my passions, too.

"Vaughn, the fight must restart whether Hayti is free or not. Do I need to remind London that there's nothing to fear of Black and White working together?"

"You wish to be a martyr, Abigail?"

"No. I need the Clapham Sect fight. If I show them the evidence Lord Worthing has collected, they'll resolve to continue."

"Does your husband send a spare backbone?" He filled his glass again. Lemon slices plopped into the crystal. "Admirable. Very admirable, but I don't see why you are protecting a murderer."

"I think Henderson capable of killing, but I don't know for sure if he did. I can't condemn him until I'm sure. And I need unshakable evidence to prove his guilt and keep myself from jeopardy."

"You believe you can find such proof?"

"I have to. I can't attest to a meeting, one I didn't attend. I can't even claim public knowledge of a secret event. That alone could cause more members to abandon Wilberforce."

Vaughn sighed and looked up to the sky. "And if you can't find proof of Henderson's guilt?"

"He'll get away with it. I can say nothing, or I'll be made the villain."

"Henderson's vouching for you saves you from scrutiny, as well as himself. Smarter bastard than I thought."

"What?"

"The man's quiet. Never trust the quiet ones. Doesn't say too much in his club. Doesn't associate much with anyone. He's protective of his sister, and now you."

"What?" With a shake of my head, I dismissed these foolish notions. "He hates me. This, I'm sure. Henderson and I do nothing but fight. That stupid fence construction was the latest battle. And if he's the killer, I'm the next woman he'll gladly be rid of."

Vaughn sat back and thumbed his lips. "You truly think he did it?"

My godfather raised his hands and mussed his short, cropped

hair, then gazed at me with such pity. "How do I free you from this situation?"

I wasn't a wretch. I wasn't my half sister. Yet, at this moment, I could picture Dinah laughing at my newest predicament. She'd be the first to spill all to our father to let him know I'd finally erred.

She'd be right this time and would savor the moment. Then she'd rally and help me.

The way I missed her, I wouldn't mind her crowing. Wouldn't mind it at all.

Yet, I had to accept that she was alive, and well . . . just didn't want to see me.

Sighing, I stretched my arms and stood. I drifted to the spot where I'd stood when Henderson lied to Duncan. My anger burned anew.

"I'll get free of this, Vaughn. This is sort of new for me, to be ensnared in an actual crime."

"True. If you'd listened to your vision, would you've been able to avoid this?"

"I don't have them like Mama. I'm not her, but I wish I had her strength. Yet, if she truly could control and master second sight, wouldn't that mean she'd be here, alive, with the loves of her life still fighting for her?"

Vaughn was silent for a long time. I heard church bells. Then his lips parted. "It hurt Magdalena not to be able to help, not always stop bad circumstances. Don't run from the gift if you have it. Learn to use its advantages."

I'd always ignored the snips of visions or future sight or precognition as the researchers and folklore gossips called these dreams. "All I saw was a silky ribbon hanging on a fence. It had blood splatters. And there was blond hair. I had no idea it foretold Juliet Henderson's murder."

"But it's eating at you. That's why you're sleeping half the day away. Young lady, are you truly trying to convince me that you're willing to let your neighbor get away with murder?"

It was gnawing at me, how everything I worked for was at risk because of Stapleton Henderson. The sooner I solved the murder and unattached myself to his lie, the sooner my conscience would become clear.

Unfortunately, to catch a smart man, I needed to lean on a smarter one. Convincing my godfather to help always had a cost.

Chapter 5

Vaughn walked with me onto my lawn. Side by side, we headed toward Saint James Park. I noticed the place was empty. "It seems oddly quiet."

"The park? No races or bird fanciers today. Bad news and mourning travel fast." He stopped right at the spot, as if his slippers knew this was where Juliet Henderson had died.

"Vaughn, what type of evidence will I need to prove a war hero's guilt? What will stand up in court? I don't think pieces of a dream will do."

"Abigail, did your second sight show Henderson killing his wife? Seeing a person is significant."

"No, I didn't. I saw neither of them. None of the actual murder. I saw wrought iron, a caught ribbon. Splatters of blood. I don't remember much else. When I saw her . . . the body with Lord Duncan, there were red stains on her fingers, a broken nail. The woman had struggled."

"Her killer may be marked?"

"Yes, but the wound may not be visible. With her state of undress, who knows where it may be found?"

He grimaced. I supposed my words sounded strange. I should explain. "Mrs. Henderson was left partially nude by the killer. Her dress wasn't torn, but unfastened. It was carefully done or even staged for the shocking appearance."

The tension on his face eased. My actual observations were more powerful than superstition. He crossed his arms and glanced at the freshly filled in post holes, then maybe again to the vacant park.

I trusted Vaughn perhaps even more than my father. Though I had doubts of when I'd become expendable, or if he'd ever truly tell me the full truth about things, I knew he thought me capable and with wits to handle the truth—the beauty and darkness of it.

"Let's head back."

We did so, but this time I stopped at my trampled garden and gathered wilted petals of my ruined tulips. "In one of Worthing's old books, I read the lust of these flowers started a financial speculation and panic almost two hundred years ago."

"Yes. Panics start by the lust of something rare. The deprivation causes many to take risks to gain treasure. That's why most gamblers lose. They can't stop. They want what they perceive to be missing."

"Like the love of an unfaithful wife?"

"Loyalty and love are a different matter. Sometimes the heart wants what it wants."

We were talking about Henderson and Juliet, not me and James, or even Vaughn and my mother. Right?

His steady gaze pronounced everyone was guilty.

When he held out his hand, I put the petal, creamy and white, against his sable-colored veins, long life veins.

"This is a tragedy. But, my dear, unless you saw the victim and the villain, you couldn't stop this."

"I do feel responsible in a way. I've been using the drops. It takes away most dreams."

MURDER IN WESTMINSTER   67

"Abigail, no."

"I didn't want to see the blonde's face. I thought it was Dinah. I didn't want to dream of my sister dying. Now Juliet Henderson is dead."

All the dread of the past weeks returned. The nightmare unfolded and unfolded until I knew it would be my sister. What do you do when you need to protect someone and can't find them?

Yet, this murder was yards away. I knew Juliet Henderson. I could've warned her. Now it was too late.

"Abigail? Abigail?"

A warm palm held my cheek. I blinked and my godfather's face came into view.

"As much as I'd love for you to trust your gift, to mine it for its possibilities, it's not a crime to ignore it. And if you were meant to see it all, you would've. Nothing can stop destiny. Don't blame yourself."

I knew this, but part of me was ashamed that I'd been a coward. I clung to his neck for a moment, a lingering moment like a little girl lost. Then I released him and again danced to the edge of the terrace, the last cobble before the muck and manure of my hedgerow and ruined garden. "It's all too late. I saw a woman running, a ribbon necklace with an emblem. If I knew Dinah was safe, that might give me courage."

Turning back to Vaughn, I was ready to beg. "Tell me where my sister is. I believe you know where to find her."

"I can't break her confidence. I'm a man of my word. And I promised Magdalena to look after all the girls, not just her, Abbie."

If Vaughn made a promise to my mother, nothing on this earth would make him break it. "Then tell me why my marrying Lord Worthing made Dinah run?"

He sat back down. "Her leaving is more than the baron.

That's all I can say. It's Dinah's truth to tell. She will when she's ready."

Another slow gulp made his Adam's apple bulge. "Your sister's almost there, Abigail. When this Henderson business is done, we'll see if she can be convinced to try again."

"She's still out there in the streets, Vaughn. Let her know I love her. That my door's open and I won't judge."

"I will, but let's get you free of this murder entanglement."

"There has to be evidence. Henderson is steps ahead of me. First, *Ali Baba,* and now he's already removed the fence."

"Abigail, your neighbor's not stupid. The magistrate must have cleared the fence's removal. Any physical evidence missed probably sits in a refuse pile somewhere."

The pendant? There was no mention of one being found. Wouldn't there be one? Why else have a ribbon necklace?

"The magistrate must think the runners have seized everything. Or he doesn't believe Henderson's guilty."

With a huff, I put my hands to my hot cheeks. "I don't like to think my neighbor is capable of violence, but I didn't think he'd knowingly lie to an officer of the court about me staying through the whole play."

Walking back to the table, I released a long, lung-emptying sigh. "I hate that he knows I can't refute his statement without putting myself under suspicion."

"Tsk, tsk," Vaughn said, and thumbed his glass. It made a solemn chime. "Duncan has political ambitions. He won't press a war hero unless he can prove guilt."

That wasn't the same as thinking a person innocent. "Is this when you tell me to be careful? I live near someone I suspect of strangling a woman. How is that careful?"

"You're the respected wife of James Monroe, Lord Worthing, the great explorer. But you're his Blackamoor baroness. You cannot risk a scandal with him away. You'll be like Hayti, cut adrift. Second chances are hard to attain."

Creaking floorboards sounded from the parlor. Someone was coming.

With Vaughn in the midst of his lecture, there was no stopping him.

"Your cousin's contracted to support Mary Edwards, Britain's human computer. Her position could be in jeopardy. All Florentina's associations have to have spotless reputations."

"Sorry to interrupt." Mrs. Smith came with a tray of biscuits drizzled with chocolate. "I hope you're not getting the mistress to be more fretful about folks' opinions she can't change. She's not a leopard. Those freckled spots won't fade her skin."

"Ah, the opinionated Mrs. Smith," he said, "still full of island fire."

"Yes. And I kept my Jamaican accent, too."

Vaughn smiled at her, acknowledging the dig at his chameleon-like nature, but it was a necessity for the ton's enforcer. "Not everything is a matter of race or birthright. Sometimes class and station matter much more. Lady Worthing is being accepted. We should want nothing to ruin her chances now."

The housekeeper set down her silver tray and picked up the half-empty pitcher of lemonade. "I see you've developed a fast liking for this."

"A little tartness does quench the thirst." Vaughn lifted his glass and she filled it.

"Sometimes it's old-fashioned rules by men. I know the navy men don't want to rely on any woman, White or Blackamoor to do calculations for the navy." She yanked her pristine white apron. "They don't see the utility of a woman at all."

"Oh, *dey* do, Mrs. Smith. The *mon* won't admit it, unless it has to do with *a bed and a backside*." Full Jamaican rolling off his tongue with the coarseness of Saint Giles—Vaughn laughed as Mrs. Smith's eyes popped wide.

She put down the pitcher, but didn't box his ears. She did,

though, cast him a withering gaze that matched the stiff starch of her high white mobcap and formal gray gown hidden beneath her apron. "Lady Worthing, you'll need to get ready for the *lichwake* this evening."

"The what?"

"Mr. Vaughn," I said, "next door they're having a gathering for Mrs. Henderson. Apparently, this *lichwake* is a Scottish tradition to honor loved ones."

Mrs. Smith picked up the biscuits and waved the platter to me. "Everyone knows Mr. Henderson couldn't stand his wife. This is him celebrating being free."

Vaughn took a treat. The edge crumbled. Chocolate smeared his fingers. "Well, we all can't be wildly in love, like Lady Worthing."

The tweak stung, but I held my face steady.

"When will the *lichwake* start?"

"Right before sundown, ma'am."

She curtsied and swept back into the parlor.

Alone again, I made myself say, "I need you to go with me."

Vaughn's mouth was open. "You seriously want to attend a party for the dead? That's not how the ton mourns."

"All the neighbors will probably go, especially the women. If I'm the only one absent, I'll look guilty. It will feed into the notion that something is going on between me and Henderson."

"Is that all? Your brow is quivering. That means you have more to ask."

Sitting back, I wiped chocolate from my hands and his. "I need you to get me everything you can about Henderson's record in the navy. I want to know what he's done, what he's capable of doing. Then get the adorable Wilson Shaw to pull what he can on everyone's finances."

Vaughn shook his head and pulled out his gold watch and

looked at the clock face. "For you, Abbie, I'll go with you to the party, then follow to the funeral. I'll set the minions to work."

"Thank you, sir."

"Unless you'd wish your father to accompany you."

I hadn't considered that.

This wasn't the kind of thing Papa would be good at. Death or even sadness wasn't something he wished to endure. "I'd rather your opinion of the people at Eleven Queen Street. You'll help me get a step ahead of Henderson and stay there."

"If he's not the killer, you'll need to stay one step ahead of whoever that is. Subterfuge is not your father's specialty." Vaughn said this with a smile. "The man's too honest. I wanted you to say your preference aloud."

When I chuckled, he finished his glass, the last of the lemonade. "You do have your mother's charm. No wonder people are ready to gossip about you. Speaking of gossip, Wilson has broken a marriage engagement to another wealthy widow. I thought this one with her twenty thousand a year would be the one."

My childhood friend liked attention, and women gave him plenty. A man with golden-brown skin, sharp wit, and green-hazel eyes was a rarity.

Vaughn stood, but he had that look of wanting to impart some last piece of wisdom.

"Go ahead and say it."

"A friend of mine was at Drury Lane last night. He saw you leave, and then saw Henderson go and come back. Your neighbor had plenty of time to return here, after cutting through Saint James Park to kill his wife or to step off your terrace after a tryst. I rather wanted you to be in an affair than involved with murder."

A friend? Vaughn had spies everywhere. He'd not drop

names. Yet he wanted to know all my business. "You question my faithfulness to James over Stapleton Henderson, the argumentative worm who only yesterday built a wall to separate our lawns."

My godfather bent and kissed my brow. "It's my fault you married too young to a man I didn't know would always be gone. I'd never have recommended the match."

Arms folded, hackles and gumption raised, I stood. "Lord Worthing and I are a logical match. He's brilliant and needed someone in his corner to champion his innocence."

"And he left you here, waiting. Not once has he taken you on one of his grand adventures."

That was the one thing I hadn't counted upon, either.

To have all the trappings of an elevation, but not much of a husband. "I'm not my mother. I'm not led by my passions. I'm satisfied."

He patted my hand. "Your passions haven't been stirred, Abigail. And the newly separated, now-widowed Henderson is a younger man, and a hero, like Worthing. If one was to say Magdalena's daughter had an archetype that might be it."

"I'm a Carrington, too. With my father's cooling blood as a guide, I'm given to reason. I'll not repeat her mistakes."

Offering his rare laugh, he bowed and started to my parlor door. "Who are you to say Magdalena made mistakes? I think she did everything exactly right."

"Wait, Vaughn." It took everything in me to sound calm, not bristling from his arrogance. "You'll be back to help."

"Of course, Abigail. I'll always support you and act to keep you safe."

"Did the third act have the actor for Ali Baba ruin his lines?"

"Yes. He did it again in the fourth, but it was less noticeable."

Henderson didn't mention that. He must not have been there to see. "Thank you, Vaughn. Be back soon. Engage Wilson."

My godfather took his gloves from his pocket, taut cream kidskins. "Happy to help. Don't particularly like the notion of a murderer next door. A discreet affair with Henderson would've eased my mind."

Burning, I listened to his footfalls, the creaks of my floor.

When calmed, I had to remember I had a killer to catch.

Chapter 6

Evening settled over Westminster like a patchwork design. The sky mottled with streaks, gray, purple, and dark blue. The air didn't smell of rain. It didn't smell of flowers, or anything much at all.

Vaughn returned to my parlor near six. He had the opportunity to confirm the address and the lease terms of Juliet's residence, Seven Watling in Cheapside. The rooms would have to be renewed in another month. Why a short term of three months, not a year or more? Happenstance or did Henderson know she wouldn't need them long? The notion of premeditated murder made my skin crawl.

My godfather stood at the terrace door. "People are starting to gather. Shall we?"

I left Teacup napping again on the sofa. Hopefully, he'd give poor Rogers no more trouble.

On Vaughn's arm, we made it outside with minimal floor squeaks. We started to my lawn and crossed the imaginary boundary between Number Two and Number Eleven Greater Queen Street.

Thinking of Juliet on that fence, the ribbon, the scarf, all my nerves bubbled anew.

"Are you all right, Abigail?"

"Yes, Mr. Vaughn. Maybe Papa isn't the only one who has a problem with mourning."

He tugged my hand closer and we stepped to a well-worn path that surely led to Saint James Park. The killer could've ridden through the unfenced meadow, a pretty place with tall grasses and bluebells, and committed the murder. Our private yards weren't secluded.

The ground leveled out as we neared the stone terrace at the rear of the Henderson town house.

A dog barked and then another answered.

"Those are his killer hounds. The ones that chase my Teacup."

Vaughn's neck whipped toward the park.

Henderson and his two dogs were there. He'd cast a stick and one of the beasts retrieved it.

His brow lifted. "Yes, those two lean fellows obeying commands look menacing."

"Looks can be deceiving, sir." Yet, I stayed watching them, wondering how my neighbor could have this carefree moment with his wife dead inside.

My father was the opposite. Not a day went by that he didn't have a toast to my mother. His grief never ended. I didn't know how to help him. The way he practically disowned me, I gave up trying.

Suddenly I couldn't go forward.

My strength left.

Vaughn's hand tightened on mine. He pulled me forward, holding me like I'd stumbled. "Don't get stuck, Lady Worthing."

"It seems easy to do."

"You're here for the *lichwake*. That's where Mrs. Henderson is, not out here."

Vaughn was right, but I'd stopped moving to keep staring at the lone figure and two dogs.

A man approached him and the hellhounds barked like they were going to eat the visitor.

Henderson snapped his fingers and the beasts stopped making any racket. The sleek animals circled, but then sat on either side of their master, not uttering another sound. They stilled like ice sculptures or glass figurines.

Impressive. A simple motion ushered such control.

The stranger and Henderson were too far from us to overhear their conversation.

My godfather grew tired of my overt nosiness and tugged me, starting me again to the house.

Unlike Number Two, Henderson's terrace led into an office, one with gray paper–treated walls. A bookshelf behind a large desk, mahogany was freshly polished with orange oil, offering a sweet, clean smell to the room.

Leaving the fireplace, Vaughn went to the bookshelves. He touched the portrait. "Fine picture of Mary Henderson."

"Yes, his sister." I wondered how she fared. She was upset yesterday.

My godfather kept eyeing the shelves and picked up a tattered book.

"Scottish poetry authored by Robert Burns." He thumbed it.

> *Should auld acquaintance be forgot,*
> *And never brought to mind?*
> *Should auld acquaintance be forgot,*
> *And auld lang syne.*

He snapped the book shut. "Well, Henderson likes Scottish literature."

"I'm going to be presumptuous and say he has Scottish roots. Something he is proud of."

"See, you two have a lot more in common. Scottish capes."

"Yeah." I was going to correct him, but Vaughn was right. "Yes. Scottish tweed capes."

He picked up another book. "Now this is interesting. It's a book on precognition, but from Scottish lore. Here I thought it was only from the islands."

"Can you put that back before someone sees?"

"Well, you should be able to tell me. You are both Scottish and Jamaican. You might have a double portion. Could be more powerful than your mother's."

I took the book from him and put it back. "How can you joke? The gift made Mama go insane."

He sobered. "There's no way for that to have happened. Your father . . . Your father's grief colors his vision."

If I knew that making Vaughn angry would make the truth slip out from the lies everyone believed was necessary to tell, I'd have him angry every moment.

But I needed his help with Henderson rather than to chase old ghosts. "Mrs. Henderson wouldn't walk around the town house to get to the yard. She'd come through here."

"If she was in the house. That would make sense."

"Ask the footmen what they saw or heard."

I put my hand on the stone bust and glanced at the plans Henderson drew to construct his fence. I noted the sloppy bookcase filled with papers and such. Turning, I saw the mirror above the mantel, sparkling and clean. I could imagine someone looking at her hair, then dashing out onto the terrace for air.

"What is it, Abbie? What can you tell about Mr. Henderson from this room?"

"That he's selfish to force everyone to come through his office to go outside. A little bit of a rude placement. And what of his own privacy?"

"I thought the same things, but maybe it's his way to control things, being able to see who enters and exits. When he returned in January, his sister, Miss Mary Henderson, also lived here. She's a pretty young woman, an heiress in her own right, maybe with ideas of courting. If I had daughters, I might design ways to ensure I knew who slipped in and out of the house."

The sister came into the study from the hall. She leaned against the doorframe. Mousy-brown hair with floppy curls and tendrils falling, with the same dark blue eyes as her brother—she looked hurt.

"My condolences again, Miss Mary. This is my godfather, Mr. Neil Vaughn. Mr. Vaughn, this is Miss Mary Henderson. I hope you do not mind my bringing company."

She shrugged. "No. My sister-in-law was popular."

Vaughn bit his lip, bowed, then headed past her, probably following the spry music, which had begun to find us.

She nodded toward his fleeing shadow. "He's not one of her friends?"

My mouth opened at such a question.

"It's true. Juliet was adored and loved by many. Is Mr. Vaughn one of her admirers?"

"No, my godfather doesn't like popularity contests." My hands shot to my face at such a flippant response. "I'm sorry."

"Don't be concerned. Many friends are upstairs. All in love with her." She looked as if she was going to leave, but spun back. Her onyx gown swung out like a bell, then collapsed at her feet. "They don't know her. Her kindness. Her large heart. My brother said you were there when he found Juliet."

"Yes. Yes, I was."

The annoyed look of this girl of fifteen or sixteen disappeared. She came to me standing inches away with her fingers clasped in front of her. "Stapleton said you were the only one to show her any dignity. Juliet was carefree, a wild spirit. I loved her so much." Mary's tears fell. She threw her arms about me.

I startled, but I had the wherewithal to embrace her, too. She was genuinely hurting. I wanted to hold her, to say sorry, to pretend even a little that this was Dinah and me reconciling.

It wasn't. It was a girl grieving the loss of a dear friend. Burying Mary in my arms, I embraced her and held on until she calmed. "The culprit will be brought to justice. It will happen."

"I had Miss Bumners launder the quilt. It looks good as new. No frays or anything to remind of the horrors Juliet faced," Mary shared.

That quilt meant the world to me. Many nights I'd wrapped up in it and read in my parlor. When I held it again, would I see my mother, her talent . . . or strangled Juliet?

Mary wiped at her eyes.

"Thank you."

When we separated, I saw Henderson on his terrace watching us.

She spirited out the door and he grabbed her, swirling her as she cried anew. Mary seemed small in his arms, swaddled against his pitch-black tailcoat. Her gown of jet crepe looked purply in the dusky light.

Servants scrambled all about them, lighting torches along the lawn. But brother and sister looked aloof, and alone. Couldn't stand seeing those sticks with fire, not after the runners last night.

I closed the light tan curtain that hung on the window.

A killer could be loving to a younger sibling. Though I refused to be taken in by his demeanor, there was no doubting that Henderson loved Mary.

The last book Vaughn touched about precognition stuck out on the shelf. I went past, not even thinking of touching it.

A double portion of troubling dreams would be horrible. My Jamaican and Scottish relatives proved bothersome enough. With a final look at this drab office, I decided to find Vaughn and get through this *lichwake* as soon as possible. Didn't think

I'd be lucky enough to stumble upon another clue down here that confirmed Henderson's guilt.

Whipping into the hall, I realized this was the basement level.

The floor plan at Number Eleven differed greatly from mine. This lower level must be partially sunk underground. The air down here was cold. The brick walls felt icy.

Walking almost back to the study, I stopped at a room framed with portraits and a pianoforte in the corner. Why were these patriarchs and matriarchs here in a place that few would see?

Perhaps the Hendersons enjoyed private concerts here.

The pianoforte was freshly polished and smelled of rich orange oil. Looking at the keys, I noticed the instrument was played often. Who was the musician, Mary or Henderson?

I kept walking. The music sounded stronger at the end of the hall. Wandering here and there, I found a storage room, no gathering. Then a wine cellar, no Vaughn. Still, the lively tempo vibrated above my head.

The sconces in here were well lit, but I saw no stairs. The interesting architecture, with white brick walls curved at the ceiling, continued. I walked down one narrow aisle and saw shelves of dusty bottles.

The maids must have missed cleaning in here.

"The Hendersons have an exhaustive collection, ma'am." The butler's voice made my heart jump and hit the low ceiling. I clutched a shelf.

"You scared me, sir."

"Sorry, ma'am." His tone wasn't menacing, merely unexpected. "Didn't mean to frighten you as you snooped, Lady Worthing."

"Yes, you did. And I wasn't exactly snooping. More lost. But these bottles are impressive."

An older man, slightly portly, stood in front of me with a smirk. "Again, sorry."

"It seems I'm at a disadvantage. You know who I am, but I know nothing of you."

"Jyles, ma'am, William Jyles. I'm the Hendersons' butler." Now that I'd gathered my wits, he did look the part—dark mantle, humbled countenance, and bowed posture that implied service. "Mr. Jyles, you've been with the family for many years?"

"Yes. Served the family in some capacity for over twenty years. Some strange happenings have always come about. This is strange and sad." He rubbed at the large bandage on his hand.

"What happened to your . . ."

"Careless. Burned myself lighting the torches last night. Too much going on. I wasn't concentrating." Jyles reached with his other arm to get a bottle of wine. "Ah, an 1803 J. S. Terrantez. It's a Madeira. Mr. Henderson loves his ports."

"You were saying, sir, you hurt yourself last night, to illuminate the lawn for the runners?"

"Yes, such a horrible spectacle." Jyles turned away and tugged at another bottle.

"Then you worked last night? Did you see Mrs. Henderson while she was alive?"

"Yes." His expression sobered. "She was full of life and volatile when I saw her. But she was always coming here, in and out. It's a shame she's gone."

The sadness in his voice was similar to Mary's. This woman, whom I'd only ever seen at an occasional outing, laughing, being the center of attention, seemed to be adored in this house. That was different from the scene she made when her husband kicked her out. I fingered a dusty bottle. "You will miss her, Jyles?"

"Juliet Henderson was a rare light. Unpredictable. Always

wanting to tease or jest. She could be crass and funny. Yes, I'll miss someone who was free and took risks to be herself."

"Jyles," Henderson's baritone floated from the hall. "Are you giving tours again?"

"Mr. Henderson, I found the baroness lost in your cellar. I haven't charged her a penny for the view." The man chuckled. He shuffled out the door with his right leg dragging.

I followed and stood next to my neighbor. "He should rest, but you're making him work."

"Lady Worthing, Jyles would want to be here serving on a night like this."

That was the sentiment I'd begun to understand. Juliet was well regarded by those who knew her best.

"Did you enjoy your tour? My family collects wine. We collect a lot of things."

"But it's dusty in there. It's a shame to have such finery and not take care of them."

He winced. Then pointed me forward.

The hall was narrow at this point and the sounds of the *lichwake* echoed above. "Laughter and refreshment are on the next landing, the street level." He made his hostlike speech, but he sort of blocked my path, slightly keeping me near.

He looked at me with the same glare he always did, the one I'd assumed was annoyance. I almost waited for him to whip out a drawing of the next meaningless fence he'd construct to replace the last.

Then I thought of the sad emotions of Jyles and Mary and decided to be charitable. Stapleton Henderson, if he were innocent, could be mourning as heavily, merely suffering in silence.

As Juliet's life within these walls was beginning to show me that appearances deceived, I took the lesson to heart.

"It's a fine cellar. My visiting it was a onetime mistake. No need to build a fence to keep me from straying."

"Then what will keep you . . . or any woman from straying?"

Unsure if he was being funny or if he'd found a new way to confuse me, I bit my lip and passed him.

"The *lichwake* is on the main level, take the stairs at the end of the hall. Your quilt will be waiting on my desk when you're ready to leave."

"My godfather, Neil Vaughn, accompanied me. He'll attend the funeral and represent the Worthing household. Again, I'm sorry for your loss."

With a dip of my head, I turned and ascended. Once I met everyone else who was close to Juliet, I'd return to my house and compare tonight's impressions with the news Wilson Shaw would bring tomorrow.

Chapter 7

The colors of the main level surprised me—brilliant white, bright gold—big panels that framed the walls were painted light colors, like light blue.

The main entry doors were guarded with handsome footmen, each probably six feet in height.

This level must be where life happened in Eleven Greater Queen Street.

Vaughn stepped to me with a goblet of something that smelled of grapes and cherries. "For you, Lady Worthing. Don't fear. It's not poison, unless it's slow acting."

"Cute, sir." I took the glass and sipped. It was unusual, both sweet and tart like spring cherries. "Mr. Jyles did say Henderson liked his ports. And this is a good vintage. Have you found out anything?"

He pulled me into an adjacent study. We settled into a corner away from the guests that kept arriving. "The footman Dillard said that Mrs. Henderson came in last night and then went to the lower level to wait for Mr. Henderson."

"So they were to meet and she was in his study. Drury Lane was set up as an alibi."

"Seems to be a popular one." His admonishment meant that I needed to be more careful. He was correct. I'd choose some obscure coffeehouse in the future.

"But the other footman, Humphrey, told me later that Mrs. Henderson liked to lie to get into the house. She'd take things and sell them off. At some point, Mr. Henderson ordered she not be admitted unless he was here," my godfather stated.

"Yet, she did enter last night . . . for the last time."

Vaughn took another sip from his glass. "This is too sweet. Don't tell Mrs. Smith, but I think I prefer her lemonade."

"Make nice with Henderson. There's a wine cellar downstairs full of bottles. There has to be a vintage for you."

He flashed a partial smile. "I'll stick with this sweet drink rather than roam about a killer's lair."

I started to leave to circulate, and Vaughn ushered me back. "Mr. Dillard admitted to having an affair with the late woman."

"The footman said this to you? Out loud on the day of her funeral?"

"No, Abigail, but I overheard him speaking to Humphrey. She had a number of dalliances with the staff and others. Apparently, a lot of others."

Looking about the parlor and the neighbors, particularly the crush of men, I wondered how many were guilty of adultery with this woman? What type of marriage would drive Juliet to such lengths?

I took another sip, feeling a headache starting to stir. It needed to stay at bay. Then I could size up people and put them into a bucket—good, bad, indifferent. It was a survival instinct that had to help me figure out who wanted Juliet dead.

"I'm going to circulate, Mr. Vaughn. Let me see if I can best your information."

"A competition, Lady Worthing. How nice." He saluted me with his full goblet.

Liking mine, I took my glass with me and left this bright white room and moved to a drawing room. Then I noticed something missing. No squeaks. None anywhere. Why were two side-by-side houses so different?

Straightening my gown, smoothing the fine pleats of the skirt Mrs. Smith had painstakingly ironed, I decided to chase the sounds of laughter.

One of the footmen that had been at the front in his dashing silver livery held trays for the maids. A buxom one seemed to catch his roaming eye. Neither of them seemed concerned about their late, murdered mistress.

Tall and with big arms, he surely had the strength to kill, but I saw no scratches on the slim neck poking from his high collar or bared wrists from his gloves.

Could the splatter of blood on the ribbon and her hands just be Julia's?

Suppose it wouldn't be that easy, though I hoped she'd inflicted some damage to the force that snuffed her light.

Come, Abigail, find the clues.

Time to move on and seek someone with more urgent motives. Why kill Juliet yesterday? Vaughn overheard the footman claim of her frequent visits. What changed and provoked her death? Perhaps showing once too often.

Had Henderson grown tired of the returning wife? Perhaps the quiet man hated her loud scenes, like the one that filled Greater Queen Street the day he kicked her out.

From the drawing room, I started into a bright parlor. An adjacent wall was painted a dead pink. Lots of molding and trim rimmed the area.

Everyone had to be here.

Even neighbors I thought had moved came tonight to the Henderson town house. I hugged, shook hands, and kept moving.

Vaughn's rumbly laugh sounded ahead. The man had slipped past me. In here, a violinist played. I could see a reel being performed after a leisurely dinner.

There were no tears.

Everyone had smiles and stories about Juliet.

This wasn't how death was viewed to stoic Carringtons or feisty Jamaicans. The joy in this room spoke to my heart. Maybe this was the correct way to mourn.

Overstimulated, overtalked, with half my port gone, I turned in the opposite direction and entered a second parlor. Pale blue walls closed in and surrounded a shiny pine box.

Candles scented the room with honey. They burned everywhere—sconces, candelabras, holders on stands.

All beeswax.

All the eight hours' length.

All about half burned.

A full day of sadness?

That seemed a long time to mourn publicly, even with playful music.

A man prayed over the coffin.

It was inevitable, my choosing this room. Death had a way of inviting Abigail Carrington Monroe to the party.

My pulse seemed normal as I moved closer to the coffin.

I wasn't anxious or actually fearful of the dead.

I merely hated what the absence did to those left behind. We were listed as *survived by* for a reason.

Clasping my elbows as if they'd fall off, I came closer to Juliet, her coffin. In the span of an hour, I'd learned more about this woman who lived next door the entire length of my marriage. She went from a name and victim to someone I wished I'd known.

A servant with gloves and a silver tray waved me forward. The closer I came, I realized it was the butler again. Mr. Jyles took my half-empty glass and exchanged it for a full one. "An 1804 vintage. Also a Madeira. Drink up, the funeral procession will start at nine."

That was an hour away. The service and then burial will be very late.

Jyles moved on and passed out more beverages.

Apparently, the *lichwake* was to get stinking drunk and sit with the dead all night until the funeral. Everyone would be good and sotted by the time the bells chimed. A late church service, then midnight burial, didn't bode well for skittish persons. Wasn't that an invitation for ghouls and grave robbers?

Grousing, and thankful that women weren't expected to attend funerals, I moved to the coffin.

This time I caught a whiff of lavender. It was strong, chokingly strong. Juliet's body must have been washed and prepared with that fragrance.

A fellow in livery stood off to the side. Medium build, late forties in age, he seemed familiar. His eyes were red.

The man seemed brokenhearted.

It took a minute, but I recognized him, remembered seeing him lead Mrs. Henderson's carriage through Saint James Park.

"Mr. Sinclair," I asked, "you were Mrs. Henderson's driver?"

"Yes, ma'am." He rubbed at his face and stepped back. "Sorry if I'm hogging the view. I think she was the finest thing ever."

Another kind accounting of this woman's life. "You didn't need to move. I was a neighbor. You sound as if you lost a dear friend."

"Come, ma'am, don't be shy. You know Mrs. Henderson wasn't shy at all." His lips turned up a little. Then they fell crashing into a frown. "I drove her here for someone to kill her. Life's not fair. She was too good."

He teared up again, and I felt worse.

I'd become standoffish this last year. The slights were at the forefront of my mind. I'd become jaded and isolated myself from everything but a mysterious theft or two for the magistrate. Looking through papers, using all of my mind to find the inconsistent statement, was fun. I never minded Lord Duncan getting the credit for solving them. He was one of the few who didn't mind my cleverness or my face. Everyone else of the ton wanted less of me—less witty, less daring—merely for an invitation.

I'd hate for there to be two versions of me, the one people knew and the one they hoped to see.

Staring at the coffin, this open box with a woman who could no longer be a friend or do anything for anyone anymore, I thought she would understand the distinctions. *I will bring your killer to justice.*

"Mr. Sinclair, you said you drove Mrs. Henderson here last night?"

He swiped at his face. "She said she wouldn't need me anymore. That this would be the last. Did she know this would happen? Some get a premonition of the end. Mr. Jyles said Mr. Henderson has books on it."

Vaughn and I had seen them. Pondering mystical or even illogical things didn't seem to match the man I thought Stapleton Henderson was. "What time did you bring the lady here?"

"About eight. Why didn't I insist on staying?" He put up a fist like he wanted to punch something, but sloshed his glass. "Sorry, Lady Worthing. Sorry."

Digging into my reticule, I offered him a handkerchief. "You need to calm yourself, Mr. Sinclair."

He took it and then swung it around to wipe his bare hands—no injuries, just a tiny scratch by his knuckle.

"Look at them, ma'am."

"Look at what, sir?"

"Look at them vultures. Gathering around the princess, now that the queen is dead. All Hail Mary."

The disdain or mocking in his voice—did he not like Miss Henderson? "Mr. Sinclair, have you been drinking all day?"

Squinting, searching for answers, he nodded. "I might have started at Olive's and kept going."

"I heard of Olive's in New Palace Yard. It has good food."

"They serve meals?" He shrugged and handed back my handkerchief. "I'll be eating there next time. They have a decent bar."

The man hovered over me with his breath tart and as foul as

the dense lavender smell of the coffin. Mrs. Henderson might still rise to be away from the stink.

His posture was wobbly. "They're hoping the princess will be like Mrs. Queen. I think some of those suitors wanted 'em both."

"Both? Miss Henderson and Mrs. Henderson?"

"Oh, yeah. Beauty and money. Both women are pretty. One with money she threw around, the other's an heiress in waiting. Hey, you think that's why she was kicked out? Two beauties can't be under one roof."

Was there jealousy between Mary and Juliet? Didn't sound that way, not the way Mary sobbed. No, this was man-and-wine explanations.

My palm lifted and found its way to my self-righteous hip. "Women can get along. And Mary Henderson is heartbroken over her sister-in-law's death."

"Well, if she seems that way to you, I'll trust you. I'm quite drunk."

He bobbled a bit and I helped him to a chair on the side.

"I can't tell if Mr. Henderson is mourning as hard as everyone else. But he seems reserved to me."

Sinclair chuckled a dry-hiccup offering. "Oh, that's him mourning. Staying away and quiet. Otherwise, he'd be on the pianoforte wailing away. When he's angry, watch out, Beethoven."

"He's active on that big box downstairs?"

"Very. They'd duel with sonatas and slammed doors. But once the man decided to kick her out, he didn't seem to be bothered anymore. She could do anything, and nothing made him angry. I thought it meant he figured her out. Juliet liked knowing she could drive someone crazy. No reactions made her anxious."

That sounded volatile and unhinged on both parts—husband's and wife's.

"Lady Worthing, when I dropped her off yesterday, she was

happy and said she wouldn't need me anymore. I thought the Hendersons were reuniting. Should've known they weren't."

"Why is that, Mr. Sinclair?"

"She was too happy. She didn't love him. She loved . . ."

"Who, sir? Who would you say?"

Something or someone caught his eye. His brow wrinkled badly. "Life, ma'am. She loved life. And he took it from her, took her from all of us." Sinclair drew himself up and left the room.

Who was the *he*?

And was *he* in this room?

I folded my arms about me. Then I lowered them to my sides. I didn't want to seem angry or puzzled. I was here as an impartial juror. As drunk as Sinclair was, he had the strength to strangle Juliet and tie her to the fence.

Someone here did it or maybe no one. But when I thought of the careful undone buttons, I knew the killer had to be here or was on the way.

I turned to Juliet for guidance, leaning on the makeshift altar.

So pale and gray, with red rouge on her cheeks.

The makeup, which had to have been lovingly applied, highlighted the dark marks to the side of her face.

"You fought back, didn't you?"

Her dresser had put a scarf about her neck. This one, heavy and garnet colored, contrasted the white muslin gown she'd been made to wear.

White and spotless.

Innocent.

"She loved scarves, ma'am." A young woman in a maid's costume, like Mrs. Smith's gray-and-black one, stood at my side.

Her face was wet. Her reddened eyes looked as if she'd only taken the briefest respite from crying. She dabbed her eyes.

"That's a lovely scarf, but I thought I heard she loved necklaces."

The woman looked puzzled; then her face cleared. "Just one necklace. Mr. Henderson made a gold *J* for her to wear when he was at sea. I think she wore it every day, always on a new ribbon."

No jewelry or golden letter was found with Juliet.

Where was it? Did the killer take it to pawn or for a remembrance?

"Your employer was well regarded, Miss . . ."

"Miss Bumners. I adored her." She took out a cloth and polished away fingerprints that mourners had left on the sides of the coffin. "Those who didn't were simply jealous of her kindness. She was a free spirit. I loved her so."

The same passion I'd heard in Sinclair was evident in this Miss Bumners. She stuck her hand into the coffin and tucked a stray gold lock about Juliet's ear. "That was her problem, I suppose. Everybody loving her, but only one could have her. To strangle her and leave like she was nothin'."

"So sorry, Miss Bumners."

She gazed at me with soft brown eyes. "You're the first to say it to me. Thank you. Mrs. Henderson, she'd noticed things."

Was that her magic and her curse, recognizing people others didn't?

"I washed your quilt, fixed the tears, and ironed it, ma'am. It was made with love. I see it in the careful stitches, the way the different colors were put together."

"My mother made it for me. I didn't want to part with it. But Mrs. Henderson needed her dignity."

Miss Bumners clutched my arm. "You gave her that. She wanted care, and the brute had to strangle her. She was finally leaving him for good. He didn't have to do this."

"You think Mr. Henderson did this?"

"No. Oh, I don't. No, I don't know. Don't listen to what I'm saying." Then she shook her head furiously. "Couldn't have been Mr. Henderson. They'd become the best of friends again, once they lived apart. He used to read her Pope's *Rape of the Lock*."

"Excuse me?"

"Ma'am, it's a play about stealing a locket of hair. Juliet had beautiful hair."

"Mr. Henderson does seem to like plays lately."

"He's become a bit unpredictable. I polish his pianoforte now only twice a week. It used to be every day."

That's a fiend, all right, now sparing orange oil for the world. I sighed; I was about to convict Henderson again based on this woman's words, and she also must've been drinking.

"Yes. The person who took her jewelry could have been a common thief, someone from Saint James Park who saw her walking alone."

"Could be, but she rarely walked by herself. And the dogs would go with her."

The hellhounds? "Did she enjoy the greyhounds?"

"Yes. They loved her, too. The dogs have been with her five years."

If she had them under control like Henderson, the beasts would bark at a stranger. The murderer must be someone known to Juliet and the dogs.

Wouldn't Rogers have said something if more than one dog barked last night?

Miss Bumners kept talking about Henderson and Juliet. I tried to pay attention, but my gaze kept drifting to the woman in the coffin.

The carefully done-up curls, the scarf covering the marks to her neck, gloves hiding the broken nail.

"Did Mrs. Henderson wear any rings? Surely, her marital band."

"Sometimes. Come to Seven Watling tomorrow. I can show you her rings. I'm supposed to pack up everything. Then Mr. Henderson can close down the rooms."

"Why so soon?"

"Something about being efficient and not wasting money."

That sounded like my fence-building nemesis.

Mary led a man out of the room. She seemed more at ease, but the maid appeared agitated.

Miss Bumners crumpled a dust rag and pushed it into the pocket of her black tunic. "I saw you gave Mr. Sinclair your cloth and he sobbed all over it. Let me wash and iron it, Lady Worthing. I'll have it ready when you visit me at Watling."

"It's no trouble."

She glared at me like I was thickheaded. "Come to Seven Watling tomorrow. I'll have it cleaned and pressed. Tomorrow about two?"

A lady's maid knew all her mistress's secrets. She'd know who the woman's lovers were, and if any had a better reason for killing Juliet than her husband. After folding the handkerchief, I gave it to her. "Seven Watling tomorrow. Yes."

Miss Bumners looked over her shoulder, then hurriedly left the parlor.

A steady crowd filled the room.

I moved to the rear and posted near the window. It had a view of Greater Queen Street. More carriages were arriving.

Mary returned. Her face was cherry red. Her dark eyes looked sad, almost lost.

I watched her mannerism as mourners greeted her. She was elegant, even stately. Yet her gaze glistened every time she turned to the coffin.

Our eyes locked and she came to me. "Lady Worthing. I wanted to thank you again for coming and for helping, and even for letting me grieve in my brother's study."

"So many people loved her. I didn't know Mrs. Henderson well. But under the circumstances . . . I wish I had."

"I don't think so." Mary's words were a whisper, but vibrating with anguish and maybe guilt. "My sister-in-law can sound

MURDER IN WESTMINSTER   95

shallow or brazen to most. But that wasn't her. That was what she showed the world as if she were acting in a play. When you got to know her, truly know her, she was loving, very caring."

"I'm sorry, Mary."

"The magistrate has arrived. He'll have more questions. I want this over." She turned to me, putting her back to the rest of the mourners. "My brother says you have the magistrate's ear. Make Lord Duncan see the good side of Juliet. Then he'll catch the true culprit. Don't let them write her off as a reckless tart."

"I'll try." It was all I could promise and keep Mary from another teary episode.

Solving three theft cases put me on Duncan's tolerated list.

Not sure if anything gave me any advantages to solve this murder when almost every man and woman seemed in love with Juliet.

Chapter 8

Mary left me when Lord Duncan came near. She circulated and chatted as if she'd run an estate for years.

But her eyes were on me and the magistrate. Did she realize her brother was the main suspect?

Duncan's hat was gone and the part in his curly hair looked combed. He bent his head to me. "So, what have you discovered, Lady Worthing?"

"That Eleven Greater Queen Street is much bigger than my house."

He frowned at my comment and I could feel a "dear lass" or "lass" coming. "I meant about the murder, lass. Who do you suspect of killing Mrs. Henderson?"

To evade the magistrate would pit us against each other. I couldn't afford him thinking ill of me or refusing to give me access to information when I, too, was on the suspect list. "Lord Duncan, Mrs. Henderson apparently wears a gold letter *J* on a ribbon about her neck everywhere. None of your men have found one. The killer must have it."

"So someone took it as a memento of the murder."

"That's what I suspect, my lord. But it might've been valuable. A horrible thief could've stolen it and her life."

"A robbery and a murder?" All the cogs must be turning in his head. He dipped his chin again. "What will be your next action?"

"I'm thinking over my options, but I will be questioning Miss Bumners in Mrs. Henderson's leased rooms at Watling Street tomorrow."

He tucked his hands behind his back. His wrinkled waistcoat of dark emerald looked better than his drooping cravat, but his leather slippers had shine. His way of cleaning up to show respect?

"How is Mr. Henderson acting?"

"Distant. I haven't seen him come up from the ground level."

"That's odd. He should be sitting with the dead. Keep me informed of anything else you learn, Lady Worthing."

"Of course, my lord." I bowed and looked demure. I hoped it would be enough to have him move on and not think me a nuisance.

The magistrate did and headed to the coffin before going into the hall. I didn't know if the man drank or if he liked sweet wine. I supposed I'd soon find out as this event kept going.

Mary stepped inside and held court with some of Town's leading men newly arrived. From the sketches in the London *Morning Post,* I recognized John Cam Hobhouse. One of my father's oldest clients Mr. Mansel, the Master at Trinity College bragged on the Hobhouse's connections and the pleasure of the son's attendance.

His family put the young man in circles with future political ambitions. An heiress for a wife would be beneficial.

Then there was Foxwell Burton. I'd seen him at a few of Wilberforce's speeches. He was a handsome young man in his twenties who had already come to champion abolition. More politicians should.

Vaughn came to me. He had another full glass.

"I thought you didn't like the port."

"When in Rome, Abigail." He squinted at me. "What is it?"

"Some reformers have arrived. It reminds me my work is not done. I need to get to Wilberforce without any more delays."

"Well, from the dignitaries I've seen tonight, he might show."

I nudged him. "I'm serious, Vaughn."

"So am I, Lady Worthing. I didn't know the Hendersons were this well connected. Here, let me go get you something to eat. There are biscuits drizzled in a raspberry glaze."

"I'll keep Lady Worthing company for you, Mr. Vaughn. It is Mr. Vaughn, right?"

My godfather dipped his chin to the young man, one of the fellows buzzing about Mary earlier. "It is. And you are the brash young preacher now heading Saint Margaret's."

"Guilty," he said with a charming grin. "I'm Mr. Samuel Benjamin. Though I don't know if 'young' still applies, but 'brash' certainly does."

His gray eyes beamed. He was of medium height with sandy-brown hair and impeccable tailoring—long ebony lapels, a perfect ballroom knotted cravat of crisp white linen.

Red-faced, cheeks burning, Miss Bumners returned. The woman looked cross as if she'd had words with someone. She swiped at the coffin with her dust rag. For a moment, she looked as if she'd head toward me, but one of the fellows hovering about Mary came to the maid and clasped her arm. The two disappeared.

"Enjoying your tenure?" Vaughn said to the equally distracted Benjamin, though it was unclear what garnered his attention.

With a hand to his crisp lapel, he lifted his chin. "Very much. I've been two seasons at Saint Margaret's, in the shadow of the great Westminster Abbey. You and the baroness should attend sometime. Or is my small church not fancy enough?"

For the briefest moment, I panicked that he'd discovered I'd been trying to visit Wilberforce at Holy Trinity.

Then the fellow beamed a wider smile. "I'm teasing, but we'd be honored to have you at Saint Margaret's anytime it is convenient. It's quite progressive."

"Progressive? In hymn selection." I knew he'd point out Olaudah Equiano and the church's history of abolition. I merely wanted him to say it aloud and take a side.

He rubbed at his chin. "At the church's baptismal font, Equiano, the African as many called him, christened his new life of worship at Saint Margaret's."

"His autobiography started a fire in hearts and minds for abolition. He'd be shamed at how things have changed. Are you saying that freedom is your progressive stance?"

"Yes. Unequivocally yes. I hope once the politics are settled Wilberforce will pick up the cause again."

Vaughn offered me his annoyed eyes. "Lady Worthing's high-strung tonight. She's distressed that there could be a killer in our midst."

Ensuring that my tone was soft and polished, I said, "The notion of fraternizing with a murderer has me intrigued and frankly concerned. Mrs. Henderson was attacked along my property. I need to know what happened."

"Someone will be caught. Justice will be done." Benjamin's gaze seemed earnest, and perhaps it was.

"This death has troubled our neighborhood. It would be nice if you, as one of the church leaders, brought comfort and unity to all."

"You are right, but I'm still trying to establish myself in Westminster."

"I suspect you're on your way. Mrs. Henderson bragged of your sermons. I think she raved on them." Was it extra wrong to fib to a minister about his teachings? Couldn't be. Not with him grinning ear to ear.

"Lady Worthing, Mrs. Henderson was a generous parishioner. I will greatly miss her assistance."

My hunch was right. He had interacted with Juliet and was partial to her. How partial was the true question.

"And where were you the night Mrs. Henderson was murdered?"

He squinted at me. "The rumors of you helping Lord Duncan are true."

"It's a hobby, sir, but please play along."

At first, he sighed like it was impertinent to question his innocence; then he said, "Ringing bells. You probably heard them. All of Westminster. I love our bells, the tones they make. I invite change ringers from all over Britain to come and practice. Did you know the bells are the primary way to communicate across the vastness of the land? Many country parishes will ring to call people to worship or to war." He flashed his pearly smile. "Perhaps I can come up with something specific, a tune that will lead Lady Worthing to our humble services."

"Thank you, sir. And do try. I'm partial to music and bells."

Mary shrieked. Awash in fresh tears, she ran from the room.

"Mourning so hard. Let me see what I can do. Excuse me." Mr. Benjamin left the parlor.

My godfather shook his head. No doubt he'd been observing every detail of the entire exchange.

"What do you think? A kindly man, Vaughn."

"Kindly and more, Abigail. This minister spread his attention to both Henderson women."

Vaughn could read my face like a law book. I saw the spark, too, when Benjamin went after the crying young woman. "Friendly to both, I suppose."

A man with Juliet's hair coloring, same with streaks of gray, barged his way to the coffin. "I just come. Say it ain't true. Not my sister. No, God. Why?"

His fists pounded the side of the coffin.

People backed away.

"I'm her older brother. She's supposed to outlive me."

Miss Bumners returned and handed him a handkerchief and then wiped everything he'd touched.

The fellow took it with hands covered in brown leather riding gloves. He must've rushed in. "Where is he? My brother-in-law let this happen. He's supposed to protect her."

"Mr. Tanner, calm down," the maid said. Then she whispered something that made him settle.

"You're a good one. Always was, Miss Bumners. Let me find the lout in charge."

The brother had asked a good question about Henderson's whereabouts. Where was the master of this house, the only person not making a scene or publicly paying respects?

Grief was a strange thing. Unsettling. Even transferable, the way my hands started shaking.

"Vaughn, I'm going for air."

"We should be starting for the services at Saint Margaret's. The men, along with any professional mourners Henderson may have hired, will accompany us to the grave."

His steady palm took up mine. "Abigail, are you well?"

"Too many people. It's too warm. I'm going home. Send word of your safe arrival home, Vaughn. There is a murderer afoot."

"Will do, but do you want me to walk you back across the lawn?"

"No. I need to be alone." With a kiss to his cheek, I started into the hall and saw the two footmen talking.

"Be prepared to be fired now," Humphrey said to the younger man. "Surprised Henderson kept you on after he caught you kissing his wife."

Dillard stopped midstep, sloshing the tray of mostly empty glasses. "I didn't mind it, but she did it to make 'im jealous. Henderson knew it. That's why he let me stay."

"Might pretty woman, Mrs. Henderson." Humphrey straightened his mantle and kept walking. "Mighty bit of trouble."

What Juliet did or didn't do, none of that was worthy of death. Still warm, growing warmer, I tugged at my collar and slipped into the stairs. At the bottom level, my face felt flush.

I sailed into Henderson's office, and everything faded.

I felt the violence of a panic attack coming. My heart seized in my chest.

Everything inside was ripping and breaking until I had to let go. I had to see what I was meant to see.

Juliet sat on this big desk. She danced up with her scarf floating like a veil. The gold *J* on her ribbon shimmered. She touched the wall of books like her arm could pass through it, then waltzed out the terrace doors.

I clutched the desk.

Breathe in. Breathe out.

Dreams meant nothing. I'd prove it and moved to the bookcase.

I pulled at a few tomes, and nothing happened—no confession fell, no mysterious letter *J* dropped.

As I put things back, I hit the picture of Mary and exposed the edge of a safe. I tugged the painting free and saw it full, square with a metal door.

Hidden in the wall—had she opened it? Was she killed for something she discovered?

The close of the terrace door snapped. Bracing, I turned and faced Stapleton Henderson, the man I believed gained the most by murdering Juliet.

The fiery look on his face indicated that even if I was wrong about him, he'd be happy to start his villainous ways by throttling me.

Chapter 9

My heart gonged and rattled against my lungs until I coughed.

Henderson stepped inside his study as I clutched the portrait of his sister to my bosom.

On the other side of the desk, he stopped. Fumes seemed to come from his flared nose. "Rifling through my things. That doesn't seem at all neighborly."

"Well, ah . . . the picture was dusty."

"Stealing old books is dusty business. Can definitely make your eyes itchy, a nose congest. Are you running a fever? Something hot enough to temporarily challenge your sanity."

"Well, if it has, wouldn't I be the last one to admit this?" I laid the picture on his desk. "This is a handsome one of Mary. Who's the artist?"

He stepped closer, posting between the corner of the desk and the wrought-iron poker of the fireplace. "My father's not for hire. He's dead."

"Then I suppose there is no further need to discuss his employment for a new project."

Henderson leaned and placed his hands by the marble bust

on his desk. If he tossed it at me, I'd be dead. "Lord Worthing said your power of observation was very keen. Did he overlook pilfering to get information?"

"I'm not taking anything, sir."

"No. I caught you before you could."

"What? What is it that you think I've come to steal? Didn't think you're stupid enough to leave evidence lying around that proves you killed your wife."

His calm gaze became blue flames. Blue was the hottest fire. It melted metals. He pounded closer. The floor obeyed him, offering up no sound.

I scooted out of his way as he tugged the safe handle. The door opened and exposed a compartment. "Look, no money. No broken fingernail."

"No gold letter *J*, but there is a little sachet inside. Pocket change? Sorry, I'm not open to bribes."

Henderson paled, checking again. His sun kissed cheeks went white. He swatted the bag and it jingled, heavy clangs. It was full of money. "The three thousand pounds she was supposed to take with her. She was supposed to have this. Someone's put it back."

This emotion was true.

Henderson was surprised this foot-by-a-foot hole covered in black velvet wasn't empty.

"You wanted Mrs. Henderson to take your money?"

"She liked to act as if she'd put one over on me. The three thousand pounds are here. My wife was going to Scotland with my blessings to divorce me. She would marry her current fantasy, poor bloke."

Feeling less scared, I moved closer and noted that the safe had none of the aforementioned things—a bloody fingernail, a letter *J*. "You didn't mind her having an affair?"

"I minded, Lady Worthing, but not much can be done about a heart that wishes to wander."

We were standing side by side. He smelled of outdoors, grass clippings, and something berrylike. The man towered over me, but I no longer feared him. "Other than this safe not being empty, is there something else I should make note of, Mr. Henderson?"

His lips curled, then flattened. "Not sure what to think. She didn't get the money. I thought the killer stole it. Now it looks as if she was killed because she didn't have the money."

"Juliet Henderson could've been in a hurry."

"Could be, but I checked last night. The safe was empty."

"When did you check last night?"

"After we found Juliet." He turned and faced me. "Did you put the coins back?"

"What? No."

"Did you kill her, Lady Worthing? Did you leave *Ali Baba* in those ridiculous Scottish capes—"

"They're not monk's robes . . . They're Scottish tweed capes."

"That's what I said."

"Oh. Most people say it wrong. But . . ."

He folded his arms, clutching tightly to his biceps. "Did you sneak from Drury Lane, come to my house, and murder my wife? You stole the money, had a change of heart, and I caught you putting the coins back."

"Why would a murderer put coins back and risk being discovered?"

Yanking the stiff-backed chair from the desk, he dropped onto the plaid covered seat. "You could've said you didn't do it."

True, but he wouldn't believe me. I pulled out my recovered theater lorgnette and held the tortoiseshell handle, flipping out the lens.

"What is that, and what are you doing?"

"Looking for a clue with my glasses. A hair or something stuck to the velvet or the sack. Something to tell us who did it."

"Well?"

"Nothing is there." No matter how much I wished for something. "A blond hair would prove Juliet had been in the safe. Nothing here."

I turned to the stoic man, who actually looked lost for once. "How did you see me leave? You don't have an adjacent box, no box at all."

"I used a friend's. I borrow it from time to time when he's out of the country. But small, tight spaces reminded me too much of my ship. Sometimes in the dark, things feel crowded, too crowded. I needed out and went to get some air in the stairwell."

My brow lifted and he surely read the doubts in my mind.

"After living a decade in tight quarters, I can't tolerate cramped accommodations, not for long. You passed right by me. I saw you and your monk friend. Pretty clever to have your maids—"

"One was my housekeeper."

He chuckled, then sobered. "After such an elaborate escape, I suppose you wouldn't be careless as to try to give the money back. No, you'd keep the money."

I pounded my fist on the desk. "You think I would kill a woman with violence, but have a conscience about money. No wonder Juliet left you."

"What?"

"You don't understand women. I don't think you understand much at all, unless it involves lines and angles."

"I like curves, too."

He turned from me and glanced at his safe. I was glad he did. Not sure I wanted blue fire aimed at me.

"Did you follow my cousin and me out of Drury Lane?"

His head tilted to me. "Yes."

It was *him,* that feeling of being chased. *Him.*

Moving to the other side of the desk, I wanted to toss the statue at him, but it looked too heavy for me. He'd probably catch it and fling it back. "You frightened me that night. I changed my plans because I felt you, someone, near."

"You felt me." Like a cannon, a fifteen pounder from Hayti's shores, his gaze shot to me. And stayed. "I won't hurt you."

Time slowed and I tried to read his secrets, his truths, maybe pieces of the life he'd lived ten years away at sea.

"I said I won't hurt you, Lady Worthing—that night or now."

Fool that I was, I believed him.

Breathing easier, I put my hand on the white marble bust. "I wish this thing could speak. He surely saw everything Juliet did in here. He saw her leave to the garden. He had to have heard what she said, maybe her thoughts."

"Yes, John Donne, please give us a poem." Henderson craned his ear. "No answer, but I doubt any of his testimony would stand in the courts."

There. That was the dry sarcastic tone I'd learned to endure. "The killer didn't put back the money. They wouldn't risk being caught. Someone else did this. Someone who didn't want anyone to know that you and your wife had made an arrangement, or that she was leaving you for Scotland."

He rubbed a hand through his dark, curly hair. "Any number of people knew. Juliet wasn't a discreet person."

"I recently heard discretion is a quality men enjoy."

"It's a gift. It is something to treasure."

"Why?"

He rubbed at his brow, forcing a part in the center of his wild curls. "One can share anything and know it's safe. That's freedom, Lady Worthing."

Talk was freeing? Maybe for those used to being free, without a stain of enslavement in their pedigree. For those whose grandmother and mother knew chains in Jamaica, like mine, discretion was a luxury. The ability to go and to be anything one wanted—those were things treasured.

"Lady Worthing, anyone today could have put the money back while I played with my dogs. The hellhounds, as you call

MURDER IN WESTMINSTER   109

them, are Silvereye and Santisma." He fisted his hand. "Anyone could be guilty, but I happened to catch you."

"For the last time, I didn't enter the safe or give you money. You're constantly trying to embroil me in something. The request to keep your dogs leashed turned into a surveyor's dispute for an unwanted fence to be built. Money disappearing, money theft, more games. All of this on top of you attending the theater last night. You're suddenly unpredictable. Nothing worse than an unpredictable curmudgeon."

His arms flexed, pulling at the sleeves of his ebony jacket. The velvet black armband looked taut, as if it would pop. "My wife's body was found on *your* lawn. That makes you involved. And you know how questions can stir. I've seen others, innocent people, struggle for justice for the crime of being in the wrong place or being seen at the wrong time. I tried to help. You have no true alibi."

Had to ignore the emotion in his voice—that sorrowful, regretful tone that felt honest. It could all be an act to make me lower my guard or, worse, empathize with him.

I spun toward the mirror and watched him watching me. "You sound noble, Henderson. The theater excuse gives you a solid alibi, too. Moreover, everyone knows Lady Worthing is a theater buff. It's an added benefit to have me as a part of your defense."

"*My* fence, *your* lawn. That's my point. We have to work together."

"The wall shouldn't have been built."

"You have your wish. It's gone. It will never return. I'll not keep myself or my dogs away from you again."

His tone held a threat, a promise, something—a mystery I refused to solve, ever.

When I worked on my breathing again, I turned. My jet skirt floated, then collapsed at my ankles. "Who do you think killed your wife?"

He pivoted and closed up the safe. "A disappointed lover, a remorseful guinea thief, but these could be two different people."

He headed to the door, began opening it. "I've wasted enough time. Must go up to formally join the *lichwake.*"

Then Henderson stopped, not widening the crack that allowed the music and conversation from above to filter inside. "Neither me nor you. Despite what you think of me or what you heard . . . I've only killed when necessary."

"In the many wars you've been involved?"

"It's ten years of military service, Lady Worthing. Something I and your husband were once both proud of."

That voice of his twisted me up. The weight of his words indicted my James and himself. "Henderson, why are you telling me this? I'm not the magistrate. I'm not a juryman."

"You're my neighbor. The wife of a man for whom I worked hard to gain his respect. I don't want his wife thinking me capable of such."

"Then who do you suspect of murdering Juliet Henderson?"

"Half the mourners upstairs have an intimate connection to my wife."

"Then that would include you, Mr. Henderson. The nature of a marriage is intimate."

"Is it?" He shoved the door closed and faced me. "Maybe when it's new."

No blinking, no shuffling in my stance, nothing to indicate a dissatisfaction with my marriage.

His hands covered his mouth for a moment. "I didn't mean to say that. Any man would hate his wife's unfaithfulness, but Juliet didn't deserve to be virtually abandoned for years. Gone so long, I made her a war widow. We came to an understanding."

"You kicked her out. The argument—"

"I'm particular about the happenings in my bed. But that night, the big argument was for show. Juliet craved attention and drama. I wasn't even here. All the footmen can attest to it. I was at my club. I stayed until Mr. Jyles sent word of her departure."

That night, hadn't I and all the neighbors heard shouts and slammed doors? "The crying, the shrieks, they were all an act to make everyone think you horrid?"

"All pretend. You, a theater buff of all people, should know acting from what's true."

"Did she give you any indication that she was troubled, that things were dire?"

Henderson rubbed his neck as he raised his face to the coffered ceiling. "No. She came and went often. We sent notes. Then I made sure to be away."

"And you want me to believe, out of the generosity of your heart, you funded her and her lovers. That's very generous. Too generous."

"I didn't kill her."

"But you know who could have."

"I have ideas." His gaze washed over me, then lowered to his desk or maybe the poet sitting on the corner. His eyes had less heat this time, but embers remained.

"Henderson, you don't believe I murdered your wife?"

"No. Of course not. I wouldn't have given you an alibi."

"You mean given yourself one. You said you left the theater. You weren't seen back until Act Three. You could have come through Saint James Park and killed her."

"I didn't kill her. I need you to believe me. I know you saved Lord Worthing from hanging. I need help. I have no one else to turn to."

I shook my head. "What does your sister think of all of this?"

His head lowered again. It wasn't Donne that he viewed, but rather the picture of Mary lying on his desk.

It struck me like a lightning bolt. "Henderson, you're protecting your sister. You think she's involved."

The look on his face told me everything I didn't want to know or believe.

"It was she who sent me a note to come home as soon as possible. I had planned to go to my club after the theater. When I arrived, she'd come from our aunt's. It was a late dinner, but she . . . Juliet."

"Mary found the body. That's why she'd been upset. That's how she knew I'd covered her."

"Juliet was already dead. Your dog coming to harass mine was the perfect excuse to find the body again and spare Mary. She can't testify. This will ruin her."

My thoughts raged, realizing I was a fool. That everything I knew was wrong. "The shock she had was pretense. Her acting was good. She fooled me."

Henderson swiftly clasped my hand. Desperation wrapped about him like the tight sleeves of his tailcoat. "She didn't do anything. I beg you, help me keep her from this trouble. She's still mourning the loss of our father. Her life has been disrupted for a year."

I flung free. "You think she did it. She doesn't have the strength to . . . strangle Juliet."

"I don't . . . No. Of course not, but she can still be accused of it. She could be convicted. I'd rather be the most likely suspect. Then, of course, you are next in line."

"Is that a threat? That you'll turn me in to Duncan? The magistrate and I have worked other crimes together. He doesn't think I'm capable of this."

"You honestly expect Lord Duncan to be fair when pressure mounts for an indictment? I know you left Drury Lane. If I saw it, someone else might have. And I'll recant my admission of seeing you there, and let the pieces fall."

Duncan was helpful now, but it did bruise his ego a bit when I cleared Worthing. Men and grudges and convenience were consummate companions—that's what my mama used to say.

"Henderson, I thought you a curmudgeon, a murderer. Now I see you are a mastermind manipulator."

"An improvement." He stepped back and touched the bust of Donne. "Mary and Juliet all say I'm too intense, but I'll swing from the gallows before I let my sister take the blame."

"And I'm collateral damage."

"Where were you heading to, Lady Worthing? Why did you need costumes and actors?"

His voice was matter of fact, entitled as if I'd tell him all.

"I wasn't coming to kill Juliet. I needed air, too."

"Fine. Keep your secret." Standing near wall sconces showed everything from the splotchy freckle on his left eye to his growing frown. "We are in this together, Lady Worthing. Maybe you'll remember that and be honest from now on."

My face felt flush. I trembled because he'd outmaneuvered me and I hadn't seen it coming.

A hand fell on my shoulder, and I nearly jumped over the desk.

"What are you seeing, Lady Worthing? Lord Worthing told me of your second sight."

James told him, him of all people? No. Not possible.

The door to the study opened and Henderson moved away quickly.

The action seemed guilty. The butler looked to the floor, with his cheeks reddening. He thought he'd walked in on us.

"Yes, Mr. Jyles." Henderson moved to the door. His face had become blank like a stone shield. "Is it time?"

The man nodded, then handed me my cleaned blanket. "Sir, we need to take the coffin to the church. The procession must start in a few minutes or the service won't be finished in time for the ten o'clock burial. Nonetheless, I think Mrs. Henderson would have liked a late-night party."

"Let me follow." My neighbor turned to me. "Lady Worthing, thank you for listening, for helping."

He dipped his chin and then went with his butler.

The door to the study closed.

I was alone and confused, burrowing my arms about my mama's quilt. What to believe? What to do?

It didn't truly matter.

I had a killer to catch.

Someone in this house murdered Juliet Henderson. And I was more convinced than ever that her husband was the killer.

Chapter 10

Pacing in my drawing room lined with portraits of the Monroe men, I circled the large table. This might be my fiftieth lap. The floor had even given up the ghost and quieted its usual noises.

I no longer merely sounded like a trapped rat. Henderson had made me one. I stopped in front of James's picture. The artist painted my husband at the docks with the sea at his back.

"I wish you were here. You need to tell me why. Why would you share something so personal with the neighbor?"

Can't control these visions? I don't even know what they mean, if they mean anything, and you told. James, why?

My husband was an intensely private person. He loathed gossip. Yet, this was the same man who needed to sail around the world and thought nothing of the talk that would arise by him leaving his new bride.

Was that it?

"Did you want me to say I needed you? Should I have humbled myself and said I was frightened at the prospects of living in your world without you?"

*And if I had voiced my fears, my dread of waking alone in a
house without my family, without you, would you have changed
your mind?*

I had to remember this wasn't a love match, but more a re-
ward for combing through record after record to find a pattern
of embezzlement that proved him innocent.

Yet, he gave my secrets to an enemy. "You didn't ask, James.
You had no right."

The picture didn't answer. It was aloof and as far away as the
baron.

Folding my arms, crinkling the half sleeves of my morning
gown, I had to admit this was my doing. I gambled and lost
everything—but an elevated name and a few friends.

That would have to be enough.

If I wasn't fully invested in proving Henderson's guilt before, I was now. Had to gain enough evidence to prove him the
villain. It needed to be thorough. Then whatever he said would
be counted as spite.

"James, will this be one of the things we laugh about once
you return, or a thing we tease when you again say goodbye?"

The door to the drawing room flung open. "Ma'am," my
butler said, "is all well?"

I wiped at my brow and swiped a curl flopping from my
eyes. "Yes, Mr. Rogers. Only talking out loud my schedule.
What is it you wish?"

"Mr. Wilson Shaw's waiting for you in the parlor."

"Very good. I'll be with him shortly."

Rogers left and I looked back at smiley James Monroe, the
Lord Worthing. "We'll finish this later."

With a shake of my head, I picked up my skirts, a spring
print of pink flowers on creamy muslin and headed to my solicitor.

Inside my parlor, I found the handsome Mr. Shaw helping
himself to jam tarts, which Mrs. Smith baked.

Licking his fingers, he bounced up and bowed. "These treats are almost enough to keep me risking my employment at your father's firm."

"Mr. Carrington would rather close his establishment than lose the valuable Wilson Shaw, the man who singlehandedly brings in more widowed clients than all the firm combined."

"Ah, Abigail, if you weren't like my sister, I'd let your flattery go to my head."

Sitting squarely in front of the sweets, he stretched in his dapper buff waistcoat and matching breeches. It made his light skin look warmer. "I don't do these late-hour assignments for anyone but you."

"I wouldn't ask anyone but you. I'm sure your latest mistress minded your absence."

"You wound me, ma'am . . . thinking I'd leave any woman unsatisfied."

"Flirt. Do you have the information?"

"Of course," he said through a napkin and the crumbs of another devoured tart. Wilson, who was the rumored by-blow of a peer and courtesan, but had been raised respectably in one of the wealthiest Blackamoor families in London, was accepted by all. Though I believed he didn't care, like I did, about not being welcomed.

After setting the cloth on his knee, he reached into his tailcoat. "Your wish, Lady Worthing."

I took a seat and waved him to start.

"Stapleton Henderson is a man of considerable means. He owns land in Somerset. His family has Mayfair holdings, but he—"

"Prefers Westminster." That must be where the aunt whom Mary went to visit resided.

"Yes. And his combined incomes bring in ten thousand a year." Wilson's brow furrowed.

I picked up a tart. "What is it, sir?"

He flipped through more of his pages. "Wondered if my charm in landing clients extended to widowers."

Chuckling, I curled my palm to him again. "Keep going, more of the good stuff."

"Yes. He made quite a few bounties in his long naval career. The man is a trained physician. He served with Lord Nelson until Trafalgar."

"Was he there? At the battle."

"Yes. Right by the admiral's side until the end. The man's a bona fide war hero."

A loyal war hero could be a murderer. Might give him license to think he'd succeed. "What about debts? Any that Mrs. Henderson could amass?"

"Ah. The missus is a different story. She has quite a few mad modistes about town. She was cut off at the top dressmaker of the season. And shunned by a jeweler."

"Did she have a passion for buying the letter *J* in gold?"

"No. But lots of pins and earbobs. See, you're spoiling this for me."

"But you're making me satisfied."

"Lady Worthing, when are we going to stop all this cat-and-mouse play and let me loose to do what is natural . . . investing all your Worthing money." His face sobered. "All this play lieutenant-magistrate stuff could get me involved in scandal and get you very dead. I wouldn't take well to that. I'd rather you be happy being rich."

"Like you're afraid of scandal, Wilson."

He folded up his notes and stuck them into his pocket. "I like to make my own scandals. I still don't want you hurt. I'd miss these little summons."

I smiled at him, soaking in his brotherly advice and flair. "Like you, I'm always careful, Wilson. Was there anything else you found?"

"Yes, our godfather told me to be thorough. There's a brother in Chelsea."

"To Juliet."

"If you already know, why am I here?"

"Sorry, please preen and continue." I ate my tart. Nothing beat a buttery crust and tangy strawberry jam or gossip. "Wilson, go on."

"As I was saying, there's a brother, an older brother, Jeorge Tanner."

"George—"

"No, Je-orge with a *J*. He's in debt. He could lose his farm in Chelsea. The noise is Juliet had been helping him, giving him small sums here and there, but had abandoned him as of late."

"Ever since she left Westminster? Henderson confessed to me that he'd still been giving her money."

"Perhaps she found someone new to spend it on."

I didn't think Henderson would lie about giving his wife money. He was trying too hard to convince me of his innocence. "Anything on the sister?"

"Mary Henderson has lived a quiet life at boarding schools since her mother died. With the father dying last year, she came to live with Juliet."

"You mean the Hendersons next door."

Wilson popped another tart, one oozing of the bright red fruit, into his mouth. "More so with the wife next door. Henderson didn't see her or spend a lot of time with her until he retired in January."

Mary was weepy-eyed the night the body was discovered—discovered twice. And she cried hard during much of the *lichwake*. She'd clearly grown close to Juliet in the time she'd lived next door.

"You've gone quiet. You must have stumbled onto something. It's your turn, Lady Worthing. You were at the 'immoral dead party,' as some are calling it."

"I met more suspects. I need you to find out about a driver named Sinclair, a Miss Bumners, the maid, and the new minister at Saint Margaret's, Mr. Benjamin. More about the brother, too.

And, of course, if you find any information about the identity of the lover Mrs. Henderson was running away with."

"Anyone else? A needle in a haystack?"

"Can you find out what Lord Duncan's thinking? Is he going to make an arrest, any arrest?"

"Oh, no, Abigail. Not going near him. I hear he can put one in jail with a simple writ of suspicion. He'll not know my name. As to the rest, I'll dig around and see what I find."

"Fine. Wilson, investigate Tanner, Benjamin, Bumners, Sinclair, and Mary. And anyone rumored to be a lover."

He reared back and closed his eyes. "What do you hope to find?"

"I'm not sure. I'll know when we discover it."

"It's the vagueness that keeps me coming back." Wilson rose and clasped my hand. "You stay safe, you hear me. Duncan's a tricky bird, but I hear he respects you. Yet, all that can change in an instant. He's a political man. Politics make everything difficult."

"I know that to be true, sir." I wiped the stickiness of the tart from my hands. "Speaking of, can you also locate the next Wilberforce meeting?"

He put his hands to his thighs, then sought gloves from his pockets. "I told you politics makes things difficult. They've all disappeared. The Clapham Sect is laying low for now." He moved and the floor creaked. "Why didn't you go? You know how hard it is to get that information."

"Dinah."

The man spun back. "Has the prodigal returned home?"

With a shake of my head, I almost released my frustrated tears. I didn't see her or make a difference in the fight of abolition. All I did was set myself up as the neighbor's fool.

"Hey. Hey." He knelt beside my chair. "Not the giving-up face."

"No, Wilson. I have new information I know Wilberforce and Hannah More can use to write more condemning pamphlets. This will change minds back to abolition, but I failed."

He rose and brushed at his knees, but Mrs. Smith kept too fine of a house for anything like dust to linger. "I'll dig and find something. Abolitionists aren't the type to sit around. Neither are you."

Standing, I looped my arm about his to walk him to the door. "See, I don't ask for much."

"If you weren't adorable and rich and my employer's daughter, I think I'd ignore you." He blocked me from opening the door. "You are Lady Worthing. Think of indulging in your station. It has safety built into it."

"Helping with abolition is what I can do with my station. That's beneficial."

"And solving the neighbor's murder, Lady Worthing?"

I wanted to say it was personal. It was. I wanted to best Henderson and do something for Juliet. "My hobby helps to pass the time. And I need to know if I'm living next door to a killer."

As we neared the doors, Florentina Sewell was announced by Mr. Rogers.

Wilson bent and kissed my cheek. "Stay out of trouble. And keep alive."

He pivoted and almost rammed into Florentina. "Excuse me, Miss Sewell."

Affixing his gloves, the man moved to the threshold faster than anything and then closed the parlor doors.

It was a little rude, but at least the two didn't fight. Oil and water, those two.

My cousin put her hands on her hips. "What's going on, Abbie? That one only slinks around to tell you how well his clients are doing or if you need him for investigative work."

"He's invested mine. I will get him to do more of Worthing's.

But the small fact I might be living next door to a smart killer is worrisome."

She shook her head violently. "Uncle Vaughn stopped by Spitalfields this morning. He shared with his sister—my mother, and fretful father the latest happenings in Westminster."

I ducked my head. "I'm sorry, Flo."

She held out her palm. "It only took three lectures and a promise not to die or be compromised to get me from there to here."

"If it's any consolation, I made the same promise to Mr. Shaw. It must be catching."

"Abigail Carrington Monroe, why must you play mystagogus?"

Insulted, I brought my hand to my chest. "A what?"

"Latin. One who's a guide to mysteries, Abbie. Lord Worthing has been away too long. If he were here, he'd stop you."

"Florentina, I walked through my doors expecting everything, hoping for restoration of my sister. No Dinah. She wasn't here. Instead, I found my neighbor's wife strangled on that stupid fence on my side of the lawn. What am I to do? I'm a suspect."

She came forward and nearly fell into the yellow tufted chair. It was something I had Rogers scrounge from one of the guest bedrooms. A necessary find when I felt how hard the sitting chairs were.

"The law will sort it out."

"I can't wait and hope, Flo."

"No Dinah, *and* you're a suspect."

"My elaborate ruse to go to the secret abolition meeting let Henderson see us. He gave me a solid alibi, but he can recant at any moment. Like I said, I can't sit around hoping."

I pushed the tray toward her with the two last jam tarts. "Mr. Shaw is doing the usual for me, looking at the background of anyone else who could be a suspect."

She stretched for the treat. "Lord Duncan knows you. He couldn't possibly think you'd be capable of killing."

My shoulders shrugged and exposed my low level of trust in my fellow man or magistrate. "At this moment in time, he's indicted no one. But if public sentiment changes, he'll charge me and Henderson. Duncan has kept the death quiet from the papers, but something like this can't be ignored much longer."

"This isn't fair, Abbie."

Stretching, I took the last tart. "If Lord Duncan doesn't get his man or woman, Henderson will destroy my alibi. I'll look guilty of aiding Henderson in murdering his wife."

"That's truly unfair. The evil fence builder."

"Oh, he's protecting Mary. Flo, she doesn't have a solid way of corroborating her whereabouts. But there is no way she could've done it, not without help."

Would a brother and sister team up for something like this?

No. Henderson wasn't the type to do something rash or something he couldn't draw up three sets of plans to construct.

Florentina finished her tart, eating it in bits, and as always savoring the sweet center for last. "If she did have a hand in it, we should track her."

Feeling useless and trapped, I covered my eyes for a moment.

In the next instant, there was light gnawing at my closed lids.

Florentina stood over me, crumbs on her face, shining a candle in mine. "What are you seeing?"

"Not much with the light burning down on me. Put it away. I'm not my mother. I don't have visions every waking moment."

She blew out the flame and set it in a brass holder on the table. "Abigail, talk to me."

"Last night, I dreamed about it. I saw her ribbon dangling in the wind. I witnessed Mrs. Henderson be affectionate to someone, teasing with the buttons of her gown. She confessed her love, and then I saw her struggle, fighting for her life. How could someone do that? She was vulnerable, physically, emotionally."

"You know who did it? It was revealed?"

"No. No other faces. All I saw was Mrs. Henderson's, and I screamed in my sleep. The terror of her death . . . Thank goodness, no one heard me."

Florentina went to the window and smoothed back the cream curtain, holding the fabric with her fingers as if something would jump out at her. "It's all down. No more fence."

"That's all you have to say? Flo, I told you what I saw. Tell me it was real or swear to me it was my imagination. But don't ignore it like some mad uttering."

"Abbie, I don't know what to say other than this is too dangerous for us."

"I have to find out who killed her. And I need to do it for her and to protect you. Flo, everything you're working on could be at risk. Your name could be linked to my disgrace. You wore the monk costume, too."

"It's capes." Florentina turned back to me, smiling like she had peace with the confusion I'd caused. "Abbie, you've never been dull. I don't expect you to be now."

She retook her seat. "Don't sell yourself short. Deep down, Lord Duncan admires your logical mind. He might understand being caught by surprise by Henderson, a man you despise."

"I hope you are right. I have to solve this for me, you, and Juliet. If I hadn't been a coward, I might've forced myself to see the whole vision. I would've seen it wasn't my sister. Then I could've warned my neighbor."

"It doesn't work like that Abbie. You don't have that kind of power."

"I wish I did, then Juliet Henderson would be alive."

"Abbie—."

"You don't know how hard it is not to think or dream at night. To want my mind to be so tired I see nothing but blackness. If I could've been brave . . . If I had . . ."

"It's not your fault. Abbie, it's not."

"I understand Mama's burden. I know why she suffered."

Flo moved to me and put her hands to my cheeks. "You're not your mother."

"No. I thought I was smarter. Thought I could protect myself and everyone by becoming Lady Worthing. It's an empty title."

"Snap out of this, Abigail. Let's be on our way."

"Where?"

"Get your papers. Wilberforce hunting. The eating house at the end of King Street is one of his favorite haunts. There's a good chance to see him and do good. And we can be bold and in the open. No disguises or sneaking. Let's go."

"No. Wait. I promised Miss Bumners I'd meet her in Cheapside, Seven Watling, at two o'clock."

"Miss who?" Florentina stretched out in the cushions. Her rust-colored carriage gown puckered about the buttons. It was made for adventure, not lounging.

"Mrs. Henderson's personal maid. She wants to show me some jewelry or something. We can ask her more questions about the wife's last few hours—what she did to occupy her time, who visited with her—before she came to Number Eleven."

"Then it is settled. We go to Cheapside to interview the maid and then we will have dinner and watch for Wilberforce. It may take several dinners before we catch him, but it's a sacrifice I'm willing to make."

I'd hug my cousin again if I didn't have to go change. I walked to the door, then turned and rushed into her arms. "Thank you for believing in me."

"You believed in me first. Even before you were fancy Lady Worthing."

Wiping a wet eye, I hurried to my room to see what my maid had pulled out for me. I knew it would be flawless and daring, for I had people in my corner who supported me even when I doubted my own worth.

Climbing the stairs, I thought how to ask Miss Bumners to name Juliet Henderson's lovers. Which one had she jilted, hurt enough to try to stop her leaving for Scotland? Was it the same person whom she'd virtually made love to before dying? I needed to know if they were one and the same, Stapleton Henderson, the man I thought took Juliet's life.

Chapter 11

When the carriage made it to Strand Street, I relaxed. We'd be in Cheapside soon. "The heavy traffic won't slow us down, Florentina."

My cousin kept shifting from arms folded to clasping the knees of her rust-colored carriage gown.

"Are you calculating our odds of surviving?"

"One in four." She sat back and slouched. Her double buttons jangled. "How long have you known Miss Bumners?"

"I've seen her over the years."

"When did you learn her name, Abbie?"

"Last night."

Florentina ducked her face in her hand. "Wait. A woman whom you were formally introduced to last night invited you over to a distant, discreet location. Oh, no. We're going to die."

"Where's the encouragement from the parlor?"

"It's still here. But the 'I don't want to die' part takes precedence."

"Flo, Miss Bumners couldn't have killed her. It takes a lot of strength to strangle someone." I whipped the loop of my puce-colored reticule. "But she could've taken money from Henderson's safe and put it back. We'll have to find out if she worked at Number Eleven the evening of the murder."

Her eyebrow went up as my words started to filter into her mathematical mind. "Wait? Money stolen. I thought we were investigating a murder. Missing money is more to my liking. You're good at those."

"The gold coins meant for Mrs. Henderson were missing, but put back some time during the funeral. These could be the actions of two different people or a clever murderer."

"If the money was put back, how do you know it was missing?"

I stopped flitting the loops and caught my reticule, trapping it against my black shawl and deep indigo coat. "Mr. Henderson told me." It didn't seem as if he lied, but it could have been something meant to distract me when he found me at his safe.

Florentina folded her hands, then rubbed her brow. "I should've brought paper. I could be writing my last will and testament."

"If something does happen, may I have that gown, dear? It's gorgeous."

She started laughing; then I did.

But I made note of not accepting Henderson's testimony as readily in the future.

We settled in and watched more streets go by.

While staring out the window, Florentina gripped my hand. "Do we have weapons?"

"What? Flo, we're going to see a maid. We can fight off buckets and pails of starch."

She leaned forward. "Ever get hit with a bucket?"

"No."

"Me either, but it has to hurt."

"We're smart, capable women. We are with our driver. Rawlins will come looking for us if we come up missing."

"That all sounds a little too late, the part about us already being missing or even dead. Do we know if Juliet Henderson's driver came looking for her?"

I smoothed my reticule, pushed away the wrinkles of the pleated fabric. A bit of lilac from the sachets Miss Bellows placed in my drawer tickled my nose. "Actually, we don't. Mr. Sinclair could've come back or found the body before . . ."

"Before what, Abbie?"

I was about to say *before Mary arrived and discovered Juliet,* but I wouldn't betray that confidence yet. "Before Henderson and I found his wife. Mr. Sinclair is a suspect. He seems enamored by Juliet. Last night he was distraught. It could be more than pure affection. It could be guilt."

The carriage stopped.

Mr. Rawlins, in his exquisite top hat and matching jet mantle with crimson braiding, opened the door of my black Berlin.

I popped out. "Coming, Miss Sewell? You can wait outside if . . ."

"If what? No, don't say. I'm coming. I'm at eightieth percentile of us surviving the interview. I'll go in, thinking I'm still in a fool's paradise of safety."

I leaned inside and grabbed the knife from the bottom compartment.

"Oh," Florentina said, "this is no joke."

"None, Cousin. Catch up."

"So you are scared, too?"

"I want to make sure we are at a high percentile of survival."

We turned, waved at Rawlins, and started to cross the street to Seven Watling.

"Ma'am, Lady Worthing, Miss Sewell, wait."

I stopped and caught my cousin to slow her. "Yes, Rawlins."

"I'm not going to park at the mews. I'm staying out here. I'll come for you in thirty minutes."

Looking at the lathered mare and silver gelding, I thought better of it. "The horse needs to be refreshed and washed down. This one is a little tart."

"True. But I'm not leaving. I'm going to turn the carriage around and stay close. I saw Mr. Henderson arrive."

Both of us had a two o'clock meeting with Miss Bumners? "Yes, Rawlins. That seems best. We'll yell out if we need you sooner."

"I'll come running, Lady Worthing."

Nodding to him, I shoved the knife into my reticule and took my cousin's hand. We had an appointment, and I needed insurance that we'd live. Florentina and I crossed the street. Didn't have to look at her beautiful, frowning face to know she'd cut our survival odds by fifty percent.

The main door at Seven Watling Street stretched open. No footmen or grooms could be seen.

That wasn't unusual for this side of town, an area where more tradesmen and shopkeepers lived. An open door . . . that was bothersome, but maybe Mr. Henderson left it that way.

"Hello," Florentina's voice warbled.

I moved forward through the entry.

Clean white walls.

Blue moldings.

Hints of lavender in the air.

This felt like last night's *lichwake,* but without the press of people.

"Not going to find her if we stay in the entryway, Florentina." I stepped in front of my cousin and took the lead. My low heels clicked on the tiles lining the hall. An open door at the end of the hall drew me.

Noise came from inside.

I raised my hand to knock, but then craned my ear to listen.

The sound of footfalls and shuffling of paper said someone was inside.

Florentina gripped my arm and I jumped, barreling into the room, stopping in front of Stapleton Henderson.

"Making an entrance, Lady Worthing."

Shaking free of my cousin and letting blood pump anew in my arm, I cleared my throat. "Sir, I have an appointment at two."

"I happen to have one as well." He looked around, his lips poking into a frown. "I thought Juliet kept a better house."

Books were scattered about. A pelisse lay along a red sofa.

It looked a little ransacked or *dog*-sacked. Teacup would definitely have fun exploring all the fabrics and surfaces.

Florentina went to the tea service; a white porcelain pot, with a rose painted on the side, shared a tray with two cups stained of tea. She touched the side. Then she popped open the porcelain top. "I was going to see if this Miss Bumners started the meeting without us, but this is cold and half drunk."

Henderson planted like a tree in the doorway, looking toward the entry as if someone would enter the townhouse at any minute. "It has to be from a day or so. So much has happened in two days."

The man seemed taller in the narrow cream waistcoat and long ebony jacket. The velvet mourning band stretched when he folded his arms.

"This doesn't seem right. Miss Bumners is compulsive in her cleaning habits. I had to stop her from polishing my pianoforte daily. Such a buildup of the orange oil made the keys slippery."

"Oranges, you say, Mr. Henderson," Florentina said in her nervous, fast voice. "My employer loves fragrant orange oil on her tables."

"Fascinating." He covered his mouth for a moment. "Why don't you ladies stay here while I search? It's narrow upstairs. I can be more efficient—"

"No." I walked to him. "We can all look together. There's no need to split up."

"Yes, there is Lady Worthing. If he's on a crime spree, let him go about it. We can come back later."

"Miss Sewell. We'll be fine. Mr. Rawlins, my capable driver is outside. He's prepared."

Henderson rolled his eyes. "I'm not a criminal. Nor have I done anything to warrant suspicion. You ladies are safe. Let's find Miss Bumners or seek the evidence she wished to show us."

"*Today*, Abbie. That's what he's saying with his eyes. *Safe today.*"

"Miss Sewell." I wove my fingers with hers. "Sir, seems we all have an appointment. There must be a reason Miss Bumners wanted us both here. I suggest we stick together and search. Lead, Mr. Henderson."

He glared down at me. "You're good at giving orders, Lady Worthing."

"And you don't mind taking them from a neighbor. The anti–fence building party."

"Is that like the Whigs or conservative Tories?"

"They're pretty much all the same since Pitt's death, cowards."

His eyes went wide at my statement. He might've even chuckled, but none of this empty talk had made us move any farther in exploring the house.

Something heavy dropped above.

Then no more sound.

"I suppose we'll all do this. Stay behind me." He picked up a candelabra from the corner, then waved us forward.

We walked out and came to another room. The small study looked untouched, with the strong afternoon sun pouring in through the open pale blue curtains.

Henderson turned and led us to the stairs. "This level is clear of visitors."

"You mean of the murderer?" My cousin's chatter was ill-timed, as usual.

"Miss Sewell, keep working on those odds. When we are down to about a twenty percent ranking let me know." At that point, it wouldn't much matter what clues were upstairs. The runners could have at it. I needed us to live to see another day.

My neighbor clutched the rail and pounded up the steps. We followed to the second floor. This one looked very much like the first, but all walls were whitewashed, no special attention was paid to the molding.

Again, the three of us stood like sheep awaiting a shepherd to call us forward.

"This is ridiculous." I barged ahead. "Miss Bumners! Miss Bumners!"

No answer.

I moved to the closest room and flicked the door open. A copper basin was inside. It was dry. No wet towels. "The bathing chamber is empty."

Henderson stood in the hall. He didn't budge, but acknowledged my statement with a nod and roll of his hand to keep charging ahead.

I slipped past him and went farther down the hall. This floor was soft pine, but had no creaks, not even with the click of my heels.

One wouldn't hear someone coming.

Then I noticed that only Florentina's footfalls and mine could be heard. His boots were silent. Henderson could sneak in here and out without anyone noticing.

"Was the door locked when you came, sir, or unlocked?"

"Unlocked. I have a key, but didn't need to use it."

"Is that usual, Mr. Henderson?"

He looked at me with his steady, flaming eyes. "I never visited after the lease was signed. She had money for a footman. What happened to her household allowance?"

His lips pursed and we all kept close together navigating the space as if something could be lurking in the reading room, a room with not a book in sight.

"The first editions of Donne she said she must have. Gone." He bristled beneath his top hat and I felt his wallet emptying.

"There's a market for such in the rookery. Saint Giles too."

Henderson made a noise. "I gave her Donne and she sold him for money."

"I think the poet will understand. I don't think he's been in a state to care of such things for over one hundred seventy-five years."

His gaze softened. "You've studied John Donne."

"Not since yesterday."

A smile appeared at my reply. But it was true. I asked Rogers about him and even found poems in Worthing's collection.

Flo touched the wall. "They're shiny. And freshly polished with orange oil."

I touched the paneling and a sheen rubbed onto my glove. "This was done this morning or yesterday. Maybe after the *lichwake*?"

Turning to my neighbor, I found him at the door again. "What time did you make this appointment with Miss Bumners?"

"When we finished our conversation, Lady Worthing. I followed my butler upstairs and met with her in the hall. She said she had some important things to show me today."

"She told me that I had to see Mrs. Henderson's jewelry. That's when I learned about her love of the gold letter *J* you'd given her."

Something conjured in his head, and he chuckled as his head dipped. He looked younger when he smiled. "First year of marriage. Everything's new. It's probably one of the few things I did that made her happy."

He clapped his hands like a gong as if to end the sentimentality he exhibited. "I asked Miss Bumners to pack up all of my wife's things. She doesn't seem to have made much progress. Hope she had no part in selling Donne."

As many times as the Carringtons moved when I was a child, I knew by heart the routine of how things had to be crated. Sheets were the last thing. They were ordered to cover the furnishings that would stay. "Not much has been done. Do you plan to dismiss Miss Bumners?"

"Not sure." He ventured inside when Florentina and I stepped out and opened the closet I'd missed. "Nothing but gowns in here."

"You were saying about the maid?"

"Lady Worthing, Mary might need more seasoned assistance. In another year, she'll be old enough to think of courtships and such. A woman with more expertise and wisdom would be good."

"You missed the flock of young men who circled her. Those men thought her old enough. And she held court. She might think she's old enough, too. What of her aunt? Can she help?"

He looked flustered for a moment. Then shook his head before leaning against the threshold. "What are you saying, ma'am, about my sister?"

"Only trying to prepare you. She's a young woman with her own ideas. See if she's attached to Miss Bumners. Perhaps she will listen to her."

Florentina sidestepped around us and moved into the hall. "Madam, sir. There are two more rooms up here that need to be checked. Then we can say we tried and reschedule."

She took the lead this time and went into the next, a bedchamber.

Finally colored walls. This one was yellow and bright and big. The signature polish smell was everywhere. Not an inch of the woodwork was without it. Shiny, well loved. Her mistress would be proud of Miss Bumners's work.

"This room looks comfortable. Bright, sunny yellow. Everything smells fresh, Abbie. I think we're upsetting ourselves over nothing."

"Then what are our odds now, Cousin?"

"Back to ninety percent."

Henderson poked at a chest of drawers, which sat close to the door. He pulled one open. "My wife's necklaces."

The drawer glittered with a gold locket, a silver chain with mother-of-pearl.

"There were more pieces. My jeweler always fashioned something for each anniversary."

"Something instead of seeing you."

"Something to let my wife know I thought of her in my absence. We weren't meant to be, but that didn't mean I had no emotions for her."

I thought of James's gift of Teacup on our last anniversary. I loved my dog, but now realized Henderson's statement could model my future with the baron—empty with meaningless gifts that note the passage of time, nothing more. I made my voice sound breathless and desperate. "Any sign of the missing *J*? Maybe she wore something else. It is possible?"

"No," he said, "she wore it everywhere."

I pulled another drawer and found pearl pins and a few bracelets, even a ruby necklace. I was confused. "Why is this here at all?"

"Couldn't sell it all? This is horrid, Lady Worthing."

"No. I mean yes, it is terrible, but if I were running off to Scotland, would I leave any precious jewelry behind? Are these Henderson family heirlooms, something with an estate entanglement that she wouldn't be entitled to?"

"No, these are pieces she bought herself with pocket change or credit at various jewelers that I must now go settle. Everything I picked is gone."

"It's still generous of you to allow her to leave with these things."

"When you want someone out of your life, you don't care how they leave or what they take. You wish them gone."

"That's a damning statement, sir."

"It's an honest one. I wanted Juliet gone, not dead. I wanted her to find the happiness she never had with me."

Florentina opened the closet. "Nothing is packed. Granted, she had a lot of clothes, but nothing looks like a woman trying to go anywhere."

"That's it, Miss Sewell. You've said the most important thing. She wasn't going away."

Henderson slammed the drawer shut. "It was another of her scenes. She was pretending, getting one of her . . . lovers worked up for nothing."

"Not for nothing. Mr. Sinclair thought she was trying to come back to you."

"Ridiculous. Juliet didn't want me." He fanned his dark top hat and stepped back into the hall. "Unless you're going to look under the bed, I suggest we keep going."

Florentina did peek under the bed skirt and then ran her hand on the bedpost. "Nothing's here."

When she popped up, we left in a single line.

There was another door, but not to a room.

The others passed it, but I stopped.

Bracing, I flung open the door.

A mop handle smacked me in the nose. Containers of polish filled the shelves. "This must be what we're smelling. One of them has leaked."

A puddle had formed on the middle shelf. It was sticky. "If Miss Bumners saw it, she definitely would have cleaned it up. This must be new. Within the last day or so."

My throat felt tight. The sweetness of orange-oil polish consumed the air.

The others had walked ahead to the final room.

Henderson held the candelabra ready to hammer someone with it.

When I caught up to them, I watched him press open the door and swing. The man struck nothing.

It was dark inside. Unlike the other rooms, all the windows had been closed up.

Florentina swept to one and parted heavy woolen curtains. "Rawlins is downstairs. I see him. Ninety-five percent."

This room was again different, with a rich orangy-red paper treatment on the walls. A big bed with a canopy filled the space. It made this large area feel crowded.

"Looks the same as all the rest, and empty," Henderson said as he stepped two feet into the room. "I think we should go."

"When we make a thorough evaluation, we shall leave." I ran my hand along the bedclothes. They were rumpled. Someone had slept here. "We're getting close, sir. Give us a moment."

His head whipped about. Then as if he were done looking, Henderson backed into the hall.

I remembered his words about the discomfort of small places. This big bed did make the room feel tight.

It wasn't orderly, but I finally saw what we should've seen in the rest of the house—bundles and evidence of packing.

Every scarf in London sat on the bedframe.

Hatboxes were on the floor.

"She likes her silks," I said.

The smell of orange was stronger in here than in the closet in the hall. "Do you see a polish spill somewhere, Florentina?"

My cousin pinched her nostrils. "Maybe the bottle initially leaked here on some linen. Something that would hold the scent."

"This place isn't like Juliet. She liked an orderly house." He sighed. "It was my butler's only compliment of her."

So Mr. Jyles didn't love Mrs. Henderson like the rest of the servants. "And you like order, sir. Something that can be drawn on multiple plans. Is there ever room for spontaneity or gaiety?"

"Yes. I'm sure I can be Mr. Fun."

His flat, unemotional voice made me laugh.

"Fun has its place," he said in a warmer tone. "I love my dogs. I'll soon start a garden. That will give me infinite pleasure, Lady Worthing. Everything has its own proper time and season."

Something in his gaze was different. Maybe he searched for something in me that would lead him to believe I trusted his words. There was some trust, mainly because he could've killed us at any moment since we arrived—and hadn't. Not sure if that was enough to build upon.

Letting him keep watch from the hall, I yanked on drawers and found more scarves—different weaves, different colors, like sand and salmon pink.

"Your wife had expensive taste. And I suppose these are the bills to prove it." I handed him a pile of recent ones I found underneath a silver shawl. From the notations on them, they looked as if they had outstanding sums.

The man flipped through them. His countenance held the same look Florentina's did when she made calculations.

"All will be paid," he said. "But with the money I've been giving her, there shouldn't be any debt. There should be jewels and servants. Who was she paying? Where was it being spent? Could money be the true cause of her death? A blackmailer who didn't get paid?"

"What, Mr. Henderson?"

He wiped at his mouth. "What if she were meeting someone she owed?"

"In your yard?" I shook my head. "That doesn't make much sense to me, a debt collector at night at her estranged husband's house."

"I'd given her money in the past. A generous allowance.

Could she have hoped I would've been home to protect her from whomever she owed? I wasn't. She didn't find the money and some fiend killed her over debts."

That was a possibility, but the way she died was too personal, too intimate with undone buttons. It was more than debt.

Would a fiendish debt collector ogle a woman he'd just killed?

Henderson craned his head to the ceiling. Nothing was of interest there, except moldings. "She once wrote to me about her brother's debts. I wonder if he still needed money."

A spendthrift woman and an alleged miserly husband, who happened to be generous to his unfaithful wife—none of this made any sense. "Everything about this is full of contradictions."

He looked at me from his perch at the door. He moved no closer inside. "My accounts will show a steady draw."

"Steady, like coerced payments?" Florentina said what I'd begun to think.

I waved a hand to my cousin and took up her questioning. "What did she have on you to make you pay money for her to squander? What secret did she know that you needed kept secret?"

His glare cut through me, ripping me apart as if I'd wronged him.

My cousin came to my side. "She didn't mean it, Mr. Henderson."

He rubbed at his neck. "This is hopeless. And Miss Bumners isn't here. She's probably back at Greater Queen Street waiting for one of us."

"Once we finish checking, we can go our separate ways." I turned back to him with my pointing finger extended. "But I will find out what Mrs. Henderson was holding over your head. Think about confessing. You know it will come out."

He hissed, blowing out hot air like a stovepipe oven. "I'll say this one more time. Juliet and I were friends. She was eloping to Scotland with my blessings. There she would divorce me and marry the new love of her life. I had no need to kill her. She was going after her happiness. That's what I wanted for her all along."

Henderson sounded impassioned, even truthful. I sort of believed him.

My cousin squinted at him and then me. "If she was going to elope, where were her bags, her packed portmanteaus? Even if she was going to get money from you or meet her lover in your yard, there should've been something found at the scene or here."

Florentina picked up a scarf and floated the ends as she waved her arms. "A woman who loves scarves as much as Juliet Henderson should've packed some. I think she had no intentions of eloping."

This was the last room. If there was any proof she would elope, it had to be here.

I stooped and searched under the bed. Nothing—no bundle or box or anything except that strong scent of polish. The floor felt a little tacky. Had polish been spilled and wiped up?

"Someone's not telling the truth." I bounced up and moved the bed skirt back into place. "I hate indicting a dead person. She can't defend herself."

My gaze and Florentina's went to the unopened closet.

"You ladies have gone silent. Is all well?" Henderson had backed farther into the hall.

"We're alive if that is what you are asking, sir." I put my hand on the door pull. It wouldn't budge. With all my might, I tugged until it opened.

A bucket looked to have fallen from a shelf to the closet floor. "This must be the noise we heard."

Moving it out of the way, I searched the shelves. Each was

lined with paper and fancy dresses. I touched a piece of the tissue and heard the crinkle of the layers. Then something shoved into the corner, draped in linen, soaked in polish, unwrapped and fell.

A rush of oily orange scent slapped my face.

But death struck my feet.

Florentina screamed as a dead Miss Bumners flopped onto my shoes, reeking of polish.

Chapter 12

Something happened to your body when a dead woman fell on your feet.

Your pulse rushed.

Your heart thudded as if it would break.

Your breath stopped, then became a rapid pant.

That had to be good, because at least I learned to breathe again.

My eyes burned.

Henderson ran into the room with the candelabra.

I had my cousin in my arms. And a murdered maid lay on my slippers.

He dropped the candelabra and came to me. "May I?"

"By all means, help." My voice was nothing but a whisper.

Henderson put his fingers to the side of Florentina's neck. "Strong pulse. Just a faint."

"That's good." I couldn't much move. This might be what "frozen in fear" meant, except I could speak.

"I'm going to put Miss Sewell onto the bed. Then I'll come back and see about you."

Somehow I nodded. "Not going anywhere."

Henderson lifted Florentina and put her on the bed. Then he returned to my side. "I suppose the scream was Miss Sewell and not Miss Bumners crying out from you two killing her."

If I wasn't frozen, I'd slap him.

He went down on his knees and turned the body. The woman's lifeless eyes stared up at me.

A rag was stuffed in her mouth.

"She's not quite stiff. She's been dead a few hours. The cloth is soaked in orange oil. She was overcome by the fumes and suffocated. Poor woman."

His voice trailed off, and he stared into the closet.

"Could you get her off my shoes? I want to try and move."

"Oh, yes." He rolled Miss Bumners to the side.

Though I was free, I still couldn't quite move. I think my heart had lodged into my legs.

Trailing his hands along her neck, Henderson surely searched for marks. "Her nails are trimmed. Nothing broken. She was completely overpowered or surprised by who did it."

"Well, I guess you don't need Teacup to scratch you again."

"The mongrel dog scratched me when I arrived. My sister has been giving him bacon to make him come to our terrace. No bacon, Teacup gives no unwarranted affection. At least the dog is clear in what he wants."

"He's a dog. How many needs could he have? I can't believe we were making light conversation and a dead woman dropped onto my shoes."

"We are up two deaths. On the third, I might open in a farce at Drury Lane."

"Henderson, please."

He pointed to the purple splotch on her face. "She's been as-phyxiated. The strong scent of orange oil and the pressure of a hand holding against her . . . she couldn't survive for long."

His hands were stained with the shiny oil, and I dug in my reticule for a handkerchief. My knife fell and planted by his shoe, almost slicing into his toes.

Gripping my sharp blade, he waved it at me. "Let's get a few things straight. I didn't kill Miss Bumners or my wife."

"Well, I didn't. Miss Sewell either. And my cousin's still right. Mrs. Henderson said she was going to leave, but nothing here indicates that she would've. You could've killed her because she changed her mind."

He handed me the knife and I gave him the embroidered cloth. "Wipe your hands."

"I didn't do it, Lady Worthing."

Waving my knife at him, I started to try and make sense of this. "If you're convinced she was going to leave you, what changed her mind?"

He scrubbed at his fingers and removed the polish, but not the sweet, oily smell. "I don't know what was going through her head. Only what we'd discussed."

Returning my cloth, he took the knife away and waved it around. "Now you answer. Did you come here to kill Miss Bumners, Lady Worthing? Or have you decided to kill me?"

"A woman needs protection from you. Too many in your circle are ending up dead. And if you didn't kill her, and I haven't, who did?" I glared at him until I couldn't stand it anymore. When I stooped to take a better look at her injuries, I noticed buttons unbuttoned on Miss Bumners's gingham checked gown. "Someone was working these buttons. You suppose the killer did that? You think he has a thing for women's breasts? Mrs. Henderson was uncovered."

"I don't know, Lady Worthing. I'm sorry."

"Me too. We're arguing and this woman has been murdered. She seemed sweet, diligent about her work. She's young, Henderson. What dreams had she yet to make true?"

"Death is inevitable. It's never fair to dreams."

Florentina sat up, fanning her face. "Oh, this truly happened."

"Yes. Yell out the window for Rawlins to go get the magistrate. Seems the good neighbors have found another body."

As she began telling our driver to fetch Lord Duncan, I stooped again to Miss Bumners. "The body is a little cool to the touch, but her arm bends with ease."

"As I said, Lady Worthing, she hasn't been dead that long. Who was Miss Bumners's eleven or twelve o'clock appointments?"

"We didn't find a diary or schedule anywhere." Florentina edged closer. "Yep. Didn't imagine a thing."

"If you or I had been early, we could've stumbled upon the murderer. You and Miss Sewell could've been in jeopardy."

"That solves things. I'm never early. My mama said to always be exactly on time. Too early, you're a burden to your hostess. Too late, you'll miss your plate and the next opportunity to dine."

"Sort of poetic, Lady Worthing."

"That was my mother." I closed Miss Bumners's eyes and said a prayer. When I rose, Henderson helped me. "Mama never missed a meal. Sir, if you had been early, you could've been killed too."

"No. I'd have defeated the devil. Have before."

Wasn't sure what he meant, or if I needed to know. "I suppose you'd have held your own with the candlestick."

Henderson looked at me as if my words were too casual, too familiar.

I gripped his shoulders. "That's it, you're a genius."

"I am, but make sense, woman."

"It's like what my cousin noted before. Two cups. The tea. She knew the killer. She was familiar. Maybe too familiar. She wasn't afraid and was caught in the murderer's web."

"That makes sense," Florentina said, and finally stood at my side. "Perhaps Mrs. Henderson found out Miss Bumners's familiarity. She didn't like a lover being with both of them."

My mathematician had to be assessing the odds a jealous Miss Bumners killed Juliet and then the lover sought revenge.

"Killed by polish," Henderson said with a sigh. "Donne would make something poetic about a maid known to polish being killed by polish."

"And a woman who loved a ribbon necklace with a *J* was strangled by it." I said it aloud, but they must've thought this, too.

Noises sounded below.

When I went to the window, I saw Rawlins leading Lord Duncan and his runners inside.

The way Henderson gawked at them, at Duncan, and then glared at me and my cousin, I felt more at risk.

Vulnerable. That wasn't supposed to happen when I was Lady Worthing. The title and access were supposed to insulate me from danger and even suspicion.

Something crashed, probably broke into a million pieces. Henderson winced. "For our own benefit, Lady Worthing, I think we need to pool our resources and go about finding this killer together."

"Lady Worthing! Lady Worthing! Where are you?" That was the magistrate's voice.

"Lord Duncan, we are up here. We've discovered another murder."

Henderson stepped in front of me. "Think on it." He moved to the hall and greeted the men.

Florentina and I were left standing by Miss Bumners, watching the runners ransack the rooms for clues or who knows what they thought was left here.

As he stood in the threshold, my gaze caught Henderson's; then he turned away as Lord Duncan ordered his men to go through every drawer and closet.

Florentina came close and offered me her arm. "It might be safer to have Henderson close to you. This killer is not playing games."

"Well, actually he is, Flo. He's using irony in his method to murder."

"No, I mean he knows the victims and has no compassion at all when he kills. These slayings are passionless, premeditated."

This was where the mathematician was wrong. These deaths were all about rage and passion.

"Florentina, I haven't needed a male chaperone in years. I'll not start now."

She leaned on my shoulder. "Well, there'll be no seeing Wilberforce today, Abbie."

My cousin was right.

Lord Duncan would take his time, examining every crook and crevice to prove to me again how a proper investigation is done.

Footsteps.

Doors opening and closing.

Runners shouting, taking stock of the rooms we'd already searched.

"It will be quite late before we leave, Florentina. Let's find a seat."

I walked past Henderson as he answered questions.

Didn't mind Duncan taking his time. That would mean I'd be good and tired when I rested my head.

Then I wouldn't think about death or wrestle with the guilt of having some sort of second sight that couldn't be controlled, couldn't let me see preventable danger, and wouldn't allow me to save a life.

The generous sunshine finally gave up on us ever leaving Cheapside. It started to set by the time we arrived at Number

Two Greater Queen Street. Rain was in the air when Florentina and I climbed out of the Berlin. My bonnet bore sprinkles by the time we made it inside.

I took off my snappy bisque-colored bonnet with the damp brim and handed it to a footman. "Flo, I can't believe we spent the entire afternoon and most of the evening with Lord Duncan."

"I believe," she said. "After today, I believe everything."

Wanting to laugh and cry, I kept it all inside. "Dinner and a bath to stop smelling like polish will do us both good."

"You think Miss Bellows can get the smell off of me? My parents can't ask what I've been up to. I'm not sure they'll continue to think me a capable mathematician if I keep smelling like shiny mahogany."

Rogers met us in the hall. "Ma'am," he said, his nose wriggling. "You have a visitor."

"Florentina, you go on upstairs and get changed."

"No. I'm too invested. And I'd never forgive myself if you were attacked by a killer, while I luxuriated in a copper tub of steamy water." She looked dreamy for a moment. "What was I saying?"

"Rogers, show us the way."

The butler led us into the parlor.

I only screamed a little when I saw Mr. Shaw with a bloody face lying on my sofa.

"No loud noises, Lady Worthing. It hurts to hear."

Miss Bellows fanned him with my huge theater fan. Her face was mottled with red and fear. I wasn't sure if she was going to swoon from the blood around his eye or his exposed bits of chest showing from his unbuttoned shirt.

Though the man was finely built—wide, a smooth pile of warm brown muscles—the bruising along his ribs looked horrid.

"This will hurt more if you keep fidgeting." Mrs. Smith applied a compress to his rib. "You took a good beating, sir."

"No beatings are good, ma'am." He whimpered. "None at all."

"What happened?"

"I found out a lot of things on Mr. Henderson, Mr. Benjamin, and a little on Mr. Tanner. Tanner didn't take my questioning so well."

Looking as lost and as horrified as she did before she fainted in the Watling address, Florentina started unbuttoning her collar. The rich rust color had darker spots.

I couldn't fathom how I looked. "Tanner attacked you? When? How?"

"First tell me why you roses look wilted." He grabbed Mrs. Smith's hand and kissed it. "Easy, ma'am. I'm begging. I don't do that often."

She rolled her eyes and went back to cleaning the deep wound to his side. Skin was torn. Red battered flesh was visible. The man had been seriously hurt.

"Wilson?" I wasn't squeamish, but the headache from the orange-oil fumes remained and thundered with new life. Couldn't rub my temples, the smells of my polish-tainted fingers would make things queasy. "An appointment in Cheapside went awry. Continue, Mr. Shaw."

My friend turned a little on the cushions and winced more. "Mr. Henderson not only has generational money, but also a good number of naval bounties. I like that legal system of pirating."

As I walked closer to the sofa, the evidence of his beating became more apparent, more hurtful. The swelling to his jaw was horrendous. Then I spied the bloody basin that Mrs. Smith used to cleanse him. The water had turned crimson.

This was bad.

Wilson had been hurt snooping for me.

My heart lurched.

"Mr. Rogers, I know you're lurking. Can you come and bring fresh water?"

"Yes, Lady Worthing." His voice sounded from the hall and was followed by my beloved squeaks.

Wilson grimaced and turned his head to me. "You can make this up to me, Lady Worthing, by seeing if Henderson is in need of a new solicitor."

"Can we wait until I can prove conclusively he didn't kill his wife?"

"Ah. My Lady Worthing has standards."

Like she couldn't stand this casual talk, Florentina stomped her foot. "Before you continue to drag out your report and tell us why you were beaten, can someone say why a doctor hasn't been called?"

"I like my suffering in silence, Miss Sewell. And I wasn't beaten. I was shot at and fell hard from my horse onto some angry boulders. I was able to get back up before the farmers did more damage. Westminster isn't that far from Chelsea. I thought it wiser not to draw more attention to our baroness and myself by seeking outside help. Someone could link all these happenings together and assume it's related to the murder."

"It is," she said. "You could've been killed, Wilson. Your insides could be bleeding and you are making jokes. My cousin too! None of you know what you're doing."

Wilson sat up and his eyes sort of spun from the effort. "Rest assured. I'm going to live. This looks bad, but I'd rather be shot at than to allow you or Lady Worthing be a target."

Before they descended into a classic squabble, I took charge. "Florentina, you go upstairs and ready for a bath. I want you to soak this day away. I'll deal with Shaw and make sure he gets medical attention."

"Fine." She flounced from the room.

"Touchy, that one." Wilson smirked and grimaced, then lay

back down. "Well, I know beneath that prickly number-focused exterior, she cares for me. That is comforting."

"We all do, sir. But this is too much."

"I got away, Abbie. I have a new story to share with someone, someday."

"Fine. What did you learn of the Hendersons? Any jointly owned property? Again, I'm looking for a solid reason for Henderson to 've murdered his wife."

Wilson didn't answer, but looked content with the feather swishing air at him. "Lovely breeze, Miss Bellows."

I took the fan from her. "You've done enough. My solicitor is appreciative. Aren't you?"

"Oh, yes, Miss Bellows. You're a dear. I feel better. I've conclusively decided to live."

"Such a teaser. And this gave me something to do other than panic." She wriggled her nose, sending her blond curls bouncing. "I smell that you will also need attending to. That's orange-oil polish?"

Offering a nod, I couldn't say more. I hated every minute of feeling like a dust rag. It became harder and harder to remind myself that my intervening was meant to solve a crime, clear my name—instead, I kept finding bodies.

"I'll help Rogers with the hot water," Miss Bellows said, smoothing her no-longer-pristine apron, "enough for one, two, three baths."

She bowed, but at the door, she looked back. "Lady Worthing, you promised a lively employment. Thank you for speaking truthfully." Miss Bellows left, and I spun to my wall of windows that showed rain.

"I wasn't given such promises," Wilson said. "I feel cheated."

"Tell me more. There has to be."

"Not much on Henderson, except there are no jointly owned anything. There's nothing in the wife's name. Even the lease at some address in Cheapside is in the husband's name."

"He won't need to rent those rooms much longer. The occupant and her maid are dead."

Wilson's demeanor changed. The smile he'd been showing us faded. "The bastard said more people would pay."

Mrs. Smith wrung out the cloth in the fresh water that Rogers brought.

"Which bastard?" I said. "Be specific, Shaw."

"Tanner, Mrs. Henderson's brother. I made it to his farm in Chelsea. I found the address from the marriage contract for Mr. Henderson and the deceased Juliet Tanner Henderson. Jeorge Tanner was listed as a witness. The brute and his gun didn't give me time to ask questions. Someone had told him tax officials were coming."

He moaned and grunted. "I haven't been targeted in a while. Guess I need more practice riding in and out of danger."

Mrs. Smith tweaked his ear. "They could've killed you, boy."

He looked up to the ceiling. "Guess he could've killed me. I'll count this as a blessing."

"I'm sorry, Shaw." I dropped the fan to the floor. "This could've been a day full of death."

"That's why I came, Abigail. This is more serious than finding embezzled money or a suicidal thief. These people are brutal. You need to stop looking into this Henderson business. I don't want you hurt."

Watching the rain pelt the glass, I followed one drop that hit another and another until it was huge. Then it fell away. "I'm involved, Shaw. There's no turning back now. Whoever killed Mrs. Henderson and Miss Bumners probably knows I had a meeting with her. Can't stop until these crimes are solved."

"I swore I wouldn't pick up a gun again. My father he taught . . . I have an appointment with a gunmaker in the morning."

His half brother's involvement with Quaker pacifists tempered Wilson's enthusiasm for flintlocks and hunting. For him to consider it now, even mentioning his distant father, showed how serious Wilson was. "The better answer is for *you* not to be involved anymore."

He gripped Mrs. Smith's hand, cupping her fingers and the damp cloth to his side. "I don't take kindly to being shot at. Having ridden from Chelsea to here, nearly falling off, shows my commitment to things. But I came here to warn you. Abigail, nothing can happen to you."

"You don't have to be active in my hunting. I'll be more careful."

"Lady Worthing, I intend to be more than careful. I intend to bear arms."

"Wilson."

"Does the baroness want to hear the rest of what I found?"

There was no way to feign indifference. Folding my arms would only bring my rank sleeves closer to my face. "You know I do."

"The brother is in a lot of debt. The contract had an odd provision of repaying the two-thousand-pound dowry upon Henderson's inheritance of his father's estate. Couldn't find record of it ever being repaid. The late Henderson died last December, and as I said, Henderson is exceedingly wealthy. With the wife now dead, not sure if that's an out clause."

Would Henderson kill to avoid paying such a sum, a small one considering his coffers? "What about the minister?"

Dropping the cloth into the basin, Mrs. Smith raised her head. "I could help with that one. The youn', handsome Mr. Samuel Benjamin has had a good rise. They say he's eyeing the Abbey."

"Well done, ma'am," Wilson said, "but did you know he comes from a small parish in Chelsea, near the Tanner family land?"

When I looked at Wilson, he had a devilish grin. He'd found the clue we needed.

"Can't fault ambition, but Benjamin is bold. He's rumored to have affairs with several important ladies in Westminster, including one Juliet Henderson."

Shaking her head, Mrs. Smith stood up. "Goodness. Poor Mr. Sinclair said she had many admirers. Who knows of this? Did Mr. Henderson know?"

"I think the man has come to answer." In the rain, on my terrace, knocking on my glass, was Stapleton Henderson, and he looked as if he had plenty to say.

Chapter 13

I let my wet neighbor into my house and did what anyone else in this situation would do. I put him to work. He was a trained physician in the navy. I had him examine Wilson.

I stood near my fireplace as the man I still slightly suspected of murder knelt next to Mrs. Smith, making sutures with hemp string to close up the bad wound.

"Lucky I kept this. I suppose it may come in handy, given today." He gazed at me, more damp from running back to his house for his leather medical bag. "No punctured lung, Mr. Shaw. You are lucky, too."

"I guess this is what luck in Chelsea feels like." Wilson hadn't lost his humor, but he looked pained and pale in the face.

"My apologies. My brother-in-law can be belligerent. Probably thought you were a tax assessor coming to count windows."

As Henderson tied off the knot of string for the stitches, my friend winced. "I'll make sure the fellows at the office are aware."

"No broken ribs, a slight bruise on the last. This wound

should heal nicely. The natural threads will dissolve. Your right lung may sting, but it's uninjured."

"Wish it knew that."

My neighbor lent him an arm and Wilson stood.

"You'll go nowhere, Mr. Shaw." I looked at him like my mother would, with my eyes locked on him as a boy being ordered to get a branch from the yard. A swift spanking would ensue.

He bit his lip, then looked at everyone. "Fine, I'll stay."

My butler lurked in the hall. "Mr. Rogers, come help Mrs. Smith. Please escort Mr. Shaw to one of the guest rooms. I turned back to Wilson. "Then Rawlins will see you home in the morning."

Mrs. Smith tugged him forward. "There's no fussin' with her ladyship, ya know."

With a shrug, my solicitor went with the two.

"They will make sure he's well taken care of tonight."

"He'll be fine." Henderson warmed his hands by the fire. They were pink from him scrubbing them clean before and after his suturing. "What do you want me to say, Lady Worthing?"

"Nothing. I like the quiet of this moment. I don't think you've ever come for a visit." I moved the basin with pink water off the table and sat on my sofa. The air smelled of wetness and blood and polish.

"Have a seat, Mr. Henderson."

"I'd rather stand." His back was toward me. His coat hung on him, big and soggy from the rain.

"Take off your coat to dry it, sir. I wouldn't want you to catch cold."

"You actually care if the killer next door becomes ill?"

"Isn't this the part where you try to convince me you didn't kill anyone?"

"I never said I hadn't killed anyone."

That didn't sound like a defense. It was the exact opposite of what I hoped he'd say. Threading my fidgeting hands together, I tried to recollect the comfort I'd gained when Henderson helped Wilson, or even how he attended to Florentina in Cheapside. "You were at war. Those deaths don't count."

"Someone's wife or mother will miss those that died." He half rotated and then caught my gaze again. "When I plead my innocence, I want you to listen. I'm not one to repeat myself."

"You came to me. You stand in my house."

"I told you, I wouldn't keep myself away from you anymore."

When he said that the day of the funeral, it was merely words. Now it felt weighty and intentional—almost a torture to be away. "Sir, I'm asking you. Did you kill your wife or her maid?"

He pounded closer. His footfalls were sure. Not a board creaked. "I didn't kill Juliet or Miss Bumners. I do not know who did."

"Thank you."

"So you believe me?"

"I want to. I don't want to judge you guilty of something because we don't get along."

"We appear to be getting along now. Something about the potential of indictments as co-conspirators has bonded us."

His almost joke relaxed me. I eased my hands to my lap. "And for a moment of full transparency, I didn't murder Mrs. Henderson or her maid. When you went up to the *lichwake,* who did you see interacting with Miss Bumners?"

He rubbed at his wet hair and paced in front of the glowing embers in my hearth. "She talked to my brother-in-law. Many guests. I wasn't that observant. Kept wondering how the starry-eyed girl from Chelsea ended up like this."

The rain started spattering again. My window glass fogged.

And I felt what I'd thought was impossible—Henderson's pain at Juliet's loss.

I waved him again to a seat. "If Mr. Tanner was beating on my solicitor, that would leave less time for him to kill Miss Bumners."

"He was at the funeral, pretty much all the male suspects were there. I suspect she was killed today, an hour or two before we arrived for our two o'clock."

"I still think that rules out your brother-in-law, but he could be working with someone."

"Then we are no closer to finding out who killed either of them."

He was right and I hated it. "How's Mary? She was distraught yesterday."

"She went to a friend's in Mayfair. The same one that's giving her the alibi."

Earlier I thought he had said an aunt. Before I could ask, Henderson shifted his stance and moved toward me.

Again, not a board made a sound. "Juliet was strangled. Her maid was suffocated, both types of asphyxiation. Someone held a polish-soaked rag to Miss Bumners's nose and mouth, and kept it there until she died. Both take an incredible amount of strength when the victim surely fought to live."

"Did Miss Bumners fight? Her nails were clean. Maybe she didn't realize until too late the murderer's intent."

He looked away, then at the chair. His hair was damp and wild. I had to break our new peace and ask about Mary. "Did you disclose everything about your sister's whereabouts? A protective older brother might easily come up with any excuse necessary to shield his sister. It's admirable."

His sad face grimaced. "Once you're stuck on something, you're loath to let it go."

"What?"

"You insisted that my dogs were threatening yours—you didn't have evidence, only a belief."

"So we are back to it being my fault that your wife was murdered on the fence you built."

"No. I'm stuck on you being stuck. But this time it's a mystery that keeps getting people killed. Lady Worthing, there's been too much blood. Let this alone before people you care about are badly hurt or die."

He started to the door with his quiet footfalls and I slipped in front of him.

"It's not that simple. Lord Duncan's not done. We've found two bodies together. You're still his most likely suspect. And I'm right beside you as a potential accomplice. Whether you like it or not, we have to work together. We're in this together. The risk is shared."

Teacup bounded into the room and snarled. The floor creaked as he bounced from spot to spot. Henderson lowered his palm and the dog jumped to him, acting like he was glad to see my neighbor.

"Henderson, please stay until the weather clears. Play with your little friend here. Then we can think more about investigating Mr. Benjamin and Mr. Tanner."

"Leave my brother-in-law alone. He's dangerous. He could've killed Shaw. I don't want to think what he and his farmhands would do to you."

"Are you saying the violent Mr. Tanner is capable of losing his temper and hurting a woman? Could he have hurt Mrs. Henderson? Was Miss Bumners killed because she knew his anger at not receiving the special marital contract payment? The two thousand pounds."

"Digging into my business, still? I said leave it alone."

"Then what about Mr. Benjamin? He's right here in Westminster."

"No. No more investigating for you, Lady Worthing."

"What are you afraid of me finding out? You think it would shock me to see someone be a brute?"

"No."

"Is it that I'll find out Mrs. Henderson was intimate with the reverend?"

He turned and his fire-hot gaze scorched my flesh. "He was. They were. I thought that the two would be leaving for Scotland. But as you found out today, Juliet had no intentions of going with him."

"Then he is our likely suspect. We could—"

"No. We can't. This is too dangerous. If you are a bored wife of the ton, do what they do."

"What's that? Have affairs with charming men because their husbands have their own mistresses or simply don't give a damn?"

"Is that what you are doing, filling up your days with interviews and finding 'facts,' because Lord Worthing has abandoned you?"

I slapped him.

It was hard and quick. And mostly unearned.

Rubbing his jaw, he put my dog into my hands, opened the terrace door, and went out into the rain.

"Henderson! Henderson, wait!"

The man kept going, not looking back, not ceding to me at all.

Regretting my actions, I almost gave chase.

Instead, I closed the door to him and the cold rain.

It was wrong to strike an insolent man who merely stated the truth.

"Teacup, your mother's done a bad thing." I stroked his ear.

With my doggie in my arms, I sat back on the couch and watched the fire until it died.

The hunger to solve this mystery wouldn't go away.

Two murders, a beat-up solicitor, and a neighbor I'd aggrieved added up to all the reasons in the world why I had to keep pushing for the truth. It had to be faced, no matter how horrid or how deadly it might be.

Chapter 14

Walking my halls, I greeted the noon sun with my mobcap and spring muslin gown with tulips, my favorite flower. Sleep in my big bed was difficult.

Not because of unwanted dreams, but my raging conscience. I needed to find a way to apologize.

Nothing that anyone said about me or my marriage mattered. It was what James and I thought. We were partners in this. We had a base, a foundation, from which to grow a happy life. That was a lot more than others could say.

But I lost my temper and slapped my neighbor. That was probably against the Commandments or something.

Henderson wasn't without guilt. He mocked my vows, when his wife had broken theirs under his nose, and apparently with his blessing.

If that wasn't the pot turning char black in the coals, I wouldn't know.

Teacup barked and followed me, whipping his fur side to side, all spry and carefree.

"Morning, baby."

He answered me with a shake of his bottom. He was a happy fellow.

Maids were cleaning all the guest rooms. I had a full house last night.

Every bit of Number Two had life. I liked how it felt having everyone under my roof.

Then I remembered a Yuletide season in Spitalfields, when everyone who'd come for dinner became stuck because of the snow. The house was packed, filled with conversations. And everyone had second and third helpings at my mother's table.

In the hall mirror, I felt her sparkling spirit looking down on me. "Mama, I can't be doing everything wrong. Right?"

It felt like it, sending my neighbor off with a slap, getting my friend beaten, finding two bodies, and, of course, no movement on abolition.

When I reached the first level, I looked for letters. None. It was rare to receive one with franking from overseas. That was another reason why I liked starting my day at noon. All the correspondence would be delivered by the time I breakfasted.

There was a card in my silver visitor bowl.

I picked up the heavy stock labeled *Neil Vaughn, Esquire.*

My godfather had arrived. More bad news? Or a lecture?

Didn't matter. He was here to add to the full house.

"Come on, Teacup. Let's go greet our guests."

When I reached my parlor, my heart lifted. Everything was clean again. The scenes of last night—the blood, the smells of polish, the sound of my terrace door slamming—could be forgotten. It was over.

Laughter beckoned from outside.

I stepped through the threshold and put my slippers onto the slate.

"Good day, Abigail Carrington Monroe," Vaughn said. "Or is it a half day?"

I chuckled and headed to the table. Florentina and Vaughn were enjoying coffee, sitting next to each other, flicking through the papers.

My cousin laughed as she read the *Morning Post* and looked fresh as a bluebell in a similarly-colored gown dotted with tiny white flowers.

Vaughn was his formal self—black tailcoat, jet waistcoat, and dark breeches. Was that powder in his hair, turning what was thick and dark into stately and old? Who was he meeting with today?

"Truthfully, it is good for Lady Worthing to decide to join us." My godfather stood and kissed my cheek. "Your friend Mr. Shaw left early. Something about a fresh cravat, a waistcoat of Pomona green, and a shave before visiting widows."

"Well, you know he loves to make himself presentable. It's a favorite thing. Wilson Shaw is always up and about early."

"Yes, he's always been known to do that. I've known you all since you were in cloth nappies." Vaughn took up a steaming mug of coffee. "And I can tell when each of you is trying to convince me, or even yourself, that all's well. It's not."

"Couldn't we look at the good this once? Like how everyone has filled my house."

"Abigail, you found two dead bodies in a matter of days. It hasn't been a full week."

"It has been rather busy."

Florentina groused and made an undignified grimace. "Flippant Mr. Shaw said we've at least eliminated one suspect, Miss Bumners. That's not quite how we should make progress."

"Ladies, she's off your list because she's deceased." Vaughn sat back in the chair and looked at me over the rim of his mug. "This looks like lots of trouble."

"Things take time, Vaughn. You know we must approach these diligently."

He pulled out a chair for me. "You think because Duncan hasn't made an arrest, he won't. That's a wrong conclusion, my dear."

Picking up the pot, I poured a nice cup of coffee, leaving room for cream and plenty of sugar. "I'm working with the magistrate. We're allies at the moment."

"Things can change in a minute. And the expedience of sacrificing a woman, a Blackamoor woman instead of a navy hero, is something that must be weighed."

Vaughn was right. I didn't want to admit or think about how much of an advantage the man I'd slapped had over me.

"It's not fair. This is all Henderson's doing."

Vaughn reared forward as if he readied to take up arms. "Can you prove his guilt?"

The challenge in his voice could have been Duncan's.

"No. While he has motive to kill his wife, I can't find one for the murder of the maid."

Florentina put down her paper and popped a piece of muffin into her mouth. She patted her lips, wiping them free of crumbs. "We're not even sure the two deaths are related. It could be an unfortunate coincidence."

My godfather set down his cup. The porcelain clacked in the saucer as his mouth held a sarcastic grin. "One victim worked for the other. They were both found by your cousin and the neighbor. In what world, do these deaths not add up to being related?"

"Math joke, Uncle? And if we wanted odds, there is two-thirds probability that the two crimes are related. I chose to focus on the piece that implies they're not."

"Which means there are too many factors to ignore." Vaughn grinned triumphantly, then adjusted the silver sleeve buttons of his cuffs. "I help my friends with their wagers. I think the bigger odds win."

My cousin's lips shrank to nothing, while her eyes pleaded with me to take up the fight.

That was hard to do when Vaughn was right. Everything felt as if the two crimes were part of something bigger.

My godfather put down his cup. "I need you, both of you, to do something for the next few days that has nothing to do with Stapleton Henderson or death."

"How can you ask that of us? If Henderson is implicated, I highly doubt he'll save me. I'm sort of stuck proving that he's not guilty, all by myself."

Vaughn's brow lifted, for I'd exposed how involved I was with the murders, and that Henderson wasn't helping.

"Have you asked him to be of aid, Abigail? Did he refuse you?"

One nod of my head made Florentina moan and sent my cousin to her calculations. It was unnecessary. My chances at failure had to rate in the hundredth percentile.

"I might have slapped the man, leaving the imprint of my palm against his cheek, all for speaking accurately about my situation with Lord Worthing. My husband is exploring the world. I'm not at the top of his mind. I doubt I'll ever be."

"Sorry, Abbie. I know you love—"

"I'm not in love, Flo, but it was the hope that Worthing and I could be."

My cousin looked at me with sad eyes. Vaughn's had no pity, but maybe something akin to respect.

"You are wise, Abigail, beyond your years." He thumbed his lips and looked up again to above my roof. Perhaps Mama had told him to go easy on me.

"Solving things gives me a moment to feel powerful. Outwitting evildoers offers a sense of control that I lack in every other part of my life. I'll figure this one out, and I don't need anything from Stapleton Henderson. If I have a question that only he can answer, I'll send for him or go ask."

Vaughn fingered his mug, working on the rim like it would make a noise. "That must mean you think the hero's innocent. You're brave, but even you wouldn't go into the lion's den to poke bears."

"That's too many metaphors, even for you, Vaughn. I don't know about him. There are times I think he's capable of killing Juliet, but he has no reason that I can fathom to smother Miss Bumners."

Tapping her quill on her ready notebook, Florentina wrote something on her paper. "Maybe that's it. Two different killers. They're connected, but it's all circumstantial. Or the true villain thinks like Vaughn—that Henderson will be indicted for both."

The notion saddened me. How do you fight for truth when a key witness simply wants to wait and see what happens? There was no way I would sit around and let my world crumble.

"Lord Duncan, I believe, is giving me time to figure things out. The answer is close. There has to be something we're missing."

Florentina looked up with wide, startled eyes. "What if Mr. Henderson is trying to cover for someone? What if he knows the killer and feels some loyalty to him?"

"He is, and it's admirable. His sister, Mary. She was supposed to be with an aunt in Mayfair, but he admitted to me that she was next door around the time of the first murder." I wouldn't go into all the details Henderson, and even Mary, had shared. I admired him for shielding her. It was what I'd wanted to do for Dinah.

"An aunt in Mayfair?" Vaughn looked puzzled. His brow furrowed with deep craters. "I didn't think the late Mr. Henderson had any living siblings."

"What about on their mother's side?"

"That would be the Proctors," he said. "I'll have to do a little research. Oh. No, no. We're going to take a moment and not investigate. Not do anything about these deaths."

I thumbed a few pages of the paper. "The reporters are not sitting around. Miss Bumners's murder is mentioned here along the fold. Nothing has yet to be written about Mrs. Henderson. I suppose Duncan hushed up that one."

"No, Lady Worthing. You underestimate the reach of Mr. Henderson. He has friends in journalistic places. The newsmen are keeping things quiet for now. Being a military hero and having old money is a formidable combination."

Indeed it was.

To stall the magistrate and the gossip rags, it had to be powerful. "Have you been able to get his military records?"

"Not yet. But I'm not sure I'm going to get it." He folded his hands together. "You need to do something else with your mind."

"Are you abandoning me, Vaughn?"

"Of course not, Abigail."

"Who's gotten to you? You're scared."

"No one has taken me aside and threatened me." He reached for my hand. "But I'm frightened for you. With Shaw being hurt, it's like my family's under attack. I can't risk you and Florentina being attached to this."

"I'm attached. I'm not moving. The military record gives me a better idea of the man next door."

The man who admitted he'd killed before, the man I'd slapped. Who was Stapleton Henderson? What advantages would he seek?

"Abigail, this could be even bigger. Consider where we are this moment. The politicians and the reporters are looking for someone to blame for all the ills of the world. We've all seen papers turn innocent friendships into dark associations."

"What are you saying?"

Florentina sighed. "What my uncle is trying too delicately to say is that these newsprint and scandal sheets may paint you as the evil temptress who has made a war hero murder for her."

The sad thing was they both were right. This was a more dangerous situation than I'd ever faced. The consequences could be dire. The slowed heartbeat of abolition could be fully snuffed if I was made an example of a free Blackamoor gone amok. "I'm not sitting around and watching my life be torn apart because of my neighbor's misfortune."

"Can you get Lord Worthing back?" Florentina almost handed me her scribe and bottle of ink. "Write him and ask him to come home."

My cousin didn't understand what she was asking. I leapt up and went to my garden. The rain had washed away a lot of topsoil. Roots were left bare.

I felt the same.

Vaughn lifted from his chair and stood beside me, like we were about to promenade through my garden. "Abigail, this is not an indictment on you. It's the world."

"The world is still too slow."

"It is, Cousin!" Florentina yelled; then her tone became softer. "But there's still good. There are still people willing to fight, like me and Shaw and my uncle."

Vaughn nodded. "You write Lord Worthing, have him come home. Take a few days to stay out of the way of this murderer, and I'll get Henderson's military records."

Would James come if I ask?

Would he tell me he's forgotten our vows?

Would he ask me to go to Scotland and end our farce and set him free?

Maybe he'd surprise me and remember the woman who believed in him when everyone else had given him over to Newgate's hangman.

Looking at my tulips, the ones still raising their heads despite last night's heavy rain, I decided I wanted to be like them. Surviving was beautiful, too. "I surrender. I'll write Lord Worthing and invite him home as soon as possible. And I'll not actively try to hunt anything more on this mystery."

Folding over the newspaper, Florentina coughed and crinkled her pages. "I'll stay out here this next week to make sure my cousin is away from danger. In fact, I'll take her to church."

"Flo, no. You don't have to do that."

"I insist. We shall go to church and repent our sins, and we'll stop making my uncle fret." The sparkle in her eyes was a revelation. She had a plan, and since I was desperate, I'd listen.

"Good." Vaughn pulled out his pocket watch. "I have a meeting. You get Worthing back. I'll keep working to see gossip misses your name."

"And you'll send a copy of Henderson's record for me? I need to know what I'm dealing with next door."

"For you, Abigail." Vaughn made a quick bow and left.

" 'Et tu, Brute.' You enjoy me backing down?"

"I do, but we gave my uncle what he needed to calm his nerves. He's concerned about each of us. He'll rest easier knowing you've become less of a target."

"Flo, what am I—"

"There's no need to stop, Abbie. We need to take a detour."

"What are you talking about?"

Slipping into Vaughn's seat, I waited for her explanation. I wanted to be cheered.

She set her paper down and pointed at a column. "Wilberforce is having an open meeting at Holy Trinity. It's designed for the public to go and hear his words. There must be a moment in which you'll be able to get him your documents."

"You haven't lost faith in me, Florentina?"

She gripped my hand. We wrestled for a moment before she let me win. "Never. You're always my odds-on favorite."

I would take this respite from the murders to push abolition. Getting Wilberforce the eyewitness accounts, which were raw in nature, would surely renew the call for freedom. It was best to make this push now, before I sat down to write my letter to my husband, discovered I was wrong about my neighbor's tolerance, or simply wound up dead.

Chapter 15

A week later, my cousin and I were on our way to Holy Trinity at Clapham Common. Rawlins drove the big Berlin across the Westminster Bridge. The bells of the close Saint Margaret's met us on our journey. My fingers itched. I wanted to know more about the minister, but I'd promised not to make any progress on the murders.

"These chimes are lighter than the Abbey's, but ever sweet. Florentina," I said, nudging her arm, "listen. They must be doing a full peal to practice change ringing."

"That's nice." She was scribbling in charcoal her computations. "I wondered if we'd hear the bells when we crossed the bridge."

The sound was marvelous, and even the lights, the lanterns that align with the stone sections, seemed to flicker to the beat.

The sun would lower soon. For now, it stood guard over Rawlins and my Berlin and spotlit the city barge below that crossed the Thames.

Leaning closer to the window, I got a good look at the men in tricorn hats busily moving people and goods across the water. If London didn't require enslavement to make things happen, couldn't the rest of the world do the same?

Florentina put her arm about me. "We lived. Almost a whole week of nothing. I think you even slept through the night."

"Driving to the other side of the Thames felt like leaving to a new world. Perhaps we should think of travel once . . . things are solved."

She pulled my arm through hers. "Now you're talking. But tonight, we'll listen to speeches, cheer with the crowd, and when the time is right, we shall go to Mr. Wilberforce and ask for a private audience. Hand him the papers, and we're done."

My cousin sounded certain in her bisque-hued bonnet that shadowed her eyes. Her tightly twisted chignon was high on her oval face. She looked lovely and confident. Perhaps she should be the baroness today.

The brim of my bonnet was wide and threaded with parrot green ribbon that matched my carriage dress.

"Teacup barked a lot this morning. Maybe I should've taken him with me."

"Abbie, the dog can't go into the church. He's like you, filled with pent-up energy. Since you kept him in the house and stopped him from visiting the neighbor—"

"It's bacon. He gives my dog bacon to make him affectionate."

"Mr. Henderson bribes your dog with bacon?"

"I know. It sounds ridiculous, but now that he's given Teacup those treats, the terrier won't stop yearning for the fatty meat."

"Well, I don't blame Teacup. Give me some apple-smoked choice cuts and I can be bought."

Passing through the warehouses, we entered the part of the area that looked more residential, more spread out.

"Did you write Lord Worthing?"

Florentina, Dinah, and I shared everything, until James proposed. Then the shared confidences stopped when my sister disappeared. My cousin and I were close, but we never talked of my marriage—all the promises and disappointments. "My mother would say a woman builds or destroys her own house."

"I remember her saying such. Is that your way of saying you didn't finish? Or that you won't?"

"I'm looking for the right words. They'll come. I'm confident they will."

She sat back and pulled her hands together about her satin fawn-colored reticule. "When you're ready and you want to talk or cry, I'm here for you."

Couldn't utter anything, I merely clutched her arm tighter.

The carriage slowed as we came to Holy Trinity. This time Florentina and I went with no costume but as our normal selves to deliver our message and to make a difference. If my days as Lady Worthing were to end, I wanted every moment to matter.

Two sets of tie bars lined the dirt road. These stood ten feet away from the wrought-iron gate that circled the church.

Crowds had started working their way around these fences.

Rawlins opened our door. "This is as close as I can get, Lady Worthing."

He handed me down. "We are on the north side of Trinity. Work your way through the little white ties, go past the wrought-iron gate to the door on the left. I'll meet you here. Unless it rains, I'll be back in two hours, ma'am."

"Thank you, Rawlins. Be careful."

He tipped his tricorn. "Little lady, I was born to be careful and to be aware of my surroundings." He opened his frock coat and I saw something small, like a blunderbuss or a pistol for dueling.

I was speechless.

"Ma'am, go on. I'll be fine or take a blackguard with me."

Florentina towed me forward. She didn't see Rawlins's weapon. Maybe that was best. I didn't want to see it.

Yet, if something did come against him, he was ready.

I needed to be. My mother had the ability to discern truth from fantasy, a lie from an excuse.

I needed to grow into that.

I needed that confidence.

I needed to find me. I was different and changed since marrying. Lady Worthing needed to reacquaint herself with bold Abbie Carrington.

The inside of the church was hot and packed with people. It felt good to see so many people coming to hear about abolition.

The masses moved along.

Regulars or those who seemed like regulars filled pews. The way they looked, with high walls like horse stalls, my thoughts again went to Rawlins. He'd worked for my parents during the good years. Then moved on to other estates when things became lean. He was the third person I hired when I became Lady Worthing.

The milling crowd pushed Florentina and me to the stairwell. With a shrug, she took the lead, held my hand, and charged the steps.

On the balcony-like landing, she said, "Seats up front in the gallery."

We claimed them before someone could ask us to move or point us to the back row. When anyone tried to make eye contact, neither of us responded. These were our seats, our place tonight, and we weren't giving them up.

"It's been fun having you about every day, Flo."

Florentina looked at me. "You let me do my calculations for my work. I'm not behind. And you serve the best tarts."

Looking out into the sea of faces, I was never more proud of this olive beauty next to me. Strong, sensitive, mathematically inclined, she was a hero in many ways.

Singing started. Many below stood with their hymnals. The music sounded sweet and strong. From up here, I could see the people standing in those tall pews, and they looked even more like they waited in horse stalls.

> *Awake, our drowsy souls,*
> *And burst the slothful band;*
> *The wonders of this day*
> *Our noblest songs demand*

The Elizabeth Scott hymn was what London needed. It was what I needed. Everyone needed to awaken to our power and not be fearful. We could have a Hayti, and all the other countries, too. We could rid the world of enslavement and still have commerce. Work could still be done.

Florentina nudged me. "Abbie, he's getting up to speak."

From our perch in the gallery, I saw William Wilberforce leave the nave.

He walked toward the transept and stood in the shadow of the high pulpit.

"The cause is still just," he said. "Though many falter. Though we are human and stained and flawed, the work of good is still powerful. It still transcends."

An "Amen" sounded from the rear. Others clapped.

He glanced around, as if taken aback by the approving outburst. "I made my first speech against the slave trade in 1789. For seventeen years, I have fought and saw men gather for a single purpose, only to lose heart and have the cause of freedom die in the seat of power."

People had to listen. He could call their souls back to action.

Florentina caught my shoulder and pulled me against my seat. "Let him do this without you falling over the rail."

He raised his arms and brought silence again to the church. "Everyone here knows my commitment. And if my good friend Mr. Pitt had lived, I'm sure that prime minister would've called for the vote. Slavery, the great sin of our time would be no more."

Applause became thunderous. Once more, he lifted his hands and tamped down the adoration.

Oh, take courage, Mr. Wilberforce. The lively energy in this church is for you.

"But I'm here to report that there's no report. No action." His pitch lowered. "The legislative session won't take up any fight on the cause of the enslaved. Everything is stalled. The fight is unwinnable now."

The air that was hot with praise grew cold and silent.

A coin could be heard dropping. A pin bouncing or my shattering heart would be loud. "Capitulation, Florentina. My hero is capitulating."

Grumbling ramped up as if the congregation had recovered from a dead faint.

"Listen. Listen," Wilberforce said. "Time. We need time. We must be patient. It's for the best. More time. More patience. Then we can try again."

The crowd hissed—some rose and raised fists. Others shook their heads and walked out.

A young fellow in those rented pews leapt up and shook the frame.

"Why is this happening? I thought it was right to own no man."

I leaned as far I could over the polished rail and drowned in horrid orange oil to hear Wilberforce's response.

It was slow, the consonants and vowels dribbling out of his lips, the way they seemed to take a whole minute to say, "Wait, we must wait. The tide for abolition will turn when the fire of

Saint-Domingue's cannons cool. Then Britain will see the government of Dessalines, who fought with us to overthrow the French, is no threat. In that day, the fight will continue. That is when we will win."

Some nodded. More left.

But I shook and stayed in my seat.

All the risks to come here.

The situation that I was in with my neighbor—was to protect the Clapham group. I risked everything merely for Wilberforce to say the battle would take time.

In a blink, I stood with James at Number Two Greater Queen Street. James no longer asked me to see him off. The man said he understood my needing to find Dinah. Then he walked away heading to his carriage—his back straight, his red jacket with the high collar he fashioned flapped as he said his goodbyes. My husband offered whispers to me that everything would be better with time, just wait.

"He can't do this." My voice was loud, but I didn't care about the stares.

Florentina threaded her fingers with mine. "It will begin again. He hasn't seen your letters. When he does, he will be bold. He'll risk his name for it."

"I have letters. The crimes—rapes, tortures that we have treaties in place to prevent happening to soldiers—but all is allowed to be done to hundreds upon thousands of men and women who are prisoners of war."

"Abigail," she said in a low whisper, "enslavement has been happening over hundreds of years. Another few months is not going to—"

"Tens of thousands are stolen every year. Flo, you like numbers, percentages. Ten percent will be killed by the conditions on the voyage. The rest will die before their thirty-fifth year."

My forehead fevered and I stared at the leaded panes of glass behind the altar. I wished for them to break, for every buttress overhead to fall and crush everything resisting abolition.

Florentina patted my arm and I was back, breathing heavily in a church of cowards.

And I knew I was one, too.

"You're warm, Abigail. People are leaving. Let's get you outside, and then you can cool down."

"No. We can't be comfortable and live extraordinary lives in London while others are abandoned."

"Then we can't give up." She put her palm to my cheek and lifted it. "We won't. Lady Worthing can change minds, even if it's one at a time."

The service had ended.

Florentina and I waited for others to leave before we moved into the stairwell.

The bells gonged. Holy Trinity had four.

As we stepped outside, the dusky moon and stars were out. My temples cooled in the night air.

People were coming out. All the fences and ties had people walking about them. Florentina and I waited for Rawlins, close to the spot where he dropped us off.

Surrounded by people, I saw Wilberforce and Miss Hannah More were surrounded by parishioners. They hadn't left yet. They held court back in the nave. The letters and eyewitness statements I had from James were in my reticule. I could give it to them, but suddenly it seemed a waste to trust quitters.

"Lady Worthing?"

"Hmm. Yes."

From the shadows stepped the new minister of Saint Margaret's, the dapper Mr. Benjamin. "So this is the church you've been sneaking off to, Lady Worthing. It is impressive, but so is my humble church."

In the dim light, he laughed, but he seemed genuinely surprised to see me. He almost appeared nervous or guilty and kept looking back to his gig. It was a small carriage, like my yellow bounder, but with one horse.

"Mr. Benjamin," I said in a sweet, flirty manner, "are you trying for another place to serve? You want to leave Saint Margaret's?"

He hooked his finger about his dark lapel. "No, I'm content at Saint Margaret's, but when I heard Wilberforce would speak, I had to come. He's a favorite."

"But we heard the church's bells." Florentina's brow furrowed. "Aren't you supposed to be minding them?"

"I oversee the start of things. I have plenty of assistants. They can practice a peal."

"A peal?" Florentina asked.

"Mr. Benjamin, this is my mathematician cousin, Miss Florentina Sewell."

"Ah, a lady who likes numbers. A peal is the number of bell positions and rings that can be counted to five thousand forty changes. My four bells can do twenty-four positions quickly. For the Abbey, using seven of their bells takes about three hours. I have all the time in the world, depending on where I'm helping."

"Time, you say?" My voice wavered.

Benjamin kept talking. He seemed more confident as William Wilberforce and Hannah More passed within feet of us.

I wanted to step to the politician and offer the reports I'd received from Antigua, but a dejected reformer wouldn't do anything with the information.

How long would others face abuse as the report sat idle on his desk?

At the end of the dusty lane, they waited for their carriage like us. Wilberforce stared in my direction, and I could've sworn he mouthed, *it takes time.*

The man wanted me happy for crumbs, to rejoice that they had not given up the cause entirely.

My glare at him had fire—didn't the crusader know my cousin and I couldn't be satisfied because we were lucky to be born free?

His driver pulled near.

More dust and rocks kicked up as his pair settled. Then he and Miss More climbed aboard and were gone.

And I ached as bad as when I discovered Dinah gone. Her leaving was a choice, as was Wilberforce's decision to wait for more favorable conditions.

"Lady Worthing, are you well?"

Mr. Benjamin had stayed near. I decided to ask him a question.

"Sir, how do you heal a disappointed heart?"

The man looked a little shaken by my question. "Not sure. It's a question I ask myself sometimes. Then I consult the Good Book."

Something moved inside his carriage. His face became red. "Excuse me, ladies. Back to Saint Margaret's." He doffed his top hat. "I hope I see you both at my church soon."

He walked off, then trotted toward his carriage as Rawlins arrived.

My driver jumped down and helped us inside. "Take us to Saint Margaret's as quickly and as discreetly as possible."

His nose wrinkled, as did his brow. "What about your 'I'm being careful' talk, ma'am?"

"I need our carriage to be fast and efficient. Can you do that?"

"Yes." He grinned, welcoming the challenge. "Very good, Lady Worthing."

Florentina folded her arms. "Why are we going there? Haven't we had enough of churches?"

"I want to see if we can tell what a minister does when he has hours to kill and a guaranteed alibi of ringing church bells."

"So you think he's our culprit? Not that we are supposed to be investigating."

"Don't know, Flo. But we have to get some more luck. If I have to bide my time, I'll help as many as I can get justice, starting with Juliet Henderson."

In my gut, I believed the secret to the murders might be in the minister's carriage.

If we could beat him back to Saint Margaret's, I'd know if the flamboyant man could be a killer and a courting one.

Chapter 16

James's stylish Berlin with the small gold *W* on the door was hardly a secretive vehicle, but at night with Rawlins driving, anything was possible.

Unleashed from all the precautions I'd put on him this past week, he made the big carriage fly.

"He's putting the yellow bounder's speed to shame." I tried not to look too concerned at how fast he turned corners.

Her face paling, my cousin didn't seem amused as bumps flung her from one side to the other.

"Do you know that hundreds of carriages flip over in a year?"

"Please, Florentina. No survival statistics."

"Abigail Carrington Monroe, we are not doing what Uncle Vaughn asked us to do. You are again investigating the murders."

"For a week, we did nothing to advance our theories. Henderson first told me Mary was with an aunt, then friends. Now he says an aunt again, when Vaughn said they have none."

I pulled closer to the window and watched South Lambeth

Row turn into Vauxhall and then to Prince Street. "We'll soon be on the bridge, and then we can slow. Rawlins must beat Mr. Benjamin to Saint Margaret's. I have a hunch."

"So we are rushing from one church to the next? Breaking that promise to my uncle over a feeling. Did you have a vision? Are we rushing to a death?"

With my palms to her cheeks, I made Flo breathe. "Calm yourself. I haven't had a vision. We are not chasing a dream, but I may have puzzled together clues that shouldn't be ignored."

Florentina held on through a turn by warehouses, where the carriage probably only had two wheels on the ground. "Perhaps Henderson might mean a friend of the family that is close enough to be considered an aunt."

Henderson was too smart to say something that could quickly be disproved. Or had the second murder shaken him so much, he confessed too much?

"Perhaps. But that still leaves us with a man willing to take the blame to spare his sister. What could the 'lass,' as Duncan would say, what could Mary be up to that would warrant such a sacrifice?"

The lights of Westminster sparked in the distance. We'd be there soon. "Rawlins will surely slow once we get to the bridge."

At least I thought he would.

The carriage drifted.

Bang.

A wheel must've hit a hole, but we kept moving forward.

My cousin gripped the back of the seat and balanced on the bench.

"Don't see a ferry at Vauxhall Yard. That's good, but if he could get the carriage moving a little faster, I suspect Rawlins might jump the Thames."

The carriage hit another dip. Florentina's cranberry hat flew to the side. Her heavy braids came down. "Abbie."

"We are almost there."

My cousin gawked at me as if she peered over my father's thick-rimmed glasses. "What are we investigating?"

"No. No second sight. Merely logic. What does a well-to-do man—a flirtatious, handsome man—do with time on his hands? I suspect he bides his time well with companionship, not just attending public meetings to find out the latest on abolition. I wish I had seen who he sat with in Holy Trinity."

I clasped her shaking knees. "I will be more careful with you, Florentina, but I have to investigate and then rationally come up with the answer. I'm not my mama. I will not depend on dreams or visions, but my logic."

"Wait. Wait! I don't want you investigating things by yourself. That's not what I meant, Abbie." She sat up and put a hand to her hip. "The burden of second sight made your mother sick. Her gift was too heavy for anyone."

"Mama handled it and helped people. She was a force of nature. At times she was like a cyclone, impossible to stop. People came to her for advice. They depended upon her."

"And that burden took her sanity, worked her straight into the ground." Florentina joined me on my seat. "We're good, Abbie, as we are. You are good. You're making a name for yourself. You don't have to keep pushing."

"Says the mathematician that's helping our ships find their way home."

"Mathematician's aide, Abbie."

"The world's not turning fast enough for you, either." But I was determined to show that my ability to reason and solve crimes was better than Mama's burden. Of course, that meant having to solve the two murders the neighbor and I discovered.

From my carriage window, the arches of Westminster Bridge loomed ahead stark and glowing in the dark.

We'd be crossing soon and Rawlins made the Berlin leap forward like it could fly. I hoped it might be more like a lumbering gull than a heavy-bottomed rooster. Though those birds could leap, they couldn't fly. The Thames was too wide to make it in a single bound.

"So, what's the plan, Abbie?" Florentina struggled up from the floor. "You're not letting Rawlins drive like a maniac, only to park at Saint Margaret's."

"No, but if we can still hear bells ringing, there's a chance we beat Benjamin." As these words left my mouth, I felt the carriage jerk onto the bridge.

My bones chattered.

Florentina's too.

The lights of the lanterns glowed, casting gold or orange rays at us as we passed each beacon.

Florentina crushed her bonnet to her bosom. She might have prayed.

"Keep sending up good words. We need to hear those bells of Saint Margaret's. Then we'll know Mr. Benjamin wasn't kidding about leaving people to change ring."

My cousin clasped the seat. "Make Abbie make sense, Lord Almighty. Sense."

"If Mr. Benjamin can have ringers working tonight when he's not at the church, then he could do that any night. His alibi goes away. He has the strength to kill Mrs. Henderson."

"And Miss Bumners."

One could hope that the two were related. Finding one killer was easier than two.

"When we get to Saint Margaret's, we'll look around and find out who is ringing the bells while the master is away."

Florentina closed her eyes. She was doing our survival odds again. They had to be picking up. We were almost across the bridge.

"What if despite driving this crazy, we've not beat the minister to the church?"

"Maybe we can interview the bell ringers as they leave."

"In the dark? Yes, that's the perfect thing for two Blackamoor women to do. Still have the knife, right?"

I did. Henderson had given it back to me, but I'd left it in the other reticule. I'd need a checklist to ensure my reticules matched the threat level, not just my outfit.

Blam.

The carriage set foot on the other side of the Thames. Soon we were on the cobbled streets that surrounded Saint Margaret's and the Abbey.

Then I heard the bells.

The tone was solemn.

The clang of four different pitches—all belonged to Saint Margaret's.

My breathing eased. This gambit across the Thames wasn't for naught.

When Rawlins pulled us into Bridge Street, then to Saint Margaret Street, I tapped my hand on the roof to stop. The carriage slowed. Horses whinnied and my driver came and opened the door. "Ma'am, I can't stay here. The mews is a few streets away."

"Let us out. We'll meet you, once we ask a few questions."

He helped me down. Florentina too, who'd pinned her crumpled bonnet once more.

"Thirty minutes, ma'am. Then I'm coming for you."

"We'll be safe. This isn't to accuse anyone tonight. It's to see if my hunch is correct."

"A hunch can get you killed. Thirty minutes."

As I clutched Florentina's hand, we walked to the back of Westminster Abbey. The lights inside made the flying buttresses look like evil dragons. That didn't scare me. Dragons like this weren't real. Fiery beasts didn't exist at all, unless one tried to get into one of the Almack's or the new Argyll Rooms without a voucher.

We found ourselves on the southward side of the Abbey, Poets' Corner. Hopefully, Chaucer and his friends entombed inside would serve as lookout guides.

"I wonder if Donne is buried here."

"What, Abigail?" Florentina froze and looked over her shoulder, behaving as if we were being followed.

"Nothing. I thought of a poet, an unexpected favorite of a neighbor."

"Concentrate, Lady Worthing. Any signs or premonitions of our demise and we need to give up."

The bells kept clanging, and I led Florentina to the front. From here, close to the entrance of Westminster, we had a clear view of Saint Margaret's portico and her burning torches.

"Fine. We made it. Bells are ringing. What do we do now?"

Didn't exactly know. "Let's see if Benjamin arrives."

Florentina leaned close. "Two Blackamoor women shouldn't be alone spying on ministers or nuns or monks. We don't even have the monk robes to try to fit in."

"Scottish capes . . . Sssshh. A moment."

Pulling out my lorgnette, my folding theater glasses, I tried to see into the bell tower.

One of the round windows was open. Someone or something passed by.

"What are you expecting to see?"

I was about to say I didn't know, when a single-horse-pulled gig came close to Saint Margaret's entrance.

A spry young man, Minister Benjamin, stepped out. He helped a woman out and twirled her around as he set her feet on the ground.

The torchlights exposed them.

I shoved the glasses at Florentina.

She caught the sight, too—the kisses and the hugs—as our

Mr. Benjamin and the neighbor's sister went into Saint Margaret's.

"Mary Henderson, out this late with no chaperone." Florentina sounded shocked.

But that wasn't the half of it.

"Flo, upon finding a body, would you be able to go all the way to Mayfair, or would you come closer to Saint Margaret's, where the friendly neighborhood minister could bring you comfort?"

"He's bringing her comfort, all right. What is she, fifteen?"

"Fifteen, brought to live with Juliet Henderson after her father died. That can be shocking. A young woman can act out when there are changes to a household."

We were silent for a few minutes, listening for the bells until they stopped. If this was Mary's true alibi, the scandal of her being alone with a man—who was also having an affair with Juliet—would be horrible. Was that enough for murder?

"Abbie, I don't think she could do it. At fifteen, orchestrate a murder? No."

"Then maybe love is allowing her to cover for a killer. Maybe she's protecting Mr. Benjamin."

She handed me back the glasses and nodded.

I wasn't sure if I was right, but I knew one person needed to be made aware.

It wouldn't be easy telling Henderson. I hadn't apologized or even seen him this past week, but he needed to know his sister courted scandal with a man who might've murdered Juliet.

Chapter 17

By the time the Berlin rolled up to my door, Number Two Greater Queen Street, it was quite late, close to midnight. I'd insisted upon dropping my cousin at her parents' home in Spitalfields.

Florentina was a good sport. We'd had a good week together. She'd done so much for me, but I needed her safe when I did my last mission. Her mother interrogated us and reminded me of how much freedom I had. A married woman didn't require a chaperone or an accounting of how she spent her time—unless her husband demanded it.

With James away, I had full autonomy over my days, my life. I liked that. I liked this new freedom a lot.

Stepping out of the carriage, I noticed how dim the lights of Number Eleven seemed.

Had Mary come home?

Was Henderson here?

Did he have any suspicions about his sister and Benjamin, the man also rumored to be having an affair with Juliet?

"Lady Worthing," Rawlins said. "Thank you for having faith

that I could maneuver the Berlin and not end up hurt or getting you hurt. I may have to get the springs redone."

"I believe in you, sir. But this is not over. Stay alert."

"Always, ma'am. I believe in you, too. Good evening, Lady Worthing."

Watching the carriage pass me and head to the mews, I had to admire Rawlins's calm. I wished I had it inside. Truthfully, everything spun.

When the footmen let me in and I'd discarded my coat and hat and reticule, I sailed past Mr. Rogers and went to my parlor.

The man followed.

"How was church service?"

"Uneventful. How about here, sir? Any commotion. Teacup?"

"He's a changed dog. I put him to bed on the pillow you have for him No one has been bitten all week."

"Bacon, Rogers?" One sniff and the crispy meaty scent revealed the truth. "Et tu, Brute?"

He put his hand behind his back, his face lighting with a sheepish grin. "Well, I took it upon my own initiative to ask Mr. Henderson how he handled the thing so well. He's good with him."

This was a traitorous act, but the excuse I needed to visit.

"Well, now I must write him a note of gratitude for apparently helping everyone with their fear of my little terrier."

"Ma'am, would you like some tea or something?"

"No, Rogers, I'm going to be up for a while. You go on to bed. I don't want to be disturbed."

He went to the door, but stayed for a moment. "I heard the meeting wasn't positive."

Holding in my frustration, I sank onto my sofa. "No. Everyone is too frightened to do good."

"This, too, shall pass, ma'am. Abolition will happen."

For this late hour and tiresome day, I offered him the best

smile that I could. "Thank you. It's just . . . everything seems to require waiting. Never knew how much I hated that."

"Most do, but things will move forward. You will see." He bowed. "Don't stay up too late."

"Good night." I waited for the door to close. Then I reached behind the sofa and retrieved my lantern. Upon lighting the candle inside, I lifted the curved handle and stepped out onto my terrace.

From here I examined the night sky, which was cloudy with only tiny glimmers. With my lantern, it was enough to see lights burning in Henderson's study.

This was my chance to be brave, ask him to accept my apology, and then tell him what I knew.

Walking across the lawn to Number Eleven felt as if I'd crossed into enemy territory. Holding my breath, thinking of the right way to sound sincere, to be sincere, I knocked on my neighbor's door.

It took a moment before I heard movement.

Then I think I heard a curse.

The door cracked open.

Henderson, in a robe, stood in the threshold. "Someone else die?"

"No. Not that I know of."

"Then good evening, Lady Worthing."

The door started to close and I wedged my hand and then the rest of me inside. "Please. I need to see you."

He didn't move, merely shut us in, and I was trapped against the framing and his chest—shirtless, cravat-less—my nose pressed into hard muscles and folds of a billowy robe. Keeping my eyes up, I didn't look down to see if he was more exposed.

Still, he remained motionless and the weight of the lantern in my hand dragged down my arm.

"Lady Worthing, I said good night."

"Mr. Henderson, I have to speak to you."

"Well, the last time we had an intimate conversation, you slapped me. I'm not in the mood to be assaulted again. Unless you have a purpose other than sniffing me, I suggest you turn around and leave."

His voice sounded raspy, like he'd awoken from sleeping.

"I had to see you. I want to apologize. And ask, what's in your soap?"

"Eyes up here," he said, and backed up. "Juniper berries are in my soap, same as in good gin."

The hardened look on his face eased, but it seemed like an eternity before he finally tied his robe. "You've come to apologize?"

"Yes. And to thank you for training my Teacup. Seems the new knowledge you've imparted to my staff has made them no longer afraid of my dog."

"So say it. Offer me a full-throated apology. Can you do it, Lady Worthing?"

"Yes."

He folded his arms. "Then do so."

Suddenly self-conscious about being in this study with a man so casually attired, I looked to his rehung painting of Mary and a tarnished rapier on his desk. At least the intricate thing wasn't in his closed fists. "Yes. I offer you my sincere apology. I shouldn't have raised my hand to you."

"And my innocence, Lady Worthing?"

"I . . . I don't think you killed both women."

Henderson grumbled, went to the terrace door, and opened it. "Good night, Lady Worthing."

Refusing to budge, I set down my lantern and glanced at the porcelain head of Donne. "Is this poet buried in Westminster?"

"St. Paul's Cathedral. His monument was one of the only things to survive of the church from London's Great Fire."

"Oh, yes. Not the old poets' section in Westminster." I nodded like this was the most interesting fact in the world.

"You're a grown, married—allegedly, happily married— woman knocking on my private study in the middle of the night, but you have difficulty looking at me. Why?"

"Shame. Shame at my prior actions. It was abominable to slap you. I'd like to make amends. We must have silver polish . . . no polish."

"You stand here, Lady Worthing, blushing. That is a blush, the darkening bloom of your cheeks."

"Some don't think Blackamoors can blush. They don't see that our skin is similar or that we can find ourselves tongue-tied in embarrassing situations."

"Do you blush for all men, or the ones you've sniffed?"

The heat in my face told my truth. Shame the devil and me. "Yes, I'm blushing because I realize how bold this must seem. I saw your light on. I know it's on most nights. I assumed you'd be working."

He tied a bigger knot in the cinnamon-brown robe. "Don't sleep most nights. I find it better to keep my mind occupied than to be restless and useless."

"Warm milk works for me. A drop of laudanum in it, if you want no dreams." Underneath the rapier, another drawing lay on his desk. Some new contraption he'd been working on. I touched it and the paper's movement, the crinkle sound, gave me away.

"Look at me, Lady Worthing. You came to me for a reason. It wasn't soap or paper." His blank expression softened when I glanced up.

A small trace of an indention showed near his lips, the place where dimples might lie if a smile became visible.

"Why aren't you sleeping? Mourning Mrs. Henderson?"

He didn't answer.

"Or maybe your father? I learned he died before you re-turned home."

Moving to his bookshelf, he picked up a tome with one of Donne's poems. "Oh, you're doing research on me?"

"Yes, I wanted to know more about a man who invents aunts to protect his sister's alibi."

"Ah, the lady moves from slaps to invading my privacy."

"It's better than cutting off your toes."

"I think you need to stay far away from me. I require all my appendages."

The slight blush now raged, turning my face to fire. "I'm ridiculous. I fully admit it. But I'm also human and hate having to prove my humanity and worth to you or anyone else."

He flopped into the chair behind the desk, then took the small pointy rapier and put it in a drawer. "I've never asked—"

"One of a dozen insulting questions about my hair or my heritage because you think it's allowed. Or I'm judged by the actions of other Blacks from another country around the world. The highest level of arrogance is when someone assumes my marriage is some charitable act or experiment."

"Sorry."

A headache threatened. I needed to quit, but the same stubborn will that brought me here to say my piece remained, anchoring my feet to the floor. "If someone knew where my sister was and that she was in trouble, I'd want to know. I'd want every little fact."

"You mean, your half sister, Dinah Carrington? The one who's run off?"

"See, my searching is an invasion of your privacy, but you feel entitled to assess my background. I guess we are both hypocrites."

He nodded in the same nonchalant manner as James. It must be something men born to privilege did. "Lord Worthing's an old friend. I served under him before Nelson. I wanted to know who'd made the confirmed bachelor come up to scratch."

"And you find his bride a wholly reprehensible choice, with poor connections and virtually impoverished by the date of our wedding. I'll have you know at one time my family was well-off."

Henderson dipped his chin again. This time he did smile. "I know everything there is to know about you." He flitted his finger along the desk. It looked like cursive the way the digit moved. "Some may call it scandalously clever, a bold usurping moment. I think it a wise, but impertinent, choice for a man married to the sea."

I wasn't expecting a compliment about myself or a true statement about James. "Before you begin to read minds or fortunes, let me tell you what I've come to say."

His dark eyes brightened, and somehow he'd given me his full attention.

"You know that my sister has run off. I wish someone had told me of Dinah's intent, that someone had warned me she was upset and considered doing something that could ruin her future. I would've stopped her from running. I would've found some way to make things right so she would've stayed."

"Sometimes leaving is best."

His eyes, indigo and enlarged in the dim light, glanced through me and claimed some hidden truth, something forgotten or wished for, which I couldn't say—like, James being away made me lonely, though I'd never known such freedom. I could go and come and be any version of Lady Worthing I wanted without asking permission.

Arms crossing my chest like a shield, I said the rest. "I would do anything for Dinah, as I suspect you'd do anything for Mary. Your sister's in trouble."

The screech of chair legs sounded. Then big, bared feet flopped next to Donne.

They didn't smell like juniper berries.

"Lady Worthing, tell me something I don't know. Amuse me. I told you in confidence that Mary found the body."

"And that she was with an aunt and later you changed that to a friend."

"My old governess. She'll back anything I say. This is not new."

"Coming back from Holy Trinity, I discreetly followed a carriage. From Poets' Corner, I snuck around the side of Westminster Abbey and gained a full view of Saint Margaret's. I saw your sister there two hours ago."

"My sister?" The bored look dissipated. "Mary?"

"Do you have another?"

He grimaced. "Not that I'm aware of."

"Were you aware that she's involved with Minister Benjamin, the man you said was having an affair with your wife? Your sister was alone with him, kissing him like they were courting, going into Saint Margaret's."

Fiery anger vibrated Henderson's cheek as a full scowl emerged. "The bastard."

I'd be frightened if it wasn't the same expression I had to mask when I learned on my wedding day that Dinah had left.

"The bastard needs to die for touching a hair on her head."

"Which her, Henderson? Mary or Juliet?"

"Does it matter, as long as he's dead?"

"Whoa." I lifted my hands—as if I could motion him to settle. I couldn't even train my dog. "We have enough bodies right now."

"Mr. Benjamin was having an affair with Juliet. He was the man she planned to run away with to Scotland. The lout has turned from mourning her to making eyes at my sister."

It was more than eyes, but Henderson was already upset. A man protecting his family could be rash. "How long had the affair with your wife been going? How long had you known?"

"Well over a year, they've been running hot and heavy. Juliet told me everything when I returned, and we decided to separate. She and I were much better friends than anything else."

Leaning against his desk with my palms flat, I started with my questions. "After you kicked her out? She confessed?"

"After she agreed to leave. She wanted to go, to do as she pleased without feeling watched."

I sympathized with that notion. Freedom was good. "You would let her stay even though you didn't feel love for her?"

"Lady Worthing, Juliet bore my name. There will always be a sense of obligation to her."

"Did you kill her?"

"No."

"But you believe Mary did?"

He said nothing, but his gaze wavered. Rubbing his palm like he'd injured it, he said, "She's a Henderson. She's capable of anything."

Saying that I was sorry didn't seem appropriate.

Nor did telling him I thought Mary innocent, for I wasn't sure if that was true.

"Lady Worthing, you've said what you needed to tell me. You can go."

He dismissed me like I was nothing, like he felt nothing, but his eyes said pain—horrible, horrible pain.

Not an inch of me moved. None. Not even my braided chignon that needed to come down and find curl papers.

"Mr. Benjamin was having an affair with your wife. He's a suspect. He had motive to kill. Juliet changed her mind about leaving with him. Duncan should be given his name."

"No. This man has no faith, making love to Juliet, then romancing my sister. He'd turn her in to Duncan as the culprit or the accomplice."

Balling my hands, I readied to leave this arrogant fool, whom I was trying to help. Instead, I breathed, made my voice calm, and stayed. "If Mrs. Henderson decided not to go, that would've upset the minister's plans. Or maybe she was upset and threatened to tell Mary of their affair? He might have killed her to keep his secret. Miss Bumners too. A lady's maid knows everything."

Slipping past Henderson, I sat in the chair by his desk. "That still doesn't explain why there were no portmanteaus. Her apartment didn't look like someone was packing to leave the country. I'm beginning to think she changed her mind. Mr. Benjamin killed her from his disappointment."

Henderson folded his arms. "There's a logic to what you are saying."

"If I'm right, this dangerous man is after your sister." I sat back and caught his gaze. "I'm stuck. I'm asking for your help. I want to be of aid to Mary."

"Let me think on it."

When I rose, Henderson already had my lamp in his hands. I took it and he drew the handle and me close. "It takes a remarkable person to admit weakness and ask for help."

"Sir, I don't make habit of admitting I'm stuck to anyone."

"Lady Worthing, I've decided. I much want your help. I'll go with you to see Mr. Tanner. We have to pursue all suspects, and I have to stop him from attacking every stranger who comes to his farm."

"You must be convincing. I don't take kindly to those who hurt my friends."

"Don't fret. I've been told that I can be convincing." He released the lamp. I started to the door, but he wouldn't let me pass. It was again him, and a mostly closed robe, and me.

"We leave at week's end at nine."

Florentina wouldn't be available. I'd taken too much of her time. "One o'clock."

"So late?" His face was near. His voice softer.

"Yes. I start my appointments then. Is there a problem with that?"

"Fine. Looking forward to it. We head to Chelsea next week. And be careful of the laudanum drops to sleep. It's a cure-all that can become quite addictive."

"That's a doctor's opinion? I wouldn't say a friend's, because the last time I was here, you threatened me."

"Well, we aren't enemies." He held the door for me and snapped his fingers as his two sleek silver dogs came to him.

"Silvereye and Santisma?" I pointed to the one with a dark circle of gray fur about his eye. "Lovely greyhounds."

He clicked his fingers twice and they sat. He made the noise again and they came and begged in front of me. "They are well behaved without bacon treats."

"I'm glad you finally trained them. Teacup is at last safe." I said this with my chin up.

And heard his laughter all the way to my door.

Chapter 18

The following afternoon, with Teacup nestled beside me on the sofa, I settled down to a little reading. My doggie had tired himself running and rolling with the stuffed ball I'd made him. It had a bell inside and my boy loved to shake it to make the noise tinkle. I brushed his shaggy coat. "Good sleepy dog."

The sun shining through the fully open curtains made the pink flowers on my print cotton gown look light, airy. Not their true shade at all.

The letter I started writing James last night was on the table. Vaughn and Florentina had both asked me to do this.

And I couldn't.

What if he said no?

What if he didn't miss me at all?

What if he returned and tried to command me like one of his crew? Could I trade independence and freedom for companionship?

What if James returned and it wasn't permanent? What if he never intended to be in London permanently? Would I be happy then?

I picked up the scribble I'd started and burned it in the fireplace.

James should know to come home.

I shouldn't have to beg.

A year and half, almost two, was too long.

Rogers came into my parlor and announced, "Mr. Vaughn, ma'am."

When my godfather indicated he wouldn't be staying long, my butler left us alone in my parlor.

"Abigail, you look lovely. Seems rising at noon agrees with you."

I kissed his cheek. "You should try it. It's fantastic for wrinkles about the eyes."

"Be kind, dear. If you strip me of my vanity, what will I have?"

"You'd have your kind heart, savvy wisdom, and incredible luck at cards."

"You're a flatterer, Abigail. And you have a bit of luck, it seems. Lord Duncan's uncle, John Campbell, the fifth Duke of Argyll, is near death. The magistrate will travel to Inveraray Castle. He'll be gone for a few weeks. That is more time for things to die down."

"It's not going to die down. It will fester. This killer will strike again."

"I was afraid you'd say that." He sat opposite me in a rich Mazarine blue tailcoat and a bottle-green waistcoat. The man must be off to look at ponies with the Prince of Wales.

He pulled papers and spread them onto the table. "This is everything that you need to know about Lieutenant Commander Stapleton Henderson. It's his military records."

The file was thick, at least half an inch. "Thank you. Is Inveraray near Glasgow, where you and Mr. Shaw were educated?"

"A day's ride from the school. Duncan passed through my ole stomping ground. Expect him back in two weeks."

He rose. "Lady Worthing. Be safe. Study this to know who your neighbor is, but keep avoiding an active investigation."

"No, two weeks is perfect to figure out this crime and hand Lord Duncan a name to indict by the time he returns."

"I thought you'd say that." He grimaced and started for the door, but Vaughn knew I wouldn't stay away from something that needed solving.

My godfather pivoted. "You'll write to Lord Worthing? I still think his presence will be beneficial."

"Hmm. Yes."

"Well, at least you didn't say no. Stay safe."

Vaughn bowed, then pushed at the door. The floors squeaked and his footfalls continued until everything shut tightly.

Stapleton Henderson knew everything about me. It was time for me to learn about the naval career that shaped the man.

Shifting through the pages, I saw Vaughn had brought everything—from his first pinning to his accounts of his service and bounties to citations and incident reports.

One letter was from Henderson.

It was my neighbor's personal account of Admiral Lord Nelson's final hours.

> *October 21, 1805, under Nelson's battle plans, his fleet grouped as smaller squadrons sailed into enemy lines. The hope was to destroy their fleet before reinforcements could sail.*
>
> *The move instead of the traditional lines took the enemy by surprise. Victory sailing under Nelson took the lead. We came under heavy fire. Cannons from the* Redoutable *and the* Santísima Trinidad *struck the hull. A second ball killed Nelson's secretary, John Scott. As one of the ship's surgeons, I knew there was*

nothing to be done when a man is nearly cut in two.

More balls fired, cutting down the wheel and at least eight marines before my eyes. I stood next to Nelson and heard him quip with his boisterous sense of humor say, "This is too warm work to last long."

The 74-gun Redoutable *and the 130-gun* Santísima Trinidad *took turns pounding our ships, but our side gave as good or better.*

Then sharpshooters manning the rigging fired onto the quarterdeck.

Musket balls passed by that the smoke choked. When the wind passed, I stepped to my side. Nelson was no longer behind me. He'd fallen.

Searching his person, I found a ball had lodged in his back. From his wheezing, I could tell it had pierced a lung.

My friend, and admiral, knew it, too. He hesitated to be taken below. The man wanted to stay for the fight. When he saw his strength fading, Nelson consented to go below. After a more thorough examination, I found the musket ball entered his left shoulder and appeared to be lodged at his sixth and seventh thoracic vertebrae. I could tell he felt it stuck in the right shoulder blade. There was nothing that could be done.

Sergeant Major Robert Adair noted the hole in my jacket. I cannot help but think that Nelson took the ball that missed me.

I set the parchment down and took Teacup into my arms. "It appears your bacon friend has been lucky."

Yet was it truly good fortune to know you lived when another person had died?

How did that shape a mind?

Would guilt become commonplace?

The dreams I fought were changing me.

And not necessarily for the better.

Looking into Teacup's furry face, I watched him snuggle with me on the sofa as if I was his world, and despite the craziness—in my head and all around Westminster—we would still be fine.

Maybe dogs didn't notice change.

There was no question in my head that I'd found someone who might understand that moment. "If only I could stand asking, Teacup."

Rogers came to my parlor. "Miss Sewell is here."

I put my feet on the floor as my cousin entered.

"Tea, madam?"

"No, Rogers. Madam and I are going out. Can you have Miss Bellows bring down Lady Worthing's emerald pelisse?"

He looked to me and I offered a nod of consent. "Why would I stop anything that has her cheered?" Then I asked Flo, "Where are we going?"

"I was cold and beastly to you the last time we were together."

"Flo, you had reason. My high-speed chase could've killed us."

"You were doing an Abbie thing. I have to understand that's you."

I shook my head. "You're right. I'm taking too many risks."

"Well, for you to acknowledge someone being right besides yourself is an important step in your evolution."

Henderson said something similar about this in his study.

"So you think I'm changing?"

"I know you're improving. And we're going to celebrate by catching a bit to eat."

"I can have Mrs. Smith make us lunch."

"She'll do well, but I don't think she can get Wilberforce over to your house to read your papers."

For one brief moment, I thought she talked about Henderson's records. But my cousin was speaking of the documents in my reticule with eyewitness reports on the atrocities James had witnessed. If Clapham Sect wrote pamphlets on them, that should shake free the conscience of Britain.

Bending to me, Florentina put her hands to my shoulders. Her golden straw–colored carriage gown, with a double row of cloth buttons, shimmied from the effort. "You heard me. Get up and get moving. I can't give you my fears. I have to let you do your calling and wait for you to shine. We're family, as close as sisters. That's what we do."

I hugged her and my doggie. This was what I needed. No commiserating over losses.

When I set Teacup down, he growled, then scurried to the back of the sofa.

I tossed him a saucy grin. "I'll only be gone a little while."

My cousin was in such a mood to go out, and I was more than ready to be a little reckless and to give a reformer the fuel to start abolition talks anew.

Chapter 19

Florentina had Rawlins drive almost to the rear of Saint Margaret's to the busy area of New Palace Yard. My maid, Miss Bellows, accompanied us and began telling stories of the latest gossip. Seems two doors down a neighbor's daughter eloped with her music teacher.

Miss Bellows gleefully spilled all the details, but all I could do was think of Mary and Dinah. I had that feeling about Henderson's sister, the same I ignored with my own—a desperation of some sort. For Dinah, it seemed like a competition or race betwixt us. Couldn't fathom Mary's. Maybe losing her father?

"What do you think of that, Lady Worthing?"

I looked up at my maid's cherry face, her wizened light blue eyes. "The cook, she's with child."

"Um. Good."

She started to laugh. "You kidder. Not good. She's unwed and it looks like the expectant father is her widowed employer."

Part of me wanted to make hand signals to Flo; then she'd catch me up. Instead, I nodded. "That is a pickle."

Miss Bellows launched into another story. I listened, but stately Saint Margaret's across the way had my attention. From here we had a good view of the back of the church and the beautiful three-paneled stained glass. I heard it dated from the 1500s.

The shade of Florentina's dress—a walking dress with double buttons on the sleeves—matched the gold in the king's crown of the window.

My cousin looked at the church and said, "It's not Sunday, Abbie. There's no need to think of church or consider returning. I think we'll have a better evening at Olive's."

Her hint wasn't subtle.

Miss Bellows shook her finger. "Don't tell me you two are spying on that Mr. Benjamin. Almost every woman on Queen Street is. I hear attendance is up. There's word he'll soon choose a Mrs. Benjamin."

I hoped his selection wasn't fifteen, and my neighbor's sister.

"Weren't there other rumors about him, Miss Bellows?" Florentina stretched against her seat. "I heard he was close to Mrs. Henderson?"

"But she was married." My maid looked disturbed. "Marriage means they live happily ever after, right? Ma'am, you and the baron—"

"Ladies, look at the panels. They're pretty. I love how light is captured in the colors."

They both did and were silent, blessedly silent.

"I'm surprised they display the glass at all," Florentina said. "With the Crucifixion in the middle pane, that's a very Catholic depiction. Where're the Anglican runners set to take the church elders into custody?" Her mood was biting and sarcastic, typical for her when she started to hunger.

"Florentina. You miss the beauty and hypocrisy of it. People are mad at Catholics simply for their faith. But this image celebrates everything before the king broke with it. Henry the

Eighth, the mad wife-swapping king, is on the right, and the first wife, Catherine of Aragon, is on the other."

Miss Bellows smoothed her dark charcoal-gray dress. She'd left her apron at Number Two. "Odd goings on in the past, ladies. There's something wrong about women being discarded for not producing heirs, for not . . . something. It's never the men at fault."

She was right, and I wondered about the concept of blame and whom history chose to count as the villain. Hayti now. Juliet Henderson later. Some will indict her for her own murder.

I slouched picking at the strings of my reticule, thinking how I'd be remembered. What was it Henderson had said about me? Scandalously clever, a bold usurper, a wise and impertinent choice.

The carriage slowed as traffic from Westminster Bridge merged with those from Parliament Street. Given two of the area's best taverns, the Exchequer Coffee House and Olive's, were adjacent, even sharing the same larder for their breads and cheeses, one could understand why people crowded.

For a moment, Rawlins picked up the pace on Saint Margaret Street. Then he came around to let us out. He looked uneasy. I hadn't seen him like that since dropping us at Holy Trinity.

"Lady Worthing, it's too crowded," he said. "I can't get closer with all these carriages. You might want to send ahead for a table."

"I'm ready, ma'am. This is exciting." Miss Bellows, who sat opposite Florentina and me, bounced down and fought through the crowd to Olive's like she worked for the king or even Queen Charlotte.

That made this impertinent girl feel special.

"The food has to be good." Florentina pointed through the glass. "Look at this crowd."

The Berlin was a big, showy beast. I liked the yellow bounder because it could get into smaller places. Perhaps when I went to Chelsea, the chaise would do.

A second glance and the crowd had grown. Tens of people. Some on horseback. A great deal more on foot. That seemed a lot wiser now. "Olive's and Exchequer are known for their meals and wines. If we get a seat, we'll not be disappointed."

Every whinny of a horse or striking of hooves made me jittery, but Rawlins had everything under control. I'd had no odd dreams to color the moment. I had nothing to fear. Nothing would happen today.

Florentina made signs in the air. I was sure it was a quotient or something.

"Miss Bellows is taking too long, Abbie. I'm beginning to doubt if Wilberforce can secure a table."

"Oh, they'll get him one. He's still influential."

From our vantage point, I could see the door opening and closing as patrons left. There had to be one table for us. "Miss Bellows won't dawdle. She's used to doing this."

Having an intermediary was a thing James and I came up with to ensure those who didn't know I was Lady Worthing wouldn't hesitate to serve us.

Some still hesitated, even at the mention of my title, but I'd not been turned away. Thank goodness, money trumped awkwardness and impertinence, even race. Well, that's how things worked in Westminster.

Nonetheless, the London world wasn't changing fast enough. If independence half a world away could frighten good people from their good intentions, I truly couldn't expect much from a waiter or tavern owner.

Better to face the battle, any battle, head on with them looking at me and my beautiful brown face. I started climbing down. "Rawlins, we'll go see what's keeping Miss Bellows."

*   *   *

Hand in hand, with her papers rolled and tucked under her arm, Florentina and I wound our way into New Palace Yard.

We avoided a rude gentleman who called out to "wenches," as he called them. "Women who paid him no attention" was what I'd call them. A horse veered and missed a suddenly stopped carriage. I did breathe easier when we made it to the tavern's door.

My maid came out, fanning her reddening face. "He's checking, ma'am, but he assured me he'd find something."

With a whimsical smile and demure eyes, I did my third favorite activity, watching people.

A fellow spit on the sidewalk and kept going. It wasn't directed at us, but it showed his limited home training. Yet in the back of my mind, I realized these were the very folks I was depending upon to open their hearts and minds to abolition.

In another ten minutes, when I thought all hope was lost, a man from the waitstaff poked his head out. "The Baroness of Worthing's party. Ah, there you are. This way."

Customary prim smile in place and a reticule with tipping pennies on my wrist, we followed him to a table in a corner.

"You'll like this one," he said as I put three pence into his palm. "It's rumored the first owner of Olive's had to remove a bust of a Saxon king in order to create this nook."

"Cozy and royal. It's a blessing." Florentina put a hand to her stomach. It was an attempt to smother a gurgle. Well, we'd waited a long time.

I sent the man on his way after requesting a pot of tea be brought and something to nibble. Sitting back, I relaxed and waited. "What are the odds parliamentary people will show, Miss Sewell?"

"Better than hoping for a personal visit to your residence."

Miss Bellows clasped the back of the empty seat. "Ma'am, do you need me to stay?"

Her ruddy face with lips thinning like an anxious child, one visiting a new place, stung me. My maid fidgeted as if she had never been anywhere.

Then I remembered she hadn't.

Since she was a spinster, society had limited her sphere. Mine would be further reduced if not for the fortune of having a respectable father and a wealthy husband.

After making eyes at Florentina, who was busy counting lit sconces and beer steins—her way of calculating potential bar fights—we agreed that Miss Bellows could join our setting. "Tell Rawlins to be back in two hours, then return. Take this empty seat beside Miss Sewell. It is out of the aisle. It's our pleasure if you stay and dine."

The glow in her cheeks was angelic, as if I'd donned a green stocking and become Father Christmas doling out presents. She ran out of the coffeehouse on borrowed wings.

"You should've said an hour and a half." Florentina straightened her bonnet. "The odds of a fight increase the longer we stay."

Shrugging, I settled into my chair and unbuttoned the collar of my Saxon blue carriage gown, which looked more lavender than blue in the dim light. "We are going to have a peaceful luncheon. No upsets or confusion."

A barmaid ran from the kitchen.

My heart pounded. I'd bragged too soon.

A man wearing a gravy-stained apron popped from the kitchen. "Ten pounds of rump roast will do."

My pulse slowed.

Florentina glanced my way. "What? What's happening?"

"I think I know what I want to eat. Roast."

She shook her head and made room for Miss Bellows. "That sounds good, but let's not get carried away. Remember we are also here for your mission with Wilberforce."

"What?" Miss Bellows's voice became pitchy. "Lady Worthing is trying to be political?"

"No, not truly."

"That's good, cause Wilberforce is on the outs," my maid said. He's in trouble. His good friend Pitt the Younger died in January. He gave more leadership in the wars than the king. I think everyone is still mourning. Everyone is rudderless."

"Tiller-less, actually," Florentina said, making charcoal marks on a small piece of foolscap. She could do more than one thing at a time.

I thought of what I'd read of Henderson's military record. I wondered about a man who'd been in service for ten years, now suddenly free of it, how did it shape him? What did he miss? Coming home to an unfaithful wife . . . whom he was now free of as well, what did that feel like? Wearisome? Strange? Joyous?

"You're in deep thought, ma'am?" Miss Bellows bounced a little in her seat. "Your brow is wrinkling. What are you thinking of?"

I smoothed my forehead, for no one need know I had concerns for my neighbor. "Mustn't do that. No early lines, as my mother would say."

"Yes, you must keep your looks for when Lord Worthing comes home. You'll be a sight for a man who's been long at sea."

Was I smiling still?

I couldn't tell. My mother had told me about men, sailors coming ashore in Kingston Harbour to visit the ballrooms, the mulatto balls, the brothels.

A man could forget he was married or perhaps become like Vaughn and my father, fall deeply in love with an island woman. Unfortunately for them, it was the same one, Magdalena.

The barmaid came and took our order, then disappeared behind the swinging door.

Jeers sounded at the door.

A group of men singing at the top of their lungs entered the coffeehouse. They were joyous in their words, but each wore crepe bands on their arms. Must be another funeral. Death, I suppose, was a constant in all our lives.

These fellows kept streaming in and upset a wobbly man carrying a tankard in his hands.

"You singing bastards. Watch where you're going."

I knew the voice and remembered the ale smell of him and lavender. "Mr. Sinclair?"

He heard me and sloshed to my table. "Number Two Greater Queen Street."

"Yes, it's me. Are you well, sir?"

"No. I burn. I mourn to the depths of my soul." His words came out like a song, along with a rush of bad breath. "Miss Bumners didn't deserve to die. I heard you found her. Tell me it's a lie."

" 'Tis true." I pointed to the open chair at our table. "Sit before you fall down."

The man swayed, then flopped. "Sorry. I can't take any more grief. First Juliet, now Bumners."

The poor drunk breathed heavily. The fumes of liquor that came from his mouth could ignite a torch.

"Mr. Sinclair, have you been here since the funeral? Did Mr. Henderson let you go?"

He flopped to one side, almost falling out of the chair. "The butler did. Does all his dirty work. Said I wasn't needed, now that Mrs. Henderson is no more. Snide fellow. He took pleasure in it. Saying those words. Letting me go. I gave them the best seven years of my life."

One hand slung the silver tankard, while the other dropped onto my shoulder.

He had power in his drunk limbs.

With a push, I had him sitting upright and balanced against

the chair back. "Sorry to hear that. I know you worked diligently for the family."

"No one, not one, ever liked me, but Juliet did."

"Not even Miss Bumners?"

Sinclair gripped his chin like he tried to have a rational, coherent thought. "Well, hard to tell. She was always secretive. She kept everyone's secrets. I think that's what killed her, she knew too much."

"I wouldn't think someone would be hurt for knowing too little." Florentina adjusted her straw bonnet and I looked at her, signaling to let the man talk.

Miss Bellows fixed a cup of tea. "You were familiar with the late mistress, weren't you? People like to gossip about the goings-on over at Eleven Greater Queen Street. Was it decadent as all the tales?"

"Miss Bellows, please." I made eyes at her, too, wide ones that surely looked of pain. I hoped she'd understand.

"Come on, Mr. Sinclair," she continued, not taking my hints, "tell us about the partying. Did she get that young miss corrupted by all the men traipsing in and out? There was fear of that, you know."

I'd never heard of this. Did people not tell me what was going on in my own neighborhood? Then I thought of my gambits and the costumes and how I purposely kept Rogers and others from knowing. I supposed I needed to breed a new atmosphere of trust in my home.

Sinclair waved his hands in slow motion. "You got things all wrong about her. Juliet was full of life. She loved Mary, and I think the war hero and the wife would've gotten back together. She talked about the person who truly loved her—the difficulties, the jealousy. People didn't want them together."

Florentina popped up from her papers. "How can you be certain of this love? I'd heard the house was volatile. Arguments all the time."

"Pshaw," he said, flinging his wrist as if swatting flies. His coat wrinkled. His face held a shadow of days. Was he in here hiding?

"That was an act. Juliet loved theat—theatri—she loved to act. She wanted the world to be her stage. You know she wanted to do plays. But her father and brother were against it. They were mean to her. That lousy brother always wanted money from her."

Henderson had told me the fights were an act. I hadn't fully believed him. I suppose that part was true. Drunks don't lie, do they?

Florentina stacked her papers. "How did she and Miss Bumners get along?"

So my disinterested cousin was listening.

Sinclair had begun singing again, something about barring the door. Then he stopped and glanced at Flo. "Good. Everyone loved Juliet. Always fun. Miss Bumners could be prickly. And sometimes I think she was jealous. She was from Chelsea, too. One girl gets elevated, the other presses corsets."

He laughed and then cried. "They coveted everything Juliet had. I heard that the man who killed Bumners hurt her something good."

"There's not much good in death." Florentina flipped a page. "Nothing at all."

"Why would someone want to hurt Miss Bumners?" I turned Sinclair's head back to me. "Why was she a threat? Something she knew? Something she took and wouldn't give back?"

"Don't know. But she was always thinking." Sinclair nursed his shiny mug, its handle glistening in the light. "She said she had a plan to tide herself over until her next employ."

"So she was going to be let go, too." Miss Bellows tugged at her shawl like she was cold. "Just not right."

Henderson hadn't decided on her employ, but the talk

among the servants was that he'd let the maid go. Who bene-fited with Bumners gone?

Sipping my tea, I pushed the notions away. I was having an outing, hoping to see Wilberforce, not trying to solve the mur-ders.

I turned again to Sinclair, who had my thick reticule and shook it. The pennies rattled. "Sounds light in there." I doubted the man had use of signed statements for abolition.

"Sir, can you remember what Miss Bumners's plans were, or whom she was to meet the night of the funeral?"

Crossing arms, he lifted a hand to support his chin. "Oh, I need to sober up to help you."

"Yes, help me help Mrs. Henderson."

"Of course." He swayed again, then popped up when an-other wave of patrons entered.

"Who, Mr. Sinclair, do you think killed Mrs. Henderson?"

He rolled his shoulders and turned his mug up to his face.

Then he looked toward the door and began to shake. Ale rained on me.

"I didn't tell! Didn't say a word."

"What? Wait, Mr. Sinclair?" I scanned the tavern and didn't see anyone who'd threaten him. "Calm down sir."

He shook his head. "Don't have 'em come after me." The panicked man charged toward the door.

I started to chase, but Florentina grabbed my hand. "Stop. He's drunk, Abbie. Let him have his fit and let the mystery solving go. The man you wanted to talk to is here. Mr. Wilber-force has entered Olive's."

Wilberforce was here, probably coming from a session in parliament. He talked to several other gentlemen.

Florentina shoved my reticule at me. "Don't think, Abbie. Go."

My cousin was right. I had James's letters with me.

I marched toward the man in the dove-gray tailcoat, the frail-looking fellow with a slight bent in his stance. He laughed at a colleague's joke. That sounded strong.

Shoulders back, head level, I approached, not as a puzzler or someone trying to solve anything, but as a revolutionary soldier. I had letters that could restart the fight for abolition.

Halfway to Wilberforce, I heard a crash.

The world slowed.

The impact. The scream.

The crunching and breaking of bones.

The thudding of people running.

The door swung open. In a glimpse, I saw what was left of a man, facedown in the dirt. A dented silver tankard lay at his arm. His arm twitched, then stopped moving.

In my head, I screamed and screamed his name. *Mr. Sinclair!*

In shock, I fled through Olive's entry and became one of the many onlookers crowding the fallen man.

A hackney driver shouted obscenities. "I didn't mean to hit 'im. He ran into my path. Didn't you see it? Didn't you? Oh, God! What have I done?"

More men pressed toward Sinclair and pushed me farther and farther back.

Didn't mind being tossed away from death. Yet, my gaze kept hoping for movement. Was a miracle too much? A kindly man who never hurt anyone shouldn't be run down by a hackney.

Wilberforce passed me. He pulled something like gilded leaves from his pocket. He read something about peace and understanding, then led the crowd to pray.

I had nothing—no peace, no voice, no warning that this would happen.

My gift, my curse, never worked like that. It never showed me anything that I could understand. I wasn't my mama.

I wished I were if it meant I could've saved Sinclair.

I slipped back into Olive's and stepped into Mr. Benjamin's path.

"Sorry, Lady Worthing," he said. "A lady shouldn't have to witness such."

My chin dipped, not in agreement, but more in shock that Benjamin was here, while another witness who could link him to Juliet Henderson had been killed.

He took my limp hand and led me back to my party. "Lady Worthing, are you well? Do I need to send for a doctor?"

With a shake of my head, I realized he'd seen me in this nook. He likely observed my talk with Sinclair. I looked up at Benjamin, into eyes that seemed innocent, but I knew they weren't.

Forcing myself to swallow, I pointed to the door. "You're needed outside, sir. Go help that driver who'll feel the guilt all his life for killing."

The minister's eyes shifted. He tipped his black beaver hat and jogged away. He went through the swinging door and exposed people kneeling by poor dead Mr. Sinclair.

How long had Benjamin been in Olive's?

Was he by himself?

Or had he come to meet with the driver to threaten him?

Seeing me and Sinclair in conversation—did that put a target on the driver's head?

Had it marked me, too?

Hands shaking, I tried to smooth a napkin over my lap. Platters of rump steak were set out. Florentina and Miss Bellow were eating, enjoying life. They hadn't seen what I had.

"Lady Worthing," my cousin said after she cleared her throat. "You don't look as if you had your talk with Wilberforce. Did it not go well?"

"No. Something stole my attention, his too."

A hymn sounded. "Amazing Grace." Some of the revelers must have gone outside to sing for the lost. The opening and closing of the front door allowed the words, the feelings of John Newton, the slave trader turned abolitionist, to flood Olive's, to find me and arrest my soul.

> *Yea, when this flesh and heart shall fail,*
> *And mortal life shall cease,*
> *I shall possess, within the veil,*
> *A life of joy and peace.*

There was no peace in me. I was in need of amazing grace. Sinclair's death left me empty with more questions, another report for the magistrate, and slices of cooked-down, garlicky rump roast growing cold.

Chapter 20

It was dark before everything finished at Olive's. The person filling in for Lord Duncan didn't ask any questions of me. Dozens of men, it seemed, saw the accident. And for the runners, it was probably preferred to take their statements as opposed to ones from two Blackamoor women and a maid.

This was a clear reminder of my position in solving mysteries. People indulged in secret, not in public. Nothing was more public than Olive's and New Palace Yard.

When Rawlins deposited Miss Bellows and me back to Two Greater Queen Street, I sent him to take Florentina home and made my maid retire to bed.

Ignoring the creaking floorboards, I went to my parlor. Teacup was there. He came to me and I bent to him. He licked my fingers as I cradled my doggie. "Missed you, boy. Did you protect everyone today?"

My curtains were open and the night looked inviting and calm.

Nothing in me was that.

With Teacup in one hand, I picked up the lantern from behind my sofa, lit it, and then went out onto my terrace.

Sitting in the dark with my simple lantern and my panting pup, I think I started to cry.

A light in the distance stung my wet eyes. Two happy dogs barking were the harbinger of a lone figure coming closer.

Henderson stood at my garden. Unlike the runners, he did salvage my flowers. He edged around them like there was a border.

His lamp shined on my face. The beam crossed, settled on my eyelids, then disappeared.

When I opened my eyes, he sat across from me. From a snap of his fingers, the greyhounds bowed before me, quiet.

Teacup wiggled and whined and then settled in my lap.

Not sure how much time passed.

The quiet felt nice. It also felt good not to be alone.

When Henderson started to move, getting up as if he'd leave, I finally spoke. "I heard a man mostly die today."

"Lady Worthing, you saw death?"

"No, but I heard it. Bones breaking. Maybe a scream. Then a gurgle for air. A last gasp. Then I saw his ghost leave his body with a final twitch. In an instant, he suffered intensely. He should've been dead, but he lingered, feeling all that pain. Then nothing. Like the nothingness out here."

"Not the same. Nature, openness, settles the spirit."

"You're right, Henderson. I definitely wasn't settled in front of Olive's." I looked over at my neighbor and caught the embers of his gaze. "Mr. Sinclair is dead."

Henderson's eyes widened. They'd ramped to full blue flame. "How?"

"Trampled."

He leaned back in the chair. I couldn't read his expression, but it felt like sorrow. "Sinclair was a loyal, lovable drunk." Henderson sighed. "Sorry you had to see or hear it."

"Can't get the noise out of my head." I caressed Teacup, sinking my fingers into his curly fur. "His death might've been a minute, but it seemed like hours."

"If it were hours, you'd hear everything from the fight to live, to slowly losing vigor, then surrender, then gone. Be glad it was quick."

My neighbor had to be thinking of Lord Nelson. There was more emotion in Henderson's voice than I'd ever heard.

Couldn't think to offer comfort or further bare my soul if I had any doubts of his innocence. "I need to ask you, one last time. Did you . . ."

Henderson stood, snapped his fingers. He and his dogs left, trudging at a slow speed toward his property.

Teacup jumped from my arms and caught up to him.

"Wait. Mr. Henderson. Wait!"

Ignoring me, he kept going. With a flick of his wrist, he sent his dogs to his fields, then went into his study.

Teacup sat at his door, scratching and whining.

I picked up my dog and knocked on the door.

On the third knock, he let me inside and Teacup ran and hid under his desk. "Lady Worthing, if you can't keep your terrier, perhaps you shouldn't have one. Some people don't make responsible pet owners."

"I'm not here for your smooth talk. I need to hear one more time that you didn't kill Juliet."

"I didn't kill my wife. Satisfied? Leave."

"Aren't you going to ask me why I asked?"

"No. Good night."

Leaning against his bookcase, he folded his arms over a Carmelite brown waistcoat. It reminded me of the ridiculous capes I'd made to escape the theater. "Please leave. I'm not quite myself."

The look in his eyes drew me; for now, I wanted to know

what that meant. Shutting the door, I heard its solid rattle and bent my head to the new plans on his desk. "A garden? Your wife's been murdered and you're making detailed drawings for a garden? You find nothing else more pressing."

"I like plants. I'm quite fond of flowers."

Though he'd said so, it was still surprising, the exacting details of his planning while we were in the midst of a murder spree. "Sir, that's the last thing I thought you'd say."

"What, not militaristic enough? Not hedonistic? You prefer gladiator sports?" Wrenching at his cravat, he dropped into his chair. "Some flowers have medicinal qualities. I learned through my travels through the West Indies. It's also a calming distraction."

"Ten years of travel, until October 1805, means you saw quite a lot."

Henderson glared at me. His gaze felt as if it sliced a surgeon's incision across my throat. "Oh, the budding magistrate has done more research."

"Thank you for the aspirations, but they won't let women have the job, let alone me."

"Perhaps you'll be the first, with your clue finding, privacy invading—"

"I don't believe you killed your wife, or Miss Bumners, or Sinclair." I clutched the back of the chair beside his desk, the one I'd sat in the last time we talked. "I merely wanted to hear your innocence from your lips."

He fingered his mouth, then looked down at his drawings. "Thank you. I accept your apology."

Hadn't exactly offered one, but if it lessened his anger and got him to help, I might even say it aloud.

"Wait. You had Sinclair on your list. You said he was run down by a carriage? You think it murder?"

"Yes. The poor fellow died outside of Olive's. He was drunk.

When I didn't see the cause of the upset, I thought the liquor made him act out. I didn't trust my instincts. I should've kept him at my table. Then he wouldn't have been frightened or pushed onto the road right into the path of the hackney."

The man I'd started to understand became the malevolent builder of fences, complete with a sinister grin. Henderson erupted in laughter.

I wanted to take every kind thought back. "How can you be cheered? You want me to think you a monster again?"

"The irony has humored me. Juliet is murdered with a ribbon necklace, one of the things she loves most. Miss Bumners, the efficient polishing maid, is smothered with orange oil. And now Sinclair, a drunk and a driver, is trampled by a hackney outside of a tavern."

He sobered and craned his head against the chair. "And for thinking I'm a monster, when did that stop?"

"Teacup. He's a better judge of character than me. He's curled by your foot and you have no bacon."

Henderson looked down at my dog leaning contently on his boot. "Our murderer has a strong sense of irony. Whoever it is, they must be a poet."

"Sinclair was drunk when he talked to me. It could've been an accident. Miss Bumners and Mrs. Henderson are the only two confirmed to be murdered."

"No. They all were murdered. It would be an injustice if this was a coincidence." He thumbed his lips. "And I suppose you have a plan to catch the killer, and you need my help?"

"No. I don't even know why I'm here."

"You know exactly why you are here." His tone went from jovial to smug. "You have more questions. You're dying to ask them."

My grip tightened on the chair back. "Yes, I want to know what you are thinking. Why haven't you looked for the killer? When Duncan returns, you will still be his prime suspect."

He tucked his arms behind his neck. "Lady Worthing, why should I search, when my busybody neighbor continues to put herself in dire circumstances to find the killer?"

"Why didn't I tell Duncan the truth? I'd be free of this. You'd be rotting in Newgate."

His face blanked, and he stood, tugging at his waistcoat. He bowed for a moment with the light of the sconces glowing on his rich, dark hair. Faint threads of silver were there, twisting and shimmering.

Then he walked to me, his indigo eyes never blinking.

His height buried me in shadows. "I've been wondering why you didn't correct me. Duncan trusts you. You could've cleared things up nicely. And I'd be imprisoned. My sister would be safe. You'd have a nicely wrapped-up murder investigation, further proving your utility to the man."

"But you said you didn't do it."

"Oh, now you don't believe me again. Is this like the Ali Baba actor? Must say I'm innocent the right way and repeat the phrase correctly, like the poor befuddled player. 'Open Sesame. Open Sesame, Abigail Carrington Monroe.' There, have I unlocked your trust?"

"I didn't watch the play, remember? How would I know if you said it right? How do I know if I let my guard down you won't use it to your advantage?"

The crinkle in his eyes said he would. "Give me the set number of times I must recite my innocence before you accept it, Abigail Monroe."

He was angry that it took me a while to believe him. "I suppose an entitled, privileged man expects everyone to believe him. For once, think of my position. All we've done is argue, until your wife died. Quarrels make nothing easy."

"Looking for ease, Abigail? You had a chance to tell your truth. Tell me, is it because you're a woman you think someone like Duncan won't accept your testimony? Or is it that being a Blackamoor woman who has married well, you believe that your soft, supple skin bears suspicion?"

I hadn't noticed until now how he kept saying my name with increasing familiarity. "What game is this?"

"Must be difficult to be you." His whispers teased my ear, the cheekbone of the side he favored. "Your mind must be fearful and constantly fighting your logic. Never trusting anyone has to be lonely."

I couldn't move or he'd know I was frightened, or worse, acknowledge that part of me believed this.

His hands went to my shoulders, close to the buttons of my collar. "This artery here would be all that's needed to kill. One slice and it's done. Much less work than strangling or smothering. And anyone, man or woman with good aim and a sharp weapon, could do it. That's how I'd do it."

Trying to be stone, trying to project bravery, I made my arms stiff at my sides. "I trust my cousin, godfather, my close set of friends."

"Do any of them know you're here, confronting a man you don't trust? This is your second visit in days."

No one knew I was here.

I was with a man who'd seen more death than many. Maybe that's why he had to laugh about it. To make sense of senselessness.

But I didn't know Henderson.

Had no idea what he was capable of; yet, I stood rigid as a board as his palms skirted my neck, his grip tightening.

"Pressing here, this spot, after a few seconds can render the victim unconscious. See, much less effort. Nonetheless, getting your victim to run out into the path of carriages, I guess takes the least amount of effort."

The pressure of his hand shifted again. I felt the warmth of his fingers teasing the fine hair along my neck. Any shift or attempt at running would tighten his grip like a noose.

"My father's old rapier is in a drawer. If it were polished, I'd show you where a proper slit would make the most effective wound. Quick and painless if the blade is sharp."

My swallow fell down the hole of my throat, sort of like tossing a pebble down a well—it made a slow descent with a distant thud.

He had nothing to lose.

But neither did I. "You didn't kill Juliet Henderson. It's taken until now for me to realize you're the type of man who would've told me, grinned at your cleverness, and not felt any remorse at the admission."

His laugh boomed, and he backed up to the other side of the desk. "You're a brave one." Then, as if nothing had happened, he picked up Teacup, cradling him in his large palms. "You're brave, like this scruffy thing. And your skin is supple."

Henderson's gaze was pleasant and unrecognizable from before, when he'd shifted into something monstrous. He cuddled Teacup, and my dog licked the hands that could've killed me. "I apologize for frightening you, Lady Worthing. I let my teasing go on too long. I'm working on restraint, but that's why we get an overcomplicated fence between us."

"Then I wonder what your garden will look like." Rubbing my neck, fluffing the wilted lace of my gown, I caught his gaze. "Look, I'll stop bothering you and we can return to never talking or even acknowledging the other exists, once we find the murderer."

"Or murderers. These killings don't all have to be related."

"No, your original logic is right. They do have to be related. I want to go to Chelsea tomorrow. I need to interview your brother-in-law. If Miss Bumners, Juliet, and the minister are from Chelsea, that could be the connection. Tanner has already savagely threatened Mr. Shaw. I'm sure he'd have killed him, if my solicitor hadn't gotten away."

"Juliet stopped giving her brother money. That would make Tanner angry."

"If she spent the allowance on Mr. Benjamin, Mr. Tanner might know that as well. The minister could be the next target."

"Can you think of a logical reason why the good reverend might want to kill Tanner? A good murdering pair should work both ways."

I shrugged. I couldn't see one. "I know you'd like Benjamin to be guilty, to get him away from Mary."

"No, I don't want him guilty if it means my sister might confess to prove her love. She's read too many of my poets and could be swayed to be overly dramatic."

"You haven't been able to dissuade her? Benjamin is wrong for her, especially with his involvement with Mrs. Henderson."

"I haven't told her that part. Mary loved Juliet." With a loud, long sigh, he dipped his head to Teacup. "When she comes home tonight, I'll tell her the rest. She's with an old family friend in Mayfair. The old woman's like an aunt."

"Be gentle with Mary. It will break her heart. And if Benjamin did kill your wife or Miss Bumners, he's dangerous."

His tone softened. "You'll give up on me, but will still try to save my sister. Admirable."

"This trail of bodies is leading to everyone that Mrs. Henderson cared about. Mary's vulnerable. Broken hearts or great disappointments can make one careless."

"Is that from experience?"

"My sister. I didn't pay attention to her pain. I've lost her. I wouldn't want that to happen with any siblings that care for each other."

"Duly noted. I love Mary very much." He handed me Teacup. "Allow me to take you to Chelsea. It's too dangerous to go without me. I can control Tanner."

"At twelve-thirty, come to my house. My driver will take us."

Henderson nodded, but his eyes drifted again to some unreadable look. "I suppose my driver and vehicle are out of the question. 'Open sesame—' "

A tap on the door interrupted. "Yes," Henderson said.

His butler, Jyles, came in with a tray and a bottle of wine. "Your port, sir. I didn't know you had a guest. I'd have brought another glass."

"Don't fuss on my account. I'm leaving. Thank you again for finding Teacup. I should trust more of what you've said, on matters of training and repetition."

Henderson's face remained blank, but his eyes lit. He walked to and held the door. "Sorry again," he whispered.

"Sir," Jyles said, putting the tray next to Donne, "you asked me to tell you when Miss Henderson arrived. She has. Shall I send her down?"

"No, I'll come up. Should I escort you back, Lady Worthing?"

I stepped outside and saw my lantern glowing on my terrace table. "My light will guide me back."

Waving me forward, he grunted. "I suspect it will."

He lingered for a moment, watching. When I'd crossed the invisible divide, he returned to his study. Yet, I felt him watching through his window.

When I stepped into my parlor, I extinguished my lamp, set Teacup free, and started to my bedchamber.

Rogers stopped me in the hall. "There you are, ma'am."

"Good night, sir."

"Wait, ma'am. You have a visitor in the drawing room."

"At this time of night? Is it Mr. Vaughn or Mr. Shaw?"

He shook his head. "It's Mr. Benjamin of Saint Margaret's."

Not exactly the person I wanted to see at this moment, now that I was beginning to think him guilty. "I suppose it couldn't wait. Show him to my parlor."

"Very good, ma'am. I will go get him."

I passed by the hall mirror and saw a woman too tired to be scared. If Benjamin was guilty, I hoped he'd had his fill of killing tonight.

Chapter 21

Walking slowly, I made it upstairs to my bedchamber without a telltale squeak. No laudanum drops tonight. I had a feeling that I was too tired to dream. That level of exhaustion made for the best sleep.

After letting my guest wait as I refreshed my face with cool water, I entered my parlor. Mr. Benjamin stood, but continued to entertain Teacup. It seemed the minister liked jingling my terrier's bell toy, back and forth, even under a chair leg.

Maybe my boy wasn't that good at judging character.

Mr. Rogers stood at attention, a good distance away, as if my little angel would lunge at him. Teacup would never do that while playing. After he was done was a different matter.

My butler hovered for a moment, but after some casual conversation about church service and hymnals, he made his way to the door without Teacup barking at him. With a hand to his dark jacket, Rogers said, "I'll have Mrs. Smith bring a service of tea."

"Is she still up, sir?"

"No one sleeps until you do, Lady Worthing. And everyone is upset about Sinclair."

He bowed and disappeared, and I felt terrible. They were up. They were mourning. And I didn't know.

"It was an awful day today," Mr. Benjamin said. "I wanted to make sure you were well. You looked shaken at Olive's."

My mother's quilt was on the sofa. I started to pull it about me, but I saw Juliet. My hand trembled.

"I knew you were upset. This is terrible."

"I'm fine, sir. I should go check on everyone. Sinclair was a favorite." I started to rise, but the minister stayed seated. "I'll wait."

He dropped the toy and Teacup charged it. The dog scooped it up and vanished under the chair. A bell would jingle every couple of minutes.

"It's not necessary, Mr. Benjamin. If you don't mind—"

"Your little terrier has a future, Lady Worthing. He'd make an admirable change ringer for Saint Margaret's or perhaps the Abbey."

"Is that your goal, sir? To reach the Abbey? It's a big one."

"Well, Westminster is a big church. The church of kings and queens."

"I was conversing with my neighbor, telling him about poor Mr. Sinclair."

"How is Mr. Henderson? He was quiet and reserved—even through what I'd call a decent eulogy at his late wife's funeral."

"He's mourning, sir. Everyone's different in how it happens, how it looks. He's heavily upset that someone killed his wife. And in such a brutal manner."

Rubbing my throat, I smelled juniper berries on my fingers. "I'm told there are a lot of easier ways to kill someone than strangling."

He looked away for a moment. "Ah. I suppose. I wouldn't know."

"Wouldn't know an easier way to kill, or you think strangling is easy?"

He bit his lips. "I think you are mixing up my words. I'm sorry Mrs. Henderson is dead and Mr. Sinclair, too."

"What about Miss Bumners?"

"I . . . I didn't know her that well, but I don't think anyone meant for her to die. Must have been some tragic accident, like Sinclair."

"That would be a comforting thought, like this quilt. But it was murder."

He shrugged. "I'm sure Lord Duncan will sort it out."

Oh, my. How classic. He didn't appreciate my opinion and disqualified it. Perhaps *this* woman should make him squirm. "Have you known the Hendersons long? I was under the impression that you all were close."

His slick smile faded. "My family knew of the Tanners of Chelsea. We are from the same area, but our families ran in different circles."

"Really. How different?"

"Well, I'm a third son with some connections. The Tanners are good, honest farm people. Not sure how a dairymaid married into the Hendersons. And with no children, there won't be much mention of her. That is sad."

Women shouldn't be brood mares to be considered accomplished. Or was that why she was murdered? Becoming pregnant by one of her lovers . . .

"She will be remembered by those she loved and those who loved her," I said, "And marrying above one's station is not a crime."

"If so, then you'd be arrested, Lady Worthing. I mean to say you've done well. James Monroe, the Lord Worthing—they will write textbooks on his exploits."

"All mothers want their daughters to marry well. Even Blackamoor ones."

He offered that nervous chuckle that most did when I acknowledged the unspoken racial truth.

"You married well, ma'am. Pity he's someone twice your age and always away."

Mrs. Smith came in, saving me from uttering a sharp retort for his condescension. Her arms were full with the silver service and a plate of sweet biscuits.

Yet, her eyes were wet with sorrow. "Mr. Sinclair was a good one. Kind. It's a shame."

"Mrs. Smith, go on to bed. My guest will be leaving shortly."

She wiped at her cheeks, curtsied, and left.

I kept calm until the squeaks said she'd taken the stairs. "I don't think anyone cares much for age differences when both parties are of legal age to make such weighty decisions. Twenty, not fifteen, I think is a good metric." I lifted the plate to him. "Take a ginger biscuit. The recipe was invented in the 1200s by Franconia monks."

"Thank you." He took one. "I meant no offense. It's well done on your part. And solving petty crimes for Worthing and Lord Duncan is to be commended." Putting a piece of the spicy sweet cookie into his mouth, he crunched and munched, quieting for a moment.

Then he made a face at Teacup, who'd poked his head out. "Delicious. And there's nothing wrong with ambition. A daughter of a famed courtesan who married one of the biggest financiers of the East India Company, that's ambition and luck. Then the luck ran out, I suppose. Then, poof, you marry Lord Worthing."

"That's the mystery of life. One minute you're up, then down. You never know what can happen, Mr. Benjamin."

He stretched and took another biscuit. "I do a lot to let those in the neighborhood know that I'm on their side. Nothing of the past matters. Only what we make of today."

"That's a very good sentiment. I thank you for coming—"

"It is my pleasure. I want you to come to my church. You haven't taken me up on my offer of a tour of Saint Margaret's."

"Is that what you did for Mrs. Henderson, take her on tours? Convince her with your considerable charms to accept your special attention?"

The happy expression the minister bore dissolved like a sugar cube bobbing in hot tea. "Sinclair was a drunk. His blind loyalty to Mrs. Henderson might have him confused."

"Miss Bumners wasn't confused. She seemed clear about a relationship between the two of you."

His gaze shifted to the right. "I can be a bit of a flirt. But if you think I killed Juliet, I mean Mrs. Henderson, you're wrong. She was married. Why would I take her from a situation where someone else is paying her bills and she can no longer afford to gift trinkets or church donations? So please be careful with your words. Rumors can be hurtful. Like if it gets out you're spending time at night next door."

"Mr. Henderson's grieving. And he needed to know his wife's driver died. Weren't you the last man to talk with him before Sinclair was killed? The poor man seemed scared that you'd seen him talking too much. Her driver would know a lot about you and Mrs. Henderson's comings and goings, with whom she visited at night."

"I didn't kill him. I'm not the hackney driver."

Setting my tea down, I put my hands to my wrinkled carriage gown, which had bits of mud from the walk to Henderson's study. "I'm showing how things can be twisted."

"But rumors won't impact you, Lady Worthing. Or the naval hero. You have fortunes and positions. For someone like me, rumors can be deadly. I've ambitions. I don't want anything to impede them."

"Then perhaps you shouldn't dally with a young girl, someone half your age. As you said, that can be rife with problems."

"Is that what Mr. Henderson told you? He's a jealous, controlling man. I think him capable of killing his wife over rumors."

"Mr. Benjamin, it's not a rumor when I saw you at Saint Margaret's with Mary Henderson."

He nodded and sank back into his chair. "You were coming for the tour. I told you I can be a bit flirtatious. It's my way to make others comfortable. I think many can misread my intentions."

"Kissing Mary at Saint Margaret's while you pay choirboys to ring the bells seems like a definitive action."

His smile widened, and I prepared to receive a trite "oh, my goodness" and a feigned blush. Instead, he stood and preened at my fireplace, showing off a white damask waistcoat. "I'm fond of Miss Henderson. She's persistent, following me. Showing up places. She knows what she wants."

"She's young. She's barely fifteen."

"I know." He ran a hand through his dark hair. "In a few years, if she remains attached to me—a man can use a wife of means."

"At least you're honest about it."

"I'm a minister. I appeal to a Higher Authority. And if I promised to amend my ways, you should consider coming to Saint Margaret's for a proper tour. It's a church with great history and passion for your causes. You meet with Wilberforce often?"

Did he know of the secret Clapham meeting I missed or the public one at Holy Trinity? I sipped my tea like nothing was wrong and that my alibi wasn't one lie away from being revealed. "Mr. Benjamin, I'm passionate about abolition. The cause is bigger than one person. It's bigger than me, than Wilberforce. Abolition has ground to a halt. I don't want to continue the delay because of some social failing of mine. People need to be free. People will be free."

"Then we agree that rumors are terrible. I think we understand each other." He moved to the door, squeaking each step. His brow furrowed and he tried to move more easily.

"They make less noise in summer and fall."

"The beauty of an old house of an established family. The good and the bad. I can't wait to see you at Saint Margaret's, or perhaps at Westminster Abbey. I want the support of a strong congregation."

"Then you definitely should squash rumors."

"Golly, a minister can dream, but I will work on it. If I serve the Church with all my might, it will make up for my short-comings. Next year, one of the Abbey's change bell directors is retiring. Opportunity is on the horizon . . ."

"I'm impressed, Mr. Benjamin. Better get those dalliances under control."

"Completely understood. I'll work on clearing up misunder-standings."

Rogers returned. "Do you need anything?"

"No, but Mr. Benjamin is leaving now. Can you show him out?"

My butler looked solemnly at the minister. "Mrs. Smith wanted to know if you were going to ring the bells of the church to-night?"

"Tell her no, but tomorrow. We've had many deaths affect-ing Westminster. It will be for all."

"I'll let her know." Rogers held the door to the parlor open.

Benjamin crossed the threshold, tugging on his pristine waistcoat. "A pleasure, Lady Worthing. See you on Sunday."

I nodded. "Wouldn't miss it."

"Capital. This is wonderful." He left my parlor.

Rogers picked up the service, but left my cup. "Charming devil."

My eyes locked with his. We were in full agreement. "That has to be the worst kind of minister."

"Yes, ma'am. Get rest, ma'am."

"You do the same, Rogers."

*   *   *

As soon as the parlor door closed, and I was alone with Teacup, he finally came fully out from the chair.

Then he ran back under when Mary rushed inside from my terrace.

She heaved. Her face was flustered. "Is he after you now?"

"What? Mary, sit. What are you talking about?"

"It's always a social visit in the evenings. That's when he's with the women in the parish. Why does he torture me?"

"Mary, calm down. You're not making sense."

"Just stay away from him. You're married. Can't you married women leave any man alone?"

I grasped her about her middle and held her while she shook. I tried to calm her, but she beat on my shoulders. "He loves me, and you all want him away from me."

She became a sobbing wreck in my arms. But I held her fast, like she was Dinah; I refused to let her go.

"Did Juliet want him away from you? Did she tell you what was going on between them?"

"Yes. She did. She said she never meant to hurt me. Then I told her I wished her dead. And she died the next week."

I looked into her sorrowful eyes. "Mary, you can't wish someone dead. You didn't strangle Juliet. You didn't kill her."

"How do I make it up to her? I wanted something horrible to happen to her. Then she suffered cruelly. She's dead. My fault. *Mine.*"

Mary broke free.

I chased and watched her run back to Henderson's door.

When I saw him snatch her up and bring her inside, I returned to my parlor and my cold tea.

Henderson was right about a few things, except his sister. She exhibited a desperate passion, more than a passing fancy for Benjamin.

It was dangerous and unhealthy for a young lady to be inclined to love someone who wasn't good for her. How desperate would unrequited love make her?

Desperate enough to kill?

And she had a brother who'd take the blame, if needed.

This was dangerous territory for me, fearing for both Mary
and Henderson.

Chapter 22

At five minutes after twelve, Henderson showed on my terrace. Dressed in dark blues, from midnight-colored breeches to an indigo waistcoat and jacket, my brooding neighbor looked handsome. He might've always been, but viewing him on my territory without annoyance might have swayed my perspective.

"You are early."

"This is not early." He stepped inside. The music of my creaking floor squeaked a little.

"How's Mary? She came to visit last night."

His brow rose. "She's distraught, like the rest of my household. Jyles told everyone about Sinclair. Then I told her about Juliet and the minister."

"Wait, your butler told them? How did he know? Did Mr. Benjamin visit your house, too?"

His gaze shifted and he looked to my windows. "Small Westminster community, I guess. But the adulterous minister was here before my sister?"

"She saw Mr. Benjamin visiting. That is why she came."

He spun back with fire in his eyes. "The bastard. Did he make threats?"

"None that I can't handle."

His hands fisted; then he shoved his arms behind his back. "Don't let him near you. I'll keep him from my sister."

This tone, dry and dark, reminded me of last night when I insulted him and he'd tried to frighten me.

I would be wary if I didn't know this anger was from his concern for his sister, even a little for me. "Don't do anything rash. Your sister's vulnerable. You saw how she was shaking."

He grunted and paced, but this time my floor decided to quiet and not squeak under his feet. "She was distraught last night. I made her some tea from kava root. That seemed to calm her."

"Is this some new discovery for your garden?"

"Yes, for the added hothouse, but the root is not new. Scholander discovered the plantings about forty years ago. Many have found it to offer clarity of thought and calmness."

"Forty years? That doesn't sound like enough time to make sure something is safe."

"It's been around for thousands of years and used by tribes in Vanuatu and Bligh Islands. But a European man is credited with its discovery."

For a brief moment, I could believe he understood my plight, those of color, or foreign descent, who get trampled in British ideals. The collegial tension in the air felt a little too chummy, too friendly. Not exactly the atmosphere I wanted when going on an expedition with him. "Captain Cook and William Bligh are two of Lord Worthing's favorite explorers."

"Hmm, a man turned pirate and a wronged naval officer. Worthing has a good sense of humor." Henderson's brows furrowed, and he shifted past the sofa and headed to the mantel. "You don't seem enthused about your husband's explorations."

Was my countenance slipping?

Did Henderson detect my annoyance at James, who should be here helping me? Today marked another month with no letter. And I hadn't finished a single draft to send to him.

"Lady Worthing?"

"I . . . Forgive me."

"Are you having a vision? Is there danger going into Chelsea?"

With a shake of my head, I dismissed the notion. "My husband shouldn't have told you anything about a few coincidences. I merely wondered where the Bligh Islands might be."

"They're called Timor now and are in the Pacific Ocean. Past the penal colony of New South Wales."

"Oh. There. That's a lifetime away."

His gaze moved from me to the mirrored glass above the fireplace mantel. We both were in it. His height and indigo attire went well with my short lilac Spencer jacket and goldenrod-yellow gown. If not for the wary expression on my face, I'd say we looked like confidants.

"Shall we go? My brother-in-law is best to be seen before dark. He can be testy."

Picking up my bisque-colored bonnet, I nodded. "If *you're* calling someone 'testy', we should hurry."

He followed me down the hall.

I heard his footfalls for a moment and then they disappeared. When I gathered my gloves and reticule, we walked out of the house to my yellow bounder.

Henderson stopped. "This small vehicle is what you've chosen? Why not the Berlin?"

"This is small and discreet."

"It's yellow and not even a good yellow, like your gown, which is more a plantain. This is like a banana."

"Nonsense. Rawlins can get us in and out of anywhere in the city before anyone notices. We look like another jarvey."

"We're going to milk country. That is fields and cows and . . . and milk. This is *yellow.* No matter how good of a driver your Rawlins is, this will stand out."

"You're expecting trouble?"

He rubbed at his face. "Lady Worthing, please."

"You know there's going to be violence?"

His countenance never changed from blank and handsome.

Rawlins bounced down and held the door.

I swept in and adjusted my skirt and waited.

My neighbor stood outside. His normal grimace now appeared pained.

"For someone fretting about the time, you seem to be wasting it."

He swiped at his neck, mumbled something, which I was sure a lady shouldn't hear, then climbed inside.

As soon as he settled with arms folded against his dark waistcoat, we were under way.

Rawlins took the route we'd used to return from Holy Trinity. "We're on Millbank now." My gaze went to Henderson and he seemed to be breathing heavily, like he had to force himself to do so.

"Are you well, sir?"

"Quite fine, I assure you."

He didn't look fine. He looked positively green.

Dropping my caution, I put my hand to his forehead, then to his reddening cheeks. "You don't have a fever. But you're warm."

He took my hand and held it to his chest. "I'm a physician. I can tell if I'm ill. But I will make allowances for this intrusion. I did say your skin is supple."

Snatching my hand away, I tucked it under my reticule. "My father's stubborn, too. He'll work himself into a raging fever rather than take time to be fit."

"Milady, I'm not your father."

"You could've sent a note. I can surely handle a visit by myself."

"Tanner's not civilized. There's a long stretch of road to his farm in dairy country. That is probably how he attacked your Shaw. Tell me what the minister said last night."

"He talked about rumors, his ambitions, and Mary."

Henderson sat up. "My sister didn't cry when I told her about Juliet and Benjamin, not until she ran from your house."

"Your sister knew of their affair, but she's desperately in love with him. I think I convinced Benjamin to let her go. It doesn't bode well for an ambitious rector to dally with someone this young."

A grunt, a flexing of his palms into a fist—then my companion relaxed again. "You should be more careful about letting a murderer into your home."

"I let you in."

"No. No, you haven't, because I'd know what you were thinking."

That was odd. But he was odd. "You know it's fine to say you don't hate me anymore."

"I didn't hate you before, Lady Worthing."

"Then why the wall?"

"You accused my dogs of harassing your terrier. You said you wanted them separated. I obliged."

"And, Mr. Henderson, you felt the natural way to handle my objections was to build a wall?"

"It served your purposes. The dogs would be apart. Kept us apart, too."

His breathing seemed to ease the more he talked. I decided I'd keep him chattering, even if I had to ignore his statements with somewhat dual meanings.

"Do you like to draw monstrosities on paper and then build them?"

"Monstrosities? The fence was elegant and an ideal solution."

"And this garden? Will it have a lot of right angles?"

At this, he chuckled. "You'll have to wait and see." He took a long breath. "Thank you."

He looked out the window. "Who do you currently think killed Juliet?"

"I don't know. We're running out of plausible suspects. I'm guessing that you think it is Mr. Benjamin."

"Since you and I didn't kill my wife, Sinclair is dead, as well as Miss Bumners, and I highly doubt Tanner would kill his sister, that leaves only one person in my mind with a great motive."

"Well, Miss Bumners and Mr. Sinclair can be or are eliminated. We're left with Mr. Tanner and Mr. Benjamin. Both have the strength to strangle or smother women, but there could be another suspect. She admitted to me last night she wanted Mrs. Henderson dead."

His gaze narrowed. "No. No. No."

"I didn't say she did, but we don't know who in your household could have overheard her. I doubt that she's been discreet with how much she is enthralled with Benjamin. Someone could tell Duncan. Despite your wanting to accept blame, the magistrate could indict you both."

"My sister didn't do it. And I place Sinclair back on the list. He could've killed Juliet and Bumners and purposely walked in front of the jarvey. Suicide might have been his way to escape guilt."

I wanted to contradict him, but he was right. I hadn't seen Sinclair get hit. He well could've done that to himself.

"Of course, Lady Worthing, if your second sight could help—"

Waving my hands to silence, I struck the seat. Unlike the soft cushions of the Berlin, the bounder was hard. Pain rippled through my wrist. "I didn't see anything."

As I wrung it out, Henderson grabbed my arm and massaged with his thumbs right where I'd whacked myself. "No need for violence."

"So says the man who wanted to choke me. No, correct that. Slice my throat."

"I didn't."

"Why my husband told you something personal about me is confusing."

"But you do have visions?"

Breathe in. Breathe out. "Sometimes. They rarely make sense. I've seen nothing but a blonde, a floating shawl, a streaming ribbon necklace. A kiss. Then cries for help."

His thumb kept working magic on my arm. "There are two pressure points on your wrist. This one is the heart line. It controls the balance of your emotions. The other is an inch or two over in line with your pinky. It regulates happiness."

The way his fingers danced and wove over my arm—I was happy, even sated.

"Now that you've relaxed, look into your dream. Can you see anything new?"

With my bonnet tipped forward, I sat back and tried to remember all the elements, but nothing came to mind.

The jostling of the roads had my knees knocking into his.

He reached for them, steadying me. "I'm not being forward. I'm trying to keep those bony things from impaling me."

"There's not a bony thing on my body."

He reared up and this time he had a smile. "No, you are rightly shaped."

A man's attention wasn't foreign to me, but most of the time, it was ill placed or simply wrong. Though my cheeks warmed at the compliment, this was one of those wrong times from the wrong man. An exploring baron should be sitting across from me saying things to make me blush, to help me remember that I was a beautiful, desirable woman. My youth shouldn't be spent waiting for love.

But that is what I'd done to myself.

My desperation to protect my family and have a more secure life away from my father's thumb meant I was away from everyone. Except for Florentina and Vaughn, I'd been cut adrift. I shouldn't be punished for marrying well.

"Now you're silent."

"I think we hit Grosvenor Row."

He glanced toward the window. Then hit the roof. Rawlins pulled the carriage onto the side of the road close to warehouses opposite the Thames.

Henderson bounced out and bent and gasped. Rawlins approached and the two discussed something. My driver nodded, then climbed back to his seat.

My neighbor remained bent over for a moment, then bounded inside.

He looked pale with his eyes closed and head back against the seat.

"The small space. Is that it? Why didn't you say something?"

"And miss this well-deserved torture? I was abominable last night, Abigail."

The breathless way he said my name was as good as "open sesame."

"I'm sorry. I wasn't thinking," I said.

"No. You were thinking it safe to be in your vehicle, where you have control. Women don't get control. Good to know that you will take it when you want it."

Glancing at him, I didn't know what to say, except I hated this picture he'd drawn of me. "Us being civil is new, but I'd never do something to hurt another person, not on purpose. How long has small places been a problem?"

"A while. Then worsened with my last battle. Something changed being in the hole with Nelson dying."

"Sorry." I stretched my hand to his.

He wouldn't take it. "When you touch me, let it be for any other emotion than pity. A slap is preferable."

My palm curled against my stomach. He felt shamed letting me see this weakness, but to me, it was one of those rare times he appeared human. Actually, that wasn't true; whenever Mary was mentioned, the man's hard exterior softened.

"Let it be known, Mr. Henderson, that I don't pity you. I'm getting better at tolerating your foul moods."

"Never tolerate a thing too long, or ever settle, Lady Worthing. We all know how poorly that can turn out."

Was he referencing his and Juliet's marriage alone, or what he suspected about mine with James?

Or worse, was that a prediction of how I'd come to feel about James the longer he was away?

"Settle in, Lady Worthing. It's a long, winding ride to the Tanner farm."

It was easier to relax now that I was mostly sure of Henderson's innocence.

Yet, the quiet left too much time to think and didn't stop the feeling that I'd missed something obvious, something that could prevent the next death.

Chapter 23

At one o'clock sharp, we reached the road to Chelsea. The famed market would be picked over at this hour. Thank goodness, Mrs. Smith came early enough to select choice cheeses and meats.

My companion still looked uneasy. He folded his arms now.

"We should've taken the Berlin. I thought it would look too presumptuous in the country," I stressed again.

Henderson opened his eyes a smidgen. "Never let fools control your actions, even ones that live next door."

"Let me ask you a question. If your wife hadn't died and she changed her mind about running away to Scotland to divorce you, what would you have done?"

"I don't know. Now we'll never know. But you, Lady Worthing, are you the type to charge in and fix a problem?"

"Yes, I'm not one to let things fester and die."

His brow wrinkled and he turned toward me. "What an odd way of looking at things. I find patience produces the same outcome, a livable solution." Henderson leaned forward and peered out the window. "You need to be careful charging forward. Circumstances and risks be damned—it tends to have repercussions."

That's not exactly how I saw things. I wanted to help, always did. "I suppose if it is the afternoon and I've had my tea, anything is possible."

This produced a rare chuckle from the man.

We bumped onto a desolate stretch of road with cows on either side. Henderson roused and looked anxious to be out of the chaise. We had to be there soon. Chelsea wasn't far.

"May I ask you something? How . . . Why did you marry Juliet Tanner? The Hendersons are very wealthy. To me, it seems you would have many options. And then there's that strange clause of repaying the dowry."

"Well, she didn't save me from a hangman's noose, if that is what you are asking."

I bristled on the seat. "Never mind. I don't know why I'm thinking of you and trying to decide if you were actually targeted by this killing. That someone did this to hurt you."

He sighed and pushed out a long, steady breath. "Think of me all you want. I'll not interrupt any pleasure of yours. And I did callously reference your circumstances, but I've always been curious if you thought your only choice to be secure was marriage to Worthing?"

Part of me wanted to be flippant and say a negated murder sentence was a shameful thing to waste. But that wasn't my motive. "Yes, I wanted security and, in a way, restoration of my family. I thought it all possible with a family friend."

He stared, then looked away, tugging on his waistcoat that had shifted and come undone by his restless movements. "I appreciate your candor, and that you offer it when it's not rightfully deserved. You are different."

"And that's worrisome to you?"

"It's hopeful, Lady Worthing." He rubbed his chin and said, "I suppose Almack's and the happy ton patronesses are where you think suitable love matches are made." He stretched his arms. "But I thought I was saving someone. Thought I gave a friend an opportunity to change her circumstance. Thought I bested my father, picking an unsuitable bride, at least in his standards."

"Then it was love?"

"Perhaps. Maybe for me. Maybe for both of us in the moment. Being away in service to king and country takes a toll. It demands a great deal of effort to keep desire burning. Then the society that she wanted to be a part of used her up and spit her out. Scandal after scandal. Affairs. All detailed in delight by my parents . . . my father particularly. I wanted nothing from him alive, but upon his death, I had access to unbelievable resources. That is why I'm giving Tanner back the dowry he scrounged up for Juliet. Because I can. And he needs the money."

Keeping my eyes low, away from his, I refused to judge his earnest statement. "Out of all this, you and your wife remained friends?"

His countenance eased. "Once your heart isn't affected, it doesn't much matter what anyone does. You're impervious to pain."

"Are you? Henderson, I haven't lived your life, but I know that no matter how we want to distance ourselves from things that hurt us, it's still there when we close our eyes."

"Perhaps that's why I don't sleep that much." Henderson opened his mouth as if to say more, but all I heard was *boom.*

Bang.

Cannons? Fireworks? Muskets?

Henderson shoved me to the ground. "We're being shot at, Lady Worthing."

The carriage ran off the road and cocked sideways against trees.

The whole thing nearly capsized. I was flung against Henderson.

He caught me, but together we were pinned into the corner. The man gasped, then grunted. "Targets."

"Rawlins?"

"I saw him . . . through the slats on the side. He dropped into the tall grass. He's safe for now. Hopefully, he has a weapon."

"A blunderbuss, I think."

Henderson groused, then gasped for air. "That's for close range. Do you have any weapons in here?"

I read his lips. They were too close to ignore, but I didn't quite understand.

"Lady Worthing, I need you to answer. Then I need you to move. The guns are getting closer. Weapons?"

"The compartment."

He pushed me off of him to his left as he went right.

The air smelled of gunpowder and Henderson's sweet juniper berries.

Pushing at the panel, he opened the compartment. His fingers disappeared inside. "Nothing but a knife? No guns? And you run around trying to solve heinous crimes with a play knife?"

"My first heinous crime. And that knife is sharp."

"Only with a lot of force. More than you can offer."

"I've been getting along fine, sir."

"All this time?" He gripped my shoulders like he wanted to shake sense into me. "I'm surprised you're still alive. Do you think your driver could stop me if I intended to get to you?"

With his fingers lashed about my shoulders, I felt small. His eyes looked haggard, tormented.

Something changed in Henderson. The gunshots, the sounds of war, were doing it.

When a shot hit the door and ricocheted above our heads, he threw me underneath him and covered me as if his body could be a shield.

"Tanner!" he called out. "It's me, Henderson. We need to talk."

More bullets answered.

"Guess your brother-in-law's still not in a talking mood."

"Next time we take my carriage. I'm always prepared. I won't let you take such risks again."

Let me?

The sound of guns, closer guns . . . the heat of him, was unbearable. I felt trapped and I had no problem with small spaces.

"Drop the weapon!" Rawlins's voice. "I shoot straight, and I won't stop until you're dead."

"Tanner! It's me, your brother-in-law. Juliet's friend and yours." Henderson yelled this over and over as he continued to shroud me from the musket balls ripping the fabric top of my bounder. "Tanner, it's me. We come in peace."

"No. You come to set me up for the killings. I didn't kill my sister or her maid."

"We know you didn't do it." Henderson gasped between each word. "Now, come on . . . Talk to us. You know who did. I want that person to pay. *Not you.*"

"Do we?" I whispered. "Do we know he didn't do it?"

"Yes, and it's always better to agree with a man shooting at you."

"Everyone stop!" My voice sounded loud, like a trumpet. "We came to see about you, Mr. Tanner. It's me, Lady Worthing."

The bullets stopped for a moment.

"I'll stop if you stop." Tanner's voice, distant and cranky, sounded as it had at the *lichwake.*

"No, ma'am, Lady Worthing. I didn't drive out here to be killed," Rawlins retorted.

I elbowed up from the floor. "Rawlins, I want you to stop. I want you both to agree to a truce. Trust me. I'm coming up to talk."

"Lady Worthing," my driver answered, "I have plenty of bullets."

"I'm coming out, Mr. Tanner. I'm a friend of your sister-in-law. Mary Henderson needs you alive. She desperately needs us to catch your sister's killer."

"The lass is a good one. Juliet loved her. Fine. Lady Worthing, come on out. But no tricks."

When I started to move, Henderson held me about my waist. "Are you insane? You can't trust him."

"I have to. The man with the gun said to come up. I have to agree, like you said."

Henderson's breathing was rapid. He needed out of this vehicle as much as I needed all the shooting to stop.

"Rawlins! We need this man to trust us." I pulled a little from Henderson and pushed open the door. It smacked the side of the bounder and stayed open.

Henderson still had me. He didn't seem to want to let go. "What are you doing, Lady Worthing?"

"Facing destiny. Don't faint on me."

He grunted and gave me a push, helping me reach the carriage door.

Wedging my fingers, I pulled half out of the cabin. "Remember me. I was at the *lichwake*. I saw you grieving. Don't shoot."

With one leap, I dropped to the ground. Didn't hear anything as I dusted my skirts, but as I stood up straight, I came face-to-face with Mr. Tanner and his smoking flintlock.

Chapter 24

Popping my hands into the air, I took a step closer to Jeorge Tanner. "You need to put the weapon down."

"I don't take orders from no wench."

"I'm not a wench. I'm a baroness. And that wasn't an order—it was a suggestion."

"Put the gun down!" Rawlins yelled from behind a tree. From the corner of my eye, I could see his jet-colored flap coat.

"I'll kill her before you can get me. Come out. Let me see you!"

That was stupid. The man had shot and nearly killed Shaw at this distance; he'd maim my driver. "Stay put, Rawlins. That's an order. I'll handle this."

Tanner cocked the gun hammer. "I said I don't take orders from no wench."

"I'm no wench and that wasn't for you. That was for my driver, who will shoot you between the eyes. Don't do it, Rawlins. I think I can reason with Mr. Tanner. We want the same thing, the truth of Juliet's murder. I know you didn't do it."

The fool must have believed my bold talk, for his finger relaxed about the barrel. "Where's Henderson?"

"Injured in the carriage. I need your help to get him out."

He lowered the gun entirely. "I didn't mean to hit him, 'less he did kill Juliet."

I took a step forward. "Listen, Mr. Tanner. You have one bullet in that chamber compared to Rawlins's two. My cousin, the mathematician, would say you have a thirty percent chance of misfire. Ten percent chance of the flintlock jamming or not firing at all. But my driver only needs to see your finger twitch. He has twice the chance of getting it right."

Tanner looked at his gun. Then lifted it again aiming at me. "Then I better not miss."

Well, if I lived to see Florentina again, I could her tell that mathematics didn't work outside of London. When I heard the hammer cock again, I closed my eyes and waited.

Thwack.

Thud.

Something dropped.

It wasn't me. I wasn't dead.

But Tanner began yelling, "You got me!"

His gun had fallen away and the man bled on the ground. My knife was half in his arm.

Henderson had climbed mostly out of the cabin. His thick thighs loomed out the door of the off-kilter carriage.

He'd pitched it and done it with such speed and accuracy that the blade looked to be inches in Tanner's arm.

"I owe you an apology, Lady Worthing," Henderson said as he took a huge breath. "Thrown with speed, this is a useful weapon."

Tanner writhed. He tried to pull the knife out, but couldn't. "Thought you said he was injured."

"Guess you were right not to listen to a wench."

My neighbor and somewhat hero jumped down from the carriage. He pushed at his hair, piling the dark curls back into place. He looked polished and unruffled, nothing of the flustered man who'd suffered a panic attack.

He strode closer. "Let me answer your question. Yes, Lady Worthing. I purposely left him alive. Are you well?"

"Yes." The word came out shaky, but inside I congratulated myself on being lucky. "I'm glad you had charity on Tanner. He needs to tell us who has him rattled. Who made him think anyone coming here has been sent to blame him for murder."

"Stupid, Tanner." Henderson bent to him and started examining the wound. "Didn't hit a main artery. I'm good."

Rawlins came out of hiding and took up Tanner's gun. "What now, ma'am?"

My driver looked relieved, but I knew him. He feared more for my safety than his own.

I folded my arms and looked up at the still-perfect blue sky. "I believe Mr. Henderson will deal with his brother-in-law. Can you get the carriage unstuck? I want to leave as soon as possible."

"Yes. I set the horses free. Let me go get them." He started to turn, then stopped. "I'd kill him for you, if you asked."

Putting my hand on his, I gave it a little squeeze. "That's why I didn't. Get our carriage righted, sir. And bless you."

Rawlins nodded, leveled his tricorn, and disappeared in the high jade grass.

"Tanner, why must you always be a fool?" Henderson sounded exasperated, but he'd pulled the blade from the man's shoulder and was using strips of his brother-in-law's shirtsleeve to stave off the wound. "This is not how you greet in-laws. Especially one here to give you your two thousand pounds."

"Why are you giving me money when you're going to say I murdered Juliet?" He then screamed as Henderson shifted the man's hurt arm.

"Because I don't think you did it, Tanner. The nice lady and I want answers. Tell her what she wants. Don't be belligerent."

The man winced. "If that's fancy talk for stupid, you're right. Should've shot through the carriage, then shot the wench."

"She's a lady." Henderson lifted his hands high in the air. "Your lack of respect says you want me to let you bleed out like a pig in the smokehouse. And keep my money. How generous."

"All right. Fine. But I'm not letting you blame me for my sister's death. I didn't do it. I have no trust of you, Henderson. Nobody from your family."

I moved and stood behind my neighbor. I wasn't the squeamish type, not till I saw the blood covering my knife. Henderson was strong and accurate.

"Lady Worthing, ask your questions of Tanner. If he's good and answers, I'll make sure he lives."

"Wait? What?" The foul man looked pale and the cloth had soaked through. "I'll answer."

"Mr. Tanner, when was the last time you saw your sister alive?"

"The day before she died. She said she wasn't going to be able to help me out for a while. She was going to leave him." He winced when Henderson tied another strip of cloth about his shoulder. "Hey, watch it. Juliet said you knew she was leaving and was good with it. I figured you were lying. All you Hendersons could lie real good."

Oh, how I wished I weren't trying to find a murderer. I'd love to know what he meant. But there was no time. I stooped closer. "Whom did she say she was going to run away with and when?"

"She told me she was leaving soon, but wouldn't give no names."

"Mr. Tanner, do you have any suspicions with whom?"

He pulled to a seated position. "Don't know. Someone she'd

known for a while. Someone I think was possessive. Had her scared once. Then she told me it was some misunderstanding. Should've followed up. Should've protected my sister."

Henderson was quiet. Too quiet. I wished I could read his mind and would know what wild thoughts were running through it. His fingers were stained red, but Tanner's wounds seemed to have slowed. "Go get stitched up." He flung a sack of coins at him. "The dowry money. Get someone who doesn't ask too many questions."

Tanner seized the bag. "Why are you being good to me? I sort of tried to shoot you."

"Because Juliet deserved better. We both failed her."

Rawlins got the horses hitched, then used their might to pull the carriage free. The cloth top of the chaise had rips where bullets had pierced. Tanner could've truly killed us.

"Field hands coming to see what is happening. Lady Worthing, Mr. Henderson." Rawlins waved us to the carriage.

"In a moment, sir," I said, then went to Tanner and grabbed him by the shirt collar. "Whom was she having an affair with?"

"A lot of people." Tanner started chuckling. "She loved to be in love. Passed the time while Henderson was away. She'd talk about being trapped in that town house for days with nothing but his staff. The fussy butler and maids, she didn't need all that, you know. She kept looking for one person to love her."

"Sir, Madam. Company dead ahead." Rawlins's warning was timely. I saw people coming closer with pitchforks.

Henderson cleaned the knife on remnants of his brother-in-law's coat. "It is time to go, Lady Worthing."

"Who killed Miss Bumners?"

"I don't know. She seemed like a pleasant woman. Her family lives on up the road."

My neighbor shifted. "We need to leave, Lady Worthing. Tanner, call off your people and no one else gets injured."

"They think the tax man has come to count windows on us. I told them that. They hate the tax man."

"We're leaving now." Henderson picked me up and tossed me over his shoulder.

"Wait. Mr. Tanner, who told you we were coming?"

"Mr. Benjamin. The minister's getting ready to leave town for a while, but said he wanted to look out for me. He said you'd set the magistrate and the sheriff on me."

"Why would I do that?" Henderson didn't put me down. He dropped me into the chaise. Then ripped off the rest of the top. "I know you didn't do it."

"The minister said you'd pin it on me because I threatened my sister when she stopped giving me money."

"I didn't know you threatened my wife." Henderson jumped off the chaise, went back to the man, and punched him in the eye. "There. But I wouldn't turn you in for something you didn't do."

He came back and climbed in beside me.

"You should've slapped him for what he did to Shaw."

"Another time, Lady Worthing. Rawlins, get us going."

My driver did.

The horses started moving as if nothing had happened. The ride had more bumps. I was sure something had bent or become misaligned when we ran off the road.

Everything was silent, but the dragging rhythm of the undercarriage.

Henderson showed me my cleaned knife and stowed it into my compartment. "What are you thinking?"

"For Mr. Benjamin to come out here and not be shot at, like Shaw or us, means that he and Tanner may be closer than we know."

"How so? Tanner could've shot at Shaw because he's a stranger or because he's . . ."

"Blackamoor? Perhaps. But even you said the man was prone to shoot first and ask questions later. He didn't do that to Benjamin. And he took the man's counsel. Tanner believed you'd come here to get him hauled away for murder."

With eyes distant or looking up at the very blue sky, Henderson sat back. "So, what are you saying?"

"I think that the Chelsea set is the key to our mystery. Something happened among the four of them."

"Four? Juliet, Tanner, Miss Bumners, and Benjamin."

"Yes. I think Benjamin planned on leaving the ministry for a wealthy woman. Mrs. Henderson changed her mind because of you. Perhaps being away, living in Cheapside, she decided she wanted you again. Remember, she came back to Eleven Greater Queen Street with no luggage. No luggage, no actual running away. It was another theatrical scene. But Mr. Benjamin couldn't accept rejection. He killed Juliet."

"Why would Miss Bumners have to die?"

"Not sure. Maybe she knew the truth. If Juliet wanted to come back to you, you wouldn't be a suspect. Her lover would be. That's the minister. The kiss in my dream. That had to be with her lover. The way Juliet was exposed. It was intimate."

Henderson was stone-faced. He didn't look convinced, but he didn't tell me my theory was wrong. "My sister will be devastated if this is true."

"Worse than that. If Benjamin is planning to leave town, he might take Mary with him as insurance. She's in love. She'd go."

"My sister. Mr. Rawlins, do hurry back to Westminster."

When I was sure the breeze wouldn't drown out my words, I turned to my neighbor. "Thank you for saving my life and proving my choice of weapon is effective."

Henderson leaned to his side, then sat back. "You're welcome." He shook his head. "And when you are ready to be trained in better methods, let me know."

I settled in and watched my bonnet sail away. It didn't matter. We needed distance from Tanner and his ilk, before someone with better aim finished filling my bounder with holes.

The wobbling, dragging sound underneath the bounder continued.

My curls frizzed in the breeze. The dust of the road choked and settled all around us. I must look a sight.

My companion next to me looked stiff. Very normal for him.

Rawlins pulled my mauled yellow carriage to the side of the road, then came around to the side. "Ma'am, Mr. Henderson, we're safe from Tanner, but we need to stop. I think something under the carriage is bent. We're close to Chelsea Market. Go over the hill and look around. Refresh yourselves while I fix things. I won't have us broken down. Or suffer more injuries."

"This wasn't your fault, Rawlins. Not at all."

"But we have to get back to town. Mary—"

"My sister is fine." Henderson jumped down and held his arm out to me. "I think this is a brilliant time to visit the market."

I couldn't help staring at his friendly gesture. "We can stay here. The market's a public place, sir. To look at us one would never guess we've been shot at or are merely tolerating one another."

He stepped back and let me exit on my own.

"I'd assumed, since we were on top of one another and you've been in my arms at least twice, we were more familiar, Lady Worthing. Pardon my assumption."

As we walked a little distance, and I was sure we were out of Rawlins's hearing, I decided to tell him what I thought. "Listen, you buffoon. We have to be careful. We're still suspects with no evidence the minister did anything. Benjamin hinted at starting rumors of neighbors visiting each other at night. He doesn't know we are at each other's throat."

"My brother-in-law is a fool, but he genuinely loved his sister. He's not Juliet's killer. It has to be Benjamin. But why would he kill Miss Bumners? Too many people knew of his affair with Juliet."

"What if they were killed by different people? That makes no sense. What are we missing, Henderson?"

We walked a little more. The vendors were visible, along with cows. Chelsea Market—all the best cheese was surely gone. "Henderson, I'm sorry. Sounds as if Mrs. Henderson was going to return to you. Guess you would have had to answer that festering question of what next."

"Juliet didn't love me. I wasn't who she wanted."

"Then explain why there was no portmanteau, why her place wasn't packed."

"It was not possible for her to return to me." He shrugged. "There's a dairy farmer we should see—that is, if he's here."

"When you say 'it was not possible,' do you mean not possible for her to return to her senses or that you'd take her back?"

In one glance, I was again scorched in indigo flames.

"Juliet and I were friends. We were not in love. Don't know whom Tanner was talking about. But save your questions for this gentleman."

An old man in a dark jacket and loose breeches and dusty boots sat between two big, pretty brown cows.

"Mr. Bumners, don't tell me you're selling your favorite beasts?"

"No. Wanted some company in the market." He cupped his hand to his eyes. Then he saluted. "Lieutenant Commander Henderson, sir, how are you?"

"Managing. I'm sorry about your daughter."

The weathered face looked away. "She was into some financial scheming." He shook his head.

"Was this last one involving a minister?"

"Naw. I wished she'd be more active in the Church. I liked her to be around more good influences."

The adulterous minister, who was possibly a murderer, wasn't what this man had in mind.

"Tell me," Henderson said, "one sailor to another. I'm looking for who hurt her. It had to be this scheme."

Mr. Bumners swallowed. "She was helping a man run off with a young heiress. The man was going to get the dowry, then abandon the girl."

"How was Miss Bumners part of it?"

"Half the fortune if she looked the other way when he wanted to meet with the girl." The old man grunted. The cows mooed. "My daughter was in love with this criminal. I told her it was wrong. 'For the wages of sin—' "

" 'Is death,' " Henderson said. He bowed his head and looked as if he'd spit fire. Then he stormed off.

"Sir, Mr. Henderson hasn't been feeling well. Do you know what would happen to the heiress?"

"Can't say that I do. But to be ruined and left in Scotland. That must be hard for a girl."

I took coins from my reticule and bought the last piece of goat cheese.

"Let it set out one more day. Then scrape it good." The man stroked the heifer with the big brown eyes.

Good, stinky goat cheese. It would be delicious with toast.

I took my parcel and went after Henderson, but not without looking back at this man grieving his daughter, hating her choices.

If I died with my sister missing—missing because she hated my choices—was that how my father would be—all alone with questions?

Henderson looked furious when I caught up to him. His indigo jacket was dusty, smelled of gunpowder and his eyes were hell's fury. "Can't believe they planned to do that to Mary."

"Which they?"

"Bumners and Benjamin. Not Juliet. She loved Mary."

"You believe Mary's the heiress? Calm down, Henderson. We talked to a grieving man. He could be twisting things up. We need corroboration."

"My sister is a target. She could be a target. But he'd get nothing. All her money is in a trust, which I administer."

"Calm down, please."

He looked straight ahead, guiding us through vendors, who'd begun to pack up. We saw lace and apples and bottles of wine.

Henderson stopped and picked up a bottle. It looked old and dusty. "This shouldn't be put in the sun. Wine should be kept in the dark."

"Then we all must be wine. I feel I'm in the dark. What are we missing? If Miss Bumners was working with a different man, not the minister, who would that be?"

After paying, he put the bottle under his arm. "Doesn't matter who. I'm killing Benjamin the next time I see him." He pushed out a short huff. "Let's head back."

The sun had started to lower. It surrounded Henderson and made me squint up at his height. "At least the day was pretty. It should be cooling."

"You're brilliant," I responded.

"I know this. But what are you talking about, Lady Worthing?"

"What if Mrs. Henderson was going to let things cool down? Let's say you are right, that Benjamin had the crazy idea of tricking an heiress for her fortune. Your wife realizes that the target is Mary. She comes to her senses and changes her mind. She tells Mary, and then Mary hates her. Mary tells Benjamin.

The minister then decides that Mrs. Henderson is a liability and murders her."

"And what if Miss Bumners knew of Benjamin's affair with Juliet, or was having her own with Benjamin? She could try to extort money from him to keep her quiet."

"The monster decides it's best to silence her for good."

I reached for his arm, the one I'd rejected earlier. "Is there any chance Mrs. Henderson had a change of heart and remembered her love for you? Perhaps she thought of how you used to care about everything she did and where she went. Could what you two had, could it have returned to her?"

Shaking his head, he said, "No. I was never like that. What is for you finds you. You may chase a little, but once a connection is made, it's there."

Henderson wasn't a curmudgeon. And I probably didn't need to seem prickly to him. "Mr. Sinclair had mentioned about her returning to her true love. If that wasn't you or Benjamin, then who?"

"Don't go getting that dreamy look about fairy-tale things, Lady Worthing. Sinclair was a drunk. I think the ale made him see rainbows where there weren't any." He started us walking. "Hopefully, Rawlins has everything in order. I need to get to Mary. When any of this gets out, she'll be devastated."

"Did anyone know of the provisions?"

"Juliet knew. I told her, hoping she could dissuade vultures."

My footing faltered. I wobbled, with one foot kicked out before my slipper landed safely on a stump.

Looking at my shoe, I saw the ribbons dangling from the bow. Juliet was the answer to all of this.

"Lady Worthing, what is it?"

"If Juliet knew there would be no money from marrying Mary, I'm sure the minister knew. That's why it was easy to let her go. Why he didn't try to defend his courtship. He doesn't want Mary without the money."

Henderson led us back to the chaise.

When he gripped my hand to help me in, I clutched his fingers tightly. "We have to get back to town as fast as possible."

"What is it?"

"What's worse than a girl eloping?"

He shook his head. "This is no time for riddles."

"What's worse is a girl who wants to elope, but her fellow has no intentions of marrying her. Then he takes back all the words you thought were loving and makes you think you were crazed."

"A harsh rejection will devastate Mary. But it would be for the best." He was gruff and resolved. The man had no idea how tragic unrequited love could be. "Lady Worthing, I know my sister."

"You didn't see her the night she visited after following Benjamin."

"She's upset—"

"You don't get it, Henderson. She's already entangled and grieving hard over Juliet's death. Mary isn't thinking straight. And you've seen what can happen when people are in low states and feel betrayed."

He'd never said anything, but he didn't have to, not now. I understood he battled with anger and depression, from Nelson's death to the war to even Juliet.

"Mr. Rawlins, are we ready to go?"

"Yes, sir." My driver hobbled as he put back on his thick jet-colored mantle. "I'll have you back to Greater Queen Street shortly."

He took a step and looked in great pain. "The whole axle and everything came down on my foot. But I can still manage."

"No, you will take things easy for now. I can get us back to Westminster."

Henderson helped him into the bounder, and then climbed onto the driver's seat. "Hope your bonnet is secure."

"It is somewhere back on the road. Just go."

Henderson meant to travel to our neighborhood, but I'd have him drop me off at Saint Margaret's, then circle back. I had a feeling that at dusk the distraught sister would be at the church trying to convince a murderer to marry her.

Chapter 25

When the bounder stopped in front of Westminster Abbey and I climbed down, despite the look in both men's eyes—Rawlins like a father, Henderson like . . . a Henderson, fire beneath an icy calm—neither could stop me.

If Mary was here trying to convince Benjamin to love her, only another woman could stop her and put her pieces back together. If I'd known that my sister was so upset that she'd do something rash, I would have stopped everything for her.

This was my chance to help someone lost.

Henderson grumbled, but then put his hands out in concession. "My sister is not here. She should've arrived home by now and you are putting yourself in danger with a man we suspect is a murderer and a schemer. This is dangerous. It's foolish."

"I'm going to Saint Margaret's. I suggest you go retrieve Mary and prove me wrong. It's something I believe you were born to do."

His glare became white hot. The deep blue of his eyes scorched, but I'd not back down.

"Mr. Rawlins, hand the baroness her knife."

My driver popped open the compartment and placed the sparkling blade, handle first, into my hand.

"The neck, Lady Worthing, is the most effective place to strike. No cravat will get in the way. An easy slit. I've shown you where to be effective."

Nodding, I put the blade into my reticule.

Rawlins started down. "Mr. Henderson, I'll be with her."

I blocked him. "No, you need to rest. And if I need to run for my life, I can't have my driver falling down and getting caught by a monster minister. Please go. There isn't time for any of this. Henderson, take him to my house."

"Rawlins, you heard the baroness." My neighbor picked up the reins. "I'll be back as soon as I can. Don't be careless or a hero."

"Go get Mary and then return for me. Hopefully, no one's here and I'll finally take a tour of Saint Margaret's."

Shaking his head hard, like it was subject to fall, Henderson made the carriage move. "The throat, madam."

Couldn't I run and hope for the best?

I waited to see the carriage turn the corner. This was the point of no turning back. Truthfully, this was me leaning into the impossible—that my womanly intuition made more sense than any gift my mother might've had. Mary was in love and would make a fool of herself to a man who only wanted money, money she didn't have.

Turning up the cobblestone path, I stood alone in front of the two great churches of Westminster. To my left was Saint Margaret's and dead ahead sat Westminster Abbey. Side by side, they looked aloof. An estranged husband and wife, close but never touching.

No crowds gathered. It was late in the day.

In case of emergency, I prepared my fast-beating heart and

both lungs to scream loud enough to draw attention from the crowded New Palace Yard where Olive's sat. Directly behind Saint Margaret's, they would hear me.

My low heels knocked against cobbles. The calm of the rhythm, this place, even the stillness of the air that seemed centuries old. This was good . . . and eerie.

The heavy shadow of Westminster Abbey's grand facade, the three arched entries, the parapet-topped columns and the two that looked like medieval princess hats dwarfed the plainer church.

I wondered if the lone clock tower housed the bells. Of course, there was no other place for them to be, not cast metal bells that weighed thousands of pounds.

Walking fast, I approached the pivot point where I'd turn toward the white stone of the smaller church. Very different from the Abbey's brown ones. I'd never noticed how the churches were built to be separate and never equal.

Taking a long breath, I stepped inside, entering Saint Margaret's, looking for Mary, hoping she was safe and not making a play for a man who wasn't worthy of her.

The door, warmed by the gorgeous evening sun, was ornately carved. With gentle pressure, like the church was fragile, I pressed inside to the nave.

Light streamed through glass windows, which were positioned near the ceiling. The brightness warmed me, but I didn't see Mary Henderson or Benjamin or anyone.

A few more steps into the silence, I saw the glass windows that were visible from the street leading to Olive's. Almost deciding I'd seen enough and Mary wasn't here, I warmed myself in the colored sunshine and trailed my finger on the walls surrounding the pews. These were high like Holy Trinity. Up close, they did look like horse pens. Was this what it took to get people to church and make them stay?

My chuckles echoed. Then disappeared.

All was still and quiet.

Moving to the wide aisle, I reached the stairs to the pulpit. Unlike Holy Trinity, the platform on which the minister preached was two stories high and equaled the height of the gallery. From up there, I was pretty sure, Benjamin could see anyone sleeping in the balcony.

With my hands holding to the side, I thought about climbing up and looking out to see if someone was hiding in the pews or crouching in a corner with tears.

That might be too much. "Hello? Mary, are you here?"

No answer.

I backed away, but ornate trimmings on the pulpit and the tall arched buttress, supported by columns on the lighter side of the nave, captured my gaze. The plaques and monuments underneath seemed scattered or disorganized.

It had to be arranged like this for a reason. Right?

Something like a hinge whined.

I turned but saw no one.

Pausing and searching, I dared not move. "Anyone here?"

Not a word was uttered. Everything remained quiet.

Missing my creaking floor of Number Two Greater Queen Street, I rubbed my temples. Henderson would be back for me. If his sister was safe at home, he probably comforted her, in addition to helping Rawlins reach his bed.

My neighbor was a doctor, after all. He might even be examining my driver. That could be the delay.

Firm in the knowledge that I was becoming melodramatic and a loon, I began to relax. Might as well look around and take the promised tour. I moved under the gallery and stood in front of a large sculpture of a woman. I wondered why she reclined here in this place, and why a small statue of a man stood at her feet.

It was intimate. Who but a partner would be touching . . . ?

Intimacy, was that it? In my dream, I saw or remembered a kiss. Whether that happened or not, I didn't know. But Juliet's state of undress, Miss Bumners's loosed buttons at her back, spoke to a familiarity between the killer and the victim.

I kept looking at this one man at the foot of the reclining, relaxed woman and realized that each victim let her guard down. My pulse ticked up, loud in my ear. It was foolish to come here alone when their killer was likely the philandering minister, who was intimate with them both.

Something creaked behind me.

I turned and saw nothing.

Typically, a lover of squeaks, I was terrified by this. It reminded me of how vulnerable I'd made myself, but I'd done this to save a sister.

Scanning from the empty nave to the transept section housing the pulpit, then to the other end of the church with the lone pipe organ, I proved to my soul I was alone with an overactive imagination.

Things shifted and moaned.

A centuries-old church had every right to sing like my floors.

Perhaps it was time to wait outside for Henderson.

Then I thought myself silly.

Putting my hands on the marble of the reclining woman, I felt the cold solid rock. I traced the cranberry veining and wondered about its origin and how it felt living eternity as a woman, stiff and silenced.

"It looks alive, Lady Worthing, doesn't it?"

Mr. Benjamin's voice echoed and I jumped.

My heart pounded hard.

It had become a chisel and would soon drive its way out of my chest.

Turning, I didn't see the minister. The glare of the sun stole my vision. Where was he?

"Oh, I hope I didn't frighten you." His voice sounded closer, but I still couldn't see him.

"Lady Worthing?"

Squinting, I finally saw Samuel Benjamin standing in the nave in the center aisle.

"Where did you come from?"

"The bells. I'm getting them ready for tonight. Where did you come from?"

"You scared me, sir. But you'd offered me an invitation to visit. I had some time on my hands waiting for friends. So . . . I . . . I hope I'm not . . ."

He neared a good seven paces away. "You're welcome. Please bring me more parishioners. What an evangelist you'd be."

"Well, I'll try. We're going to Olive's again. This time I hope it will be less chaotic, less deadly."

"Yes. I performed the service for Mr. Sinclair."

I didn't know, not that women were allowed—such an awful tradition keeping women from funerals because men believed we were too weak to face death. We faced it all the time, simply trying to bring life into the world. "Sir, who attended?"

"A brother and the male servants of the house. Sinclair was greatly loved."

"I trust you did another good job."

He was three pews away. "I tried, Lady Worthing. It feels good to do good."

On edge, feigning bravery, I waved him to the statue. "Sounds as if you haven't felt like that in a while."

"I haven't." He hooked a hand about his olive-green tailcoat and joined me at the unusual statue. "Well, this is Mary Dudley. She was one of Queen Elizabeth's most loyal friends. This fine woman acted in her stead for diplomacy, even nursed the queen through illnesses."

"Why is she here and not with the queen in Westminster?"

"Elizabeth lies in eternal sleep with her sister, Mary, whom she executed."

"So much for sisterly affection." I placed one hand on the cold marble and the other on my reticule, my fingers wrapping the knife's handle. "And the man at her feet?"

"Well, Lady Worthing, that's Dudley's husband, Henry Sidney, at her feet. But this is all a memorial. They are interred in Penshurst."

"That's a lot of trouble to have their memories here. I wonder if they are at rest." I swallowed and tried to sound calm. "I wonder about those murdered souls. Do you think they find rest?"

"I'd like to think that everyone can find rest. I need some. I'm thinking of taking a sabbatical."

"That's unusual for one serving less than a year."

"Almost a year, but even ministers need to go away for perspective to hear the counsel of the Lord. I haven't been quiet. I'm restless."

With a nod, I took more steps to my left, putting more room between us. "Reflection is good. But I don't think a guilty conscience gets rest."

He didn't look my way. "There should be forgiveness. King David was forgiven."

My hands sweated. "You think you'll repent enough to be forgiven for your affairs?"

"You mean by Miss Henderson? I haven't told her my plans."

It was now or never to see if I could get him to confess. Henderson had to be back any minute. He'd been gone long enough. "Yes, and the two women from Chelsea."

"What are you talking about, Lady Worthing? You know how rumors can be wrong."

"But this is not a rumor. I talked to a grieving father. Mr. Bumners said—"

"Yes, I was having an affair with his daughter. That proves nothing."

"So Mrs. Henderson and her maid and Mary."

He ran both hands through his hair. "It's not as bad as it sounds."

"Tell me how it's not. Two women who should be friends, might've been friends, meet violent ends. They're from the same area of Chelsea that you are. Milking families."

"It's a shame about Ann and Juliet. We all knew each other from Chelsea. We all knew the Hendersons and their money. Have you become Mr. Bumners's new emissary or Henderson's? I'm leaving town, ma'am. What else do they want?"

"A father wants to know why his daughter's dead. A husband wants to know who killed his wife and her maid. You're the connection. You were intimate friends to both. Ann trusted you."

"I didn't kill Juliet. I think you, Lady Worthing, need to go on to dinner and forget these absurd questions."

My satin slippers didn't budge, but his did. He started walking away.

"What of Miss Bumners? You were close to her. You were intimate friends. She made tea the night of the funeral. Did you console her, teasing with the buttons on her collar?"

He stopped right next to his pulpit. "Lady Worthing, please go."

"Ann Bumners knew all about your affair with Mrs. Henderson. She helped with your plans to romance Mary Henderson."

With his palm slapping the stair rail, he spun and faced me. "You don't know what you are talking about."

"What came first, the plan to turn Mary's head for her money, or Juliet?"

"Juliet Henderson was a rare spirit. Her infectious laugh made you burst. But she didn't love me. She had at me to keep me from Mary. Ann knew of that matter—all those wrong reasons. I loved Juliet more than anything."

Hadn't expected a full-throated confession of love. "You didn't kill Mrs. Henderson."

"No. I might've wanted to, the way she teased, but no."

So Juliet wasn't running off with the minister. "But Miss Bumners . . . Did she tell Juliet of your initial plans for Mary?"

"Yes. She ruined things."

"You came over to Mrs. Henderson's apartment in Cheapside to make her pay. Miss Bumners expected you. She was formerly your co-conspirator. Did you chat friendly over tea? Did she make up for your loss, slipping you into Juliet's bed?"

"Ann wanted what Juliet had. I found it hard to forgive her. Juliet would be alive if we'd run away together."

"Miss Bumners wasn't going to be silent. She'd told her father your plans. She'd told Mrs. Henderson. You couldn't risk her telling anyone else. You overheard her invite me and Mr. Henderson to Cheapside."

Gritting his teeth, he shook his head. "Has Henderson put you up to this? He'll do anything to keep suspicion away from him. With this ridiculous theory, what do you get out of it? Have you taken to the new widower, bonded with him, since you're virtually one yourself?"

"Miss Bumners knew everything. The maid had to be eliminated. She planned to expose you to Mr. Henderson and me the day after the funeral. Who wouldn't believe you capable of murder if you could hurt a girl barely fifteen in the worst way?"

"Never. Mary is young and impressionable. I didn't hurt her. And I had plenty of opportunity to do so, the way she chased me. You don't know what you are talking about."

"Fine, don't tell me. I know it all. And when Miss Bumners's father tells what he knows to Duncan, you'll have to answer to him. Good day, sir."

I turned.

A creak announced advancing footfall.

The murderer was coming for me.

Chapter 26

I dashed between pews. Where did one hide in a church?

"Lady Worthing, slow down. Let's come to an understanding."

Dodging, then back up and changing direction, I avoided the lanky man's reach. "No, thank you. The women who understand you are dead."

When we were little, Dinah, Flo, and I tried not to get caught sleeping. Dinah would sit with us on the last pew. We were all the same. I needed to live long enough to tell her we could be the same loving family again.

"There is nowhere to go. No one is expected for hours. You were stupid enough to come snooping. Lord Duncan's magpie trying to solve another crime for him."

The distance to the door from me was thirty feet. Didn't think I could outrun him.

He came for me.

One turn and I saw him leaping over the tops of the high walls, bouncing on the cushions.

"How are you going to kill me, Benjamin? There's nothing ironic here." Except the abolition history. I spied the font used for Equiano and ran the other way.

Benjamin was on one side of the last pew. I was on the other. He kept shifting toward me and I countered. "Perhaps you should surrender, sir."

"Or perhaps you'll fall and bust your crown at the font where Olaudah Equiano was baptized. There isn't enough water in it to drown you, and dumping your body in the Thames isn't quite baptism, but it will have to do."

"You're not a very good minister."

"And you're not good at minding your own business. Can't you see you leave me no choice? I don't want to do this."

He leapt and grabbed me by the neck.

The knife.

I couldn't get ahold of it.

Couldn't breathe.

The doors blew open.

Henderson and Mary came in.

Benjamin dropped me to the ground.

"Not a minute too soon." I filled my lungs and crawled away before he could get his hands on me.

"Then it's true," Mary said, crying. "You're a monster."

"Mary, it's not as it looks. This was their plan to keep us apart."

"Killing Juliet and Miss Bumners, and now trying to strangle Lady Worthing. Were you going to kill me later?"

"No, Mary," he said. "Things are all mixed up."

"Liar."

Henderson helped me to stand. "I figured my neighbor would get you to confess. She's good at pestering people."

Benjamin started to laugh. "If Juliet and I had eloped months ago, none of this would have happened. Juliet loved me and I her. It was her idea to use this one for her twenty-thousand-pound dowry."

"Months ago? We've been courting since I came in December. Waiting for me at the baptismal. Walks home. Rides in your carriage. All that time it was just the money. I forgave you because . . . men can't help being attracted to her. I thought it just flirtation. But you made love with Juliet and kissed me for my dowry?" Mary ran past me and slapped him. "Juliet would never hurt me. She tested you to see how much of a liar you were."

"Mary, it's not—"

She wrenched back in horror. "I knew she was killed because of me."

Crying hysterically, Mary pushed away from him. I thought she'd flee out the doors, but she went to the tower, instead.

"Mary, come back!" Henderson went to go to her; but from the way he glared at Benjamin, I knew he'd not let him escape.

"Please, sister, come back."

"No, Stapleton. I'm going to lay another death at his feet. I'm jumping from the tower."

I pulled out my knife and gave it to Henderson. "Keep him busy and alive. I'll go get her."

For a second or even less, he smiled. Next he had Benjamin in a headlock.

It was dark at the end of the hall, but I saw the stairs leading to the tower. "Mary. Mary, come back."

The corridor was dark, like Drury Lane's, but I hoped my eyes adjusted. "Mary."

When I cleared the last step, the room in which I stood was empty. No Mary. No window.

"Henderson!" I yelled at the top of my lungs. "Make him tell me how to get to her."

"We're coming up."

Murmuring and cursing rose from the floor as I pressed on every door and each squeaky floorboard.

The minister would be no help, or Henderson was strangling him. I started beating on every piece of wood. Toggling a slotted window, I let the setting sun inside.

The rosy-purple light exposed something that looked like a hidden door. I thrust it open, exposing a narrow staircase.

Climbing it made everything creak. I hoped I didn't fall through the floor.

Finally at the clearing, I found four ropes threaded from the ceiling. Each hung with its ends wrapped, almost like a slipknot or noose.

Then I saw her bathed in pink light. Mary had a thick round casement open. If the girl climbed through it, she'd fall to her death.

"Please move from there. Come back down to me and your brother."

"From here," she said, "you can see the Thames. Samuel kissed me here. It was my first kiss. Then we watched the sun lower onto the river. It was romantic."

"Mary, please. He's not worth it. Come away from there."

"No, Lady Worthing. Convince my brother this is not his fault."

She pushed feetfirst onto the casement and dangled her legs, her white satin slippers dancing against the sky.

Chapter 27

In Saint Margaret's bell tower, I witnessed Mary Henderson as she half dangled out the window. "No. He's not worth it. You are worth everything."

In a flash, this was Dinah, the night before my wedding, standing in the door to my bedroom, begging me not to marry. I let her go. I didn't fight then and there, or let her know how much I loved her and how marriage didn't change us.

In a blink of my eyes, I went after a sister. I leapt at the window and grabbed ahold of Mary, snatching her by the shoulders. "If you go, I go, too."

"Juliet tried to tell me he only wanted my money. I wanted her dead for taking Samuel away." Mary sobbed. "Sorry, Juliet. My sweet friend. I don't deserve to live."

The whitewashed walls and dirt-brown oak floors absorbed the light this open window allowed around us.

"No escaping, Mary. No more running." My reticule flung out to the sky and sailed down. "You can't jump, Mary. You can't do this."

"Let me go, Lady Worthing. You were right. Go on and gloat. Go on, Lady Worthing. Tell me how stupid I was to believe Reverend Samuel Benjamin could love me. Too young, not pretty enough."

"Never, Mary. You're beautiful and spirited. I'd rather be wrong in this matter than to have your heart broken. Men like Benjamin are made to lie. They're charming. You were charmed. This isn't your fault. He targeted you. Be glad you know before he ruined you."

Tears started to flow harder, harder. The floor squeaked below my feet as I tried to drag her back in.

"I'm ruined. I loved him, and then I turned on the one person who tried to tell me the truth."

I pulled her a little more inside. But she locked her leg on the sill.

"I thought Samuel would see how I was always his champion. I thought if I were persistent and worldly and dramatic like Juliet—"

"You mean like sneaking into his carriage and showing up in Clapham?"

"Mr. Sinclair would drive me wherever I wanted to go."

"And the friend or aunt in Mayfair?"

"That's my old governess. She's old and will agree to anything. But I was there with her before I went to visit Samuel."

"Did you both discover Juliet together?"

"No, he dropped me off. I heard your dog. I went to get him. And I saw her."

Mary cried hard. What she said sounded like the truth, but she couldn't attest to Benjamin's whereabouts or what he did before they met.

"I wanted him to notice me. Then he'd know I was the one."

"Look at you, Mary, beautiful girl. My mother, she'd say this is only the first of a hundred mistakes. You can't give up. You have ninety-nine more to go. A charlatan made a play for you. Your heart will heal."

I kept my embrace tight, not slackening for a moment. "He's a brutal killer. Mrs. Henderson, Miss Bumners . . . He may have tricked Mr. Sinclair into running into the streets. Don't let him claim another life. Come on. Come back inside. Your best revenge is living well. You get up and breathe the fresh air and be free, make those other mistakes. He'll never be free again."

My hold on her hadn't slackened, but then she unlocked her legs. She stopped kicking her feet in the air, stopped moving altogether.

Mary leaned on me and then pushed backward. By the time I released my next gasp, we were fully inside the room.

She held on to me. And I held her, mussing those brown curls that fell everywhere. I'd saved one sister today. "We will get through this. I'll get you through this. I promise. I'm not going anywhere. I'm your neighbor."

As if this were Dinah, I looked into her eyes. "There's nothing that you can ever do that's worth destroying your life. Any day, any moment you need me, I'm here. I'll show you the way out of darkness."

"I'm angry at him." Mary broke from me. "He killed her. He needs to pay."

She ran at top speed and started pulling the ropes. Like a drunken bell ringer, she yanked and shifted and tugged on each rope until the bells rang.

Holding my ears, I shouted, trying to get Mary's attention. "What are you doing?"

Each of the four bells answered and rang out *chaos, chaos, chaos.*

The way the ropes jerked Mary off of her feet, I knew the force she created was tremendous. Maybe it would burn up all her anger.

Benjamin and Stapleton entered. My neighbor kicked the minister forward. He looked horrified. "Stop! You can break the bells, crack their supports. These century-old bells can be ruined."

Mary grinned nothing less than the most magnificently evil look I'd ever seen. "Then that should happen on your watch. Consider it a parting gift from me."

"Mary, stop," Henderson said. "It's jerking you. You can break your arm."

"Samuel Benjamin let me pull the bells before. Tell them how this was one of the places you'd bring me to convince me we were in love. When my brother told you, you'd never see any of my dowry, you still couldn't tell me the truth."

Running across the black-stained pine floor, she started alternating her position and ringing them faster. The spinning rhythm sounded out of control.

"Mary, stop. These bells are old. The floor's not as solid as the one below. Everything is weak compared to the weight of the bells."

She didn't heed him. If anything, his warning made her speed up. Her light blue gown and lace floated as she ran and rang and sailed from side to side. The slats on these windows, like the ones in the bounder, let in dusk's light.

"Lady Worthing, Mr. Henderson. Please stop her before she causes damage."

Her brother grunted, stepped forward, and tried to grab the rope from her, but she dodged him. Mary worked herself and the bells into a faster frenzy.

The creaking overhead grew louder. It now sounded constant and deafening, breaking.

"Mary," I said, no longer wanting to encourage her, and growing more frightened by the noise above, "you might want to slow down. Three people are dead because of him. Let's not add any more to his tally by having these bells fall on us."

"I didn't kill Juliet. Miss Bumners was an accident. I didn't mean to kill her. She wouldn't be quiet. I didn't touch Sinclair at all. Something spooked him or he was an unlucky drunk."

"Mr. Sinclair was a kind man. He never meant harm to anyone." Mary shook her head. "And how many more have gotten caught in your web, you smooth-talking minister?"

I tried to grab Mary, but Henderson caught me. "Let her have her say. Hendersons tend to bottle things inside and let it eat us alive."

"Tell him everything, Mary," her brother said, and clapped, "while you have the chance."

"You're all insane. This is church property. Not mine." Benjamin lunged at her.

Mary jumped out of his reach. "My sister-in-law changed her plans because of me. She couldn't run off with you. She'd never hurt me, like you. Juliet teased you, but she wanted me to know you were horrible. That's why you killed her."

He leapt at her, as he'd tried to leap at me. As if to swat him like a bug, she flung the thick braided jute at him.

The long, stretchy cabling caught Benjamin's neck.

Something above snapped.

The man was jerked fast to the ceiling. His body trembled in midair as he slammed against the roof. He stayed there, motionless, caught against the rafters.

Henderson grabbed his sister and buried her face against his chest.

And I stared at the lifeless minister, the rector charged with the bell ringing of Saint Margaret's, dead by the pulls.

Henderson rocked Mary. "Sis, two women, maybe a third person is dead because of him. He won't hurt you anymore. Juliet can now rest."

That was the unsettling part. I knew for certain Benjamin killed Miss Bumners. I wasn't sure he'd killed the others.

Chapter 28

Lord Duncan sat in my parlor making notes. "Lady Worthing, I came from next door."

"Eleven Greater Queen Street? How are they doing? Did you make an arrest?"

"Now, hold on, lass. You ask a lot of questions, but no. No additional arrests. I'm satisfied that Mr. Benjamin is our culprit. He killed Mrs. Henderson when she refused to elope with him and then Miss Bumners. She tried to extort him over his various dalliances, and the man thought it easier to be rid of her to keep her silent."

He put down his pen and looked at ease while I paced. Something wasn't right. Florentina should be here. The math didn't add up.

Benjamin admitted to killing Miss Bumners, but none of the others. He should've admitted to Juliet's. He had nothing to lose.

"Lady Worthing, after visiting my uncle and watching him die with peace, I think we all need to search for what makes the soul calm and satisfied. I'm satisfied that your logic has helped me solve this crime. I'm quite pleased."

"But Mr. Sinclair? Something frightened him."

Duncan sighed. He looked tired having ridden three days straight, after his uncle's funeral. "Mr. Sinclair is a known drunk who frequents Olive's. You were there, but you didn't see anyone push him. Or are you changing your statement of what happened that night?"

The man filling in for Duncan asked nothing, but I'd written down what I'd witnessed and sent it to Duncan's office. "You read my note? You just returned."

"Yes, Lady Worthing. I take everything you've penned seriously."

A Blackamoor giving testimony on anyone of another race was rare, but legal, and I shouldn't challenge and ruin the rapport I had with the magistrate.

I shook my head and kept pacing, loving the creaks of my floor. My mind raced and reviewed every step. "I feel like I'm missing something. The gold *J* of Mrs. Henderson's ribbon necklace was never found. We've had no confession."

"Ma'am, I have interrogated poor Miss Henderson and Mr. Henderson. They both attest to confronting Benjamin. The minister had motive and even admitted to smothering a woman. He's guilty, Lady Worthing. I'm sure of it."

Leaning against my fireplace, I gave credence to it for a moment and tried to remember my dream. If I saw Benjamin, I'd let everything lie. But I didn't. I wasn't convinced he did it.

The magistrate stood, threw on his dark cape, which covered his black mourning band. He stretched with both of his lanky arms reaching up to my ceiling. "Unless you have evidence, conclusive evidence, Lady Worthing, I'm closing this case."

"Lord Duncan, I don't have anything other than a feeling."

"Well, I had a feeling that Henderson did it. But you'd not work with a man who'd kill a woman. Juliet Henderson suffered. Ann Bumners suffered. As far as the crown and I are concerned, I have their murderer. Well, the coroner does."

I walked him to the door. Mr. Rogers gave him his hat and gloves. "Lady Worthing. You're getting too emotional. Sometimes things don't add up. You'll learn that if you continue to dabble in solving mysteries."

"You won't stop me, Lord Duncan?" It came out like a question, but it was more a statement. This was my calling, my way of helping, using my privilege for good. "I want to be of service."

He smiled a little, like a proud teacher to a protégé. "For now, but Benjamin is our man. And he is being punished by eternal damnation. If he'd lived, he'd hang and face the same fate. You have to admit a certain efficiency to things. Benjamin was guilty."

He tipped his hat to me.

When my footman opened my door, Mr. Vaughn came inside.

I said goodbye to the magistrate and followed Vaughn to my drawing room.

When I closed the door, I saw my godfather pacing, almost as I had, but under the shadow of Lord Worthing's picture.

"Vaughn, what is the matter?"

"Abigail, I give you information to help you *avoid* problems. Rawlins told me about the gunfight with Tanner and now a hanging in Saint Margaret's."

"I was perfectly safe. Mr. Henderson was with me."

He stared at me, then maybe through me, like he wanted to address someone else, someone who wasn't there. "Listen to me, Abigail. You've been lucky. You need to take time to rest and leave your neighbor alone."

"Vaughn, I can't. I promised him I'd help his sister. Benjamin made her confused. He took all her self-confidence."

"What is Henderson doing to yours?"

"Excuse me." I put a hand on my hip, on my wrinkled dress, still rife with grass stains and smelling stale like old drafty wood.

"He takes you places where they shoot at you."

Wagging a finger, I lifted my arm. "*I took me.* He insisted on coming along. Probably best that he did. The man kept me alive, and Rawlins from killing."

My godfather rolled his eyes, then shifted toward James's large portrait. "You need to be back, sir. Then save my goddaughter from herself."

"Yell louder, sir. Don't think Worthing heard you from the other side of the world."

Teacup came into the room and offered a happy bark.

My godfather ignored my terrier and kept with his interrogation. "And Saint Margaret's?"

His tone sounded harsh. Teacup barked as if the dog didn't like his tone. I didn't care for it, either.

"Again, I went by myself and confronted Benjamin. Henderson and his sister joined me later and sort of saved my life. Though I do know where to strike with my knife—that is, if I can free it from my reticule."

He groaned and ran a hand through his powdered hair. It left a stain on his gloves. "I give up, Abigail. You've an answer for everything."

I didn't. If I did, I'd know who truly killed Juliet Henderson.

Vaughn took off his formerly white gloves and bent down to my terrier. "Can't you get through to her?"

Instead of allowing himself to be petted, Teacup bit Vaughn, then took off running down the hall.

"Oh, dear. Sorry, Vaughn."

He wrung his hand out. The skin was barely broken.

"Let me get you cleaned up, sir."

"Lady Worthing, I'll do it, so the glove won't irritate it. Then I will let it get air, nothing better to heal a scratch than air."

"What about a burn?"

"Yes, a burn too. That probably needs more air."

"Then you'd not cover up something that was freshly done?"

He peered at me again, but this time with sympathy. "Are you seeing something, Abigail?"

"No, a stray thought." I clasped my palm, remembering the one man who covered his hands in tight clinging gloves after he said he'd been burned. It could be a coincidence. "Do you know anything of Mr. Jyles?"

"No. You're not trying to hire him to replace Rogers, are you? I thought you liked Rogers."

"I do. My butler is a good, honest man. Not everyone is. Let me go get Mrs. Smith and get you cleaned up. Then you can give me more warnings I won't listen to."

"Abigail, tell Teacup I'll remember this. Oh. And, Abigail, your sister." He sighed as if the world sat on his chest. "Dinah went and saw your father, and then she moved on from my contacts. I don't know where she is anymore."

Frustration welled in my throat. It was hard to swallow when all I wanted to do was cry. But my soul was spent. Helping Mary, going over every detail with the runners, and then again with Duncan, took all my energy. There was none left to generate pity for me. "Let me go get some soap and water for you. I need to clean up that scratch Teacup left. I hear if you give him bacon, he forgives on demand."

I started to the door; Vaughn's voice, low and powerful and reassuring, reached me. "I'm sorry, Abigail. I'll keep looking. I found her once. I'll find her again."

My eyes leaked a little, but my resolve came as sure as my shifting floorboards—the homey sounds, the creaks that I'd become used to and were here for me always. "Stop looking,

Vaughn. Dinah knows where I am. When she's ready, I'll be here. I'm not going anywhere."

I left my godfather under the watchful eyes of my husband's portrait. That seemed fitting—the one meant to watch out for me, along with the man who actually did.

Later tonight, I'd seek the one I had to help. For I was sure I knew who killed Henderson's wife.

Chapter 29

It was well past ten when Vaughn left. Teacup and I sat in my parlor. My half-written letter to James lay on the table in front of me.

I saw light glowing outside.

"Teacup!" I rubbed his cute little face, swiping his gentle brown hair this way and that. "I think you need a walk. Don't you, boy?"

He offered a happy, low bark, one that wouldn't awaken my household, which had retired. I took my lantern from behind my sofa, threw on my Scottish tweed cape, and went out into the night.

It took a good couple of minutes to catch up to Silvereye and Santisma at the end of our property in Saint James Park. The dogs bounced about until Henderson snapped his fingers.

Even Teacup obeyed and settled between the big greyhounds.

Their master held his lantern out to me. "Lady Worthing. We need to stop meeting like this. Someone might die."

His words sounded eerie in the quiet night. "That's not funny, you know."

"To each his own."

We started walking together. Teacup played nice with the two bigger dogs. I only hoped Henderson had bacon to continue to encourage the good behavior.

"Let me guess," he said, and flicked my collar, "you're going to another secret meeting again? What, no theater first?"

"No. We've had enough drama today. But I have a question for you. You must search your memory. The night of the *lichwake*, did all the servers wear gloves?"

"Yes. Except for Miss Bumners."

"Her hands had no injuries. You bore some, but those were Teacup's scratches to the skin by your thumb. It was clever of you to do that. You knew that Mrs. Henderson had put up a fight. My dog's scratches could point suspicion at you. How did you know that she fought?"

The light of my lantern glowed on his silent face. A minute spun by before he answered. "When Mary found Juliet, I checked for a heartbeat, a pulse, something to tell me she might still live. I found nothing, but I noted her broken fingernail and blood on her hands. I suspected it wasn't just hers."

He rubbed at his neck. "You're not back to thinking I did it? I thought we'd grown past our general distrust."

"I know you didn't do it. Remember? You'd tell me. But I think we've overlooked who did do it." I took a deep breath. "Do you know how Mr. Jyles hurt his hand that night?"

"Jyles's hand was injured?"

"During the *lichwake*, there was a bandage under his glove. He said he'd burned himself."

"Burned himself? How? Was he lighting a candle?"

"He said he lit torches that night and was careless." I took up Henderson's hand. "Right here in the fat skin by his thumb."

"That's a hard place to burn, Lady Worthing. My footmen light stoves, the fireplaces. Even the sconces. The runners lit torches out here. Not one of my servants was used, to prevent them from hiding evidence."

"That's what I thought. Mr. Jyles is guilty, but I don't have a motive."

"You need to stop your fact finding, Lady Worthing, and go get a good night's sleep. Those are doctor's orders."

"You're not my doctor. And why aren't you concerned that a man who violently killed your wife is free? He could get away with this."

"Lady Worthing, we don't have evidence. Any gouging marks have probably healed. No wound. No conviction."

Needing to do something other than strike Henderson to make him take me seriously, I stomped in my short boots and picked up Teacup. "You want me to give up. We should tell Duncan."

"No, Lady Worthing. Everything is settled."

"You and Mary could be at risk."

"No, Juliet's death was personal, emotional. Jyles harbors none of that kind of animosity toward me or Mary. I thank you for your concern, but the matter of Juliet Henderson's death is closed."

My heart roiled with injustice. "I don't understand. Are you so afraid of renewed scrutiny that you'll let a killer go free?"

With a snap of his fingers, he turned and walked away with his dogs.

"Henderson? Henderson?" I caught up to him right at the point where that stupid fence had ended, where Juliet had died. "Is that it? Are we done?"

"Let me handle this. If Jyles is guilty, it will eat at him. Justice will be served. Now go on to Number Two, and I'll go to Number Eleven, and we'll speak of this to no one."

I walked past him. "Why did I even bother?"

"Because you care, Lady Worthing. But you have to respect when someone has boundaries and tells you no."

He was right. And as I couldn't make Dinah talk to me, I couldn't make my neighbor take seriously a threat that only I saw.

"Make sure you keep living," I said. "Teacup needs more training."

"I intend to live a long time. Good evening, Lady Worthing."

We separated and went to our respective houses. When I made my way back inside my comfortable parlor, I said an extra prayer for Henderson's household. Something wasn't right, but it wasn't my place to fix it.

I needed to put my attention to what was mine and what had problems. Pulling out my ink, I started again on my letter to James.

Chapter 30

Florentina swept into my parlor. "Are you still under house arrest, Lady Worthing?"

"I'm not under any arrest or even suspicion. It's been two days since Lord Duncan closed all inquiries into Juliet Henderson's and Ann Bumners's murders. He's satisfied with what we've learned."

"Who can believe a handsome minister was behind it all?"

I didn't think he was, but since Lord Duncan's runners hadn't come for Jyles, I supposed the minister would continue to be blamed for everything. "I'd like to know if Mr. Benjamin frightened Mr. Sinclair. I wish I had paid more attention to what was happening in Olive's that day."

"Abigail Carrington Monroe, my Lady Worthing, will you let this go? You solved another peculiar incident, and the inquiry is closed. Nothing will bring that unfortunate soul back."

"None of them will come back. Death is final."

Florentina took Teacup from my arms. No one was afraid of him anymore. Though I was again at odds with my neighbor, he still kept training my baby.

"Mr. Henderson has made this little thing tame. He's an angel."

The dog or the neighbor?

As if all of this sweet talk was too much, my terrier sort of offered a low growl. He stopped when I shook my finger.

"You look unsettled. You're not trying to get out of our meeting. Mrs. Edwards took great effort to arrange it for us. I don't want to beg off. My employer will be disappointed."

"No, it's not that. We're going to be away. I sort of wanted to stay and see if I'm needed. Something could happen, and I should be here."

My cousin put her hands about her neck, rubbing; then she rolled her shoulders. "Nothing is going to happen. The guilty man is dead. Lord Duncan found the long piece of ash wood, the pull, broken. Without that board, the heavy cast-iron bell made a full rotation and jerked the ropes to the ceiling. Nothing could stop that. It was accidental."

Well, for what he did to Mary and Miss Bumners, maybe it was Samuel Benjamin's judgment. "The irony continued. The bell-ringing rector strangled by church bells does fit. Sad and fitting."

Teacup made a happy bark when Florentina approached the window. "I don't see another fence or a bonfire or a line of mourning revelers trampling your lawn. Can it be that you and the neighbor are at peace and that Mary has found it as well?"

"I saw her yesterday. She holds herself responsible. The poor girl wanted Benjamin to hurt for what he'd done. Then she caused the bell accident. It was a coincidence, but on top of Juliet's death . . . only time can fix a broken heart or rid her of guilt."

"Sounds as if you need to take a bit of your own advice. My uncle told me that Dinah has run off again."

There was nothing to say. My sister made her choice, and I wasn't it.

Putting Teacup on the floor, Florentina came and tugged me to stand. The lace on my peach-colored gown fluttered as she whirled me. "Lady Worthing, go get dressed to go out. I need you to wear something that says I mean business. We have an appointment."

"Yes."

"You don't seem excited." She put her face to my cheeks. "You can't know everything any more than you can control everything around you."

That's pretty much what Henderson had said. I wrapped arms about my cousin who was here—and the best friend a girl could have. "Help me select the most suitable thing to wear. Miss Bellows says she heard puce will again be the color of the season."

"It's hard to kill purple."

Loving every one of my parlor floor squeaks, I walked with my cousin to the hall. Arm in arm, we headed to my closet to find the proper Lady Worthing outfit that would guarantee I'd be heard and get abolition moving again.

This appointment, as Florentina deemed it, was actually a two-day trip to Somerset. Miss Bellows accompanied us, making travel easier. That is to say, it was a reassuring sign of peace and harmony for our colorful trio. When stopping at the coach inns that Rogers had taken the liberty to prearrange, we had no trouble.

It was a lovely trip in my Berlin, lovely and safe. I'd given Rawlins my blessing to outfit it and the yellow bounder with as much weaponry as he liked.

I hated the notion that he might be called to use it, but remembering the reception in Chelsea, one could never be too careful.

My Berlin entered Somerset around noon. The green hills

were such picturesque land. I felt as if I'd fallen into one of the fairy-tale books Mama and my father read to us as children.

Soon we arrived at Barley Wood—a large house set on a sizable plot of emerald land hosting sculpted gardens.

"You want me to come with you, ma'am?" Miss Bellows stopped her latest embroidery project, something with wonderful tulips, and lifted her smile to us.

"No. I can do this." I smoothed my puce carriage gown and eased out of the Berlin, with my reticule full of letters.

My cousin had resourcefully arranged this visit.

My title eased the opening of these doors.

But I, Abigail Carrington Monroe, needed to stand on my own. I was ready for this mission.

The papers about the horrors James witnessed had to be written about and disseminated to the general public. People would be swayed. The accounts in the right hands could ignite the nation's soul.

When Florentina came down from the carriage, I pointed her back to the seat. "Miss Sewell, you can stay, too. You've done enough. I don't want to put your reputation at further risk with your employer."

"Nonsense, it was she who helped me write Miss More for an invitation. Turns out this abolitionist has a heart for women doing unconventional things. And I want a better look at this place, Lady Worthing. Miss More owns the house and the acreage outright. This is an unmarried woman who has the income to do want she wants, when she chooses. *That's* freedom, Abigail."

I heard Florentina's heart, and possibly the future she desired, in her words. "Then come along. I'm strong enough to do this alone, but wise enough to want company."

"To battle, Cousin."

A servant in a sprig print apron and matching mobcap let us into the house. "Miss More is expecting you. Follow me."

Similar planks of varying widths lined the floor, which was a deep chestnut color. They didn't squeak as loudly as mine, but I did like the occasional noise when we shifted and turned a corner.

This big house was magnificent. A drawing room had a curved ceiling framed with a dark wood lattice structure, which reminded me a little of the buttresses of Saint Margaret's. This room had burnished panels along the walls. Everything was well cared for. "Magnificent house," I told the servant.

"Yes. Miss More and her sisters have hosted many special guests here. I think we can get up to a hundred in these two rooms. But I'm leading you to her gardens. It's her favorite spot."

Soon we stepped out onto a stone terrace. Beyond it were hedgerows shaped like the rectangular walls of a box. Everywhere there were flowers—red, pink, yellow. And lots of daffodils.

"Puts my garden to shame, Florentina." But not the one that Henderson had drafted.

It had been two days away from Westminster, but I thought of him and Mary and hoped they were well. I prayed his way of dealing with things kept them safe or proved me wrong.

My cousin chuckled, but I could see her thoughts calculating the income necessary to afford all of this.

"Miss More," our guide said, "Miss Sewell and Lady Worthing to see you."

"Sit," the famed abolitionist said. "Lucy, bring refreshments."

"That's not necessary, Miss More. We don't wish to take up a lot of your time."

"As you wish. Please." She waved her hand to the two simple wood chairs sitting close to her.

Florentina and I sat and waited for this activist and good friend of Wilberforce to examine us.

Rumored to be in her sixties, the older woman, who possessed a face lightly weathered by sun or time, regarded us with sharp brown eyes.

A frilly mobcap of white lace balanced the sharp Mazarine blue of her walking gown. The hue said spry, even fashionable. This was different from the austere reputation I'd heard she possessed. "You women are welcome. When my friend sent the note of two Negresses wishing to meet with me to discuss abolition, I didn't know what to say. We're trying to get the politics moving again. We were close. Then things changed and circumstances in parliament changed, too."

I wanted to say the change was a country of free Blacks and a cowering of the public at the potential of having a free society. But my mother said something about honey and flies and fools—so I said nothing about this. Instead, I sought to be polite. "Were you also a good friend of the late Mr. Pitt?" I asked, knowing that Wilberforce had taken the man's death hard.

"Not as good as some of my colleagues. And my poor Wilberforce, it sent him into a depression that he only now seems to be moving past."

Sad feelings and guilt had a way of rotting things from the inside.

"Your garden, ma'am." Florentina clasped her hands, then released them, putting her palms to her side. "It's quite beautiful."

"Yes. I love my land. There's an air about the place, the mint and the heather, that's tranquil. It is different from the turmoil of London. But you didn't come for tips on my plantings. Tell me the purpose of this visit."

With my hand about Florentina's arm, I decided it was now or never to speak. "We've come to help. I know that you've written pamphlets for the cause of abolition. I have written testimonies from visitors to the islands of Antigua and other colonies in the West Indies of the cruel practices of enslavement."

I dug into my reticule for James's letters and official statements supporting what he'd documented—the separation of mothers and babies for profits, the horrendous beatings and punishments for the simplest things. When James described the hot-sugar treatment—the literal burying of a man up to his head and dumping boiling sugar slurry over him, then leaving him to hungry ants—a part of me broke inside. I knew these had to be used to remind everyone what was at stake. "You've written pamphlets before on the cruelties. These new accountings, the brutal realities, will remind London of its heart."

"Why can't you do this, dear? You're articulate. You could do this. Olaudah Equiano published his memoir, which framed these sins in such a powerful way, seventeen years ago."

"But these aren't my stories. My husband witnessed them. These accounts are from White men, ones who saw or were actually involved in the trade." With my fingers steepled, I leaned forward. "You're a voice for the movement. Your words made things happen."

Miss More looked at Florentina and me. I saw hesitancy, as much as hope, in those eyes.

"Ma'am," I said. "To be honest, the scrutiny on my life is a bit much."

"Any woman that's different gets attention."

"True. But some openly want me to fail, and if I do, I'll be used as a symbol of why equality doesn't work. Hayti is the reason the abolition movement has stopped all around the world. I don't want to be the reason for more failed progress."

Miss More took the documents. "I'll look over these. I will do my best."

"That's all I can ask." I rose and curtsied. It wasn't protocol, but a queen offered a queen respect. I believed this woman had a good heart. I almost heard the cogs turning in her brainbox. Several pamphlets would be made.

"Ma'am, rest assured that when I find my way to make a difference, I will, even if I have to do it in secret, like the Clapham Sect."

Miss More's eyes met mine. She nodded and I filled with more hope.

Florentina followed me to the door leading into the house. I turned one last time and watched this woman reading and weeping at the treatment James had penned.

My anger at him for leaving didn't feel bad at this moment. It was for the greater good.

We walked back the way we came. My heart felt lighter. I'd given the papers to the right person, a woman. I knew she'd make things happen.

I decided to be a woman who brought change to Westminster.

Epilogue

Hearing his employer play a maddening round of Beethoven, William Jyles chuckles to himself. This was like old times.

He needs things to be like they once were. With Mr. Henderson back settling into town life, perhaps this will be a good change for them all.

In an hour, everything quiets, with his employer sequestered in his study with a port and an old book about period weapons. Number Eleven Greater Queen Street seems boring. Miss Mary, the poor child, is away at her old governess's. Her grief makes everyone in the household suffer unbearably.

But there isn't much William can do but wait and hope everyone will forget Juliet Henderson's murder. God, he misses that woman. She was fire and life.

Saddened beyond belief, he finishes taking inventory in the wine cellar, and before going back up to the main level, he decides to see if Mr. Henderson requires something.

He pokes his head into the open study. "Do you need anything, sir, before I turn in?"

"Feeling poorly, Jyles?" Henderson waves a fine short rapier.

It's shiny and sharp, one of his late father's. And newly polished—the man finally got to it. He lays it atop the dusty book
he's been reading. "I've heard from one of the maids you
haven't been yourself since Mrs. Henderson died."

"It's your pianoforte. It took me back to some of the great
rows you and the lady had. Very spirited conversations."

Two fancy goblets sit adjacent to the bust of Donne. "I miss
Juliet, too. She had a lot of spirit. She didn't deserve to die."

"Yes, the beastly minister."

Henderson stands and opens a bottle of port from his side-
board, filling the two glasses. Pushing one to William, he says,
"Let's toast, to the late Mrs. Henderson."

As William looks at the fine liquor in the glass, he swirls it,
watching the wine grow legs, the drips that show the strength
of the dark liquid.

Before he can take a sip, Henderson lowers his glass right at
the point of the rapier. "Not yet. Let's talk."

Talk? He shrugs, staring at how sharp the weapon is, and
wondering how many people Walker Henderson skewered
with the blade. "About what, sir?"

"My sister will return tomorrow. Then she'll be at the neighbors' for tea, around three. Remind the new maid."

"Yes, I'll do so. Sir, should we make a toast? This is one of
your special ports. They are delicious."

"Not a port, but a very fine beverage. One of Juliet's fa-
vorites."

William's mouth salivates. His employer has the best taste,
and who doesn't mind a free indulgence at the man's expense?

Henderson drums his fingers on the desk. "Mary will spend
more time next door, I think. Lady Worthing will be a good influence."

"So no more fence building and feuding with the little magistrate in Number Two?"

"No," Henderson says. "Lady Worthing is not someone to be away from. She fascinates me."

"So now that the wicked witch is dead, the neighbor with whom you fought mercilessly over dogs is someone you wish to know better?"

"Juliet wasn't wicked. And first impressions can be wrong. I was steered by your cartoonish version of the baroness."

That sounds as if Henderson has seen some of Lady Worthing's reported admirable qualities. That can be dangerous. "There's a line between adversary and friend. It can be thin, sir. A stem can have both a rose and thorns."

Chuckling, Henderson points the rapier at the waiting chair. "Funny. And poetic. If you must throw these barbs, let me see your face as you say them. Then I'll know if it's a jest. And get off that leg. The gout bothering you?"

Only Juliet noticed. Only she cared. "No. Hasn't bothered me in weeks."

William places the port on the desk next to Donne, then sinks into the chair. This is perfect, except for the weapon pointing at his chest. "Lady Worthing is close to Lord Duncan. Having a magistrate about . . . Well, your father wouldn't have it."

"That would only be a concern if I was guilty of something." He toys with the rapier spinning the point, then picks up his goblet. Looking dead at William, he then sits the goblet down with a thud. "And it's lucky for everyone I'm not my father. For the first time in a long time, I've no demands on me. I'm totally free."

William lifts his glass and offers a toast. "To freedom."

Henderson waves his hand over the rim and again stops him from drinking. "Not yet."

"You must want to say a few words. For the household, sir. We should drink to the household. The chaos is gone."

"This is a special blend, Jyles. Look at it and imagine the hints of honey and almonds. There might be the toasted heather, but no one ever knows the exact recipe for heather ale."

"Then we should drink, sir."

"No, Jyles, this is a wine of choice. We should celebrate how clever you are. I have a clever and dangerous butler."

"Me?" He chuckles and again tries to feign shock. "Not me, sir."

"Yes. How long had you and Juliet been having an affair? Was it over many years or this last one?"

William swallows hard.

He doesn't know how much Henderson knows of his love for Juliet.

The longing and exasperation and passion had been stoked by the naval officer's long absence and William's own need for excitement. He holds the crystal in the air and watches the shimmer of the candles on the glass. "You're not a man given to rumors. Let us go back to celebrating that you're not swinging from the gallows."

"But one of us in here should."

The cold tones he's seen Henderson reserve for others are now directed at him.

William's lips smack the rim, but Henderson grasps it and brings it down.

"What is it, sir?"

"Lady Worthing put all the pieces together, pieces I'd overlooked in my grief. I wondered about the bandaged wrapping the next morning, but forgot to ask. You told Lady Worthing it was a burn from torches. It wasn't. Juliet scratched your hand badly in the violent struggle."

William rubs at his wrist and the scab, which has healed up nicely; the bloody gold *J* of Juliet's ribbon necklace had gouged him deeply. Her fingernails did damage, too, but his long sleeves hid most of it.

"You knew my wife was thinking of going away with the minister, but you also knew the fiend was courting Mary."

"Benjamin tried to have them both. He convinced Juliet of it, that they'd have Mary's dowry and carry on the affair in Scotland."

"So you murdered Juliet because you were jealous?"

"I didn't mean to. I only meant to frighten her away from Benjamin. In a way, I protected Miss Mary, too. I did you a favor."

"The reappearing money in my safe was a nice touch. Only you and Juliet knew of it. And my dead wife couldn't put it back. There was a slim possibility that Mary did, but then the helpful baroness next door reminded me of your injured hand. Juliet marked you as her killer."

"Mr. Henderson, please. I wouldn't—"

"Indeed, you should've had a better lie. Why did you do it?"

His eyes dart about the room. He seeks escape, but he also remembers every moment with her in this room. The taste of her pouty lips. The softness of her skin. How she fits in his arms. How he couldn't stop her from being with others. How he couldn't stop choking her. "I didn't . . ."

His voice is weak, and his palms are perched in the air wrapping about an imaginary throat.

"Didn't what, Jyles? Didn't love my wife, my Juliet? Didn't want her with anyone else."

All the arguments and passion spent in this house swirls in head with visions of Juliet. She was . . . is his obsession. "No could have her."

"Say it Jyles! Admit it! You killed Juliet."

Suddenly this burden is too great. He has to confess. "I hoped Juliet would change her mind when she saw the minister only wanted money. But she didn't care. She wished to throw away the rest of her life on a fool. She couldn't run away with him. No one should have her."

"Mighty entitled of you, given that Juliet was my wife and was leaving with my blessings."

Taking a large breath, William eases the tightness of his collar. "I didn't want you implicated. I'm glad the wench next door found another convenient killer to blame. Old Benjamin strangling in bell pulls ended everything. It's all over."

Henderson smiles, then stands and pokes at his book spines. "You set a lot of things in motion that killed not only my wife but inadvertently her maid—"

"Minister Benjamin did that."

"It's still entwined with Juliet's death. And what of poor Mr. Sinclair? You had the man thinking he was next."

How does he know? Had Henderson heard their conversation at the *lichwake* when he'd threatened Sinclair?

Turning with his hands to his hips, his fine black waistcoat's sliver button jangling, Henderson glares at William. "Funny thing. Juliet didn't bring a portmanteau with her. She wasn't going to elope. It was another of her scenes to test your love. And you proved her right. Right to death."

William feels his face sweating. The images of what he's done—her lips, their final kiss, her begging to live—haunt him. Had jealousy clouded all? He's killed the woman he loved, one who'd actually chosen him. Everything in his chest rips.

"You deserve to die for what you've done. I should see you twisting in the hangman's noose."

"What are you going to do with these ideas, sir? It can't be proved. It will start people talking again. Lady Worthing might not be able to clear you."

"And you'll lie to save your neck. Right, Jyles? You'd have me hanged to save your worthless hide." He tsks with his lips. "Dangerous butler."

Henderson walks around the desk, posting close to William's chair, sitting almost in the same spot as Juliet had that awful night. "You've been too clever until now. You definitely won't be lucky in a minute."

"What?"

"Lord Duncan is upstairs, reading your confession."

"No. I didn't write—" Then Jyles remembers this is Walker Henderson's son, the man who ruled the darkest parts of London. How hard would it be to get a forger to pen such a note?

"You have two choices, Jyles. You can sit here and drink a special blend of port and die from a quick, painless heart palsy—or confess to Duncan and then be hanged at Newgate in a few weeks."

"I'll say you put me up to it. That you wanted her dead."

"You can do that, and you'll know that every Jyles in the city will suffer. My father knew where every sister, cousin, and nephew of his employees lived. It was his way to ensure loyalty."

"No, sir, you bluff. You're not your father."

"Test me!"

Walker Henderson would make anyone and everyone suffer. How different can the son be? He picks up the glass and stares at the ruby liquid. "How is it tainted? Does it hurt?"

"Toxins from my neighbor's tulips. When they take hold," Henderson's voice becomes lower and slow, "you will feel nothing. Eventually your heart will stop. You'll die an easy death."

"You jest?"

"Perhaps. Perhaps not. But you shall be punished. Juliet Henderson was mine to deal with. She was mine. And you murdered her. I'll avenge her."

Steps pound outside the door.

"Mr. Henderson, Lord Duncan's runners have arrived. The magistrate wants to enter with them."

That was the bloody footman Dillard. All the servants that William commands will see him, their superior, hauled away.

He is desperate to save face. "Couldn't I surrender at his offices, or does the poison work too fast?"

"Too late." Henderson goes again to his bookshelf. "Come in."

"Better to die with dignity." William takes the glass and downs every last bit. "There."

Henderson nods. "The glass was left here since the *lichwake*. Butler and dirty dishes, done in? Ask the dead reverend about irony when you meet him in hell."

Duncan enters the study with three burly runners.

The magistrate, with his brow raised, eyes Henderson, then Jyles. "William Jyles, I've come to hear your confession. You killed Juliet Henderson."

Knowing he'll die and wanting that last rush of excitement, he stands up boldly. "Yes. I did it. Juliet bewitched me. I was in a jealous rage. I didn't mean to kill her. But her laughing at me, her parading of her lovers, even the damn bells that night, got to me. I lost my head."

He starts to the terrace door, but feels his heart seize. "I wanted her to suffer. She said she chose me. I should've believed her."

He gasps for air, then falls.

"Must be having a palsy," Duncan says, waving his hand over William's face.

Henderson comes and helps William into a chair. "I think his stomach is upset from the burden of guilt."

Duncan folds his arms. "William Jyles, you've confessed to killing Juliet Henderson. Did anyone help you?"

A weird sensation moves through him as he prepares to answer. His head feels light, but he wants to take credit for what he's done. "I did it alone. I was her lover, the only man she truly loved."

The magistrate nods and points to his runners.

They seize both his arms and make William stand.

Henderson stands quiet. His face is blank. "What will happen to him?"

"He'll be charged by the crown and sentenced. He'll hang before month's end."

"I won't . . . Mr. Henderson."

"Jyles, you'll get no aid from me. My family has been decent to you all these years. I'll see you hang at month's end, to watch you twitch and choke until your breath stops."

The staid Lieutenant Commander Henderson acting the part of an injured husband. Juliet would clap, finally seeing him look angry. William will play along and act contrite, waiting to succumb to the poison.

The magistrate put his hand to Henderson's shoulder. "I'm truly sorry. It seems the lady next door was right. There was another villain."

"I have to go apologize to Lady Worthing. She said to keep looking for the killer, but I dismissed her."

"Persistent woman, but I've never seen a finer mind. Henderson, tell the baroness I'm sorry, too."

"Will do." Henderson picks up the glass of the special port he's poured for himself and drinks.

The half smile he shows says everything William doesn't want to hear. Henderson, indeed, will watch William swing from the gallows.

"Take the bastard from my sight, Duncan. No easy death for you, Jyles. You shall have the same as what you offered Juliet— to have your air cut off—asphyxiated by the hangman. That's what you deserve."

Trying to fight, to punch, to run, William suffers a strike to the gut from one runner and a blackened eye from another.

Henderson throws open the door to the hall. Footmen and even some maids line the corridor. They gasp at the sight of William being led away.

"A moment. Please. I beg . . . I beg of you." He tries to compose his dignity, but he's been tricked by the liar. William's last days will be spent jailed in rat-infested Newgate. There he'll rot until his execution. Then he'll feel everything, from the heavy jute wrapping his throat to his neck jerking and snapping when the New Drop, the platform beneath his feet, falls away.

"There's a third option, Mr. Henderson."

William breaks free, grasps the old rapier, and drives it into his gut.

He closes his eyes and waits to see Juliet again.

Author's Note

I hope you enjoyed this first installment of the Lady Worthing mysteries. This is my homage to all the things I love about murder mysteries and crime fiction, but set in the world of Regency era fiction.

A junkie for the Old Bailey's criminal proceedings, I intend to bring you crime fiction and detection with an amateur detective—puzzler or mystagogue—trying to define her place in a world where women, particularly women of color, struggle for agency.

Racial harmony is something that has been a struggle since the beginning of time. My approach is to balance the good and bad of the era, to show the more inclusive side of history. Settle in and enjoy real places, true histories, and actual persons who lived during these times—all playing a part in these mysteries. This will be fun.

As always, I do a lot of research to build these inclusive narratives, and I've added some of my notes for you.

Want to learn more? Visit my website, VanessaRiley.com to gain more insight.

End of Abolition Movement Because of Haiti
When Saint-Domingue became freed in 1805, under Jean-Jacques Dessalines, all the abolition movements in the world stopped. The fear of Black rule stunted everything. It took more than a year for the cause to start moving again.

Mary Edwards
Mary Edwards is considered the first human computer. She calculated positions of the sun, moon, and stars for the nautical almanacs for the British Navy. She was one of the few women paid to do this and was paid at a man's rate for her work.

Lord Nelson
Viscount Nelson was an admiral in the British Navy. He is one of Britain's greatest naval heroes, who led the decisive naval victories against France and Spain. The nation mourned his passing in a state funeral.

His death as depicted comes from the records of the attending physicians and officers of Nelson's ship.

Olaudah Equiano
Olaudah Equiano was a former African slave sold into enslavement at age eleven. He was baptized in Saint Margaret's font in 1759, and eventually bought his freedom (from a prominent British merchant, Robert King, in Montserrat) in 1766. Equiano, also known as Gustavus Vassa, became a prominent figure in the campaign for abolition. His 1789 memoir, *The Interesting Narrative of the Life of Olaudah Equiano; or, Gustavus Vassa, The African, Written by Himself,* details his life and hardships and helped crystalize the plight and savagery of enslavement.

Hannah More
Miss More was a playwright and active campaigner for abolition. She wrote poems and pamphlets.

William Wilberforce
Wilberforce was a politician and activist for abolition. He was a member of parliament.

Clapham Sect
Clapham Sect was a secret organization of evangelists who campaigned to abolish enslavement.

William Pitt the Younger
William Pitt the Younger followed in his father's footsteps into politics. He was eloquent and savvy and one of the most powerful and longest serving prime ministers. He was good friends with Wilberforce. One of Pitt's regrets was that he didn't get abolition done before his death in 1806. He was also given a state funeral.

Saint Margaret's
Founded in the twelfth century, Saint Margaret's Church stands on the grounds of Westminster Abbey and was consecrated in 1523. The church is dedicated to Margaret of Antioch. The east window above the altar contains the oldest stained glass in the church and dates between 1515 and 1526. The middle section depicts the Crucifixion. The left and right, when standing inside the building, reverse when looking from Saint Margaret Street, commemorates the marriage of King Henry VIII and Catherine of Aragon. The church was known to have strong ties to abolitionists. Saint Margaret's has four bells and only one bell tower.

Westminster Abbey
Westminster Abbey was consecrated in 1065 under the direction of King Edward the Confessor. Since 1066, Westminster Abbey has become the church where coronations occur. Sixteen royal weddings have occurred there since 1100. It is also the burial site for kings and queens, generals, poets, and other famous artists. Westminster has ten bells and two bell towers.

Westminster Part of London
Westminster is a central part of London, which extends from the River Thames and includes Saint James Park, up to Oxford Street. It houses many of the palaces and House of Parliament.

Drury Lane Theatre
Drury Lane Theatre is one of the royal theaters and dates back to 1663. It has burned down and been rebuilt several times: burned in 1672, rebuilt in 1674; demolished in 1791, rebuilt in 1794; burned down in 1809; rebuilt in 1812.

Ali Baba and the Forty Thieves
This play, about a young man that happens upon a treasure guarded by forty thieves, was first performed on April 8, 1806.

Olive's
Olive's was a coffeehouse, which was more of a restaurant with history-filled niches around the building.

Mulattoes and Blackamoors During the Regency
The term "mulatto" was a social construct used to describe a person birthed from one parent who was Caucasian and the other of African, Spanish, Latin, Indian, or Caribbean descent. Mulattoes during the Regency period often had more access to social movement than other racial minorities, particularly if their families had means.

The term "Blackamoors" refers to racial minorities with darker complexions, which included mulattoes, Africans, and West and East Indians living in England during the eighteenth and nineteenth centuries.

Mulattoes and Blackamoors numbered between ten thousand to twenty thousand in London, and throughout England, during the time of Jane Austen. Wealthy British with children born to native West Indies women brought them to London for schooling. Jane Austen, a successful contemporary writer during this era, in her last, unfinished novel, *Sanditon*, writes of Miss Lambe, a mulatto from the West Indies. Austen declares that this fictional heiress was a very wealthy woman, and her wealth made her desirable to the ton.

Mulatto and Blackamoor children were often told to pass to achieve elevated positions within society. Wealthy plantation owners with mixed-race children, or wealthy mulattoes, like Dorothea Thomas from the colony of Demerara, often sent their children abroad for education and for them to marry in England. Read more about a woman who defies prior notions of agency for Black women in Georgian and Regency times in *Island Queen*.

Regency Colors

Many colors popular during the Regency are mentioned, such as Saxon blue, which is a grayish-lavender hue, and Pomona green, which is an apple-green color.